Margaret Jones was a foreign correspondent for the *Sydney Morning Herald* for many years and worked in the Far East before coming to London in 1980. she has published one novel and one work of non-fiction. She is now literary editor of the *Sydney Morning Herald* and is working on a new novel.

The Smiling Buddha

Margaret Jones

CORGI BOOKS

THE SMILING BUDDHA
A CORGI BOOK 0 552 12730 2

Originally published in Great Britain by
Hamish Hamilton Ltd.

PRINTING HISTORY
Hamish Hamilton edition published 1985
Corgi edition published 1986
Corgi edition reprinted 1986

This book is set in 10/11 pt Times

Corgi Books are published by Transworld Publishers Ltd., 61–63 Uxbridge Road, Ealing, London W5 5SA, in Australia by Transworld Publishers (Aust.) Pty. Ltd., 15–23 Helles Avenue, Moorebank, NSW 2170, and in New Zealand by Transworld Publishers (N.Z.) Ltd., Cnr. Moselle and Waipareira Avenues, Henderson, Auckland.

Printed and bound in Great Britain by
Cox & Wyman Ltd., Reading, Berks.

From this we can deduce a general rule which never or rarely fails to apply: that whoever is responsible for another's becoming powerful ruins himself, because this power is brought into being either by ingenuity or force, and both of these are suspect to the one who has become powerful.

The fact is that a man who wants to act virtuously in every way necessarily comes to grief among so many who are not virtuous. Therefore, if a Prince wants to maintain his rule he must learn how not to be virtuous, and to make use of this or not according to need.

And here it has to be noted that men must be either pampered or crushed, because they can get revenge for small injuries but not for grievous ones. So any injury a Prince does a man should be of such a kind that there is no fear of revenge.

– Niccolò Machiavelli,
THE PRINCE (Il Principe)

CHAPTER ONE

We saw our first wounded man when we were still about two kilometres on the Thai side of the Khamla border. He had an oozing wound in his chest, and looked unlikely to survive it. Two other men were carrying him on a blanket, moving at a fast jogtrot and though his eyes were closed, his head moved constantly from side to side. As the car slowed to pass him, his lips drew back in a grimace, and he gave a harsh, protesting cry.

I turned to look at my husband. David was very pale and a muscle was jerking in his neck. 'Are you all right?' I said cautiously, and Dom, the Thai driver, turned round in the front seat, watching us both.

David's spectacles were fogged with sweat and he took them off and wiped them carefully with his handkerchief. Without them, his eyes, blinking, looked almost blind. I rarely saw him without his glasses, for even in bed he kept them on until he had actually turned out the light, and the opacity of his eyes was always a shock.

'Of course I'm all right,' he said impatiently. 'It's the heat, that's all. This car is like an oven. I told you we should have got something with air conditioning.' He looked at me as though it was my fault. In fact he had said nothing of the kind.

For a thin man with no burden of surplus flesh, David felt the heat as a special personal torment. His skin could not stand the sun, and I knew that as soon as we left the car he would put on the discreet Panama he carried now on his lap. With his tall, slightly stooped figure and his tailored cotton jacket and slacks, he looked like some scholarly explorer of colonial times. One might expect to see him making sketches of temple ruins in a notebook.

It was certainly very hot. We had left the Grand Hotel in Bangkok at six, an hour before the angry dawn broke, for we had a three-hour drive to the border ahead of us, the last part over atrocious roads.

Dom was waiting for us in his old Ford, the one he kept for ferrying visitors to the border. He did a good business, for no one – not even the press corps – wanted to risk his own car on the last section of road which frequently came under murderous mortar fire.

As we came out of the air conditioning of the Grand, the clammy wetness of the pre-dawn enveloped us, and I felt the first runnel of sweat start inching its slow way between my breasts. April is a brutal month in South-east Asia, and for once I almost wished I could be transported back to the grey English university town where David and I lived in mutual infelicity.

It was a rough ride to the border, and David hardly talked all the way, leaning back with his eyes closed, pretending to doze. He was not asleep, however, for I could feel the tension in his body when I was thrown against him on a rutted stretch of road.

After we met the wounded man, he made no further show of drowsiness. He sat forward watching the road, and when we saw a field hospital in the grounds of an abandoned school, he called to Dom to stop. A Red Cross medical team, in green gowns and masks, was treating a couple of dozen wounded, mainly women and children. They were from the border camp where, we had heard, there had been fighting yesterday.

Dom got out and spoke briefly with some border guards who were watching the team at work. He came back with unwelcome news. 'Things not so good,' he said. 'Thirty killed at the camp yesterday, another twenty today. You want to go on?'

'Yes, go on,' David said tersely. His voice was strong,

and he looked neat and assertive as he stood beside the car, the patches of sweat under his arms the only blotch on his elegant tailoring. But his appearance of calm could be misleading. I was, at that time, still very gauche and easily frightened by other people's scorn or displeasure. But I was strong and bore discomfort with ease, and I suspected, though it had not been put to the test, that I was much less physically timid than David.

We had still seen no sign of the official cars carrying Prince Soumidath and his party, and it was clear we ought to push on fast if we were not to miss them.

As the old Ford jerked protestingly over the pot-holed roads, the back of Dom's neck looked strained. He had given up his regular job at the Grand Hotel limo pool to take journalists, minor officials and visiting diplomats to the border, and already he had, he said, made enough to put a deposit on a farm near the airport. But with the fighting spilling across the border into Thailand, and the regular shelling of the road leading to the camp, there was always the chance he would not live to enjoy life as a farmer.

The only reason we ourselves were making this sweaty and possibly dangerous journey was because Prince Soumidath was visiting the border camps under the protection of the Thai Army.

It was the nearest he could get to his own country where his cousin Prince Vouliphong now ruled, installed in an American-backed coup while Soumidath was injudiciously taking a short holiday in the villa he kept for himself in the South of France.

David did not really want to go to the border, heat, dust and blood being not in his line. However, his next-but-one book was to be a study of Soumidath and the complexities of South-east Asian politics, so he could hardly miss the opportunity. This trip would do him quite a lot of good with his publishers.

Despite some help from the Prince's aides, we had

had trouble getting passes for the border, for the situation was deteriorating fast, and the Thais were growing impatient at having to protect day trippers. As we showed the passes at the final Army checkpoint, I heard the heavy crump of shells.

I was standing close to David and felt, rather than saw, the jerky tremor which ran through his body. But his voice was calm enough. 'Mortars?'

'Tanks,' said the NBC cameraman checking in with us. Half the press corps was up that day, because of the reports of fighting and the Prince's visit.

Ahead of us, as we got back into the car, I saw a dust cloud which could have been the Prince's party. It was the height of the dry season, and we had left the farming areas behind and entered a vast, reddish plain with a few spindly trees. The brazen sun beat down, and large carrion birds wheeled in the sullen haze above.

'Poor country,' Dom said. 'No water here.' It was hard to believe we were still in Thailand, for the whole area was as barren as a lunar landscape.

Three armies were encamped here, the Thais on one side, the official Khamla Army on the other, and roaming somewhere in between, the Free Khams, commanded by the warlord, arms dealer, and black marketeer, Sarr Mok. What law and order there was in the near-anarchy of the border camps was provided by Sarr Mok's men, but as his price he channelled off the major part of the supplies of food and medicine provided for the camps by the Red Cross and other aid agencies, and sold them to the nearest buyer. It was a lucrative business, and Sarr Mok had many rivals trying to cut in on it.

We were nearly at the border when I saw movement in the heat and dust ahead. The last trace of coolness had gone from the morning, and the heat was intense, the sun clanging down on the earth like an anvil. A little way in front of us, dark figures were wavering in the landscape, as though in a mirage, and as we bumped up the dusty road, two long columns of refugees came streaming towards us.

'Uh,' said Dom uneasily. 'More trouble at the camp.' On cue, there was the sound of shots not far off, then silence.

The exodus across the plain was amazing, a Biblical epic. On each side of the road, a straggling line crept forward, thousands of people on the move. Small, dark-skinned, baked almost black by the sun, they inched forward, moving like ghosts in the haze. Women bore silent children, men carried old people on their backs. The stronger children carried most of the family belongings, usually no more than bundles wrapped in cloth. A few, more prosperous, pulled carts, groaning between the shafts like beasts. There were no animals. Perhaps there was no feed for them, or they had been eaten long ago.

'Where are they going?'

Dom shrugged. 'Nowhere for them to go. They sit here for a while until the fighting stops, then they go back to the camp again.'

David stirred uneasily beside me, and I saw what he was looking at: the soldiers. I watched with intense curiosity as a group of them urged the pilgrims on, sometimes with blows.

These were the famous army of Sarr Mok, the Third Force said to have received some support from the Americans, even though Washington was also holding up the unpopular régime of Soumidath's cousin in the capital. 'Having a bit each way,' the cynics in Bangkok had said.

They looked more like bandits than soldiers, mostly very young, and dressed in a ragged assortment of uniforms, as though they had been stripping the bodies of half a dozen armies. There was nothing amateurish about their weapons though, M-16s and AK-47s carried over their shoulders and clearly looked after carefully.

They stared at us as the car lurched by, and I saw

their blank, ancient young faces. Beside me, I could feel David's unease, and he cleared his throat, looking for some loophole.

'Are you sure you want to go into the camp? It could be risky.'

'I'm not worried.' Nor was I now, after that first moment when I had seen the men with the guns. I was on edge, but excited. When I travelled with David, most of my time was spent in dingy Asian hotel rooms, waiting for him, and no one knew what it did to my spirits.

David looked at me without expression, but I could see he was angry. He wanted me to be afraid, so he could have an excuse to turn back, but I was not prepared to accommodate him. 'Go on,' he said curtly to Dom, who grimaced and accelerated.

We drove through a broken-down gate, and into the camp itself. I had seen refugee camps before, but compared to this they were paradise. Thousands of people huddled on that plain in the brazen sun, with no shelter except rough lean-tos of straw matting they had built themselves. There were a few more ambitious huts used by the Red Cross for the distribution of food, and for an emergency hospital. In the centre, there were the remains of what had been the biggest structure of all. Dom told us it had been Sarr Mok's headquarters, but it had been mortared by one of his rivals that day, and now there was nothing there but a smouldering ruin.

Out of the corner of my eyes, I could see people digging a mass grave, and beside it was an untidy pile of bodies.

'Don't go over,' said the *New York Times* correspondent standing beside me. 'They're starting to stink already.' It was true. Even through the dust-laden air, I could smell a persistent, sweetly sickening stench. The birds circling above the camp smelled it too, and came lower, waiting their chance. One plummeted as I watched, and was driven off with stones and shouts.

After the shouts, there was nothing but silence. Even

the ubiquitous radios of Asia were missing, long since sold, I supposed, to buy food. No children cried, though there were many babies in their mothers' arms, the corners of their mouths and eyes black with flies. The people squatted in their low shelters on the baking earth, waiting for death in the form of hunger, or stray shells from the fighting deeper inside the border, or the cross-fire of bullets and mortars in the struggles of the warlords to control the camp.

We saw ahead of us the cluster of cars which had carried the Prince and the official party. Around the Prince clustered the aides who had fled from Khamla when Vouliphong took over, and joined him in exile in Hanoi. With them, incongruously tall among the small, neat Khams, was a European, his fair head bare in the sun.

'There's the so-called Political Adviser.' David's voice was tight with resentment. If he was to get anywhere with Prince Soumidath, it would only be with the help of Peter Casement, and asking favours was high on his list of dislikes.

'Why so-called? The Prince relies on him a lot,' I said mildly.

'He's a bloody poseur.' David took off his glasses, and looked at me more closely than I liked. Normally, I think, he saw me as no more than a familiar blur, but he was unexpectedly shrewd when his interests were threatened.

'Why are you so interested in him?' he said sharply. 'You hardly know him.'

'I met him a couple of times in Hanoi while you were busy with briefings.'

I had not told David about the evening at Soumidath's. He had heard about the border trip from his Vietnamese contacts.

David's mouth hardened and he would have said something more, but at that moment, the silence broke in the camp and we both forgot Peter.

The Prince was now walking among his people, and a great moaning went up, a kind of keening which broke into a repetition of the Prince's name: 'Soumidath! Soumidath! Soumidath!'

He moved among the little low shelters, weeping, talking in floods of that strange, word-swallowing, glottal-stopped language which few outsiders can ever master.

The tears ran down his dusty face onto his elegant embroidered shirt. He made no attempt to stop them, smiling, sobbing, shouting with a mixture of anger and joy to see his people again, pressing filthy hands stretched out to him, embracing as many eager bodies as he could.

The Prince was a short man, but taller than most of his countrymen. The life expectancy in Khamla was about forty-eight years – in normal times. Malaria, dysentery and plague were endemic, and the fighting and the failure of last year's harvest had resulted in malnutrition of epic proportions. But I was not prepared for the stick-like babies, and the patient, elderly faces on bodies which should have been young. Like the Prince, I could have wept.

'Where is Sarr Mok?'

We were back at the cars, and the Prince was no longer weeping. His usually smooth olive skin was suffused almost to blackness with anger. None of the aides said anything, for they were silent with shock. Some of them had been travelling with Soumidath when the coup came, and they had not seen their families since. For all they knew, their wives, their children, their parents, were refugees, squatting in the dust like the people here.

Seeing their paralysis, Soumidath turned violently to Peter Casement. 'You! Go and find out.'

It seemed an odd way to address a political adviser, but Peter showed no sign of resentment. He put a firm hand on the arm of the Prince's *chef de protocol*, and marched him into the camp to interpret. Within a few minutes, they were back.

'He's down the road, taking shelter in one of the Thai Army fire-posts.'

I saw Soumidath's face again as we got into the car. In the politics of South-east Asia, he is sometimes taken as a bit of a joke because of his liking for pretty wives – he was at that time between his third and fourth marriages – and his passion for playing the saxophone at his own dancing parties. People forget, however, with what skill he kept his country out of war from end of World War II (when it was overrun by the Japanese) right up until the time when his absence from the capital allowed his younger cousin Prince Vouliphong to seize power with CIA backing. It was with Vouliphong's tacit consent that the Americans bombed sanctuaries in the north-east of the country and so drove many undecided Khams into the arms of that uneasy coalition of peasants and intellectuals which was to become famous as the Khamla Liberation Front.

The rumour in Hanoi was that Soumidath was poised for an all-out attempt to seize back power, and that morning I was prepared to believe it.

At the second fire-post back along the road, we found what we were looking for. The soldiers at the gate, awed by Soumidath's cavalcade, waved us through, and the cars drew up.

I had never seen a warlord before, and I am not sure what I expected: somebody gnarled and savage, I suppose. Sarr Mok was sitting at a rough table in the shade, a young aide beside him. They were both drinking coca-cola, poured into tumblers full of ice. It looked rather like a bizarre version of a TV ad.

Sarr Mok was not gnarled and savage. Like most of his countrymen, he was small and slender, with a smooth face, though he must have been over fifty. He was dressed in a clean white shirt and dark cotton trousers, and the ubiquitous sandals of the country.

Unlike his aide, who was twitchy, he looked cool and relaxed; at least until he saw Soumidath get out of the car, when his face changed, and he rose at once to his feet.

He did not advance to meet the Prince, but remained standing in the shade. Soumidath walked silently towards him, his face set. Behind, equally silent, came his entourage. Peter Casement, David, and I stood uneasily to one side. Peter nodded briefly to us, but said nothing. It was not a moment for greetings.

Then, when Soumidath was almost on top of him, Sarr Mok gave a sort of groan. Very slowly, in slow motion, as though the movement hurt him, he went down on one knee. Soumidath with equal slowness, held out his hand, and Sarr Mok touched it to his forehead in homage.

I was astonished, though I suppose I should not have been. Khamla, though strategically important in South-east Asian politics, is a very small country, with less than three million people. The Royal House, in the present line, was established in the eleventh century, when Soumidath's remote ancestor, King Laovongsa, united a number of warring fiefdoms and built the Great Temple of Vangkhorn as the centre of his empire. The temple-city has since crumbled, but the ruins of the temple itself remain, an architectural masterpiece and one of the wonders of the world.

Various branches of the Royal House have fought each other over the centuries, but the main blood line has remained constant, and the kingdom itself survived assaults by the Burmese and the Vietnamese, and colonisation by the French.

Soumidath was nothing more, after the coup, than a deposed head of state, a royal pensioner in the capitals of South-east Asia, but his person remained sacred to the Khams, even to his enemies.

Sarr Mok's gesture of homage had failed to placate Soumidath. The Prince took one of the rough chairs and sat on it as if it were a throne, while Sarr Mok stood before him. Soumidath did not raise his voice. Normally high-pitched, it seemed to have sunk to a low monotone, but whatever he was saying, it evoked some powerful interdictions, because both Sarr Mok and his aide turned an ugly shade of red. I saw that the young aide's legs were shaking.

David and Peter Casement were talking to each other in a muttered, desultory exchange, though Peter's main attention was concentrated on the Prince. I stood uneasily by myself in the blinding sun until a hand on my arm drew me under the shelter of the Army guardhouse.

'Come into the shade. You'll get sunstroke if you stand there.'

The man was himself in shadow, and at first I did not recognise him, then I saw it was the lanky American cameraman we had met at the check post and later at the camp. I knew his name well. Harry Greene: a veteran of Vietnam, he was famous all over South-east Asia, a solitary photo-journalist who celebrated war and death like a poet.

He did not, candidly, look anything like I had expected. With his hair *en brosse*, and his bush shirt and camouflage trousers, he seemed dressed for a part in a war movie, though I liked his humorous eyes, and his ironic smile.

'What is the Prince saying?'

'I can only guess.' Harry Greene was raiding a stack of coke bottles and some dirty ice stored under a water tank at the side of the guard house. 'He's presumably cursing Sarr Mok for the condition of the people at the camp.'

'Is it his fault?'

'Sure. He's getting greedy. The people at the camp are on starvation rations because Sarr Mok and his boys seize most of the food and medical supplies which come in and sell them off across the border.'

'What will happen to the camp people?' Harry handed me a tin mug of coke and I drank it thirstily, not caring about the dirty ice he had thrown in.

'Christ knows.' He leaned back against the side of the guardhouse. 'There will be no harvest this year, because there has been no planting. And what country will take them as refugees? There was enough trouble with the Viets, but many of them were middle-class. Nobody is going to want thousands of diseased and starving peasants who wouldn't know an indoor john if they saw one.'

His tone was calm, even cynical, but long hard lines suddenly showed on his face, running down from his nose to his mouth. I remembered films of his I had seen on the Vietnam war. They were miracles of powerful understatement.

Soumidath's diatribe had now been in progress for some time, and, looking at Sarr Mok, I saw that he had actually appeared to shrink in stature. Suddenly, the Prince stopped, and his face relaxed. He gave his characteristic high-pitched laugh, and motioned Sarr Mok to sit down.

Within a couple of minutes, the two men were talking quietly, heads together, over fresh glasses of coke brought by the little aide whose knees, I saw, were still shaking.

Harry Greene laughed. 'Typical Soumidath tactics. First the blast, then the glad hand. He's now persuading Sarr Mok that if he will only reform, discipline his army, stop being a black marketeer, and swing his support behind Soumidath, they can march together to a great and glorious future.'

I looked at him in astonishment.

'The Prince wouldn't deal with a man like that?'

'The Prince would deal with anyone, even the devil, to get his country back on its feet, and stop the fighting. He would even have dealt with my countrymen, whom he distrusted most of all, but Washington preferred his princely cousin, and dumped him. He won't forget that in a hurry if he gets back to power.'

He raised his head and stiffened, like a dog on the alert, as there was a shout from outside, and an army truck drew up with a screech. 'Let's go and see.'

The sun blinded me for a moment, then I saw the soldiers were throwing heavy bundles from the back of the truck. Each landed with a dull thud, the last one at my feet when I came up. Then I saw they were not bundles, but dead men, and I stumbled backwards against Harry.

'Don't let it worry you,' he said abruptly. 'They're dead. Past caring.'

They were certainly very dead. They were young men, not more than twenty. Their hands were tied behind their backs and each had a third eye, a bloody hole in the middle of the forehead.

Their bellies were already swelling in the sun, and I caught the same sickening sweet smell I had smelled at the camp.

Harry was talking rapidly to the soldiers.

'Sarr Mok's men,' he said, turning to me. 'When he escaped from the camp this morning, they covered his rear to let him get away. Looks like the opposition caught up with them.'

He stirred one of the bodies with his foot. 'Poor sods.' Then somewhat awkwardly, 'Why don't you go back into the shade? I'm going to get the camera from the car.'

When he came back a little later, I was sitting on the edge of the tankstand. I had soaked a handkerchief, and wiped my face and hands. I felt slightly nauseated by the heat and the smells, but otherwise quite calm. Perhaps David was right, and I was basically cold.

Soumidath was still cajoling Sarr Mok, his hand on his arm, and Sarr Mok was smiling obsequiously. His eyes looked hard, though. Peter Casement was talking to the young aide, and David was standing watchfully in the background. He would have to ask Peter for an interpretation later: he would hate that.

Harry sat beside me, and filling a tin mug with water, upended it over his curly brown head. He looked across at the negotiations.

'The Prince is wasting his time. The only thing Sarr Mok really understands is black marketeering and banditry. He'll pretend to go along with Soumidath, but he's not going to give up a lucrative trade in misery for the sake of patriotism.'

He stared at Peter Casement, now close to the Prince's elbow. 'Now, that's a fascinating guy. He always turns up when you least expect him to.'

I said carefully that I heard Peter was writing the Prince's biography, and Harry laughed.

'You don't think he is?'

'Maybe. As a sideline. I think he's setting up as a latter-day Machiavelli, myself. The adviser and arbiter of princes.'

* * *

David had been frightened by the events of the day, but also excited by them. I could see this in the way he moved restlessly round our room in the Grand Hotel, ostensibly tidying his already neat belongings, making a few offhand remarks about our travel arrangements for Hanoi. I lay in bed watching him, thinking how the air-conditioning and sanitised splendours of the Grand made doubly ironic what we had seen that day.

David came and sat on the edge of the bed, staring at me. He was, as always, dressed in cotton pyjamas, buttoned to the neck. I had, in five years of marriage, rarely seen him naked. He was as modest as a Victorian husband, though I suspected the real reason was that he was not proud of his thin, almost hairless body, with its concave chest and rounded shoulders.

He also disliked me going naked, and this had made me self-conscious and anxious, although my mirror told me that, as the angularity of my girlhood receded, I had a good, strong, straight body with no blemishes except, perhaps, the patchwork of a fading tan.

Now that we were back in the air-conditioning, David had stopped sweating. His skin was pale and cool, his eyes hidden behind his glasses, and his hair, still damp from the shower, had been neatly combed back.

'Are you tired?' he said in a low voice, and I knew at once what he intended.

I said nothing, trying to keep antipathy out of my face, and he slid into bed beside me and turned out the light. I heard the slight clink as he took off his glasses, and put them on the bedside table, then in the darkness, his dry cold hands began to move over my body, and his breathing quickened.

This perfunctory caressing was David's idea of foreplay, but I knew it would not last long. To do him justice, I believe that every time he made love to me, if you could call it that, he started with the idea of rousing and pleasing me, but there was some devil in him that made him want to hurt instead, and the rigidity his very touch produced in me was the quickest way of arousing it.

Our sexual life had been disastrous from the beginning. When we married, I was that increasingly rare thing, a virgin, and my deflowering was bloody, and as distasteful to David as to me.

I had no standards of comparison and for a long time I thought my failure to respond was my own fault. But one did not need to be either practised or expert oneself to grasp, in the end, that David's frantic, fumbling haste in bed, at best clumsy and lacking in consideration, at worst verging on brutality, was hardly the best technique to produce satisfactory results. I suppose it was because in everything else he was so icy, so disciplined, so life-denying, that the undignified, near-sadistic scramblings in bed were the result.

David's brother-in-law, who was a psychologist, said to me one night at a party when he had had too much to drink that David had all his life denied the Dionysiac principle, and sooner or later he would have to pay the price. Well, the price was already being paid, but it was mainly me who was paying it. David had long ago decided – or convinced himself – that I was either frigid or a lesbian, and I no longer argued.

The next morning we were due to fly back to Hanoi, but I came down again with another bout of vomiting and diarrhoea which afflicted me from time to time in Asia. David said, probably rightly, that I deserved what I got because I bought cold drinks from dirty crones in market places, and ate, when I had to, at roadside restaurants. We had stopped in a little town on the way back from the border and Dom, Harry Greene and I had had curry and rice and a bottle of local beer. David had sat by rigidly, drinking Chinese tea, but refusing to eat. He never, if he could avoid it, ate outside hotels, and the smell and noise of markets appalled him.

David was well known as a mildly left-wing academic, of a trendy and acceptable sort; that was how he made what reputation he had. But his dislike of the pulsing mass of humanity which Asia demonstrates at its most dirty and vociferous remained ineradicable. Even the sort of physical contact which is inevitable in Asian crowds upset him.

I sometimes thought that if David followed his natural inclinations, he would be somewhere to the right of Kublai Khan.

He was furious that I was not able to travel, but my illness was only too apparent. He could hear me being agonisingly sick in the bathroom, and the thought of my repeating the performance on the plane reconciled him to leaving me behind. I started to feel better immediately he had gone, lying back between the Grand's beautiful white sheets, dozing in the delicate chill, waking to phone room service for tea and bread and butter brought by a cheerful boy openly soliciting a tip. The Grand was a nice change from the Hua Binh, and I was safe for a glorious three days until the next Hanoi plane went.

* * *

The last person I expected to see in Bangkok was Peter Casement.

'I thought you had gone back to Hanoi with the Prince.' I said incredulously.

'I had some business to finish up here. And you? Playing hookey?' The extreme paleness of his eyes gave him that wary, watchful look which was so characteristic, but his smile, flashing in his thick beard, was lighthearted and boyish.

I told him I had been ill, but I could see he did not quite believe me. 'You look rather well,' he said, laughing, the odd phraseology implying a compliment. It was true. When I looked in the mirror that morning, I had seen my holiday face.

He had come across me sitting in the garden of Jim Thompson's house, that exquisite tribute to the taste and skill of a collector which is one of the great sights of Bangkok, though less well known than the spectacular wats and palaces. His presence there had astonished me. I was sufficiently new to Asia to be a tourist, but I would not have thought sightseeing was his role. He was very quick, and caught my unspoken question.

'I knew Jim Thompson slightly,' he said. 'Whenever I am in Bangkok I come here, and light an incense stick in the garden to his memory.

I raised my eyebrows. Jim Thompson, who resurrected the Thai silk industry after World War II, had disappeared in the Cameron Highlands in 1967, and had never been seen again. He had served as an intelligence officer in the war, and there were many theories about his disappearance.

I wondered in what capacity Peter had known him.

Peter touched my arm lightly. 'Have you been round?'

His fingers brushed my skin, no more, and he at once took his hand away, but I felt my neck reddening, and it was a moment before I could answer him.

'Not yet. I'm waiting for the English-speaking guide.'

No one is allowed to go round Jim Thompson's house alone, presumably because there are so many exquisite small objects lying about which could be easily pocketed. But Peter went to the guardian on the desk, who, after a moment's hesitation, recognised him and shook hands. There was a short conversation, then he called me over.

'They know me here. Special guided tour for one person.'

It was, as usual, a stifling morning, but the house was so beautiful I forgot the heat. 'It's made of seven Thai houses he brought from all over the place,' Peter said. 'He was the most dedicated collector I have ever known.'

The dark teak-panelled rooms are, as any tourist who goes to Bangkok will tell you, brilliant with the colours of the Thai silk which Jim Thompson began making again after the war in the old houses across the *klong.* The house is full of marvellous things: Chinese blue and white porcelain, Kampuchean stone figures, stone Buddhas, Burmese wooden statues. The house speaks in every line of elegance and beauty and grace, and it melted the hard core of sullenness which my present life had bred in me – a tough aching thing which I felt sometimes like a growth under my heart – and I smiled at Peter Casement as though I was nineteen again.

'That's better,' he said. He sounded obscurely relieved. 'You not only look rather well. You look very well indeed.'

We drank lime juice and soda water at the Grand Hotel's swimming pool, then went off to have lunch at a small restaurant where, Peter promised, I would not have to eat curry.

I asked him about Jim Thompson's disappearance, but he said he knew no more than anyone else, that he had gone out for a walk one day in the Cameron Highlands, and had never been seen again.

I looked at him cautiously. 'He *is* rumoured to be some sort of spook.'

Peter's eyes, usually so light, became guarded and opaque. 'I wouldn't know about that,' he said easily. 'It was a bit before my time.' Then he smiled across the table at me. 'I think he was really just a guy who had Asia in his bloodstream, an upmarket version of the Asia bum. There's a few of us about now. I'm one. Harry Greene's another. We hate the place, but we can't get away from it.'

When I said nothing but continued to stare at him, he frowned and shook his head. 'Don't make a mystery out of me, Gilly. I'm doing a bit on the side for Soumidath now, but in real life I'm just an ordinary working journalist.'

'Are you? Some people think – I have heard it said that you are something else again.'

'What?' With his face set in rigid lines, he looked a hard man, harder than I had thought.

'They say' – I used the French *on dit* to make it sound less personal – 'that you are playing Machiavelli to the Prince's Prince.'

'Do they, indeed? Well, I won't pretend the idea is without its attractions. The rules are all laid down, and they are still viable after 400 years.'

'I didn't think they worked out so well in practice.'

He sighed. 'That's because you are dealing with fallible material: with flesh and blood. Soumidath knows the rules of conduct for princes and they are not so different for Khamla as for Florence. But he's too squeamish to follow them through to the natural conclusion.'

I was surprised. Soumidath's treatment of some of his political opponents was not exactly tender. The commander-in-chief of the Khamla Liberation Front, now at his headquarters at the Great Temple of Vangkhorn, had fled the capital, it is said, just a few steps.ahead of the executioner. Burial alive is a normal method of disposing of enemies in Khamla.

'The Prince is more squeamish than you?'

'Certainly.' He looked at me with a kind of intensity that made me slightly embarrassed. 'I am not squeamish at all. If you want power, you cannot be delicate. Soumidath will have to learn that lesson in the end. There is a limit from which he always draws back.'

'Do you want power?' I looked at him cautiously.

'Not for myself. But I want to be in the position to manipulate someone who has it. The secondary exercise of power is often more effective than primary. Hence the persistence of the *éminence grise*.'

We both fell silent. His light-heartedness of the morning had gone, and I felt he was, in some way, stripping himself before me. Then he laughed, and the tension lightened.

'Finish your mango. I'm talking too much, and I must be off about the Prince's affairs.'

* * *

I had expected a solitary few days, but that evening I ran into Harry Greene in the lobby and we had a drink by the pool. The warm darkness was full of buzzing mosquitoes, and the air was heavy with the scent of Bangkok smog. But at least the worst of the heat was over. I told Harry I had lunched with Peter, but not what he had said. I was curious to ask if Peter was married.

'Not that I know of. His sexual habits have always been a mystery.' He looked at me carefully. 'He is sometimes thought to be a homosexual. But I wouldn't know.'

I got up abruptly and said I must go, the mosquitoes were killing me.

CHAPTER TWO

I had first met Peter Casement in Hanoi, at the burning of the old Queen, the mother of Prince Soumidath. It was an inconvenient time for her to die: the Festival of the New Year, Tet, had just begun, and the Prince kept rigidly to the sacred and profane ceremonies involved. They reminded him of home, and kept his spirits up in this alien city. But the Queen's death came on the turn of the moon, and all the rites had to be cancelled.

It was an awkward place as well as time for Soumidath's mother to go to meet her Makers. (The Royal Family were officially Buddhist, but Soumidath, like the rest of his countrymen, believed in a plurality of gods.) The Queen was a long way from home, and she had made her son promise to lay her ashes to rest in the Great Temple at Vangkhorn, but there was, at present, no way of getting her there, the Great Temple being otherwise engaged, as the headquarters of the National Liberation Front.

The Prince made the best of things, as he always did, and borrowed a small disused temple from his hosts for the ritual burning. The day before the cremation, there was a lying-in-state to which the whole diplomatic corps and a few hangers-on like us were invited. I wanted to laugh when the Prince's *chef de protocol* addressed David as *Excellence*. But he pinched me so hard on the wrist that the tears came to my eyes instead. It was more suitable to the occasion, but it annoyed him just as much.

The Queen's corpse was on an open bier, covered with a thin embroidered veil, and surrounded with sweet-smelling flowers, very necessary in that climate.

The custom of the Prince's country calls for the bodies of persons of rank to be sprinkled with rare perfumes. In Hanoi, these are somewhat hard to come by, and the Prince had clearly demanded that his household sacrifice precious items of the toilet table. There was a little array of half-empty bottles near the bier, and we sprinkled the Queen Mother with Brut, with Chanel No. 5, and Ma Griffe, with eau de toilette, and with after-shave. I saw some of the aides turn pale as the elegant bottles, so painfully acquired and hoarded for use drop by drop, were upended over the corpse.

The burning took place at a disused temple near the city, said to contain a relic of the Buddha's frontal bone. A special little white pavilion with a golden dome had been built in the grounds, a miniature version of a burial stupa. Under the dome was the flower-laden bier, and at its head stood the 400-year-old Smiling Buddha, which normally presided over the Prince's reception rooms.

The Prince and two of his many sons were receiving guests, dressed in ceremonial funeral gear: pure white, with long overtunics, and loose skirts drawn up between the legs with a band to form a sort of trouser. The Prince had shaved his head, and looked unusually grave and monkish. With his short round body and his full lips, he resembled the royal Buddha at the head of the bier, and I noticed he glanced at it anxiously from time to time as though seeking guidance. It was a particularly sacred object for the Royal house, and legend said the line would end when the Buddha was lost or destroyed. The Prince was a superstitious man and hauled the Buddha with him everywhere. He had had a special travelling case made for it, and it formed a normal part of his luggage.

There was a fair turnout for the occasion, though not of course the full diplomatic corps, sympathies for the

Prince's cause being more or less divided along big-power loyalty lines. The Soviet Union, the United States, and China were all busy meddling in the internal affairs of the Prince's country. Apart from the Ambassadors, there were the tiny resident press corps, a few foreign experts, and David and me. I thought we were the only outsiders until I saw a man sitting by himself, quite apart from the rest of us, in a special cleared space behind the Royal party. He looked a big man, though presently, when he stood briefly, I saw he was not particularly heavy, but lean and powerful, with a tightly curled fair head, and most unusually for that place, a short curly beard, darker than his hair. He had such a watchful, nervous look that I thought he must be a security man hired for the occasion. Then I dismissed the idea, for the Prince was as safe here as in his own palace; no, safer, for there (before his cousin took his place) the assassins were always waiting in the shadows. The Prince had some friends, but many enemies, and not without cause. The growing band of guerrillas in the *maquis* testified to that.

The man apparently did have some connection with the Royal entourage, however, because I saw one of the Prince's sons lean back and talk to him. The movement also caught David's eye, and he turned in his direction. I heard him draw in his breath sharply.

'For God's sake!' he said under his breath.

'Who is it?' The chanting of the Buddhist monks round the bier stopped for a moment as I spoke, and my voice sounded louder than I meant it to be. The British Ambassador turned and gave me an impatient look, and David said in my ear: 'Be quiet! I'll tell you later.'

The ceremony went on for a long time and meant very little to me. The afternoon was warm, the chanting hypnotic, and I had difficulty in staying awake. Then the Prince made a speech about his mother's great merits in Kham, French and English, and the audience, after some hesitation, politely applauded. It is very difficult to know the protocol for these occasions, but it seemed the right thing to do, for the Prince beamed and clapped back in the Asian fashion. When we all rose to file past the bier and place a flower on it, the fair-haired man did not join the shuffling queue but kept his place at the rear of the Royal group. David was very close behind me and because I usually know what he is feeling (if not necessarily what he is thinking) I picked up vibrations of extreme irritation. As we sat down again I glanced at him in surprise. As far as I knew he was not angry with me (at least, not more than usual) and there was nothing in his immediate circumstances to provoke him. He had been made welcome in Hanoi, and was getting as much access as he could legitimately expect to the sort of material he wanted. I could only assume his emotion was due to the fair-headed man.

I was a little worried that they were going to burn the Queen Mother before our very eyes, and indeed, if the ceremony had been at home, they would have done. Open-air cremation is the custom of the country. However, the Prince must have decided that the smell of burning flesh might be too much for the diplomatic corps, or else his hosts had urged caution. At the end of the ceremony, when dusk was falling, he walked slowly to the bier and lighted the ceremonial candle which symbolised the cremation of the body. At the same time, he lit hanging strips of incense, and the sweetly acrid smell rose in the darkening air. The stone Buddha smiled in the light of the Prince's taper, and the thin tinkle of chimes came from the disused pagoda. For a moment, everything was still. I felt a sense of profound melancholy and would have liked to take David's hand, but did not. Then we all rose thankfully to go, shuffling into line according to precedence, David and I last, following the press.

* * *

The fair-headed man caught us up just as we were getting in the car.

'I heard you were here,' he said abruptly to David, offering no other greeting. Nor, more surprisingly, did he shake hands, but stood off a little, watching both of us carefully. I noticed again that air of nervous expectancy which had drawn my attention earlier.

Beside me, I felt David's stiffness. He nodded just as abruptly as the other man, then, seeing him staring at me, made a reluctant introduction. 'My wife Gillian. Peter Casement.' David was the only person who ever called me Gillian, with a soft 'g'. My family and my friends called me Gilly, and I always felt that Gillian was someone I barely knew.

The man did put out this hand then, first to me, then, very cursorily to David. His grip was strong yet light, and his fingers were unusually long and sinewy.

'I read your book,' he said to David. '*The* book, I mean, not the earlier ones. I suppose you are doing a follow-up?'

David flushed. *The New Catalyst: Asian Communism and the Future* had made his name and opened many doors to him (though the Russians hated it, of course), but he was surprisingly shy about it. There had been a few gibes in the learned journals about academics who twisted facts to support theories, and – even worse – sacrificed their integrity for the sake of hard-to-get visas. Though these had mainly come from colleagues who would never get such visas in a million years, David had taken them to heart. He was, according to his lights, honourable.

As David did not appear to be going to answer, the man turned to me with an easy politeness.

'Mrs Herbert.' He looked at me with that odd intensity. 'How do you like Hanoi?'

'Well enough,' I said cautiously. 'We haven't been here long.'

His ear was very quick. Years of living in England

have smoothed out most of my accent, but something remains.

'Australian?' he said. 'Funny. I wouldn't have expected . . .' He stopped.

You are quite right, I said silently. Most people don't. David is so bloody, up-tight, frigid English, at least on the surface, people expect a suitably matching wife, not a big-boned Australian with a recognisable accent and an ineradicable talent for saying the wrong thing at the wrong time.

'What are *you* doing here?' David said at last.

'Writing the definitive biography of Soumidath.' Peter Casement's own accent was puzzling. Predominantly American, of course, but with an odd overlay. 'I've been commissioned by –' he named a leading New York publisher. 'I thought you might have heard.'

Irish, but north of the border, that rasping Ulster accent I always found so hard to understand.

David was rigid with anger. He had himself been developing the idea of a biography of the Prince – that was one reason we had come to Hanoi – and he was only waiting until we got back to London to put up the proposal to his publisher.

'A bit premature, aren't you?' he said angrily. 'We have no idea yet how this whole affair is going to end.'

Peter Casement smiled. 'No. But I promise you I'm going to be there when it does. In at the death, as you might say.'

He opened the car door for me ceremoniously.

* * *

'A bloody journalist!' David said furiously. 'A bloody journalist to carry off something like that.'

'Some publishers think journalists make livelier biographers than academics.' I knew what sort of biography of Soumidath David would write, full of footnotes and quotes from Engels. He was quite good on political theory, but hopeless on people.

'Who does he work for?' I added hastily, when I saw he was working himself into the sort of rage he indulged himself in only in private, and with me.

'He used to work for AFP – Agence France Presse. That's probably how he met Soumidath. The Prince has always been very close to the French journalists.' His mouth tightened. 'I suppose Casement got a hefty advance.'

The sort of advances given by New York publishers were a continual source of envy to English academics, who had mainly to make do with honour and glory.

'He's Irish?'

'Irish? Yes, of course he is. Can't you hear his blasted hybrid accent? I think his family came originally from Belfast, then he went to live with some relatives in New York after his parents died. They were mixed up with the IRA or something of the sort.'

I looked at him in surprise. 'How do you know all this?' Other people's family backgrounds were not David's strongest suit. He found it difficult to remember even the names of his nephews and nieces.

'We were marooned together once in a hotel in Vientiane during the monsoon,' he said reluctantly. 'Casement got drunk one night, and talked on and on about Belfast. I couldn't stop him. He would have gone on until dawn if he hadn't passed out. I'd given up listening by then.'

I wonder how much luck Peter Casement had drawing *you* out, in that long, wet interlude in Vientiane, I said silently to myself. Not much, I bet. But I was interested in what David had told me. It was odd to think of that self-contained man I had met at the funeral maudlin and talkative, forcing his confidences on a stranger.

David had now lapsed back into moodiness, drinking Hanoi beer which, apart from the vodka and mineral water I was playing with, was the only thing available.

The vodka was Russian, and palatable enough, but monotonous as a steady drink.

We were sitting in what our Vietnamese hosts engagingly called our suite at the Hua Binh hotel. The hotel itself was a relic of colonial days, and in its day it had probably been very grand. But now it was gloomy and dank, and full of rats, which frisked brazenly along the corridors and ate our toothpaste out of the tubes.

Our suite was a long, dark room, with a table, a couple of chairs, a sofa and a standing lamp at one end, and three tiny single beds draped with dusty mosquito nets at the other.

A mysterious little room which may once have been a dressing room led to a dark bathroom almost filled by a large tub into which water could rarely be coaxed from rusty taps. It is one of the ironies of Indo-China that while natural water lies all around, in rivers, lakes and paddy fields, reticulated water, even drinkable water, is so precious and hard to come by.

I hated our room, because unlike David, who was always out at some ministry or other, I spent so much time there. It was almost impossible to read by the half-watt light bulbs, and the continual bleating of car horns outside made it a waste of time to try to sleep in the hot afternoons. I was usually driven out eventually to make another circuit of the dusty streets, or to take a book down to the Lake of the Recovered Sword. It was here that a giant tortoise had arisen at some time in early history, offering a Vietnamese hero a magical sword to fight the Chinese. In view of the present state of Sino-Vietnamese relations, this seemed quite appropriate. I was sure David would work the legend into his next book.

The least agreeable feature of sitting by the lakeside was the crowd of small children I always attracted. I have nothing against children as such, but, having no common language, our conversations were limited to suggestions that I was Russian, and my repeated denials. I carefully learned how to say 'I am an

Australian' in Vietnamese, but this brought only blank stares.

On days when I was feeling a bit scratchy, the children's insatiable curiosity and their habit of tweaking at my arms and giggling drove me mad, but I never had the heart to shout at them. Peter Casement, when he came up to me by the lake the day after the burning, had fewer qualms. He advanced on the milling children like a mock ogre, waving his arms and bellowing, and they fled, laughing.

'I saw you from the road, and came over,' he said, with the abruptness which was his stock-in-trade. 'Don't let the kids harry you like that. I'll teach you a few Vietnamese curses which will send them packing.'

He sat down on the park seat without invitation. Seen up close, he was older than I first thought, probably late thirties. He had unusually light eyes, a very pale grey with large black centres, and his steady stare was disconcerting. He was sitting still, but he was not relaxed. I noticed again that emanation of nervous energy I had felt at the cremation.

We sat in silence for a moment, then he seemed to feel he had finished examining me, and relaxed slightly. 'Tell me . . .' he said, the Irish strand in his accent dominant, 'tell me, what's Herbert's next book going to be about?'

I flushed. 'I don't think he would particularly want me to discuss it.'

'Quite right,' he said amiably. 'I might purloin it. Though if it is going to be a study of Soumidath's role in South-east Asian politics, he's a bit behind the times. My biography is going to be the last word on all *that*.'

I laughed. He was a bit off the mark, though, as I say, David was looking to Soumidath as his next-but-one subject. His present project was an examination of Sino-Vietnamese relations, from the eleventh century to the present day. He was very keen about it, believing he could present a balanced assessment, but I thought it was suicidal. At present, he had good access in both China and Vietnam, each believing he was their man. An objective summing-up would please neither.

'Cat got your tongue?' Peter Casement said. Then, when I still said nothing – I dislike being teased – he changed tactics.

'*The New Catalyst* was a remarkably successful book,' he said smoothly. 'I was quite envious.'

So were all David's colleagues, especially as no one suspected he had a major book in him. His previous work consisted of scholarly monographs on South-east Asian historical themes. Then, at a time when China was becoming trendy, and the Vietnam war had focused world attention firmly on the region, he brought out a book which was both well researched and reasonably popular, on varieties of Asian communism, and the possibility that they would coalesce into a Third Force, to counter-balance the domination of the superpowers.

The book was naturally praised by the Left, but oddly enough, also by the Right, which saw it as a solemn warning. Visas to hard-to-penetrate countries were there for the asking. David even made some money, enough for future trips. It is true that after the book was published, the Sino-Vietnamese split made a united Asian communist front seem somewhat less probable, but this didn't appear to worry either David or his hosts. His reputation was now made, even though his theory was obviously wrong.

Peter Casement seemed to have decided it was not very profitable discussing publishing history, and changed direction. 'Where did you meet Herbert?' he said. 'In England?'

'No, in Sydney. David lectured in South-east Asian history at Sydney University for two years. I was his student.'

He raised his eyebrows. 'I wouldn't have thought that was his line – getting off with undergraduates.'

I was terse. 'He didn't. We didn't even go out together until after I graduated.'

'Still . . . cradle-snatching!' He smiled for the first time, a flash of gaiety in his curly beard, and the words became inoffensive.

'Not really.' The age gap was not so great. David was about Peter Casement's age, ten years older than I am.

'And now you are a provincial don's wife. How do you like that?'

'I manage,' I said primly. In the interests of truth I was prepared to go no further than that, and if he had pressed me, I might even have elaborated. I hated it quite passionately, remembering the high, bright skies of Sydney, the harbour racy with yachts, the tearing high spirits of the southerly buster arriving on cue on summer evenings, the soft nights and the balmy winters. I hated our grey university town, with its tight protocol and Sunday morning sherry parties, and the other wives always complaining about their *au pairs*.

'Have you children?' he asked curiously. 'Do you work?' His pale eyes watched me very closely as though the answers were important. It was probably just a trick, or a mannerism, but it made me flush. I was unused to being looked at. I don't think David had really seen me for years, and in any case he had the abstracted look that weak sight and thick lenses give.

I was half-tempted to tell Peter Casement to shove off and stop prying, but I was reluctant to be left alone again. 'We have no children,' I said shortly. 'And I work in the sense that I do a good deal of research for David and type his manuscripts.'

As for children, I knew quite early in our marriage that I didn't want to give David a child, and I made sure I did not. He didn't seem to think about it one way or another. We never even discussed it, but I noticed his nephews and nieces tended to keep out of his way on rare family visits. As for a job, I was equipped for nothing except teaching in a private school, which I would detest, or working as a secretary.

'So you travel with your husband?' Peter Casement was still looking at me intently.

'Sometimes.' The present trip was intended to be a breathing space, a chance to see if anything could be done about David and me. I had not realised, though, how difficult life would be in Hanoi, with nothing to do but wait in the gloomy hotel.

It was getting late, and I was increasingly aware of the insistent giggles from the crowd that had reformed a little way off, adults as well as children, to watch the two foreigners sitting together on a park bench. Again and again I heard the sibilant whisper *lien xu:* Russian.

In the west, the huge red inflamed eye of the Asian sun was moving steadily towards the horizon, nearly ready to vanish, as usual, in a murk of thick dusk. At this time of year, Asian sunsets are impressive, but undeniably menacing.

Peter Casement saw my impatience, and stood up.

'Let's go for a drive,' he said. 'Then come and have dinner with me. Unless you are busy?'

'Hardly.' I would have dined alone, had I dined at all. David had at last achieved the invitation he had long been fishing for, a dinner with a junior vice-premier. It was hardly Pham van Dong level, but it was progress.

'As long as we don't go to the Cuban hotel. David is having an official dinner there.' The hotel was actually the Thang Loi, but as it had been built with money, material and workmen donated by Havana as a fraternal gesture, it was generally known as the Cuban hotel. It had air conditioning, but also rats.

'Not likely. We can do better than that. There are still a few unreconstructed restaurants left in Hanoi. Would you prefer the Dog, the Chicken, or the Fish?'

I got thankfully into his car, a new white Toyota. 'The Chicken.' It sounded the most innocuous, and my stomach was still tender from earlier encounters with Vietnamese chillies.

I saw the little crowd was converging on us, and wound up the windows rapidly. Their intentions were clearly benevolent, but David and I had once been mobbed, and the car nearly over-turned, in Tientsin when a huge crowd became hysterical at the sight of foreigners, in China at that time fairly rare.

It was still a little early for dinner, even in puritanical Hanoi, and we drove aimlessly for a while, within the ten-kilometre limit. Peter Casement said nothing, and after a glance or two at his profile, I fell in with his mood, watching the late afternoon crowds out of the window.

Hanoi continued to surprise me. It was my first visit, and I had expected to find a grim, scarred city, showing the traces of bombing. But what the Vietnamese still called Johnson's war and Nixon's war – the two great bombing offensives – had largely spared the centre of the city. The main American targets (intentional and otherwise) were the Long Bien bridge, the railway station, the railway yards, Bach Mai hospital, and the big residential area, Kham Thien Street.

So today Hanoi remains a ravishingly pretty French provincial city full of charming pink villas set in shady gardens, and garnished with lakes, pagodas, and temples. As in the rest of South-east Asia the clamour of car horns is deafening. What used to be called sola topees are *de rigueur* for male wear, and the girls, though their white blouses and dark trousers are a uniform, sway along on their little backless slippers, manifesting their femininity with every glance. There is no unisex here.

That night, Peter Casement took me into a new area, a maze of back streets where there was no trace of colonial influence. Dark, ramshackle wooden houses leaned against each other as though for support, oil lamps flickered, and there was a pungent smell of rotting fish.

We went through a shopfront and up a flight of rickety stairs to a sort of loft, protruding slightly over the street. We were the only customers for dinner, and an old woman sleeping on a straw mat in the corner woke, greeted us briskly and went through a low door at the back, shouting in Vietnamese.

We sat on hard benches at a rough table overlooking the street, and presently a young girl came with bowls and chopsticks and glasses for the bottle of French wine Peter had produced from the boot of his car. He spoke at some length to the girl in Vietnamese, making her giggle.

'Your Vietnamese sounds good', I said enviously. I have absolutely no language ability whatever. 'Where did you study it?'

'I didn't. I picked it up.' He was struggling with the cork with an inadequate opener. 'Don't look so sceptical. It's true. I'm a language freak. Two or three weeks in any country and I can make a fair fist of a conversation.'

I must have still looked doubtful, for he laughed. 'There's no merit in it, you know. It's like being able to play music by ear, or solve complicated maths problems in your head.'

I was to learn later that what he said was quite true. To my knowledge, he spoke French, German and Italian fluently, Japanese and Russian moderately well, and could muddle along in Mandarin and Vietnamese. He had even picked up some Kham, a notoriously unspeakable language.

Dinner came. Rice, with some bony chicken. It was really not much better than the Hua Binh, but at least the surroundings were different. Peter Casement took the trouble to be impersonal, talking easily about the politics of the region, and about Prince Soumidath's efforts, so far unsuccessful, to regain power in the country his ancestors had ruled for centuries.

As David had guessed, he had met the Prince when he was working as an AFP correspondent, and for the present at least, he was enrolled as a sort of aide, with the title of Political Adviser. 'It won't last, of course,' Peter said, 'Soumidath will get tired of me and take up with someone else. He always does. But I'm making the most of it while I have the chance.'

He was silent. In the street below, the girls swayed by, a pedlar with some baskets tinkled the melodious chimes attached to his carrying poles, the faint sound of Vietnamese music came from a distant radio.

It was immemorial Asia. With the calm night, and the unaccustomed wine, I felt relaxed and peaceful, and for once, in harmony with the city. For the first time, I began to understand the Asian indifference to the importance of individual life, the submersion of the self within the overwhelming whole, the unchanging nature of time. The night, with its gentle airs and sounds, and its faint, rotten-sweet scents, had a mesmerising effect. I think we sat for a long time, saying nothing, and I woke from a half-dream with a start when at last Peter said abruptly that it was time to go.

He said he would drive me back to the hotel, but on the way he turned up a side road, and I saw we were outside the Prince's official residence. The Vietnamese had turned over to him a handsome if decaying building which had been the French Embassy before the new one was built.

Using some of the funds he had providently sent abroad, Soumidath had refurbished it quite elegantly, Peter Casement told me. He took my elbow and urged me inside, and, still half-hypnotised by the night, I did not protest. The residence was indeed impressive, in an eccentric sort of way, for the Prince's taste was eclectic. French antique furniture jostled with a few modern pieces, with scrolls and Chinese bowls, and priceless Indo-Chinese bric-à-brac from all periods. I saw the legendary Smiling Buddha of the House of Khamla presiding over the reception room, and was struck again by its resemblance to Soumidath.

Though the night outside was relatively cold, I broke

into a gentle sweat as soon as we walked inside. It was stiflingly hot, and heavily scented with flowers, for the Prince only flourished in a hothouse atmosphere. He sat at a low Chinese table playing bridge with three of his aides, while a phalanx of relatives and sycophants draped themselves in decorative poses around the room. Soumidath looked bored, and he threw down his cards and stood up beaming when we came in, bowing over my hand.

'*Monseigneur,*' Peter Casement said in French. 'May I have the honour to present Mme Herbert,' He added some explanation about David in rapid French, which I could not follow.

As I waited for him to finish, I smiled nervously down at Soumidath. Do Asians, I wonder, mind us looming over them as much as we dislike towering? Or does our awkwardness merely confirm their belief in the superiority of short, neat packaging? I am on the tall side even in Western society. In South-east Asia, I feel like a giant. I looked sideways at Peter Casement, who was a good head taller than any other man in the room, but he did not appear disconcerted. Physically he was a very self-contained man, with a lean figure and well-shaped head, not at all awkward.

Soumidath, to my relief, was obviously glad to see us. He held my hand briefly, inquired after my health in French and English, and insisted we all drink champagne. To make conversation, I complimented him on the beautiful objects with which he had surrounded himself, but this seemed to plunge him into melancholy.

'Ah, Madame,' he said, his smiling mouth turning down, 'I do what I can, but it is a miserable place here. When I am back in my own palace, you should visit me to see how my family has lived for – oh, for many hundred of years. It is very fine, the Three-Tiered Palace, is it not, Peter?'

'Magnificent, *Monseigneur*,' Peter said, with the very

faintest trace of irony. He had told me at dinner that for the last few centuries the Royal House had been indefatigable collectors of *objets d'art*, often by simple requisition from their richer subjects.

After the second bottle of champagne, the Prince declared it was time to dance, and he put on the record player the music he still preferred, big band recordings of the Fifties. As I was the only woman present, he whirled me round the floor determinedly, then passed me on to a succession of tiny aides, each of whom sedately danced me the length of the salon.

Peter Casement, sitting upright on one of the salon's uncomfortable sofas, seemed convulsed with some terrible inner mirth, though his face was impassive. My head was whirling with heat and champagne, and when the last aide deposited me on the sofa beside him, I was almost sick with embarrassment and anger that he had got me into this position. Then he turned to me and smiled, and to my own surprise, I smiled back. What did it matter, after all? I wasn't an awkward teenager any longer.

A phone rang loudly in an anteroom, cutting through the music, and an aide went to answer it. Soumidath seemed suddenly tense, and he cut the record player off so abruptly that the needle scraped across the record. In the silence, we could hear the aide repeating something in Kham in the next room, and Soumidath came towards me and kissed my hand abruptly.

'I must deprive you of your escort, Madame,' he said. 'My colleague and I have matters to discuss. One of my drivers will take you back to your hotel.'

Before I could collect myself, one of the aides had me at the door. I looked back, and saw that the smiling buffoon the Prince often liked to play had vanished. Instead, there was a hard, middle-aged man, who looked like the commander-in-chief he had been. As I went out, I heard him say to Peter in French: 'The message has come. We can go to the border when we wish.'

CHAPTER THREE

The nights in Hanoi were interminable. I used to go to bed early, for there was nothing else to do, and lie in the hot darkness, listening to the thin singing of mosquitoes and the occasional scurry of a passing rat. Often I would wake hopefully thinking it was dawn, because there were lights and voices in the corridor. But my torch told me it was only midnight, and another fraternal delegation was coming in late from a reception at an embassy.

I had only been back a couple of days from Bangkok when David had left on a trip to Saigon, recently renamed Ho Chi Minh City. The Vietnamese had refused to let me accompany him, saying the long journey down, over rutted roads and bombed bridges, was too rough for a woman. I could hardly shame David by pointing out to our hosts that my stamina was much greater than his, so I saw him off with what grace I could manage.

It was still very early when the car came for him, but the thick, turgid air made us sweat, and David had to wipe his glasses with a handkerchief already soggy. He hated the heat, regarding the physical manifestations it forced on his body as an invasion of privacy. Just before he got into the car, he gave me his usual reluctant peck on the cheek, but drew back at once when he tasted the salt on my skin. My husband had an oriental dislike of kissing and never used it as a form of love-play. It took me a long time to get over the way he turned his head away from mine when we first slept together.

The third or fourth night after David left, I forget which, I was lying fully dressed in the dark, under the mosquito net, when there was a sharp rap at the door. I answered it, blinking.

Peter Casement was there, unexpectedly formal in a lightweight suit, and, most unusually for that climate, a collar and tie.

'I've come to invite you to a *soirée* at Soumidath's,' he said quickly, seeing my confusion. 'Sorry about the short notice, but some people have come unexpectedly from the liberated areas, and he's putting on a party for them.'

I felt a physical lightheartedness rise in me at the thought of escape from an evening at the Hua Binh, as though he had offered me a glass of wine. Then I looked down at my jeans and T-shirt, conscious that I hadn't bathed since morning.

'Can you wait until I wash and put on a bit of make-up?' I asked awkwardly, resenting his freshness. His cleanness in that sweaty climate was something I had noticed before. His hands, on the rare occasions when he had touched me, were always dry and cool.

He looked me up and down. 'Oh, I'd do a bit more than that, if I were you,' he said carefully. 'Have you a long dress with you, by any chance? The Prince likes a bit of formality. Even the Viets will be in collar and ties tonight.'

He was making me feel gauche, not for the first time. I had an impulse to say to hell with him, and Soumidath too, and to take refuge in the sullenness which was becoming chronic with me. But I met his eyes, and he smiled at me, and said softly: 'Oh, come on, now.'

My blackness fled. 'I'll see what I can do, if you give me half an hour,' I said, laughing. 'I haven't got much with me, but I'll try not to disgrace you.'

'Good girl.' He turned at once to leave. 'I'll see you downstairs when you are ready.'

It was quite a grand party considering it had been put together at such short notice. The salon was stiflingly hot with so many bodies crammed into it. There was a respectable number of ambassadors, most of whom would have had to cancel engagements to come, a few senior ministers, and a large number of bureaucrats, and, of course, every foreign journalist in Hanoi.

Soumidath had even asked all the Khamla students in the capital to make up the numbers. The women in their national dress were like the exquisite lacquered puppet figures you could buy in the shops. It was a pity the Prince could not have resurrected his mother for the occasion. I had heard what a formidable presence she had made, seated in a heavily gilded armchair, wearing a good many of the jewels the Royal family had been collecting over the centuries, diamonds, rubies, emeralds and pearls being the safest and most portable investment for a royal house which had had its ups and downs.

I was sorry the lights were so bright because they showed up the creases in my long linen shift, which had looked better, on the whole, in the dim mirror at the Hua Binh. Still, I had tarted it up with the heavy gilt necklace and earrings David had bought for me in Chiang Mai, in an inexplicable fit of generosity – or possibly because the bruises on my arms had been rather noticeable that day – and Peter Casement had been approving when I came down.

It was so hot in the salon I could feel the sweat starting to trickle down my bare legs. I was glad I didn't bother much with heavy make-up watching the little rivulets of moisture parting the thick powder on the cheeks of the Eastern European women.

Even the heat, though, couldn't deaden the feeling of excitement and anticipation in the room. It was heady with the perfume of the waxy white flowers in huge Chinese vases all round the salon, and Vietnamese waiters in white jackets, presumably hired from the hotels for the evening, were handing round glasses of champagne. I knew from experience it would be both sweet and warm and took one reluctantly.

'Now, now,' Peter said, reading my thoughts with an accuracy I resented, 'you can't expect Bollinger in darkest Hanoi.' He took my arm and steered me towards the centre of the room.

The crowd parted slightly and I could see Soumidath sitting on a dais, flanked by two men wearing dark blue Mao-style jackets buttoned to the neck. As I saw their faces, I knew at once who they were, and I was human enough to feel a slight malicious pleasure at how angry David would be when he knew what he had missed.

We were looking at two men who were at that time the most legendary in Asia, the leaders of the Khamla Liberation Front: Son Sleng, the commander-in-chief of the Khamla People's Army, and Ieng Nim, the party chairman and self-described president of Free Khamla.

Their faces were well-known throughout the world from newspaper photographs, but they were particularly familiar to me, for only a week before, with David, I had sat through a Foreign Ministry showing of a film on life in the liberated areas. These two faces had been seen over and over.

It had been a bizarre film, a sanitised account of a brutal war, with dedicated leaders living austerely in jungle camps, friendly soldiers helping peasants to bring in their crops, noble doctors conducting apparently bloodless operations on photogenic soldiers in spotless field hospitals.

The diplomats had snorted about it afterwards, because everybody knew that particular war was, even by Asian standards, bloody and degrading beyond the worst predictions.

In every frame of the film, Son Sleng and Ieng Nim had appeared, not in the neat blue suits they wore now, but in bush shirts and trousers with, round their necks, the curious pink and white checked scarf which was their trademark. The film commentary said it was used to wipe away sweat, or could be used in emergency for bandaging wounds. To me, it always looked like a teatowel

Behind the trio on the couch stood three soldiers of the Liberation Front wearing field khaki and the familiar pink and white checks. Each held a weapon, an incongruous sight in that perfumed salon. Two had automatic rifles, M-16s by the look of them, and one a grenade launcher. They would have seemed menacing had not each been tied with bright red satin ribbons, ending in broad and careful bows.

'Captured weapons. A present for Soumidath,' Peter Casement said carefully in my ear. 'All those guys were in the jungle yesterday, wading in mud and blood.'

He brought me up to Soumidath who kissed my hand without rising, helped by his elevated position on the dais. Son Sleng and Ieng Nim both half-stood and shook hands, as behoved soldiers, first with Peter, then with me. They were small men, with delicately shaped hands, but their palms were hard and calloused, and I saw Ieng Nim had one finger missing, the stump still raw and angry.

The low, sonorous voice of a gong spoke from the back of the salon. It was clearly a signal for action, as it is in Chinese opera, for Soumidath got to his feet and silence fell.

'You know who these comrades are,' Soumidath said rapidly, in English then in French. His high-pitched voice was even higher with excitement. 'They have come to us from the liberated areas, and they have brought the weapons you see, as gifts.'

He reached behind him impatiently, snapping his fingers, and one of the soldiers handed him an M-16 bedizened with its bright red ribbons. Soumidath waved it jovially round the room, his finger squeezing the trigger. Some of the diplomats involuntarily stepped back, and a very old ambassador, standing beside me, closed his eyes and whispered *'Merde!'*

Soumidath laughed and held the weapon high for

inspection. 'American-made,' he said with satisfaction. '*Venez, venez*, you may look more closely if you doubt me. It was taken from the bodies of soldiers of the puppet régime, the men who lick the arse of the United States to stay in power.'

Those diplomats in the salon whose countries might loosely be described as allies of the United States looked thoughtfully into space, but there was no stopping Soumidath. He launched himself on one of the marathon tirades against the perfidies of Washington for which he had become internationally famous. His French had become too rapid for me to follow in detail, but I knew the broad outlines of the story.

Soumidath had plenty of justification for his anger. His graceful balancing act on the high wire of international diplomacy had kept his country out of a war which was engulfing Indo-China. He was dealing with China, with the United States, with the Soviet Union, taking some aid from each, making concessions where he had to, playing one off against the other with all the delicacy and skill of which, despite his exhibitionism, he was capable.

But the United States was nervous about his off-stage approaches to the Marxist Liberation Front – Soumidath left no avenue unexplored – and cut the high wire under him, backing his far-right-wing cousin, Prince Vouliphong, in a coup which made Soumidath an exile. Soumidath had never forgiven the Americans. He saw, as they apparently could not, that by this single act his country would be plunged into a decade of blood, misery and starvation, and so it turned out to be.

The temperature in the salon was rising steadily, and most of the Europeans were pale and sweating. I passionately wished we could sit down, but there seemed to be no chance of that. Mercifully, Soumidath seemed to be coming to the end of his diatribe against the Americans, and reaching what for him was the point.

'I rejoice,' he said, 'and you will rejoice with me, that

Son Sleng and Ieng Nim are with us tonight. It gives the lie, does it not, to all those stories put about by my enemies that I wished to have these comrades executed as traitors? Or indeed had done so?'

He laughed, and we all laughed appreciatively. Son Sleng and Ieng Nim, who so far had sat impassively through the Prince's monolgue, gave wide grins which made them look very boyish. Everybody saw the joke, for it was well known that only a few years ago, the ups and downs of politics being what they were, Soumidath had indeed sent the executioners to the two men.

They had escaped only because one of their agents, in the Royal household, had given a last-minute warning. Soumidath had almost had a seizure with rage when he heard they had fled to the *maquis*, or so it was said.

When everybody had stopped laughing, he turned and gracefully drew both men to their feet, embracing them warmly, and standing with his arms round their shoulders, as though for a group photograph.

'When I return to my capital and our affairs are settled,' he said, 'this man' (he hugged Son Sleng) 'shall be my Prime Minister, and this other (it was Ieng Nim's turn) shall be Minister of the Interior. I shall be Head of State, a roving ambassador for my country, travelling to Europe, to the United Nations to put our case for aid for the great task of national reconstruction.'

He beamed with satisfaction, embracing the two men again, and at some invisible signal, a band in an alcove struck up the Khamla national anthem. It was a moving moment, carefully stage-managed, and no one could resist applauding when the anthem was over.

'Thank God for that,' I said when the band began to play selections from ancient musical comedies, and we were free to move about, the tension turning to chatter. Someone at the end of the salon had been brave enough to open a window and a little fresh air came through it, stirring the atmosphere which was now heavy with ambassadorial cigar smoke.

I looked back. Soumidath, Son Sleng and Ieng Nim were surrounded by a crush of diplomats, but I saw their faces briefly. All were smiling, but Ieng Nim's face was impassive and secretive. He was not, I thought, a man I would like to cross.

'Why did the Prince say Ieng Nim would be his Minister of the Interior?'

Peter groaned. 'A bad joke, and one he may have to pay for. Ieng Nim has a long memory.'

'Yes, but why?'

'The Minister for the Interior is always the sinister figure, the man who runs the secret police, who arranges assassinations and executions and midnight arrests. Ieng Nim is notorious for the way he deals with prisoners, even in a war where neither side is too tender. Soumidath was, in effect, offering him the job for which he seems suited.'

'Then he wasn't serious?'

'Oh, he was serious enough, and the bastard would take the job and enjoy it. But Soumidath would get rid of him as soon as he could, and they both know it. The Prince wants to keep Son Sleng, because he could work with him, and he is a great hero in the liberated areas. But not the other.'

'He looks dangerous,' I said idly, watching the group at the top of the room. Ieng Nim was silent, while the rest of the men talked animatedly.

'He is,' Peter said, sounding suddenly weary. I noticed how pale he was. 'Believe me, he is.'

* * *

I have always been a poor drinker, and three or four glasses of bad champagne in that heat was enough to make me indiscreet. When Peter drove me back to the hotel, he would have left me in the lobby, but I took his hand and drew him firmly towards the stairs.

'Don't go,' I said, laughing, 'Come up and have a

drink. No, don't worry' – he was gesturing rather crossly towards what passed for a bar at the Hua Binh hotel, and which was now firmly closed – 'for once we have something to offer. One of the French diplomats who left last week sold David half a dozen bottles of wine.'

He hesitated, looking at his watch. 'It's late.'

'Please,' and again, 'Please.'

He gave me a curious look then, without another word, he followed me up the stairs. The room, so melancholy when I was alone, looked more cheerful when we put on the lights, and Peter started opening the wine while I washed the dusty glasses in the discoloured, lukewarm water which came from the bathroom tap.

'God knows what David will say when he finds we have drunk his precious wine,' I said, putting the glasses down. I meant it as a joke, but it was not altogether, and Peter caught the undertone.

'You're afraid of him?' He really had very odd eyes, close-up, the lightest, clearest grey I had ever seen.

I laughed. 'Not tonight.' I drank quickly, feeling the wine sink gratefully through my blood. As I have said, I am a poor drinker, and an embarrassing side-effect is to make me amorous.

Five years of marriage to David had left me more or less frigid when sober, but a few drinks at a cocktail party tended to revive the sort of feelings I would really, under the circumstances, prefer to do without.

David had always moved very swiftly to break up any lighthearted relationship which seemed to be developing. He had never made any comment, probably because an acknowledgement that I was even capable of an amorous flirtation would contradict his own beliefs about frigidity, but he had always been there, sliding between me and any attractive man with whom I laughed or talked, insisting that it was time to go home.

Well, he wasn't here tonight. I poured myself another

glass of wine for courage, and sat down again, very close to Peter. He was unusually silent, watching me with a white, shut face. There was no sound in the room except the high-pitched whining of mosquitoes, and the darkness at the edge of the standard lamp seemed absolute.

I did not understand why Peter looked at me like that, but I did not really care. His left hand was on the sofa beside me, and I took it deliberately in mine and held it up to the light, admiring its shape and the way the lamp made a nimbus round the elongated fingers. Though he remained unmoving, a small jolt of something which felt like static electricity ran between us, and I saw by his eyes that he had experienced it too.

I was disconcerted by the strength of my own feeling, but for once I was not going to retreat. It was obvious that one of us was going to have to make a move, and as he showed no signs of doing so, even when I twined my hand in his, it would have to be me. For once, I felt relaxed and self-confident, my body damp with heat and anticipation, the wine singing in my head and producing a very pleasant dizziness.

I put my mouth tentatively to his, but his lips remained shut, and I felt a slight movement of withdrawal. But I was too aroused to care, and I pressed hard against him, my arms around his neck. He murmured something I could not catch, and his lips parted and I felt the heady, frantic movement of his tongue in my mouth.

We clung together, sweaty with heat, his tongue exploring my mouth and my ear, his warm, sweet breath moving over my damp cheek, his hands tight enough to bruise, but unlike David's with no desire to hurt. I must have been drunker than I thought, for a kind of fireworks display began to go off in my head, and I shook violently in Peter's grasp.

Peter got to his feet with some difficulty, as the whole of my weight was on him, and began to draw me towards the bed. I stumbled after him, kicking off my sandals, laughing and dizzy. At the bedside, I started trying to peel off my dress, but my hands were clumsy.

'Help me!' I said frantically.

He pulled my dress down again, and with a quick movement, pushed me onto the bed and sat beside me, holding me firmly pressed against the pillow.

'Listen.' His voice was hoarse, and he cleared his throat and started again. 'Listen, dearest Gilly. You're a lovely girl, but I don't go to bed with ladies who have had a drink or two too many, and will regret it later.'

I tried to speak, but he put his hand over my mouth and shook his head. I could barely see his face in the dimness, but his touch was repudiation enough. He was at a great distance from me, and wary.

'Don't say anything now that you will be sorry for tomorrow.' He got up and started towards the door. Over his shoulder, he said: 'When I am gone, get up and wash your face. Take an aspirin if you have it, or you'll have a head in the morning. Sleep well.'

He was gone. I lay in the darkness for a while, listening to the thin high singing of mosquitoes, then slowly and painfully I began to weep.

CHAPTER FOUR

David came back from Saigon with a gap in his front teeth. He had broken a crown, and the jagged bit of tooth remaining made him look rather ridiculous, like a malevolent clown. He was in a great deal of pain and in a furious temper as well, so we flew out to Thailand as soon as we could get an exit permit. David's interest in the great Asian socialist experiment did not extend to trying out socialist dentistry. He could hardly wait to get to Bangkok, to consult one of the western dentists there.

Money was going to be tight because of the dentist's bill, so instead of staying at one of the antiseptic, international hotels in Bangkok David preferred, we were reduced to a sleazy, third-class one down in the area of the great wats, light years away from the westernised business and hotel centre.

I liked it, because though it was shabby, it was also cheerful, with long communal tables in the odorous dining room, full of Thais and noisy foreign couples with backpacks.

David managed to get us a small, separate table in the corner, as local table manners upset him, but for me it was still a big improvement on the gloom of the Hua Binh. While David was out, I even made friends with two young Americans doing Asia on the cheap, and we went together to the Temple of the Dawn, and to shop for fruit in the markets.

The market stalls were irresistible, piled high with mangoes and papaya and durian, and bright spiky fruits I could not even name. It was stiflingly hot under the tin roof and the aisles were a mixture of dust and bird droppings, but the noise and bustle and cajoling of the stallholders were a delight to me.

While I was waiting for some mangoes to be weighed, I glanced up one of the aisles and saw a tall European some distance ahead. Europeans were few and far between in the market, and very conspicuous. It was impossible to miss this man, for he stood head and shoulders over the Thai women shopping in the market.

'Peter!' I called, and without thinking what I was doing, I started to push my way towards him, ignoring the American girl, Jan, who was asking me something. I was targeted on Peter, as though a magnet was drawing me. The crowd was thick and claustrophobic, and the air was dense with the cloying richness which the piles of fruit exhaled. I began to feel dizzy, and my limbs turned heavy, as though I was in a nightmare, but I still struggled on.

Then someone stood hard on my foot, and the pain made common sense return. I stopped fighting the crowd, and turned back to where Jan and her boyfriend were waiting for me. I was embarrassed and alarmed by what I had done. What had begun as a physical attraction to a personable man seemed to be turning into an obsession.

When we came out of the market, I saw Peter again. He was standing patiently while an Asian woman piled up his arms with parcels of fruit and vegetables. She was so much shorter than he and she had to strain up to reach, and he was laughing at her and making some sort of a jovial protest. It was a scene of accustomed domesticity and intimacy, which clearly had been played out before.

When Peter's arms were full, the woman called to a young boy who was throwing stones at a fence, and gave him the rest of the parcels to carry. The three of them set off down the street, and I saw them pick up a taxi at the corner.

Peter had not noticed me for his back was turned, but

I had seen the woman quite clearly. She was not very young, probably in her middle thirties, and she was nothing at all like the slender Asian girls with the faces of experienced children that foreigners usually took up with. Foreign correspondents, in particular, tended to acquire these girls, some of them Vietnamese or Lao refugees, claiming them on expenses as interpreters.

This woman was not one of those. As well as being past her graceful youth, she was dumpy and thick-waisted, and would soon be fat. Her face was rather heavy, and too much made up, and her hair, instead of falling down her back in a dark river, was stiffly permed and set. The child was large for a Thai, and quite light-skinned. He could easily have had European blood.

The sight of Peter tamed into domesticity shocked me. He looked very unheroic, and I had cast him in a heroic role.

But, unreasonably, I felt a burning, squeezing pain in my breast, as tangible as indigestion or heartburn. It took my breath away for a moment, and Jan exclaimed and asked what was wrong. 'Nothing,' I said, 'the heat. Let's go back to the hotel.'

Harry Greene had said Peter Casement was sometimes thought to be a homosexual. I had considered this, and though I believed it unlikely, I was keeping it in reserve as a comforting explanation for what had happened in Hanoi. It would do to salvage my pride, if nothing else. But it did not look as if this theory would hold up.

* * *

David's new tooth was expensive, but it was lucky for him after all. If he had not broken it, we would not have been in Bangkok at a time when someone in Washington DC decided that Prince Soumidath was getting far too favourable a press, even in exile. The mandarins of Foggy Bottom clearly felt that their protégé, Soumidath's cousin Prince Vouliphong, needed a boost, and the world should be shown there was nothing rotten in the state of Khamla.

At least, that was the interpretation the cynics of the foreign press corps put on the discreet message which came from the Royal Khamla embassy in Bangkok to a selected few foreigners, suggesting that if they cared to apply for visas to visit Prince Soumidath's former capital, they would be unlikely to be turned down.

Of course, the issuing of visas was the business of the Khamla embassy itself, but no foreigners except American advisers had been into the country for months, and the sudden opening-up was a surprise. 'Big Brother over at the US mission vets all visa applications,' Harry Greene said when we met him at a British Council reception. 'For a long time now, they've been turning everybody down flat. I've been to see Mr Vinh at the Khamla embassy a dozen times, and he always smiles and says, "Not convenient. We are not ready to receive you."'

'Why are they changing the policy now?' David said abruptly.

Harry shrugged. 'Who knows? The word here is that there has been a lull in the fighting. The Reds want to consolidate their positions in the liberated areas, and the Chinese seem to have been holding off on arms shipments to them lately. I know for a fact the airport hasn't been mortared for a month.'

I saw David perceptibly flinch. He had talked freely, on a visit we had paid to the Royal Khamla embassy, of his wish to go to the capital. It had seemed safe enough, as he knew no visas were being issued.

But now, whether he enjoyed it or not, he was going to be one of the small party of journalists and businessmen who were to be the first foreign visitors to be officially received by Prince Vouliphong. Harry was going, and to my surprise and pleasure I had also been invited. David had for once offered no objection. I think he wanted some moral and physical support.

If it was true that the members of the party had been vetted by the US Embassy, I could quite see why they wanted David. A trendy academic with good connections in other parts of Asia was ideal for their purpose, provided they could convince him the present régime in Khamla was relatively stable, and that Prince Vouliphong, even if a stopgap, was a better bet than either the volatile Soumidath or the Khamla Liberation Front.

David had a briefing at the American Embassy with a couple of political officers before we left, and I think they were able to guess without much trouble what was the right line to take. I came over to the embassy to pick him up in a taxi, and I heard one of the men ushering him out saying solemnly: 'We're trying to look at it in the perspective of the history of the region, Dr Herbert. That's the important thing.'

David knew he had to go to Khamla. He had never been there, though he had written extensively about it, and it was the embarrassing gap in his Asian experience. But he was very uneasy just the same, fussing about malaria pills and his expired cholera vaccination, and asking me constantly if I would find the trip too rough.

I knew what was the matter. He was haunted by Harry Greene's throwaway line about the Liberation Front mortaring the airport.

* * *

I met Peter again before we left. Harry Greene had invited us to pre-dinner drinks, and he and I were sitting in the bar of the Grand Hotel, waiting for David to come back from the British Library. I liked Harry enormously. He had an obsessive interest in war and death, but he could easily be persuaded to put this aside and talk about the more attractive aspects of life in

South-east Asia on which he was an expert. He treated me with an off-hand friendliness which made me very comfortable with him, and even David admitted that he was an interesting chap, for David a very high compliment.

Harry was telling me an absorbing story about an encounter with a tiger in a Vietnamese minefield, and I did not see Peter come up behind us. He gave me a European half-bow, and thumped Harry robustly on the back.

'So you are going to see the Three-Tiered Palace and the sacred elephants!' he said, smiling. 'Lucky you. I tried to gate-crash the party, but they won't have me, of course.'

He sat down and made easy conversation, talking of temples I should visit if I got the chance, and urging us to give his best regards to the *patron* of the Roi Soleil. 'It used to be one of the best restaurants in Asia a year or two ago,' he said wistfully. 'I don't know what it's like now. It probably serves hamburgers and pickle, and pastrami on rye.'

He seemed quite unselfconscious, but also rather preoccupied, and after a few minutes, he turned politely to me and asked if I would forgive him for taking Harry away. 'Only for a moment,' he said. 'We have some unfinished business.'

I thought Harry looked surprised, but he rose without protest, and went over to the other side of the bar with Peter. By the time he came back, David had arrived, and was complaining about his cholera vaccination. He was quite incurious about the fact that Harry had not been with me, and he did not see Peter.

I, on the contrary, was very curious, and Harry met my eyes uneasily. When David was ordering a drink, he leaned over and spoke quietly. 'It was nothing much,' he said. 'He wanted me to take a message to a friend of his, that's all. Peter always likes to make a little mystery out of things.'

CHAPTER FIVE

No one was mortaring the airport when we arrived, but as the Trident came in low over the jungle, we saw the scars of previous attacks beside the runway, and the burned-out skeletons of buildings on the edge of the field. David said nothing, looking out of the window with a stone face.

It was peaceful enough as we emerged from the plane into the steaming, Turkish-bath day. A large cheerful man from the US mission and a neat protocol official from the Palace were there to meet us. In the bullet-scarred airport building, children in national dress with clownish circles of rouge on their cheeks gave each of us a bouquet of flowers. They held our hands in claw-like grips while we posed, rather reluctantly, for a group photograph. David, I could see, hated it.

The rest of the group was cheerful, full of the easy camaraderie of acquaintances thrown together in exotic surroundings. There were a couple of agency bureau chiefs from Bangkok, a *Washington Post* man doing a flip through Asia, a woman from *Time's* Hong Kong office, three out-of-their-element businessmen, and David and I.

Old Asia hands say the Prince's capital is the prettiest and most elegant city in South-east Asia, and so it looked, as we drove through to the guest house. Bangkok, these days, is caught up in the march of Progress, and the noise and traffic jams are nightmarish. This little city by contrast had the quality of an agreeable dream, the air languorous and scented with frangipani, the creaking of ox-carts more insistent than the angry buzzing of Hondas.

There were a few western-style office blocks in the centre, and we passed a military barracks on the way from the airport, but the city had largely escaped the curse of the Soviet-style blocks of workers' flats which blight cityscapes in China and Vietnam and North Korea. The local style of architecture was two-storey houses in dark wood, very similar to the houses in parts of Thailand, but there were also signs of French colonial influence: pink-washed villas in large, overgrown gardens, blazing with bougainvillaea and poincianas. Heavy, sweet scents erupted into the moist air, mingling with the ripe-rotten stench of the canals.

'Ah, the smell of Asia! Themes and variations,' Harry Greene said, sniffing the air with a gourmet's passion.

We caught a glimpse of the Three-Tiered Palace in its lush gardens embellished with small pagodas and spirit houses. In an enclosure, two of the Royal elephants swung their trunks moodily. But Harry craned out of the minibus window to look at the raw, ugly perimeter fence that ran round the palace grounds. 'That's new!' he said.

The fence looked as if it was electrified, and the dark snouts of mounted machine guns were visible through weapons slits in the concrete blockhouse at the palace gate. Prince Vouliphong was clearly not fond of people dropping in, for as well as soldiers in the blockhouse, two men with M-16s stood guard at the gateway. They were very smart, with the Royal arms on their cap badges and shoulder boards, and as well as the M-16s, they wore sidearms, and carried heavy wooden batons painted white. 'Welcome to Khamla,' said one of the businessmen, with a nervous laugh.

The guesthouse was agreeable, or at least I thought so, a long rambling white villa in a big garden. It may have once been a diplomat's house, for there were signs of former grandeurs here and there. The original furnishings, however, had long since vanished, and each room was equipped only with a small bed draped in mosquito netting, a cane chair and table, and a few hooks for hanging clothes. There was a stained wash-basin in my room, but it did not surprise me that nothing came out of the tap. I wondered how the American advisers liked life in the capital.

The common bathroom was stone-floored, with a drain in the corner. There was no shower, but a large stone jar of warmish water stood in the centre of the room, a saucepan-like tin ladle hanging from a hook on the wall.

I stripped off my sweaty clothes and stood ladling water over myself. I was in tearing spirits, for David and I had been given separate rooms, the narrow beds ruled out cohabitation, and there would be lively and interesting people to talk to at dinner.

* * *

Prince Vouliphong gave his promised reception for the foreign guests on the second night of our stay in the capital. It took place, of course, in the Three-Tiered Palace, which was as sumptuous as Peter had promised. We had had a job getting in, being held up at the gate while the soldiers gave the men a body search and turned out the contents of the small handbags the *Time* lady and I carried. 'You can't blame them. The Prince has already been shot at twice, and one of the Palace limos was blown up last week,' Harry said. 'Lucky for him he wasn't in it. There wasn't much left of two of his aides and the chauffeur. Very nasty.'

David said nothing, but one of the businessmen, a fat, jolly silk importer raised his eyes and gave a mournful wail. 'What in hell are we doing in this dump?' he said. 'I can hardly wait to get back to New Jersey.'

Prince Vouliphong received us in the Long Gallery, its dark panelled walls hung with scrolls, rose-and-white vases writhing with gilded dragons lined up the length of the room, *objets* in jade and ivory scattered on small tables. The Prince stood at the end of the gallery waiting for us. Behind him I saw, to my amazement, the Smiling Buddha of the Royal house.

There was no mistaking it. The Buddha sat with one hand folded on his lap, the other straight and stretched forward, in the position known as *Touching the Ground*: Earth is called on to witness the Holy One's resistance during his ordeal at the hands of Mara the Tempter.

Harry was walking beside me, and I touched his arm and started to speak, but he had already seen where I was looking. 'No, it isn't what you think it is,' he said in a low voice. 'It's a copy. Vouliphong had it carved when he took over, and he swears it is the real one, but it isn't. Soumidath has that. But the fortunes of the Royal house go with the Buddha, so Vouliphong has to put on a show. It deceives most people.'

'How do you know Soumidath has the real one?'

He shrugged. 'Obviously I can't be one hundred percent sure. But I've got a good nose for a phoney, and this bastard is certainly one.'

As we came closer, I saw that Vouliphong had a disconcerting resemblance to his Royal cousin, and that they both, as I had noticed before, resembled the Smiling Buddha. But Vouliphong's smile was anxious, and he looked rather like a middle-aged child on its best behaviour.

His wife was with him, a small fat woman dressed in a wrap-around silk gown and an astonishing display of rubies and emeralds. A couple of officers stood behind them, in full dress and wearing sidearms, though they were so decorative I assumed their role was symbolic. I noticed the US embassy man who had met us at the plane hovering watchfully about.

The Prince shook hands all round and made a short speech of welcome in French so slow and careful that even I could follow it without difficulty. He might resemble his cousin, but he had nothing of Soumidath's effervescence, and ability to switch to any one of three languages without knowing he was doing it. Nor had his *soirée* anything of the style of an evening *chez* Soumidath. It was heavy going all the way, with laborious conversation and plodding dissertations on the beauties of the capital by aides whose French was so heavily accented that I could hardly understand them.

Vouliphong moved slowly round the room, doing his duty by the visitors. By the time he got to David and Harry and me, he was beginning to look rather despairing. I remember Peter Casement had told me he had not exactly chosen greatness, but had had greatness thrust upon him, when the Americans decided Soumidath should be replaced.

Vouliphong would not have been their choice if there had been anyone better, but he had certain negative virtues: if he was not the people's idol, at least he was not unpopular, he could be pushed around, and he was willing to accept American aid and American advisers. Above all, he had the blood royal. His superficial resemblance to Soumidath was useful on visits to the more remote areas, where the pheasants didn't even realise the head of state had changed. They still sank to their knees, touched their foreheads to his hands, and called him their father.

I was only half-listening to what the Prince was saying when, to my astonishment, I heard David mention Peter's name. Even now I don't know why he did it. A sort of malice, I suppose, in the hope of hearing something disagreeable.

He had his reward, for the Prince's moon-face flushed with anger. 'A dangerous man!' he said loudly. 'An assassin!' It is a powerful word in any language, but in French it has even more vigour than in English. *'Assassin,'* Vouliphong repeated, stressing every syllable.

David's glasses provide his eyes with a useful shield,

but I could see his pleasure. 'Surely not,' he murmured in a deprecating voice.

The Prince misunderstood, and felt he was being doubted, or perhaps royalty is not used to being ever so slightly mocked. In either case, his anger increased, and he spoke so loudly that his aides, and the hovering American, came edging up nervously.

'You speak now of a man who turns my cousin's thoughts to murder,' Vouliphong said. 'I think they have told you that twice hired killers have tried to shoot me, and last week a bomb was planted in the car which was to take me to a reception at the American embassy. It was a Daimler, the only one in the country.' His face contorted with the pain of loss, and Harry Greene's sardonic mouth twitched at the corner. He was probably thinking of the aides and the chauffeur, blown to bits.

'Are you suggesting, *Monseigneur*, that M. Casement arranged this?' David asked politely. Even he sounded a bit incredulous.

The ubiquitous American – his name, I think, was Rick Dawson – slid easily into the conversation. 'No, no,' he said. 'I'm sure His Highness doesn't mean that at all. There are still a few wild men out in the bush, unfortunately, and we have an incident now and again. But we're getting on top of it. The capital is now secure. There will be no more bombings.'

The Prince remained obdurate. 'I have told you it is Casement's doing,' he said, addressing Dawson as if we were not there. 'There is proof. The man confessed . . .'

'No proof at all.' Dawson had his hand on the Prince's arm. He turned to us. 'The guards misunderstood something a prisoner said when they were, uh, questioning him. Come over here, Sir, you haven't met our guest from the *Washington Post.*'

In the car going back to the guest house, David was unusually cheerful.

He talked easily and with good insight about the

Prince's chances of staying in power for any length of time. Then, just as we reached the guesthouse gate, he turned and looked hard at me.

'I told you Casement was a *sale type*,' he said forcefully. 'Now perhaps you will think again about consorting with him.'

I felt anger run through me like an electric shock, but it was a clean and liberating anger, not the sullen kind which turned me dumb. I did something I had never done before, and laughed at David.

'Consorting!' I said contemptuously. 'You make a few normal conversations sound like a criminal offence. And if you believe that rubbish the Prince was talking just now, you are a fool.' I mimicked the Prince's accent. *'Assassin!'*

David was so surprised that he stumbled getting out of the car, and I laughed at him again.

Later, when I was drifting off to sleep, he scratched softly on my door, and when I did not answer, came cautiously into the room and stood looking at me. I remained silent and still, and he could not see my face through the folds of the mosquito net. He said my name carefully a couple of times, then very slowly went away, closing the door behind him.

* * *

Harry Greene had looked pale and sweaty at lunch, and begged off a trip to an irrigation area which had been arranged for us. When he did not appear at dinner, I went to his room and found him lying under his mosquito net shivering with fever.

I pulled back the net and looked at him closely. His skin was damp and pallid, his teeth were chattering, and his eyes glistened alarmingly in the dim light the single ceiling bulb provided.

'Malaria,' he said, clutching the sheet round him. 'It's all right, it won't kill me. I've had it half a dozen times.

Can you get me those pills from my bag? My legs seem to have gone on me.'

I gave him the pills and some boiled water, and looked at him doubfully. 'Shouldn't I get a doctor?'

'No need. All I can do is sweat it out.' His body shook so violently that the bedframe rattled. I touched his skin and it was burning hot. He was breathing as hard as if he had just run a marathon.

I made up my mind, and got up from the side of the bed. 'You're very sick. I'm going to tell the guest house manager and get him to ring the hospital. They must be used to dealing with malaria here.'

His burning hand closed on my wrist. 'Wait. This fever is a bloody nuisance. I have to go to see somebody tonight.'

I laughed, and freed myself, though not without an effort. 'You're not going anywhere tonight, except possibly to the hospital. Your friend will have to wait, or come here to see you.

'He can't come here. And it has to be tonight, he can't stay in town any longer than that. He lives up country.' Harry dragged himself up painfully. He had spoken coherently enough, though he was trembling so violently that the words were distorted and hard to understand.

He was half-standing now, trying to drape his nakedness in the sheet, and I saw that he was in high fever, his eyes brilliant with delirium.

I pushed him back on the bed. 'All right,' I said. 'Don't worry. Tell me his name and I'll get a message to him.' I thought he was talking about some resident foreigner whom I could ring from the guest house.

Harry was still struggling to get up. 'In the bag,' he said, his breathing laboured. 'In the bag. A brown envelope.'

It seemed dangerous to thwart him, so I went to his travelling bag and found the envelope, a plain sealed one with no address, I brought it to him, but he thrust it back into my hands.

'Someone must take it,' he said. 'It was a promise. I promised . . . If it is not delivered tonight, it is no good.'

'All right.' I took the envelope and tucked it in my shirt pocket. There seemed little point in arguing with him. He was shivering and burning in my grasp, and I wanted to pass on the responsibility to someone more competent. 'Tell me where your friend lives,' I said patiently, 'and I will take him the letter myself, after we find a doctor for you. It's a nice moonlight night for a stroll.'

He seemed to hesitate. Then, pulling me down again onto the side of the bed with his burning hand, his mouth trembling so hard I could hardly catch what he was saying, he gave me the directions.

* * *

It was indeed a nice night for a walk, a soft slow scented night, the heat withdrawn a little way off behind the barrier of night coolness, but still ready to pounce.

I walked very slowly so the heat would not catch me and make me sweat, but I could not stop my palms growing moist, or control my rapid breathing.

I had had some trouble getting past the guard at the guesthouse gate. He tried to argue with me about going out, but we had no common language, and in the end I just pushed past him and went. Short of shooting me, there was nothing much he could do about it.

It was a stupid thing to do, to act as Harry's courier, and if it had not been for David, I probably would not have gone.

After I had persuaded the guest house manager to ring for a doctor, I had gone to David's room, along the verandah from mine. I wanted to tell him Harry was ill, and I might even have told him about the envelope. But as I came in the door, he looked up from his notes, and said irritably: 'Do you want anything in particular? I have to finish this paper tonight.' It was not so much his words but the sudden flash of something like loathing I saw in his eyes which made me turn and go out again without even replying.

I knew where the Temple of the Hundred Buddhas was, barely a kilometre from the guest house, near the turning on to the road north. Our guide had pointed it out to us when we travelled to the irrigation area, and we had been promised a later visit, for it was one of the most important and ancient shrines in the country.

As I came up to the main gate, I took the envelope from my pocket and held it in my hand. I did not know what was in it, and I did not particularly care. Obviously it was not an ordinary social message or the sender would not be using the temple as a post box, but I did not care about that either.

The temple lay long and deserted in the moonlight, the writhing shapes of the roof guardians outlined against the milky bowl of the sky. Under the projecting roof itself, I could see the pale outlines of the one hundred Buddhas side by side like sentinels.

I should have been afraid, but the harmonious night with its sweet airs calmed me and my breathing slowed. I stood in the half-shadow, under the temple roof and above me the blind-eyed Buddhas smiled their curved stone smiles.

I had been told someone would be waiting for me to take the letter, but I could see nothng. Then a faint current of air came down the avenue of Buddhas, and brought with it the clove smell of the local cigarettes. I heard a rustling movement somewhere ahead, then saw the tip of a cigarette glowing near the last Buddha.

As I came closer, a man stirred and cleared his throat. I could just see in the moonlight that it was a young monk in a saffron robe, his head shaved, his arms and one shoulder bare.

I moved deliberately out into the moonlight so he could see me, and heard him give a sudden anxious groan. He had probably not been expecting a woman, and my dark slacks and shirt had given him no warning. He half-shrank behind the Buddha, and I was afraid he would go away.

'Come on, I won't bite,' I said, showing him the envelope. He still hesitated, though. Perhaps he was at a stage of his novitiate when any contact with a woman was forbidden. Then I heard someone speak abruptly behind him. There was another man, not a monk, but a dark figure in bush shirt and trousers, in the shadows behind the Buddha. I could not see his face.

Whatever he had said, it seemed to give the young monk courage, for he came forward and gingerly took the envelope from my hand, backing uneasily away as soon as he had it.

'Don't be afraid,' I said in careful rehearsed French. 'The messenger who was sent is ill. I have come in his place.'

He looked at me blankly, and I suppose he either did not speak French – many of the younger people did not – or he did not understand my accent. The local brand of French is a dialect in itself. But the man in the background gave a half-bow of acknowledgement and said, *'Merci,'* in a low, hoarse voice.

They clearly were anxious to be rid of me, but I hesitated for a moment, peering into the dark shadows behind the Buddha. The second man had a solid, chunky outline with something familiar about it. But his face was completely hidden under a peasant's conical hat, and he kept his head well down.

Just as I turned to go, though, he held out his hand to the young monk to take the letter, and it was illumined for a second by a change in the dappled pattern of moonlight. His hand was mutilated and one finger was missing, leaving a wound still raw and ugly.

Walking back to the guest house, my breath came so fast I felt dizzy. It produced a not unpleasant sensation of terrible glee.

We had been assured by our hosts there were no elements of the National Liberation Front within 200 kilometres of the city. But I had just delivered a message to Ieng Nim, its second in command, at one of the main centres of the country's official religion. I remembered that Rick Dawson had said. 'The capital is now secure,' and I laughed aloud.

The guard at the guest house pretended not to see me when I returned. He had obviously not reported my absence, rightly assuming he would be in deeep trouble for failing to stop me.

I sat on the verandah in the moonlight for a little while, breathing in the scented night, then I went to bed, but I did not sleep for a long time.

* * *

Harry looked better the next morning, though his skin was a greyish-yellow. When I went in, he was propped up on a couple of pillows drinking tea, and he looked at me warily.

He answered abstractedly when I asked how he was. 'Not bad, a bit weak,' he said. 'It was a short, sharp bout this time.'

I sat down in the room's one chair, and waited for him to make the next move. He took some time about it, obviously unsure how to begin.

'I gather I was a bit freaked out last night,' he said at last. 'Candidly I don't remember much about it.' He cleared his throat and tried again. 'Did you see an envelope lying about anywhere? I seem to have lost it.'

I laughed. 'You didn't lose it. You gave it to me and I delivered it for you. To the temple, as you said.'

He closed his eyes and groaned. 'Christ! I was afraid of that.'

I was doubtful of him. 'Do you really not remember?'

'Sort of. But I was hoping it was a bad dream. It can happen, with fever. You don't know what's real and what isn't.' He sat up and looked at me more closely. 'You're all revved up this morning, aren't you? You enjoyed that little excursion last night?'

'Why not?' It was true, of course, I could feel a slow dangerous burning excitement beneath my skin. '*You* obviously find taking risks a turn on.' I had seen the white scars of old wounds on his body the night before.

'Yes, but I didn't think . . .' He saw my look and decided not to risk finishing the sentence. Then he sighed. 'Well, it's done. But I think we had better both forget about it.'

'All right.' I got up and looked at my watch. It was nearly time for our hosts to collect us for the day's excursion.

'There is one thing I want to know, though,' I said carefully, at the door, 'The message was sent by Peter, wasn't it?'

Harry slid down further in the bed, closed his eyes, and shook his head from side to side in an impatient gesture which might have meant anything. I started to ask him again, but then the doctor came into the room, busy with handshakes and '*bonjours*', and the sound of a horn from the garden told me the minibus was waiting.

* * *

I can never get used to Asian heat, the sullen enemy which waits at the edge of the verandah, advancing as the brief dawn coolness evaporates, only retreating again a little way when darkness comes.

All that long day we tramped through villages, looking at cottage industries, with no chance of the usual lunchtime shower and siesta. Sweat ran down our bodies in rivulets, dripping down on to the dusty ground. The men's shirts stuck to them as though they had been caught in rain storms, and I felt the slow torture of heat rash starting beneath my arms.

By the time we returned to the guest house, it was well past sunset, and I was too tired to do anything but take a bath and sit on the verandah drinking cold tea. David, who did not care for this sort of thing, had pleaded the need to work on his notes and so escaped the excursion. He looked fresher and composed, though he grew annoyed when I would not come with him to dinner.

By nine o'clock I couldn't keep my eyes open and went to bed. On the way, I glanced through Harry's door, but the room was empty and the bed made. He had either been taken to hospital or was well enough to get up. In either case, I felt no more responsibility for his welfare.

It was probably because I went to bed early that I woke so easily later, or perhaps it was the moon which disturbed me, glaring though the curtainless window and turning the room white. The moonlight was so strong that I could see the face of my travelling clock through the mosquito net: three o'clock, and I was already wide awake.

I had been lying for a while trying to will myself back into drowsiness when I heard a faint chinking noise from outside, as though two pieces of metal had briefly touched. Then another sound, thin and sibilant, like a whistle.

The sounds were so furtive in the quiet night that I moved with instinctive caution, sliding carefully from under the mosquito net, going silently to the french doors leading out to the verandah.

For privacy, I had left them only a little way ajar, but I could see out over part of the verandah and the garden. The huge moon flared in the milky skies, but because of its brightness, there were dense patches of shadow dappling the garden like camouflage.

I thought I saw somethng move in one of these dark patches, then a moment later, I was sure. I could just make out the dark figure of a man with the triangular outline of an automatic rifle slung over his shoulder.

It could, of course, have been one of the guards, though they usually wore only sidearms. But I was certain it was not, the man's movements had been too cautious. Still moving quietly, on bare feet, I went to the door leading into the corridor, with the intention of waking one of the others. I thought I would try Harry's room before David's. Even in a post-malarial stage, he seemed a better bet.

But as I started to turn the door handle, I heard the sound of feet in the corridor, slapping sofly but unmistakably in sandals. The darkness became a threat, and without thinking I put my hand on the light switch, and the weak bulb on the ceiling flickered then brightened.

As the yellow bar of light appeared under my door, the footsteps stopped, then suddenly, without further caution, broke into a run, and men's hard voices broke the night silence.

What happened after that happened very quickly, so that, looking back on it afterwards, I remembered it as one of those ancient silent movies with speeded-up movements.

I still had my hand on the door knob when the door itself was pushed open so violently that I was sent sprawling backwards, and landed on the bottom of the bed.

Three people ran into the room, two men and a woman, all in the ubiquitous black pyjamas of the region, and Vietnamese-style Thousand Miler sandals. The woman's long black hair was caught with a leather thong and hung over one shoulder.

One of the men, the older of the two, had an AK-47 over his shoulder, and he came close as I lay half-on, half-off the bed and jabbed it hard and into my side, motioning me to be still. Then the woman came up and looked at me intently. She said something I could not understand, and nodded her head.

Reluctantly, the man with the gun drew back, and the three of them ran to the door and into the corridor, their feet slapping softly. I got up shakily, for the jab of the rifle had winded me, and followed them. It might have made more sense to stay where I was, but I did not think of it. I was shaken, but I was more excited than afraid.

By now other lights had gone on, and doors were open. In the corridor, the man with the AK-47 was covering the other three foreigners, who slept in this section of the guest house: the *Time* lady, and two of the businessmen, the silk importer from New Jersey, and the big cattle breeder whom we all called Tex because that was where he came from.

There was no sign of Harry, nor of David. I could see David's door further down the corridor, and it was firmly closed, though he was a very light sleeper, and was certainly awake.

Making sure the gun protected her, the woman went quickly up to the three foreigners. She ignored the *Time* lady, but carefully inspected the faces of the two men, as though she was picking out somebody at a police identity parade.

Then she shook her head again, and spoke to the men, gesturing at David's door. For the first time I felt afraid, and started forward but Tex held up his hand warningly. 'Don't do anything, honey,' he said urgently. 'Don't risk it.'

David must have locked his door for it did not open when the woman tried it. But the wood was thin and the lock fragile, and it gave at once when the men put their shoulders against it. Though we were grouped to one side, we could see David standing just inside the doorway. He had a rigid look, as if he had been turned to stone.

The two other foreign men were minimally dressed for the hot night. The silk importer wore only underpants, and bulky Tex was in a short Japanese *yukata*, obviously hastily thrown on. It had fallen open, and he was trying nervously to sash it. But David, typically, was buttoned to the neck in neat pyjamas. I saw incredulously that he had even put on his slippers.

No one said anything for a minute, though David's lips were open, trying to frame words that would not come out.

Then the woman gave a low exclamation, and made an unmistakable gesture to the man with the rifle. He raised it, and I saw he was not going to threaten this time. He was going to fire.

At the same moment, David came to life, grasping the door with the energy of despair, and trying to slam it. He moved so fast that the executioner was taken slightly off balance, and the bullets slammed into the edge of the door, with David just behind it.

My ears were ringing with the noise of firing, and I could not be sure whether David had been hit. He was agile enough, though, and he began a stumbling run across the room to the window. In his haste, his slipper caught in the edge of the bamboo matting, and he fell face downwards and lay there. His whole body was shaking, and his fists were drumming on the floor.

With a grunt that sounded like contempt, the executioner moved forward, turned him over with a kick, and straddled him, his finger on the trigger. David's mouth was open, saliva running down his chin, and he moaned: Please! Please!'

The man laughed, settled himself more evenly on his widespread feet, and drew back his body slightly to get a better aim. David stopped moaning, and nobody moved. The room was so silent I could hear the dripping of the neglected fountain and the faint creaking of the incense strips in the spirit house in the garden.

I automatically put my hands over my hears to avoid hearing David die, but the deafening crack which came almost at once seemed to be from somewhere behind me. The man with the AK-47 leaped briefly in the air, and a gaping, bloody hole appeared in his back. I could see the white of bone appearing through the shredded flesh.

Then he fell forwards very slowly onto David, the AK-47 jammed between the two bodies. The outward rush of David's breath as the body hit him was quite audible.

I was very close to them both, and I was showered by a thick red rain which flew through the air. When I looked down, the front of my nightgown and my bare arms were splashed with gouts of blood, and small fragments of bloody flesh. When I tried to brush them away, they stuck to my skin as though pasted on.

We all stood in a tableau like images, then we looked at Tex. The pocket of his *yukata* was blackened and smouldering, and he was pulling something from it.

His meaty hand came out, grasping a heavy, old-fashioned pistol. Self-consciously he cleared his throat. 'Well, she's just about an antique, but she still works,' he said.

The two black-clad figures as immobile as the rest of us, suddenly moved. The woman threw herself on the dead man, trying to get the rifle, but it was trapped underneath his heavy body and she could not move him.

Then she raised her head and cried out as we heard the thud of boots in the corridor, and she and the second man ran for the window. But they were too late. Two of the guards were in the room, one struggling to get his pistol out of the holster, the other more efficiently armed with a short-snouted sub-machine gun.

There was no doubt what they were going to do, and I shouted at them in protest. 'Don't, they are not armed.'

The leading guard ignored me and fired. The two black figures danced briefly like marionettes as the bullets struck them, then were thrown back against the wall by the force of the firing. Both seemed to jerk slowly to the floor, painting broad swathes of blood on the wall behind them.

The guard with the pistol, anxious not to be left out, walked over, kicked the man's body, and fired into his face at point blank range. Blood and brains sprayed out and spattered his trousers, but he laughed and walked over to the woman's body, raising the gun again.

'No,' I said furiously, catching his arm. 'No!' He was very young, only a boy, and though he stared defiantly at me for a moment, he lowered the pistol and, shrugging, turned away. I looked down at the woman's face, and saw that, relaxed in death, she was much younger than I thought, probably not much over twenty. Her face was unmarked and looked open and innocent. Her eyes were open and there was still light in them, though as I watched it faded.

I heard a new voice and, looking up, saw Harry in the doorway. 'Sorry I'm late,' he said incongruously. 'Those damned pills! It took me a while to wake up.'

His skin was still a ghastly colour but he looked alert enough, glancing at the carnage in the room without expression. 'Aren't you going to get your camera?' I said savagely.

He looked at me thoughtfully but said nothing, then he went off to help Tex, who was pulling the body of the executioner off David. David had been silent, but as they lifted the weight from him, he began to moan loudly. His glasses were, as ever, firmly in place, and I could see tears running down his cheek beneath them.

I had not thought he was hurt, but the front of his neat pyjamas was covered in blood. Harry whistled, and roughly tore the pyjama jacket open, buttons flying everywhere. David's chest, narrow, white and hairless, was completely unmarked.

Davids' moaning had changed to a sort of bleat, embarrassing for all of us.

'For God's sake, man, shut up,' Harry said roughly. 'You're not hurt. You haven't got a scratch.'

But then I saw there was a dark, spreading stain on David's pyjama trousers, and I knelt again, trying to undo the carefully tied cord. Harry took my wrist and pulled me away. 'Let him alone,' he said, 'he's only pissed himself.'

It was true, I could smell the sharp, acrid smell of urine. I got up with a gesture of distaste, which I could not quite conceal, and Harry looked at me with fury.

'Don't be so damned censorious. Everybody pisses themselves at least once. I've done it many more times than that.'

As he went to the door, his body grew suddenly flaccid with fatigue. 'Get your husband into one of the spare rooms and clean him up,' he said, without looking back. 'I'll ask them to send a doctor to have a look at him, just in case.'

The other foreigners had vanished, and the guards had gone, presumably to get help with the bodies. I was alone with David and two dead men and a woman. The room stank of blood and urine and the smoke of firing.

I knelt down beside David and talked to him, trying to urge him to his feet. But he lay without moving, no longer sobbing but weeping silently, and when the doctor came, we had to carry him to bed between us.

* * *

An unhealthy yellow dawn came up over the garden as we sat in the reception room waiting for the vice-premier, and thunder knocked behind the swollen clouds.

The vice-premier was taking his time but then, plucked from his bed, he probably was having difficulty getting his thoughts together. He was coming, the guest house manager said, 'to apologise to you, madame for this little affair'. He gave me an unhappy bow. I heard a laugh behind me, and somebody said, 'Boy, that's one way of putting it.'

We had all washed and changed, and looked unusually neat. The cook, rising to a moment of crisis, had found some real coffee, the first we had had, and though it was loaded with sugar I drank it gratefully, feeling myself come alive.

David was not there. The doctor had given him a shot and when I looked into his room he was lying on his back, his mouth open. He was snoring, something he rarely did.

Harry came in after the rest of us and threw himself into a chair. 'I was going to miss the vice-premier, but then I smelled the coffee, and I couldn't resist it,' he said cheerfully.

We had all been sitting in a stiff silence, but he sounded so normal, I could see everybody start to relax. Harry at once took charge of the conversation.

'First things first,' he said, drinking his coffee with a grunt of pleasure. Then, putting the cup down he looked at Tex. 'Where the hell did you get that old Luger? You couldn't have brought it in at the airport, the metal detector would have picked up something that size.'

Tex looked slightly ashamed. 'I bought it here.' He looked round at our incredulous faces, and nodded. 'I surely did. I found it in that leather shop near the Palace. They sell hand-tooled holsters there, real nice stuff, and I was buying a couple for my sister's boys. I tried on one of them, and said, for a joke, to the old guy who was selling me the holster, that all I needed was something fancy to put in it.'

The coffee had brought out the sweat, as it had on all of us, and he wiped his face carefully. 'Well, you know how it is here, they'd sell you anything. Real good capitalists. The guy reached under the counter and brought out this old tool. He even had a clip for it.'

'It's way out of its area,' Harry was leaning forward, his face intent. 'Did he say where it came from?'

Tex shook his head. 'We didn't have much common language, I guess, but he said something about it being left behind by a soldier. That would be a while ago.' He shifted uneasily. 'It was a fool thing to do, buying it I mean, but I couldn't resist it.'

'You're a gun collector?' Harry was smiling.

'Sure, most of us are in our part of the world. Anyway I was cleaning and loading it last night to make sure it worked, and I left it on top of the bureau. When I heard all the rumpus early on, I slipped it in my pocket, just in case.' He looked at me, and his face hardened. 'It was as well I did, ma'am, or your husband would be dead right now.'

I flushed, for I had said no words of thanks to him, and started to mumble something, but then the vice-premier came in. Full of apologies and alarm, he shook hands vigorously all round, though when he came to me he kissed my hand, an appropriate gesture for a might-have-been widow. There was a pause while he gave us presents, pushing them anxiously into our hands, as though he was reassuring frightened children. There were silk scarves for the *Time* lady and me, rather ugly porcelain vases for the men, and records of local opera for all of us.

Then, the formalities over, he sat down and waited warily for one of us to speak. Now that the charade of apologies and presents was over, he looked both tough and wily, an oldish man with cropped grey hair and a scar pulling down the corner of one eye.

Harry, as I expected, did not waste much time on politeness. 'They were Liberation Front guerillas, weren't they? Son Sleng's people? We were told there were none of them nearer than a couple of hundred kilometres up the river.'

The vice-premier smiled without warmth. 'The main forces are there, certainly, in Luong Tai province. No large groups can move without our knowledge.' He gestured impatiently. 'But how can we stop two or three people slipping through the villages, dressed like farmers . . .' His voice trailed away.

Tex leaned forward. 'Sure, we understand that. That's how it went in Vietnam. But why were they gunning for Dr Herbert?' He looked at me apologetically. 'Sorry, ma'am, but there's no doubt they were. They had a good look at the rest of us, and we weren't their flavour of the month.'

The vice-premier's eyes were cold and careful. 'I think you are right,' he said. He reached over his shoulder, and the aide standing behind him put something in his hand. It looked like a small photograph.

"See this, madame,' he said, showing it to me. 'Do you remember who took it?'

It was an ordinary snapshot, of the type which might have been taken by a street photographer. The bottom part was heavily bloodstained, and the blood was still damp. It stained my fingers as I held the picture.

The upper part was quite clear, and showed David and myself standing outside the hotel in Bangkok. I recognised the entrance behind us. Someone using a thick felt pen had drawn a line through my face, as though cancelling me out of the picture, but David was very recognisable. His head was up, and the sun glinted on his spectacles.

The vice-premier was waiting, but I shook my head. No one, as far as I knew, had taken our picture, or certainly we had not posed for one. Harry reached over, took it out of my hands, and exclaimed. 'Where did you get it?'

He hardly needed to tell us, for the blood gave us the answer. 'It was found on the body of the woman who was killed this morning,' the vice-premier said shortly.

I was still puzzled. 'But why my husband?'

Harry answered first, while the vice-premier was still collecting his careful English.

'We were the first foreigners to come in for a long while and if the visit had gone well, it would have been a nice plug for the Vouliphong faction. Come to glorious Khamla, it's safer than New York City. That sort of thing. So Son Sleng sent in a team to screw it up, with David as the main target.'

'He is right, madame,' the vice-premier said. 'Your husband is an academic, a specialist in the region, a man of influence. His voice counts for much. Also, he is British, and . . .' He hesitated, unsure how to finish.

'And the British have no finger in this particular pie, so could have been expected to be sacrosanct,' Harry said cynically. I must have still looked doubful, for he shook his head at me.

'Come on, Gilly, who cares if a journalist or a businessman gets knocked off?' ('Thanks a lot,' said Tex and the silk importer in unison.) 'But a nice high-minded British academic would be at least a seven-day wonder. Diplomatic protests too, I shouldn't wonder.'

The vice-premier got up. I think Harry was upsetting him. 'The expedition for today is cancelled,' he said formally. 'Please let us know if you wish to stay and complete the programme, or if you wish to leave.' He bowed to me. 'The doctor will call later to look again at your husband, madam,' he said. 'But he assures me there is nothing wrong except perhaps a little shock.'

* * *

Breakfast was an omelette laced heavily with chilli, so I pushed it aside and had some papaya and a glass of tea. When I went back along the corridor, the blood that had been there earlier was washed away and there was no sign anything had happened a few hours before.

David was still asleep, now lying on his side and

breathing quietly, so I went along to Harry's room and pushed the door open without knocking.

He was lying on top of his bed, wearing a Burmese-style longyi knotted round his hips. He was reading a magazine but put it down at once. 'Do come in,' he said sardonically.

I sat down on the edge of the bed and looked at him. A long white scar zig-zagged over his ribs, and I ran my nail down it, not gently. 'Where did you get that? I thought you were supposed to be a cameraman.'

He pushed my hand away. 'In the great battle for Hue. Cameramen get shot up too, sometimes, or hadn't you heard?' I continued to look at him, and he hesitated, then made up his mind.

'If you think that letter was anything to do with last night's business, you're crazy. It was a message about a new shipment of Chinese arms, nothing more.'

'The message was from Peter?'

'From Peter, or the Prince, what's the difference?'

My voice sounded surprisingly detached. 'Why did you carry it?'

He shrugged. 'I owe Peter a favour, a big one. He got me out of real trouble in 'Nam once. And if you think delivering the letter is on my conscience, forget it. I've been too long in this region to take sides, I take what is known as the historical view. Like your husband.

'I would call it amoral, not historical, and nothing would be on your conscience, because you haven't got one. I think you enjoyed what happened here this morning.'

He caught my wrist and pulled me down hard as I was getting up. 'Are you sure you didn't?' he said softly. 'For someone who nearly lost a husband a few hours ago you look remarkably animated. Not like the old inhibited Gilly at all.'

For a moment, our lips met, and I let him hold me. But his mouth was hot and dry, the corners cracked, and he was beginning to shake again. I pushed him away and got up.

'You bastard!' I said, my voice as steady as I could make it. 'You cold-blooded bastard! You sent me off with a message to kill my own husband, didn't you?'

He called my name angrily, but I went out without looking back.

CHAPTER SIX

David slept most of the morning and I sat on a chair just outside his door. I did not think he would particularly want me there when he woke, but I had nowhere else to go.

After a while, I fell asleep myself and dreamed of Joshua, as I always did when I was disturbed. It was the same old dream. I was stumbling with painful slowness, my limbs heavy as death, through a maze of dark corridors.

The passageways smelled of damp and corruption, but there was also a whiff of Caporals, so I knew Joshua was somewhere ahead of me in the darkness. I called out to him, as I always do in the dream, and he shouted back, but the words were slurred and mutilated, as though he couldn't shape them properly.

I began to run for I knew if I could catch him, he would take me out of that place, and I was very afraid of the darkness and the rotten-sweet stench.

Then I saw he was just ahead of me. He turned and said my name though I could hardly understand it, holding out his arms to me. But then I saw his face, and I pulled back, screaming.

He had come from his grave, and his face and the hands which closed on my arms were festering with the bluish-purple marks of putrefaction. His upper lip was eaten away, showing the gum, and his long equine teeth smiled. His tongue, swollen in his open mouth, struggled again to form my name. Where his eyes should have been there was nothing, though some white thing moved and wriggled in the sockets. As he bent over me, I could smell the fetid ripeness of decay welling from his throat.

I woke on cue, sobbing and drenched with sweat, threshing about in the long chair on the verandah. There was no one, thank God, to hear me, except an incurious gardener digging a bed some way off. I looked inside David's door but he was still in a drugged sleep. He hated my nightmares, saying they were the sign of an undisciplined mind.

Joshua was my uncle, of sorts, the husband of my mother's half-sister. My own parents were old, my mother in her late forties and my father over fifty when I was born, both of them aghast at so late an arrival after years of childless marriage.

My mother wanted to have an abortion, and when no reputable doctor would do it for her, she tried gin and hot baths and jumping off tables. My father told me that, when we came home from my mother's cremation, and he was tearful and unusually ready to talk to me.

My mother was also convinced I would be imbecilic, late babies being subject to that sort of thing. It should have been a relief when I was born with the usual number of arms and legs, but she never really forgave me for being born at all, and carried her grudge with her until she died of cancer of the uterus when I was sixteen.

Nature knew what it was doing when it kept that marriage infertile, as neither partner had any talent for parenthood. My father was silent and preoccupied, and he found a small child about the house alarming.

My mother was never overtly unkind, but as long as I can remember, she kept me physically at a distance. She disliked being hugged or kissed, and made this painfully clear.

Probably the worst thing, though, was the restraint put on my spirits through living in a house with oldish people used to quiet, peace and order. Oddly enough, coming from that parentage, I was by nature a healthy, boisterous child, ready to give affection, and craving it in return. Squeezing what might have been an extroverted personality into an unnatural mould made me shy and convinced of my own unattractiveness.

In the summer holidays, though, my whole life changed when I went to Melbourne to stay for a few weeks with Joshua and Marion. Large, sloppy, fair, loving Marion was the antithesis of her half-sister, my mother. I can't imagine how they came to share even one parent.

She and Joshua had three noisy sons who tolerated me as they would a frightened puppy. Joshua and the boys took me camping in the mountains while Marion lay at home in bed reading novels. She was too fat, she said, for a sleeping bag.

I loved Marion and the boys, for with them I could shout and run without anybody telling me to be quiet. But I worshipped Joshua, who would not let me call him uncle, and who hugged and kissed me on any excuse or none, too much, perhaps, as I grew older.

Until I was quite old, Marion would let me crawl in with her and Joshua into their double bed where they lay late on Saturdays and Sundays, drinking coffee and reading. The double bed was to me a phenomenon. My parents had not only single beds but separate rooms.

Joshua used to sing in bed, but then he sang everywhere, in his loud, rich, untrained voice. When I was small, he sang, specially for me, his theme song:

> Joshua fit the battle of Jericho
> Jericho, Jericho
> Joshua fit the battle of Jericho
> And the Walls came tumbling down.

In my nightmares, he sings it still.

Joshua was, as I have said, a great hugger and kisser, and I was mad for physical affection. When I was fourteen or fifteen, however, his embraces seemed different, and though I wanted his affection just as much, a vague sensation of guilt and embarrassment began to manifest itself in me.

Marion must have seen what was happening. One Sunday morning she came into the bedroom and found me on the bed with Joshua who was too lazy to get up. I had been teasing him to let me look at the book he was reading and he began to wrestle with me playfully as he had often done when I was smaller. 'Let her alone,' Marion said, quite sharply for her. 'She's not one of the boys, and she's too big for that sort of thing anyway.'

Looking back, I suppose I was in love with Joshua. Certainly I sometimes felt some alarming responses when he touched me. From this distance, I can't quite acquit him either. Probably this is why, in the last year or two of his life, he too began a process of rejection. It was very kindly done, and I think Marion insisted on it, but there was a feeling in the household that I no longer belonged.

The boys were older, busy with their own affairs, more impatient with me, and less willing to include me in their activities. Marion was vague and good-natured as ever, but Joshua himself, on the last holiday I spent with them, seemed out of sorts and out of temper. He was growing heavy and red-faced in middle age, and he coughed a lot through the smoke of his pungent French cigarettes. Once, when he snapped at me, I asked what was wrong.

'Life is wrong,' he said gloomily. 'I'm growing old. You are turning from a child into a woman. It's all a great mistake.'

A few days later he had a stroke, and lay in hospital, plum-faced and stertorous, trying occasionally to say something through his distorted mouth. The doctors told Marion that if he survived he would be partly paralysed and unable to speak, and I prayed every day he would die. When he did, a week after the stroke, I became hysterical with guilt and anger, and had to be dragged off his body by Marion and the doctor.

It was the last time I showed any public manifestation of grief. I have learned, to a large extent, to control my feelings. But I can't stop Joshua coming out of his grave and into my dreams.

My mother died within a year of Joshua and I did not weep at all, though her illness was prolonged and unusually painful. As a gesture, though I felt very little, I tried to take her hand when the doctor said she was close to death. But, though she was almost too weak to move, she pulled it away, adamant to the last. Just as she died, she turned her head to look at me. She had said nothing for hours, but now she spoke quite clearly. 'All your fault,' she said.

During the years at university, I did not have many friends either, mainly because I was running the house for my father. He wanted dinner served promptly at seven each night, and he did not care for visitors. I no longer saw Marion and the boys. After Joshua's death, she moved to Perth where most of her family lived, and contact dwindled to occasional letters, then to Christmas cards.

Of course I had some social life, it would be impossible not to. I went to a few parties, and I went out with a few boys in my own year, but I mainly seemed to attract people as shy and awkward as myself, and my love life was limited to nothing more than an occasional fumble in the back seat of a car.

I was sexually backward for the time and place, but I was also in the wrong style, angular and short-haired at a time when girls were in caftans and Indian cottons, beads and thonged sandals, with long hair flowing to their waists. I hated sitting for hours on stools in smoky bars, I didn't like pot, not from prudishness but because it made me frighteningly disassociated.

I was not exactly belle of the year, or any year, come to that.

It was, however, at university that I met David. He was something of a rarity, an English don lecturing in

South-east Asian history, and because of his aloofness and his occasional flashes of icy wit, he became a cult figure on campus. Male students copied his waistcoats and his trendy gold-rimmed glasses. Female students ran a book on who would be the first to seduce him, into indiscretion if nothing else.

None of them succeeded. David was not the sort of man to become involved with one of his students, and the braless, long-haired girls with their golden summer skins affected him not at all. The more untouchable he made himself, the more desirable he became, and I think there were one or two dangerous moments for him in tutorials.

I took no part in the contest for Dr Herbert's affections, though like the rest of them I found his cold charm fascinating. In spite of everything, I was quite romantic, and I came to see him as a sort of Svengali figure. Once or twice I saw him looking at me in a frowning, intense, way as though he was trying to weigh me up. The only real encounter I had with him as a student was when we met by chance in a coffee shop, not the one on the campus. He came and sat with me and talked for an unexpectedly long time, asking me in his meticulous way about myself and my background.

I was mesmerised and flattered. After I had been married to David for a while, it was easy to forget how charming he could be in those days, always remote and distant, of course, but promising unimaginable revelations if the ice were ever to melt.

We met again by chance after I graduated, when he came into the bookstore where I was working. He asked me out to dinner, and that was the beginning of that. At the end of a year we were married, my father having been efficiently disposed of by David, who organised the sale of the house and sent him off to live with a younger sister who was widowed and glad of his generous civil service pension.

I don't know what David saw in me. I think he decided in his methodical way that it was time for him to marry, and it would be useful for his career if he did. Presumably even he had sexual needs and like St Paul thought it better to marry than to burn. He did not want a too-lively wife who would make demands on him, and he must have known by then that most women would be dismayed or repelled by his sexual technique. He told me once, in a moment of anger, that sensible men preferred prostitutes, as they were much less trouble.

My lack of close relatives pleased him, for he did not want a family of interfering in-laws. I also think he mistook my character, seeing a shy, rather silent girl who could be moulded to his liking, and who would do the limited amount of entertaining he thought necessary without filling the house with noisy friends. He also knew I could be quite useful to him as a secretary and research assistant, and so it proved.

What David failed to see, however, when he married me was the core of obstinacy which made me totally unmalleable, however much I went through the ritual gestures of being a suitable wife. He also could not guess that inside me was a very different sort of person waiting to get out.

The emergence of that person had, however, been hindered by a long career as a rejectee. My mother started it, Joshua took my confidence away at a dangerous period, but I had no one to blame apart from myself for becoming involved with David, who took an active and sadistic delight, right from the moment of our marriage, in turning away when I made any timid offer of affection, physical or otherwise.

Peter Casement's rejection in Hanoi should not have surprised me either, but somehow it did. All through that long day, as I waited for David to wake, I felt a slow, burning resentment at the memory.

CHAPTER SEVEN

David and I flew back to Bangkok the next day. Our hosts put us on a plane with many expressions of regret that our visit to Khamla had been cut short, but with tangible relief at our departure.

David had so far refused to speak to me or to anyone else about what had happened at the guesthouse, and the doctor had said he might still be suffering from shock and it would be unwise to press him. He insisted that he felt well, but he had a staring look about his eyes which I did not like.

On the plane coming back, however, he began to feel nauseated, and by the time we reached the hotel, he was convulsed with abdominal pains. The hotel doctor told him it was an unusually severe fit of gastritis, and that he must stay in bed for at least a week. It would be very unwise, he added, to travel to Hanoi again, as David had half-intended.

David did not want me in the room with him, saying that the only thing he needed was sleep, so I went out early and came back late, spending my days alone sitting in the courtyards of temples pretending to read the guidebook, or taking buses round the main tourist sites.

I was glad of the indifferent chatter of the guides, and the anonymity of the tourist parties. Later, I could hardly remember what I had seen, or what temple we had visited, for I was totally preoccupied with my own unhappiness.

David would soon be going back to England, and it seemed to me that I could not go with him. My whole being recoiled from the idea, though what had happened in Khamla had very little to do with it. All that had done was to force me to look at my own feelings with more honesty.

What I had to do now was to decide how to fight for my own survival. There was no doubt in my mind that if I gave in and flew back with David, I was lost. Living with him sapped my will and made me increasingly dependent, though I was beginning to see that the fault was partly mine. My compliance, though only partial, made David more cruel than he might have been with an older, stronger partner.

And yet, though our life together was unhappy, some element of the old fascination remained, and that was where the danger lay for me. I felt like a prisoner who, though the door was partly open, could not summon up the resolution to break free.

There was also a serious practical difficulty. I had quite literally no money of my own – when we were travelling, David handled the travellers' cheques and paid for anything I wanted to buy – and if I left him now, I would be penniless on the streets of Bangkok. What is more, I knew beyond any doubt he would not hesitate to use this weapon against me.

The only way out that I could see was to write to my father and ask him to lend me the air fare to Sydney and to finance me until I could get a job. He would not be pleased, for his own resources were limited, but I hoped that he would not refuse. I was still not sure, though, that I had the courage to face David, or the will to survive the struggle which would follow.

Coming back from a river trip, exhausted and on edge, I hardly heard the desk clerk when he said a gentleman was waiting for me in the bar, and he had to repeat himself. I assumed it would be Harry, but when I stood uncertainly at the bar entrance, a big red-faced man came up and introduced himself.

'I'm Bill Geraghty, a compatriot of yours,' he said, shaking hands. 'I run the AsiaNews agency here. You probably haven't heard of it. It's not exactly Reuters size.'

As it happened, I had. Someone at the Australian Embassy had told me about a Sydney man who had started a small multi-media agency and was expanding fast. I was at once wary, because I thought he might have heard about the shootings at the guesthouse, but if he had he didn't mention them. Instead, after we had sat down in one of the dark banquettes with some drinks, he offered me a job.

I was so tired and nervous that I thought it was a joke, but he appeared to be perfectly serious. What he wanted, he said, was someone who could type, take phone-in copy, handle tapes if need be, and do odd jobs around the office. 'We had just got our last girl going great guns when she walked out on us,' Bill said. 'She claimed she was fed up with Asia, and was going back to Milwaukee to get married. That's the trouble with this place. Nobody settles.'

I looked at him carefully, and liked what I saw. Overweight, with what had obviously once been an athletic body now run to fat, he had an air of cheerful honesty which was hard to resist. He smiled broadly at me, and some of the strain fell away and I smiled back.

'You do realise I've had no experience of the sort of agency you are running?' I said. 'In fact, I've never worked in an office at all.'

'That may be, love, but to be honest I'm desperate, and at least you look as if you can read and write, which is more than I can say for the temporary help we've got at the moment.' He watched me shrewdly. 'I was told you were a very bright girl, and that you might be willing to stay in Bangkok for a while.'

'Who told you that?'

He cleared his throat. 'Harry Greene is an old mate of mine. We handle film for him now and again. It was his idea in the first place.'

I opened my mouth to say I couldn't take the job, that

I was either flying back to England with my husband, or returning to Sydney, where I belonged; I was still not sure which. Instead, I had a sudden physical sensation of release, and I heard my own voice asking, quite calmly, how much salary he was offering, and when he would want me to start.

I thought Bill looked nearly as surprised as I felt, but his broad flushed face split in a smile, and he thumped my knee. 'Good on you, love. How about starting tomorrow? We'll talk about money when I find out if you can type.'

I did not tell David about the job for two days. By then he was up and dressed, and looking more or less his ordinary self. He had been poisoned, I think, not by what he had eaten and drunk, but by his own abject shame.

When I came in in the evening, hot but euphoric – I had successfully survived every test Bill had thrown at me, and we had negotiated a salary of sorts – David looked at me with careful suspicion.

'Where have you been all day? I wanted you this afternoon to go and pick up some tickets. We're booked on BA tomorrow for London.'

I could not have done it a week before, but that day, at my insistence (though with much grumbling) Bill had paid me a month's wages in advance, and the knowledge that the money was in my handbag made me feel strong and light-hearted.

So I brushed past David, barely looking at him, and went into the bathroom. 'I've got something to tell you, but I need a shower first,' I said before I closed the door. 'And I'm terribly thirsty. Can you order some drinks from room service?'

I took a long time in the shower, washing my hair under it, and letting the lukewarm water stream over me until all the heat and tension of the day was washed out of me.

When I came out, David had, against all custom,

done as I asked. Drinks were on the table, and he was sitting in an armchair near the window with a gin and tonic in his hand. He looked me up and down as I stood barefoot in my dressing gown, with my wet hair dripping on my shoulders.

'What's the matter with you?' he said resentfully. 'Why do you look so happy?'

It was so like an accusation that I began to laugh, and then I could not stop. I sat on the side of the bed, convulsed with laughter, purging myself with it, not caring that people passing in the corridor could hear me, taking no notice of David telling me to stop, that I was making an exhibition of myself. At last my breath caught uncomfortably, and the laughter turned into a fit of coughing, so that David had to bring me a glass of water to halt it. He handed it to me with cold politeness, but I saw that his hand was shaking. For the first time in our relationship, I had frightened him.

'I am happy,' I said, as soon as I could speak. 'And do you know why? I'm not coming back with you, David, I'm staying here. I've even got a job, so I don't have to ask you for money.'

He came very close to me, without speaking, and for a moment, I thought he was going to hit me. If he does, I said to myself, I shall not bear it, and he must have seen this in my eyes, for after a long pause he drew back and went to the window.

With his back to me he stood staring into the hot dusk. Then he spoke over his shoulder. 'Is it because of what happened at the guesthouse?' His voice was flat, but I knew how much it must have cost him to say it.

I was as honest as I could be. 'No. It has very little to do with that. You know the reason I cannot go back with you as well as I do. It is because you are killing me.'

I thought he would question this, but instead, turning, he looked at me with close attention and, I thought, something like comprehension.

'You're changing,' he said tiredly. 'You're moving

away from me. I've seen it happening right from the beginning of this trip. What is it you want, Gillian?'

In a way, I did not like the way things were going. I would rather, now, that he had struck me, for a defeated David might sap my resolve. 'I want my own life. I don't want to be your appendage. That is why I must leave you.'

He sat down again and reached for his drink, but so clumsily he knocked over the glass. It was the sort of accident that always happened to me when I was nervous, but never to David. He made no effort to retrieve the glass, but let it fall to the floor, watching the stain spread on the pale carpet.

Without raising his eyes, he said: 'I know you've been unhappy, but do you think it has been easy for me? You do all I ask you to do, yet at the same time you resist me in everything, and have always done, right from the start. When I touch you, I feel your body stiffen with antagonism. You make me a worse man than I am, Gillian.'

I could hardly believe what he was saying to me. It was the most intimate conversation we had had in five years. 'I am aware of what we do to each other,' I said wearily. 'That is why I believe we will be better apart.'

He got up and began to walk up and down. 'Is there someone else?' It was obviously painful for him to ask and he stumbled on his words. 'I've sometimes thought you and Harry Greene . . .'

I laughed, 'Good God, no, I'm not Harry's type at all. No, there isn't anybody.' This was true in a literal sense. I did not count the fact that, despite what had happened in Khamla, the phantom of Peter Casement haunted my waking hours and my dreams. His image was implanted in me like an irritant I could not dislodge, and if I was honest with myself, I would have to acknowledge that staying on had something to do with this obsession.

David turned and faced me and we stared at each

other in a long silence. Then he took his glasses and fiddled with them and I knew by his ungarded eyes I had won at least a temporary victory.

'Well,' he said in a low voice, 'I have to go back, but it won't hurt if you stay on for a few months. There are a few things you can look up for me while you are here.'

* * *

When we parted at the airport, David kissed me on the cheek with great delicacy, and at the same time tried to push an envelope into my hand. I knew there was money in it, so I pushed it back. I had already refused, despite his considerable anger, to take a monthly allowance from him. He wanted to argue now but I shook my head. 'You'd better go, they're boarding.'

He gave up at that and, picking up his cabin bag, went to the departure lounge entrance. 'Let me know when you are ready to come home,' he said uncertainly, and was gone.

So easy after all. I wondered why I had not done it years before.

* * *

My flat in Bangkok was very small, but so was my salary. When any of us complained, Bill Geraghty told us we were working for the future, not the present. 'Give it another year or two, kids, and we'll be in the money,' he said expansively.

If my flat was small, I still loved it. It was the first time I had lived by myself, and to go home at night and close the door and be alone was inexpressibly pleasing to me. It was in a modern block, basically one room with a divan bed in one corner and a kitchen in a cupboard. The bathroom was American style, nearly as big as the main living area, and I never got tired of the needle-spray shower.

Waking up alone in bed and remembering where I was was a daily pleasure.

I am a fast and very accurate typist, because David insisted that his manuscripts be perfect, so after a bewildered few days I had no trouble coping with AsiaNews. We worked long hours, and at the end of the day or night whoever was about went for drinks and a meal, Bangkok being the sort of place which stays open twenty-four hours a day.

The heat was not as brutal as it had been earlier in the year, and despite the extended shifts, I felt full of ferocious energy. Twice a week I insisted on the evening off so I could go to conversation lessons with a fierce, stringy Frenchwoman who lived down near the museum, and who had preserved her Parisian accent intact after thirty-five years in Asia. She drove me mercilessly, saying I had a good grammatical foundation but an appalling accent. That was true enough, and I had always been inhibited by David standing by my side, silently wincing whenever I opened my mouth. Now that barrier was removed, I progressed rapidly, and Madame even said one day that I no longer sounded so much like a Spanish cow.

I was not sure why I wanted to get up my French, except that I had been humiliated by my inability to communicate in Vietnam and Khamla. Anyway, it stretched my mind and absorbed some of my energies.

One night I saw the Asian woman who had been with Peter in the market when I was walking back from my French lesson. It was quite late, but the crowds were still thick and she was moving purposefully through them. I began to follow her, careful to stay a little way behind. What I was doing was irrational, and I was ashamed of it, but that did not stop me.

She paused briefly at the Erawan Hotel, and I thought she was going in. Instead, she went just inside the gate and lit a candle at the spirit shrine, where petitioners come twenty-four hours a day to pray for a child or health or fortune, for a lover or for a death. In the candle light, she looked younger and prettier than I remembered, and she was wearing a Thai silk dress with a low neck and very high heels that made her legs slimmer. I had not made a mistake, though, it was the same woman.

She came out and turned into a side street and walked for a few minutes until she came to another hotel, much more down-market, with rock surging out from the bar juke-box.

I followed her in as though I was sleepwalking. She sat down in a corner of the bar, ordered a drink, and began calmly to make up her lips. I sat down too, but no waiter came, so after a minute or two I called one impatiently. He looked at me oddly, but took my order.

When the drink arrived, so did a fat man in a Hawaiian shirt who had been standing at the bar. He was an American with a flat mid-western accent, and he was well on the way to being drunk.

'Mind if I sit with you, honey?' he said, not waiting for an answer, sliding clumsily on to the banquette beside me, his thigh jammed against mine, I did not answer, or even try to move away, but after he had met my glance for a moment or two, he shifted uneasily.

'I thought you and I might have a drink together,' he mumbled. 'Maybe I made a mistake. Maybe you're waiting for someone.'

I nodded slightly, still looking at him. Whatever he saw in my face made him very uncomfortable, for he got up at once and started lurching back to the bar. Halfway across, he turned. 'If you come to a place like this, lady, what do you expect?' he said plaintively.

I ignored him and turned back to watch the woman in the corner. She was now talking to another man, a small, sharp-faced European, and I saw her carefully write down something on a damp beer mat. He studied it, and did some rapid calculations beside it, converting it, I suppose.

Then he shook his head. The music from the juke-box stopped, and I heard his voice, the accent unmistakably South London. 'Too dear,' he said. 'You're over-pricing yourself, my darling.'

He got up and strolled away, and the woman sat on patiently, husbanding her drink though the waiter hovered, touching up once again her rouged lips. I took my drink over and sat beside her, watching her as her face shivered with surprise and she moved her chair a little away.

'Are you waiting for Peter Casement?' I said cruelly. It was a safe gibe, for the Bangkok grapevine said Peter had gone to Europe with the Prince, in an attempt to drum up support and finance.

She shook her head stupidly. I wondered for a moment whether she spoke English, then I remembered that she must, if she was negotiating prices.

'You're a whore, aren't you?' The word didn't come naturally, but I used it deliberately. Then, when she still did not answer, 'A prostitute. A bar girl.'

She made an effort, and spoke. Her English was fluent enough, and her accent was better than most.

'It is not your business,' she said. 'Who are you? Are you from the European mission?'

I smiled. 'Not from the mission. But I know Mr Casement and I have seen you with him.' The absurdity of sitting in a bar in Bangkok discussing Peter with a prostitute was beginning to rob me of composure, and so of my advantage over her.

It was hard to know where to go next. 'I would like to know what arrangements you have with Mr Casement,' I said stumblingly, listening with incredulity to my own voice.

She saw my embarrassment, and it restored her courage. 'Go away, madame, I do not wish to talk to you,' she said. 'What I do is my affair, not yours. Go and ask Mr Casement, if you want to know anything.'

She beckoned the waiter as she spoke, and he came

and stood beside her. He said nothing, but I saw the two calm Asian faces, ranged against me. I put the bahts for my drink on the table, and went without another word.

* * *

We were fifty kilometres or so from the border when we came to our first checkpoint. That is rather a pretentious way of putting it, for it was only a felled tree dragged partly across the dusty road to make us slow down. Two men were standing in the shade beside it, in torn and patched khaki, with the pink-checked sweat cloth of the Liberation Front round their necks.

Both had automatic rifles, and as Harry braked, one of them fired, jerking upwards at the last moment, so that the shot cracked like a whip over my head. 'It's all right,' Harry said as I ducked. 'They just want to make sure we have grasped the point.'

'Are they going to do that all the way?' I was beginning to see the uses of the checked cloth, for the sweat was running down my face, making runnels in the dust. My back was already aching from the jolting over the rough, rutted track that passed for a road, but I had no intention of complaining.

'Probably. They tend to shoot first and ask questions afterwards.' Harry put his hands briefly in the air to show he was unarmed, then pointed cautiously to the pass he had taped to the windscreen. We had been given it at the last moment and neither of us could read it, but we were told it was a safe conduct which would take us right through to the Great Temple.

'The only problem is that the sons of bitches can't read,' Harry said under his breath, as one man puzzled over the pass, and the other covered us with his rifle, moving it slowly from side to side in a way I did not care for.

But the pass also bore something more valuable than

writing, the Prince's own seal, a large circular encrustation of red wax, the antique characters of the chop deeply indented. The first man studied it, then came round to make a cursory inspection of the Land Rover's contents before waving us on.

Harry had turned up again when I had been working at AsiaNews for three months. By then, I had learned to do most of the jobs round the office – Bill tried me out on sound, on dubbing and a little producing – and I was both confident and relaxed.

David and I exchanged occasional, noncommittal letters. I did a small research job for him at the library, and, meticulous as ever, he sent me a fee. Nothing was said about my coming back.

Harry was in good spirits when he came into the office. He had been in Burma, and had brought back some lovely film: a boys' festival at the Shwe Dagon pagoda in Rangoon, a journey by river boat up the Irrawaddy, an operation against guerrillas in the bush.

Burma was hard to crack, and we would sell the film easily to Big Brother, the international photo-agency which had put some finance into Bill's operation, and which would withdraw it without notice if he showed signs of failing. Harry was famous enough to have sold the film himself without using the agency, but he was an old friend of Bill's and wanted him to survive. If nothing else, he was loyal to his friends.

Apart from a formal inquiry about David, Harry said nothing about what had happened in Khamla, and I was glad of that. We went out to dinner and the cinema a couple of times, and our old, easy relationship was back again. The strains which were threatening it seemed to have disappeared.

When he and Bill asked me rather formally to have a drink with them in the Grand bar late one night, I had a feeling something was about to happen. Harry seemed unusually pleased with himself and ordered a bottle of good French wine.

'I'm going to the liberated areas,' he said, raising his glass in toast. 'The word came through today.'

'To Khamla?' I looked at him in surprise. 'Where exactly?'

'To the Front headquarters. The Great Temple itself.'

I groaned with envy. It had been years since any ordinary visitors had been to Vangkhorn, and the temple complex was said to be falling into irrevocable decay.

By the time the war was over – if ever – and the archaeologists were allowed back, years more would pass before it could be reopened. It was even better than the Pagan site in Burma, Peter had told me, and I would have given a great deal to visit it.

Then something else occurred to me. 'Did Peter arrange this trip for you?'

Harry laughed. 'No. He has disappeared without trace. Nobody has seen him for months, or at least they say they haven't. The Prince himself sent a message to the government-in-exile in Hanoi, and they passed it on to the mission here.'

He filled my glass and looked at me carefully. 'How about coming with me? Cheong' (he was talking about the Chinese-Malay sound man who worked with him) 'is down with hepatitis, and is out of action for the foreseeable future.'

I looked at once at Bill. 'You need some field experience,' he said uneasily. 'We can manage with casual help for a week or two.'

He obviously did not want me to go. I was very useful round the office, and it would be a struggle to manage with someone new. But Harry was an old friend, and a very valuable property. I saw Bill would not cross him.

'If you are worried about your job, don't be,' he said, with better grace. 'It will be here when you come back. We aren't trying to ease you out.'

I looked back at Harry and shook my head. 'I can't do

what Cheong does. You know how little experience I have had.'

'I know, and candidly, if I could get anyone better I would. But I need someone right away, and there is just nothing else offering. At least you have some idea what it is all about.' He put his hand lightly on my arm. 'Don't worry. I'll do most of it myself, but you can make yourself quite useful.'

Bill smiled encouragingly. 'You can probably do a couple of standups.'

'Right,' Harry said. 'I want to do something on the women, and I'd like you for the voice-over. It should go down quite well.'

I must have still looked doubtful, for he grew impatient. 'Oh, come on, Gilly! You're not afraid, are you? I thought you were a pretty tough lady.'

'How will we get over the border? I don't imagine the Thais are issuing permits.'

He smiled, knowing he had won. 'Easy. There's a whole area where nobody even knows how the border runs. A child could do it.'

He was right. We crossed just before dawn, in the Land Rover, with the monkeys in the jungle coughing like old men starting the day, and a bird or two screaming hysterically.

After the first checkpoint we had less trouble, the men – and sometimes women – beside the road growing more relaxed the deeper we went in. I was nervous about driving over the rutted track but Harry made me take the wheel for long stretches. I gritted my teeth as we lurched in and out of potholes, but he would not relent. 'You need to know how to handle this thing in case anything happens to me,' he said bluntly.

Though the distance was not great, the road surface was so bad we made slow progress, and we had to camp out the first night. I was on edge with tiredness, and uneasy at the way the hot darkness pressed in at the edge of the light from the campfire, waiting for something.

Harry misunderstood my mood. 'If you are wondering whether I am going to rape you on this trip, forget it,' he said lightly. 'This is strictly business.'

'I hadn't thought of it.' I got up stiffly, my legs aching and unrolled my sleeping bag, ignoring him as he sat by the fire, smoking. He was still there, a hunched, dark figure, when I fell asleep.

We came to the Great Temple towards sunset on the second day. The high stupa which is its centrepiece is on a slight rise, and I saw it against the reddened sky before we came to the outskirts of the ruined city. Its dark silhouette was fretted with the ascending terraces for which it is famous, and it rose to a peak like a thin flame.

At the very top there were small dark shapes which seemed to be moving. Harry saw them too. 'Monkeys,' he said. 'The whole place is swarming with them.'

The buildings of the ruined city began to rise from the jungle, like rocks from a green foam. Harry slowed as we came to a barricade, a high one made of logs which blocked the whole road.

A rough hut served as a guardhouse, and a dozen or so men and women were grouped beside the barrier, waiting for us. Some wore black pyjamas, some green and brown camouflage uniforms, but all had pink-checked scarves round their necks. Their guns covered us as we jolted to a stop.

A girl came forward to inspect the safe conduct, but when Harry spoke to her in French she shook her head. The seal seemed to reassure her, and she gestured to us to get out, still with her rifle trained on us.

As we climbed down, an older man came out of the guardhouse. For that area, where we had seen mostly men and women in their twenties, he was indeed old, fifty at least, with a spiky grey crew cut and silver rimmed glasses. One of the wings was tied on with fine wire, and his khaki uniform was stained and dirty, but he managed to look oddly professorial.

He spoke to Harry in fluent French, with hardly a

trace of the local accent. 'You are Mr Greene? We are expecting you. I think you have a letter for me.'

Harry put his hand out of his pocket, moving carefully as the guns swung to cover him, and drew out a sweat-stained single sheet. He glanced sideways as I stared at him. Nothing had been said about a letter.

The man took it and read it slowly, then smiled. Despite his broken teeth, it made him look much younger. He offered Harry his hand. 'I am Penn Thioen,' he said. 'The commander in chief has asked me to look after you when you are here.'

He turned to me looking slightly puzzled. I realised that in my bush shirt and trousers, my face streaked with dust, and a bush hat pulled well down I could have been anything, so I took off my hat and smiled politely.

'Ah, madame,' he said, relieved at identifying my sex. 'We did not expect a lady, but we welcome you.' He turned back to Harry. 'The lady is your wife?'

'So much for women's lib in the liberated areas,' I said under my breath. He must have understood some English, for I saw a slight spark in his eye, which instantly disappeared.

'No, I am not,' I said patiently. 'I am the sound recordist of this team.'

Harry grinned, for I had been insisting all the way I was nothing of the sort, but Penn Thioen bowed and shook hands. He was a small man, and his grasp was so dry and light it was like touching a leaf.

'My apologies, madame,' he said. 'I was just a little surprised. We do not have much suitable accommodation, but we will try to make you comfortable.'

He motioned us back into the Land Rover, and got up very agilely himself on the tight-packed gear on the back seat. The rifles slowly came down, and a couple of the men pulled aside a heap of branches at the side of the road, revealing a narrow track around the barricade.

As we bumped into the temple complex, a shot rang

out somewhere down the road. 'It is nothing,' Penn said quickly. 'One of the fighters shooting for food. There is little trouble round here.'

Dinner was unexpectedly good, certainly a great deal better than the tinned corned beef and dried apricots we had had at the camp the night before. We ate rice, and a bony but sweet river fish, with a bitter green vegetable I could not identify. There were plates of fresh pineapple and the bright orange papaya of the region.

Even more unexpected were the bottles of Scotch whisky down the centre of the table. I do not like spirits, and I only played with my glass at the first toast. Harry gave me a warning glance across the table, and spoke rapidly in English.

'Stop making faces and drink up. This is specially in our honour.' I obediently took a deep gulp, and felt the warm fire in my veins easing my aches, so I did not hesitate again.

The dining hut was long and low, straw roofed, with the sides partly open to catch what breezes there were. Son Sleng sat at the top of the table, Ieng Nim at the other end, with me beside him. It was quite a formal occasion, with eight or nine men and a couple of women in clean shirts and trousers, the group leaders of the liberation army. They did not use terms like companies or battalions, Son Sleng said in his welcome speech. They were guerrillas, as Chairman Mao had said, swimming like fish in the sea of the people.

Ieng Nim made polite conversation with me but showed no sign of recognition. I reminded him that I had met him at the *soirée* at Soumidath's residence in Hanoi, and he acknowledged this with a slight bow. No mention was made of the meeting at the Temple of the Hundred Buddhas, and I had no idea if he realised who I was.

He had been given the job of making the toast to me, and as he went through the ritual compliments, I watched his hand holding the glass, the mutiliated stump where the finger had been red and inflammed.

I was so tired the whisky went straight to my head, and by the end of the dinner I sat in a soft haze, smiling when anyone spoke to me, but hardly bothering to talk. Harry was in much better shape, drinking toast for toast with Son Sleng, and making them all laugh with his rough, ungrammatical, but enviably fluent French.

When all the attention was concentrated on his end of the table, Ieng Nim leaned forward and spoke softly to me. 'I have seen you looking at my hand, madame,' he said. 'It distresses you?'

I shook my head, trying to concentrate. The weak electric lights had been turned out as the dinner neared its end, to save generator fuel, and bush lanterns were brought by the young men and women who had served us.

Ieng Nim thrust his hand forward so that the lantern light fell right on it. It was certainly an unpleasant wound, yellowish and with a slight rim of pus. A faint sweetish odour came from it.

'It will not heal,' he said. 'We have no proper drugs.'

'How did it happen?' He seemed to want a reply and I could think of nothing else to say.

He shrugged. 'An amputation in the field. It was badly done, but we had only medics, the surgeons had been killed.' He drew his hand back and sighed. 'The finger is no longer there, but I can feel it. It gives me great pain. Many nights I cannot sleep for it.'

I might have felt more sympathetic had I not remembered David falling and sobbing in the room at the guesthouse, and the dead girl with the light fading out of her eyes as I watched.

* * *

I am not usually fond of the early morning, but the next day I woke before dawn, without a headache despite the whisky, and at once conscious of where I was. Harry and I were sharing a hut, but in deference to the conventions a rough partition of straw mats had been erected beside my camp bed while we were at dinner. I could hear his breathing on the other side of the screen.

The birds were starting to shout, so I knew the dawn must be close. I got up cautiously, pulled on a shirt and trousers, and taking a towel, went down to the river. In the dusk the night before, Penn had pointed out to me the sandy spit, a little upstream and behind a rough barrier of bushes, where the women bathed.

The camp was stirring behind me, and as I undressed, the first of the women came down. They looked unfamiliar without their uniforms, strips of patterned cloth round their bodies, and their long black hair streamed down their backs.

They held back at first when they saw me, so I hastily waded out into the tepid, milky water.

I am an excellent swimmer – it is my only physical accomplishment – and when the sloping bottom fell abruptly from under me, I struck out strongly, letting the current take me, then swimming back against it. There had been no real chance to wash properly since we left Bangkok, and my pores were ingrained with dust, my hair matted with it. The flowing river stripped the dust away, and with it the aches and slow fatigue of my limbs.

The women had grown bolder and were now bathing naked in the shallows, washing each other's hair, and wringing out the long strips of batik cloth they used as sarongs. They were still keeping a wary eye on me, so for the moment I stayed in the middle of the river, turning on my back and floating.

I grew up in a watery city, within easy reach of the surf and the harbour beaches, and water is a natural element for me. I have no fear of it, even at home when the huge Pacific surf is running. This river was gentle, despite the current, and I felt an exquisite sense of release, limbs weightless, cut off from sound and sensation in this pale, silent aqueous world. The river surface was a yielding but strong bed, and I lay on my back looking upwards into the milky sky, still veiled with the frail mists of the morning, the sun as yet only a threatening red eye behind the heavy frieze of the trees. I could have stayed so for ever.

At last I heard someone calling to me from the bank, and turned and swam reluctantly in. One of the women came out to meet me, wading through the shallows, admonishing me in bad French. She was saying something about it being dangerous to go so far out into the river, that I would drown. There was no risk of that, but I laughed and let myself be persuaded to come out of the water.

The women had got their courage back by now. One or two of them spoke a little French, and they gathered round, asking how old I was, where was my husband, and how many children I had. They were on their best behaviour, but some of the younger ones couldn't help giggling, keeping their hands over their mouths. I saw they were amused at my size, at my white skin, and at the roundness of my breasts, nothing remarkable by Western standards, but much more obtrusive than their own tentative half-moons.

A few months ago I would have been embarrassed and anxious to escape, but since David and I had parted, I had felt, day by day, a much more exuberant personality pushing its way to the surface. So I didn't run away, but sat down on the sand spit to dry my hair, and turned their questions back on themselves.

The older ones did most of the work around the camp, they said, or went on porterage trips to bring in supplies and ammunition. The younger girls were usually fighters, joining the guerrillas when they were no more than sixteen or seventeen, and marching with the men. They said it was a good life, though they complained that they were usually given the older and less efficient rifles, which kicked back against their shoulders and left them continually aching and bruised.

I could see the bruises on the smooth brown skin. Some of them looked fresh and angry, as though there had been recent fighting. When I asked them their faces closed and they said, as Penn had done, that all was quiet in the area.

The long dining hut was deserted, but the women took me to the cookhouse where the fighters were lining up for breakfast. I was hungry, and ate some rice with a little dried fish on top though I would have preferred fruit. The tea was strong and dark, and made by pouring hot water on coarse leaves which swelled up and clogged the bottom of the mug like seaweed. It was, if nothing else, invigorating, and I took a mug back to the hut for Harry, in case he was not up.

He was sitting on the side of the camp bed, holding his head in his hands and groaning. 'Jesus, I've got a hangover,' he said. 'I must be getting out of practice.'

I put the mug down beside him, and he drank thirstily, wincing as the hot metal burned his lip. 'You put away a fair bit last night,' I said callously. 'What do you expect?'

He raised his head carefully and looked me up and down. 'You're too good to be true this morning. You look as if you've just come from a health farm. If you feel as bright as that why don't you go and finish unloading the Land Rover?'

I laughed and went out. It was true, I had rarely felt better, or more in control of myself. I felt that I could do anything.

* * *

During the first few days we were at the camp, Harry kept me busy. He did not spare me, and I spent most of my time manhandling heavy equipment, doing some sound work and, as he had promised, the occasional standup. I was not skilled enough for him and he often grew impatient, but I was learning.

I had free time in the early morning, however, for I was always up before him. After I had bathed in the river, I usually took some fruit with me and climbed slowly up the terraces of the great stupa while the freshness was still left in the dawn. Even from the first terrace I could see over Vangkhorn, the ruined city, the bleached bones of its palaces and minor temples emerging through the thick dark sea of the jungle.

I knew its history by heart. Soumidath's ancestor Jawarath II had started building it in the eleventh century, dedicating it to Shiva because he believed he was the incarnation of the god. A couple of centuries later, the Royal family (and their subjects, willy-nilly) were converted to Buddhism, so the temples, built for Hindu gods, grew a strong Buddhist overlay.

In the case of the great stupa, the centre and heart of the complex, this marriage of two themes has produced a harmonious whole, a miraculous, gentle blending which both calms and excites the spirit. The narrow terraces winding from the huge, solid base to the thin stone flame at the top are intended to symbolise the human progress through a succession of lives, each incarnation growing by degrees less self-seeking and material, until at last, at the very top, Nirvana is achieved.

Each day I climbed slowly, exploring with eyes and finger-tips the marvellous friezes with which the terrace sides are decorated, some half-obliterated by time and weather, some startlingly clear, with gods and demons and dancers and ceremonial processions led by sacred elephants frozen in stone and time.

At each new level, wider platforms jutted out, and on these, sitting, legs folded and gazing gravely out over the city, are the serene stone Buddhas of Vangkhorn. As I climbed I paused beside each of them, touching the stone which even at dawn still held the heat of the sun.

A number of the figures were mutilated, others brutally eroded by the centuries. Some had been neatly decapitated by colonial archaeologists, and the priceless heads are in museums throughout the world. Those who remained were both grave and smiling, but they all shared an immemorial calm as they looked out over the temple complex. They had been there for many centuries. They would be there when all of us now at the camp were dead, and the ebb and flow of bloody struggle was forgotten. Once I would have found that thought alarming, but as I sat on the topmost terrace, sharing the Buddhas' view, I felt a sense of disassociation which lifted me, like the ascending terraces, on to a remoter plane.

'Asianisation!' Harry said with a snort when I later tried to explain it to him. 'Mystical rubbish.'

The monkeys who lived on the stupa did not like my presence at first, and chattered and scolded me, but after the first day they seemed to become reconciled and sat, a silent audience, beside me when I came to watch the day grow over the green sea of the jungle.

The mornings were not always peaceful. Once or twice I heard distant shooting, and one morning, when I was particularly early and the mists still lay over the trees, I saw a party of fighters, forty or fifty men and women, leaving the camp and moving south. All had rifles over their shoulders, and one or two carried grenade launchers.

When I came down I told Harry what I had seen, and he went off to inquire. 'Sarr Mok's men have been giving them a bit of trouble,' he said when he returned to the hut. 'They don't usually stray into the liberated areas, but Sarr Mok has got a new sideline. He's woken up to the fact that there is big money in antiquities, and he has sent out parties to look for anything they can find: stone heads, hands, bits of columns, that sort of thing.'

I was angry, thinking of the mutilated Buddhas. 'Who buys them?'

'Dealers. Museums. It is so hard to get stuff from this area that nobody asks questions. Even small fragments of stone can be sold to tourists if the right sort of patter goes with it.'

He was right, of course. David and I had more than once been offered questionable antiquities in Thailand when we visited the archaeological sites. David always turned them down on practical as well as ethnical grounds. 'How could you possibly be sure they are genuine?' he said scornfully, though I confess I was tempted more than once.

'And these parties, like the one I saw this morning, are sent out to drive Sarr Mok off?'

'So they say.' Harry looked uneasy. 'I'm not altogether convinced because they categorically refused to let me go with the next one. Sarr Mok may be part of it but I have a feeling something else is moving out there.'

He finished the bowl of rice he was eating and stood up. 'Come on. We're doing some footage with Son Sleng and Ieng Nim this morning, and I want to get set up early.'

CHAPTER EIGHT

Wherever we went and whatever we did those first few days, Penn Thioen was always there. As he had promised when he had met us at the camp entrance, he was ready to smooth our way, making whatever arrangements Harry needed, interpreting where necessary, cajoling or bullying the shy camp people into being cooperative. He did it so unobtrusively that we tended not to notice him after a while, simply accepting him as part of the background.

The day Harry filmed the interview with the two commanders was actually a rest day in the camp and we finished early. Harry went swimming with the men, and I took the chance to climb up again to the top of the stupa, to watch the sun begin its slow, angry slide towards its quenching in the dark sea of the jungle.

I heard the monkeys chattering as I climbed, and as I reached the pinnacle, I saw a shadow cast across the terrace. Penn Thioen was there, squatting on a ledge at the base of one of the larger Buddhas. He had a book on his knee and, despite his black pyjamas and his home-made sandals, he looked, as I had noticed before, professorial.

He watched me calmly through his mended, silver-rimmed spectacles, beckoning as I hesitated. 'Sit, sit, madame,' he said. 'I see you have found my favourite place. It is very good to escape here from that' – he gestured to the camp far below, his mouth turning down – 'from that small purgatory.'

I was still wary, like the monkeys which drew close to watch us, an attentive but careful audience. 'I wish you would speak English to me. I think you do speak it.' My

French was becoming more fluent daily, but sometimes I grew desperately tired of floundering through unfamiliar thickets.

He shook his head. 'I understand it quite well, but I will not speak it, my accent is too bad.'

'Worse than my French accent?' I said, laughing.

'Much worse. But if you wish, you may speak English to me, and I shall reply in French. So we shall understand each other very well.'

He made a small reproving noise when he saw my glad look. 'I should not make this bargain at all, it is bad for your French. But here, and only here, we will accommodate each other.'

He turned and looked out over the camp again, and for a moment we were both silent. I could hear the faint rustle of the monkeys behind us, and one of the smaller ones gave a brief cry, to be instantly cuffed by its mother.

'Why do you call it purgatory?' I said carefully at last.

Penn smiled. 'It is not paradise. But it is not hell either. Somewhere in between, perhaps. Heaven or hell are yet to come, no one knows which.'

I was surprised at his terminology. 'You are a christian?' There was, I knew, a small, somewhat heretical christian group in Khamla, relic of missionary days.

'No, no, I am – what? A lapsed Buddhist, perhaps. But I spent some of my youth in France, and I lived with a pious family. I could name as many christian saints as you.'

'You took your degree at the Sorbonne?' It was a guess, but a safe one. Boys from well-off families of his generation would have been sent to be educated in France, as indeed Soumidath had been.

'Yes. In political science.' He turned away from me and looked out to the west where massive clouds were assembling for the evening's spectacular farewell to the day. 'I could have stayed in France. It was fashionable at that time to have people like me on university faculties, and I had several offers.'

'But instead you came back?'

He passed his hand over his spiky grey hair, and gave me a half-apologetic smile. 'I was somewhat idealistic as a young man. It seemed to me to be wrong for intellectuals to leave the country, as so many had already done.'

'And you ended up here? It hardly seems the right place for you.'

He gave me a surprised look. 'You are very blunt, madame.' A silence fell between us but then he laughed. 'Of course you are correct, war is not my natural *métier.* But it is all quite recent, you know. I lectured peacefully enough at the university for a good many years, until our present troubles came upon us. Then, like others, I had to make a choice.'

'And you chose this? A Marxist rebellion funded by rival communist powers?'

He swung round impatiently. 'Do not be naïve, madame. Think of the choices. As a lesser of evils, I would have preferred Prince Soumidath to remain as head of state, for he rallied the peasants behind him, and he kept us for years out of the big powers' surrogate wars. The present régime I cannot tolerate. Vouliphong is even more corrupt than the worst of those who surrounded Soumidath, and he is now no more than the tool of the Americans.'

'And Son Sleng and Ieng Nim?'

'They are cruel, but they are patriotic. They call themselves Marxists for want of a better label, but they are really only leaders of a populist movement. Now they are ready to accept arms and *matériel* from both the Soviet Union and China, but when the new Khamla emerges, it will be neutralist, independent, outside any of the Asian blocs. We will build something quite unique. You will see.'

'You are assuming the Liberation Front will win the war.'

Penn got up and stretched. 'Yes. It will be sooner than you think. Even the Americans cannot prop up Vouliphong much longer. Let us go down, madame. It will soon be dark.'

As we reached the bottom of the stupa, the sullen sun made its abrupt exit, and the warm darkness closed around us. Picking my way over the rough ground, I felt confident enough to risk an indiscretion.

'How did Ieng Nim lose his finger?'

Penn sounded surprised. 'Why do you ask? It happened last year. He was with a raiding party, and got separated from the rest. The RKA' – he meant the Royal Khamla Army which retained its name despite a change of princes and a heavy input of American advisers – 'took him prisoner, but they did not know who he was. They thought he was an ordinary fighter for he had no papers, and, of course, we wear no badges of rank.'

'And they shot his finger off?'

'No. They were questioning him about the location of the rest of the party, and to encourage him, a soldier smashed his finger, joint by joint, with a rifle butt. He escaped that night during a counter-attack, and when he came back to us, the finger has hanging down like' – he searched for a simile – 'like bloody string. He cut it off himself with a knife, as we had no doctor with us.'

I exclaimed, and I felt rather than saw him turn and look at me in the darkness. He cleared his throat.

'Since then,' he said carefully, 'I think he has become worse.'

'Worse?'

'More cruel.'

* * *

I was on the top of the stupa when the planes came in soon after dawn, so I had a grandstand view. The monkeys heard them before I did, and began to shout harshly, a sound quite unlike their usual high chatter.

At first they were nothing more than moving dots against the pale sky, then the rising sun caught the metal and I saw them clearly. They were American-made fighter-bombers, the red and blue insignia of the Royal Khamla Air Force visible on their sides as they came in low over the camp, jets screaming thinly.

They made one low run, then turned briefly and came back again. In the moment before they let go their rockets, I had a panoramic view of the whole camp. The mists had cleared and the sun was up, and I could see with unusual clarity.

Smoke was rising from the cookhouse, and the fighters making their way to it for breakfast seemed frozen, looking upwards, as though a film had stopped. Son Sleng was half-in, half-out of the doorway of the headquarters hut, a pistol in his hand. I could see our own sleeping hut, with the Land Rover parked outside. Harry was standing by it, also in a freeze-frame, in the act of pulling something out of the rear seat.

Then the rockets screamed in, and the scene dissolved in dust, flames and confusion. The cookhouse was hit and blazed instantly, and I saw one of the old cooks running out, his clothes on fire. There was too much dust and smoke in the air to be sure what was happening, but I thought I glimpsed Harry dropping and rolling a few yards before lying still.

The planes turned and flew very low along the river. I could not see what was happening from where I was, but at this time of morning both men and women would be bathing there. The sound of explosions and of screams came up very clearly.

There were a couple of anti-aircraft guns at the camp. Son Sleng had been promised SAM missiles, but they had not yet arrived. The crews must have been so much taken by surprise that they had not been able to reach the guns in time, and the bursts only began to show up in the sky as the planes retreated, out of reach.

I am not a coward, but I was beginning to learn prudence, so I stayed where I was for some minutes, until I thought it was unlikely that the planes would return for another run. There were shouts and cries from down below, but after the scream of the planes and the whine and crunch of rockets and bombs, silence seemed to hang over the camp.

I began to hurry down, but the footing was slimy and treacherous, so I had to take it slowly, as I usually did. In any case, my legs were trembling, and my heart was beating so rapidly it was hard to breathe.

When I ran into the camp, the first person I saw was Harry, sitting on the step of the hut. His face was covered in dust, and he had a bleeding cut on his forehead.

'I'm all right,' he said at once. 'A bit of temple wall flew off and hit me, but it's nothing much. I was knocked out for a minute.'

He got up unsteadily, supporting himself on the hut wall. 'Bastards!' he said. 'There's supposed to be an unwritten rule that they don't bomb anywhere inside the temple complex. Even that lot don't want to wipe out nine hundred years of their own history.'

I left him and ran through the camp towards the river. The damage was less than it had looked from above. A couple of huts had gone as well as the cookhouse, and – a far greater loss – some trucks which had just pulled out from the shelter of the trees had been hit and were blazing. People were lying on the ground outside the hospital hut. I could not tell whether they were dead or alive.

It was at the river, as I knew it would be, that the carnage had happened. The men's black pyjamas and the women's patterned cloths were still lying on the bank, where they had taken them off. The milky brown water was clear in the centre of the stream, but there were reddish stains on the sandbank, and in the eddies which broke against submerged trees. The bodies were already being taken by the current, moving slowly downstream in line, the girls' long black hair streaming behind them.

I saw something moving in the shallows at the women's bathing place, and waded round the brush barrier towards it. It was Linh, one of the very young fighters, a pretty girl who was so shy I could hardly get anything out of her but giggles. She lay on her back in the shallows, her still adolescent body unmarked. There was blood on her neck, and when she turned slowly to look at me, I saw her hair and the back of her head were matted with it. I tried to lift her, but she cried out and died. I watched the light go out of her eyes, as I had done with the girl in the guesthouse. Linh was younger, but they were very alike.

The river seemed kinder than a scratched grave in the jungle, so when I was sure she was dead, I gave her body a slight push that took it out into the stream, so that it joined the others in the bobbing, watery procession.

Harry was shouting for me as I came slowly back to the camp. 'Where the hell have you been?' he said, shouldering the camera. 'We've got work to do.'

I pushed past him, and went round the side of the hut. After I had been sick, I felt better and I washed my face in the rainwater butt, and rinsed my mouth out, careful not to swallow. When I came back and sat on the hut step, Harry handed me a half-full mug of cold tea.

'Here,' he said more gently. 'The first time is always the worst.'

I drank it, then stood, picking up the gear. 'Where do you want to start?'

He looked at me as if I had passed some sort of test. 'Good girl,' he said, and started towards the burning huts.

* * *

It was a hard day. When Harry had finished filming, he

went to help the men do what they could with the damaged vehicles, and I worked in the hospital hut with the doctor, making myself useful at the unskilled and dirty jobs. They were so short of dressings that used ones had to be washed out and used again. The casualties, they said, were light: four dead besides the ones in the river, a dozen more wounded, though not too seriously, two unlikely to live. Of these, one was the old cook whom I had seen running from the hut, the other a young fighter whose leg the doctor had amputated. He had internal injuries as well.

When there was nothing else for me to do, I sat with the two dying men, keeping the flies off them. 'If we had a proper hospital, and proper drugs, I could save them,' Lonh said. 'But not here.' He was a young man, only a few years out of medical school, but today, his face streaked with dust and sweat, his shirt and trousers bloody, he looked middle-aged.

In the late afternoon, he sent me away, telling me to get something to eat. I was reluctant to go, but he insisted.

At the sleeping hut, Harry was packing his gear and stowing it away in the Land Rover. 'Get your stuff,' he said briefly. 'We're leaving.'

'Tonight?' I sat down heavily on the step, my legs trembling with fatigue. 'Can't we wait until tomorrow? That road is bad enough by day.'

'The planes will be back tomorrow. Son Sleng knows that, so he is pulling out tonight. They can't risk having the headquarters wiped out, so they are going south.'

I got up wearily. 'But we are not travelling with them?'

Except for my gear, the loading of the Land Rover was almost complete. He was a very neat packer.

'Not likely. I've got everything I want and obviously the sooner I can get the film back to Bangkok the better. It's lovely stuff.'

I thought of the bodies in the river and the men dying

in the hospital hut, but I said nothing. From his own point of view, he was perfectly right. But as I was stuffing my spare shirts into a duffle bag, I heard a couple of shots from not far away, and came stumbling out. They sounded as if they had come from the hospital.

Harry saw my face. 'They were going to die, anyway,' he said abruptly. 'They couldn't take them with them, what would be the point?' I shook my head, unable to speak, and he put his arm round my shoulder, gripping me hard. 'It's always happened, you know,' he said. 'It's an old, old custom.'

We were almost ready to go when Penn came up to the hut in the dusk. 'You are loaded? Good,' he said, looking at the Land Rover. 'We are leaving in an hour.'

'Where will you go?' He was the only person at the camp I would be sorry to part from.

'To the southern headquarters. It is not far, no more than three days on the road. You will not find it, though, as comfortable as here.' He laughed, gesturing at the rough hut.

Harry pulled the tarpaulin taut over the gear in the back seat. 'Sorry, Penn, not this time. We are going back to Bangkok as fast as we can make it. I have some film to deliver.'

In the growing dusk it was hard to see Penn's expression but I thought he looked uncomfortable. I put out my hand to say goodbye, and he took it, hesitating. But I heard Harry cursing under his breath, and saw that Ieng Nim and half a dozen men, all carrying rifles, were coming up behind Penn.

'Get in quickly,' Harry said, pushing me towards the Land Rover, and, letting Penn's hand go, I scrambled up. Harry moved round to the driving side, but he was not fast enough. At a word from Ieng Nim, two of the fighters barred his path. One shoved a rifle into his side.

Ieng Nim came round the Land Rover and spoke to me in his soft, slow French. 'I am sorry, madame,' he said. 'But we cannot let you go yet. You must come with us to the south.'

I did not answer, staring at him, but Harry was red with anger. 'Why the hell do you want us? We are no use to you.'

Ieng Nim put his hand on the side of the Land Rover. 'We have lost some vehicles, as you know. We can make good use of this one. Three or four men can ride in the back, and it can pull a trailer.'

'Take the Land Rover, and let us walk back, then.' I groaned under my breath at the suggestion, and even Harry, putting it forward, sounded half-hearted. Carrying gear, it would be a long and nasty journey. I was not sure I would make it.

Ieng Nim laughed, but it was Penn who answered. 'Do not be foolish,' he said, sounding scandalised. 'Our own fighters will no longer be patrolling the road to protect you, and Sarr Mok's men will either pick you off for the pleasure of it, or take you prisoner and ask for a ransom.'

Harry nodded. We both remembered a couple of recent cases of abduction by unidentified armed men. One victim had been returned unharmed, the other had never been seen again, despite a sizeable ransom being paid by his family.

'Okay,' Harry said resignedly. 'If the Land Rover goes south, we go with it. But I want to get back to Bangkok, and it had better be soon.' He climbed into the driving seat, and I saw the look of relief on Penn's face. Ieng Nim gestured, and four of the fighters got up behind, balancing on the tight-packed gear.

'Thank God they are small and light or we would never make it,' Harry said, starting up savagely.

As we drove south, they put us in the middle of the convoy, between two trucks. The track was narrow, and the jungle pressed in so closely at both sides that the branches whipped at our faces. There was no chance of making a dash for it: there was nowhere to dash.

Harry rarely spoke as we drove, he had enough trouble keeping the over-loaded Land Rover from veering wildly on the deeply rutted surface. I tried taking over a couple of times to give him a break, but I had neither the skill nor the strength to keep up for long. My wrists were so wrenched by the effort of steering that they began to swell, and Harry, without complaint, took the wheel again. At night we were both so tired that we did not bother to make a fire or cook. Harry opened a tin of beef stew and we ate it cold, with some dried fruit afterwards. The sleeping bags were packed, so we simply lay down on the ground side by side and slept at once, not waking until the camp stirred at dawn.

At dusk on the seond day, a tremendous storm broke, the first I had seen in the jungle. What we could see of the sky through the trees turned a virulent yellow, and thunder began to rattle abruptly, louder than machine-gun fire. I love storms, and I laughed with excitement when the jagged white lightning lit up the jungle like a brilliant midday.

'You'll laugh on the other side of your face when we get struck,' Harry had to shout to make himself heard above the crash of the thunder and the advancing drumming of the rain, now almost on us.

The noise was so enormous that the men squatting in makeshift shelters in a clearing by the side of the road did not hear us until we were on top of them. It was almost dark, but a lightning flash showed them brilliantly illumined, quiet with shock at first, then jumping up and groping for their weapons. I had seen their patchwork, anonymous uniforms, and I remembered the day at the border with Soumidath.

'Sarr Mok's men, I bet,' Harry shouted in my ear. 'Poor little sods, they won't have a chance.'

They obviously thought so, too. There were no more than twenty of them compared to our formidable convoy, and they did not wait to argue, running for the shelter of the jungle, taking only their weapons and leaving their stores behind them. Our fighters let off a few rounds, but they were half-hearted about it, and the bad light and the teeming rain gave Sarr Mok's men some protection.

They disappeared almost instantly when they reached the trees, the undergrowth closing round them. At the very last, though, a man at the rear of the party turned with an angry gesture and I saw he had a grenade in his hand. He lobbed it wildly, without taking aim, then crashed into the undergrowth after the others.

I did not hear the grenade go off for it coincided with an almighty crack of thunder right over our heads. It must have exploded quite near the Land Rover though, for the fighters at the back threw themselves face down, thudding into Harry and me as they did so.

I felt a pain in my left leg, but everything had happened so quickly I did not fully register it. It was only when the order was given for the convoy to halt, and I slipped and fell in the mud as I was climbing down from the Land Rover, that I realised I had been hit. There was a jagged tear in my jeans, and blood was streaming down my ankle.

'What is it?' Harry said, coming round and pulling me to my feet. Then he saw my leg, and called loudly for the doctor.

Lonh came at once. He was on the truck behind us, riding with the wounded. Between them, he and Harry got me to the clearing, and under one of the makeshift shelters the departing guerrillas had built for themselves.

Lonh slit the leg of my jeans and bent carefully over my leg while Harry held a pocket torch. Lonh whistled softly. 'Not very much, I think, just a flesh wound. But there is a small piece of metal which must come out. You must hold very still.'

He motioned to Harry, who at once put his full weight across my thighs, at the same time imprisoning my wrists. 'I am sorry I have no local anaesthetic, madame,' Lonh said politely. 'But it will only take a moment.'

I felt it as the probe went in, and for a second I was violently nauseated. But Lonh was, as he promised, very quick, and when Harry let my hands go, he put a small, bloody sliver of metal into my palm. 'A souvenir,' he said, smiling. 'Now I will dress your leg, and I think within a few days – a week perhaps – you can walk again without trouble.'

* * *

Penn had been right when he said the southern camp was not as comfortable as the Great Temple. It was a very rough affair, with only enough huts for the leaders. The rest of us had to camp out. Harry unpacked the little one-man tents we had not so far used, but I found mine uncomfortable and claustrophobic and preferred to lie on top of my sleeping bag under a tree by the side of the small stream which supplied us with drinking water. Bathing was forbidden because the water supply was so small, and I had to make do with a modest wash after dark.

Food was scarce at the camp, only a bowl of rice with a little dried meat or fish morning or evening, and Harry would not let me supplement it with tinned food from our store. 'That may yet come in useful,' he said enigmatically.

I should have been bored and unhappy, for on Lonh's orders I spent most of my time lying down, my leg carefully wrapped in a protective swathe of plastic over the bandage. 'You are young enough and will heal well,' Lonh said. 'But we cannot risk infection.'

I thought of the rim of pus on Ieng Nim's finger, and the sweetish smell which had come from it, so I did exactly what Lonh told me. Harry, who was prowling about like a caged animal, marvelled at my patience.

'You should be going out of your mind!' he said.

In fact, I was not bored, and I was rather happy. The fretfulness and resentment of the years of my marriage had fallen away, and I felt calm and empty, watching with interest the life of the camp and the detachments of fighters coming and going.

I had not had before, in my whole life, a long period where I had nothing to do but think. It pleased me to observe during this time of reflection that human beings are, after all, capable of change, and in my own case, a new persona seemed to be tentatively emerging. Mrs Herbert, Dr Herbert's awkward wife, Gillian, was receding into the background day by day; or, more accurately, I saw the whole process in my mind's eye like one of those Victorian illustrations of deathbeds, with a bright new soul rising up from a discarded body. I could only hope that the new Gilly would be better and stronger than the old one.

Looking back on my marriage, I discovered I had almost stopped hating David, for I now acknowledged that he had been right in saying the fault was partly mine. My acquiescence, though it was only on the surface, had made him more of a bully. We obviously should never have married, but if I had stood up to him right at the beginning, our life together might have been less tormented. I was not sure, however, even of that, because it was only when I began to live alone and to be financially independent that I fully understood how trapped and helpless both of us had been in our festering marriage. Now, even lying on a dusty river bank with a gashed leg, with the possibility of dying in the company of Son Sleng's fighters, I felt strong and cleansed.

If, from time to time, Peter came into my mind, I thrust the image angrily away. I did not want to replace one emotional bondage with another. Now that I had rid myself of David, I would be stupid to allow myself the luxury of an attachment which at best was futile and, at worst, dangerous.

Watching Harry moving round the camp and admiring dispassionately his strong, wiry body marked with its battle scars, I thought it a pity there was no physical spark between us, no sign of the heavenly electricity.

He could put his arm round me, as he often did, and the only sensation I had was a feeling of warmth and friendship. The chemistry of physical attraction remains a mystery, but I would no more have thought of sleeping with him than I would with Penn Thioen.

I thought that when I went back to Bangkok (though in the circumstances that was by no means a certainty) I would take up the occasional invitations from men which came my way in AsiaNews and which, so far, I had always turned down. Despite myself, my body yearned after Peter. I would see what an encounter or two with an agreeable stranger would do to ease it.

Penn spent most of his time with the two commanders in the headquarters hut, but when he could, he came and sat beside me, especially in the first few days before Lonh let me get up and hobble about. We talked in our usual mixture of English and French, and he was very patient, coaxing me on so that I needed less and less to fall back on English.

He talked a good deal of what would happen when the war was over and a new régime was installed in the capital. He was so convincing that I came to accept this would happen, though at the moment the odds were heavily against it.

'Will Soumidath come back as head of state?'

He nodded. 'We will need him, in the beginning at least. I think he will head the government for a few years, then, when he sees the country is stable, he will retire.'

'And no one will succeed him? The royal line will come to an end?'

Penn grimaced. 'You think this is a pity after more than a thousand years, and so do I. But the days of princes are over. None of Soumidath's sons can hope to rule.'

Remembering the few occasions when I had seen Soumidath in action, I thought Penn was being optimistic. A graceful retirement to the South of France did not seem in Soumidath's line, nor would his sons give up without a struggle.

'Even in the short term, it will be a bit of an anachronism, won't it?' I said. 'A prince at the head of a socialist state!'

He laughed. 'Asian socialism comes in a number of forms, as you know. You have travelled in China, and Vietnam, and Laos, and seen how it varies: Marx would not recognise any of it. In the first few years, ours will be a very simple kind. We will concentrate on land reform and the breaking up of the big estates, and getting the peasants' children out of the fields and into schools. Literacy is our worst problem.'

I nodded. On our last trip, we had seen children of no more than eight or nine working not only in the fields but in the small sweatshop factories in the back streets of the capital.

'And you will take no help from outside?'

'Nothing with strings attached.' Surprisingly, he brought the phrase out in English. 'Obviously we will want economic aid, but we will get it from the IMF or the Asian Development Bank, not from the big powers. We have had too much interference already, even in Soumidath's time. The new Khamla will be a member of the non-aligned bloc, but it will be in nobody's sphere of influence. Nobody's.'

Harry came up with a cup of tea for me, and Penn at once rose to go. He liked Harry, but he told me that he did not find him serious. 'Mr Greene likes war but not politics,' he said. 'With me, it is the other way round.'

Harry watched him walking over to the headquarters hut. 'Poor bastard,' he said, drinking his own tea.

I looked at him, puzzled. 'Why poor bastard?'

'They will work him ragged now and squeeze every idea out of him, then, when they are back in power, goodbye Penn.' He made a staccato noise with his tongue, like a small boy imitating a machine gun.

'Rubbish,' I said angrily. 'Why would they do that?'

He lay on his back and stared up at the sky. 'Intellectuals are very expendable, hadn't you heard?'

I had willed myself into such a state of calmness that I was astonished at the revulsion which swept over me. 'How can you be such an icy bastard? Don't you feel anything for these people?'

He rolled over and looked at me curiously. 'Sure. I'm not as callous as you think I am. But I've seen a lot more of this sort of thing than you have, Gil. You don't live long in this part of the world with a bleeding heart.'

He was probably right, but I could not yet stay completely aloof from what was happening round us. Up to the time of the air raid at the Great Temple, I suppose I would have described myself as apolitical. I had enough historical perspective to distrust revolutions, knowing that nothing is more certain than that every revolution eats its children.

But I suppose I had really stopped being objective when I had held a dying girl in my arms on the river bank, and seen the pale water turn rosy with blood. With my intellect, I knew that the leaders of the new Khamla would be as corruptible if not as already corrupted as those they would replace. But I had an irrational faith in the Prince. There was a quality in Soumidath, despite his exhibitionism, which seemed to me nothing more complex than an obsessional patriotism. He saw himself quite literally as the Father of the People, the name the peasants gave him when he toured the countryside. It was the compelling passion which drove him, and I was able to understand without any difficulty why Peter had attached himself to him and made himself his servant.

I had also come to love Penn Thioen, with the

affection of a niece for an uncle, or a pupil for a revered teacher.

The ideas of basic socialism suited to an agrarian economy which he had outlined to me seemed to echo the simplicities of the early days of the Chinese revolution, when Mao Tse-tung, in the caves of Yenan, was planning to draw his 'beautiful pictures' on the clean-swept pages of the new China.

I doubted whether these pure aims would prove any more enduring in Khamla than they had in the People's Republic, but at the same time I fiercely wanted Penn and others like him to survive the civil war, to come to power in the capital, and to give the Prince his chance to resume his high-wire balancing act.

But then, at night, as I lay looking up at the night sky through the web of branches, and listening to Harry's strong, slow breathing beside me, I heard a faint sound and saw in the light of a campfire Ieng Nim prowling round the camp, moving almost silently, speaking in a low voice to the fighters on watch.

I turned on my side in the warm darkness with a feeling of dismay. For each Penn Thioen in any revolution, there are a dozen Ieng Nims, all of them deadly.

* * *

By the third day I was limping around the camp, but I could not move far or fast. Lohn congratulated me on the clean look of the wound, and said the throbbing in my leg should soon ease. In the evening, I hobbled back to the sleeping place, and I saw Harry watching me thoughtfully.

'How is it?'

I eased myself carefully down on to my sleeping bag. 'All right, but it still hurts like hell. I don't think I am going to be doing any long hikes for a while. Thank God we've got the Land Rover when we do move.'

He looked at me for a while without speaking, then he got up slowly. 'Stay there and I'll bring you some food. I hear we have some fresh meat tonight with the rice. The boys shot a couple of wild pigs.'

The pork was strong and gamey, but after a diet of dried fish it tasted delicious. I wiped my greasy fingers on the grass, shared a rare cigarette with Harry, then crawled under my mosquito net. Fuel, even for oil lamps, was very short, and the camp went to bed soon after dark, and got up again with the sun. It made for some very long nights.

I woke instantly later when Harry touched my shoulder, shaking me cautiously through the mosquito net. 'Hush, it's only me,' he said in a low voice. 'I just wanted to let you know I am going.'

I sat up, wide awake. It was much too dark to see his face, and I was not sure whether he was serious. 'Going? Going where?'

His dark shape squatted beside me on the ground and he spoke so quietly I could hardly hear him. 'I didn't tell our hosts, but I know this area reasonably well. Soumidath had a hunting lodge not far away from here, and I've walked over a lot of it when I was here before. You wouldn't think it, but we are only fifty kilometres or so from the border, and there's a Thai village just on the other side. I can easily make it on foot.'

'But I can't.' It was a statement, not a question.

He gave an almost inaudible laugh. 'No, my love, you can't. I don't think you could anyway, even with two good legs, because I'm going to travel very fast.' he took my hand and held it briefly. 'As soon as I have gone, they will start thinking about letting you go. They know I will create a stink as soon as I get to what passes for civilisation in these parts. If I stay, we could be here for weeks.'

'So you are doing the best thing for both of us!' I was so angry I could hardly keep my voice down.

'Right on!' he said lightly. 'I bet you a bottle of best

bourbon they put you in the Land Rover when your leg is a bit better and give you an escort to the border.'

It didn't turn out quite like that, but, broadly speaking, Harry was right. No one knew he had gone until the next morning, and I thought, all in all, they were rather relieved. Both of us were becoming something of an embarrassment. They didn't send me to the southern border, though. Instead Penn came to tell me that the headquarters was moving back to the Great Temple. From there, they would give me an escort along the western route, and I could drive back into Thailand without difficulty.

I was surprised. 'What about the planes? Won't they come back and bomb again?'

Penn shook his head. 'We have heard on the radio that Prince Vouliphong has given an undertaking the raids will not be repeated, because of the risk of damage to the Great Temple. There have been many protests.'

'I can imagine.' Vouliphong must have been deluged with cables from learned bodies and environmentalists all over the world. His advisers would have taken notice of them, if he did not. It was all very convenient for the Liberation Front.

I rode back to Vańgkhorn in some style, in the back of the medical truck. We came into the camp in the evening, and it was rather like coming home.

What I craved more than anything was to swim in the river, to wash out the ingrained dust of the days at the southern camp. The doctor might forbid it because of the danger of infection, so I did not ask him, but went at once from the hut to the women's bathing place. In the late afternoon light, the river ran calm and broad and bleached of colour, the dark trees crowding to its edge, the jungle silent.

There was no one there but me, and the ghost of Linh, and I hesitated for a moment before I stripped, remembering the red scum on the water, and way she had turned to look at me before she died. But I was, as

Harry had said more than once, becoming very Asianised, and with a sigh I let my clothes fall on the sandspit and waded out, turning on my back and letting the water take me.

* * *

When I came to the dining hut that night, I saw Son Sleng and Ieng Nim were talking to a tall European, with very close cropped hair. The man turned and came over to me, taking my hand, but it was not until he spoke that I saw it was Peter Casement. He had shaved his beard and his fair hair was cut so short it resembled an animal's pelt.

With his beard gone, he looked younger, and a stranger. He must have seen the shock in my eyes, and mistaken it.

'It's me,' he said, shaking hands. 'You are seeing the revised Peter Casement. I thought I needed a change of image.'

I could not speak or even smile, but stood there frozen, like Lot's wife. I had believed that I would not see Peter at the Great Temple – Penn had said he was still in Europe and was not expected back for some time yet – and that if we did meet again, it would be in more impersonal surroundings in Bangkok. I did not want to see him in this place where, though we were surrounded by the activity of the camp, our very non-Asianness, our physical and mental dissimilarity to everyone around us, linked us in a kind of intimacy, like two people enclosed in a transparent glass sphere.

I also recognised, with despair, that at Peter's touch, even in only a brief handshake, the calmness and equanimity of the days at the southern camp had vanished as an illusion vanishes. I was as disturbed as ever by Peter, hypnotised by him, physically betrayed by his proximity.

I don't think this was love, or if it was it was not the

comfortable kind, and I saw not much hope in it. Presumably the sexual and emotional starvation of my marriage had made me vulnerable. But I still did not understand why I had fixed on Peter, who clearly did not want me, and who was watching me now as I stood tongue-tied with a wary look which I knew only to well.

When I still said nothing, he became voluble enough for both of us. The cautious look faded, and I could see he was in tearing spirits.

'Well, you're thin,' he said, looking me up and down. 'But it suits you well enough. A thin, brown gypsy! I wouldn't have recognised the prim and proper Frau Doktor Herbert. How is your leg?'

'Much better.' I kept my voice level, though even his presence there had stripped me of calm. 'I shall be able to walk back to Bangkok soon.'

He laughed. 'You won't have to do that. If you will give me a day or two's grace, I will drive you back myself. You would have a job handling the Land Rover with a lame leg.'

I started to reply, but Son Sleng called to him then and he went at once, touching my arm lightly. 'I'll see you later,' he said over his shoulder.

We had a good dinner that night in celebration of the return to the camp and also, presumably, of Peter's arrival. There was some sort of local crayfish with the rice, and bowls of papaya and mango. The whisky bottles were out, and Peter sat at the top of the table with the commanders, drinking with them glass for glass.

I was stuck between two solemn young fighters who did not speak French, and when Penn saw this, he came and sat beside me, making them move. I smiled at him in gratitude for his courtesy, and he looked at me carefully.

'You smile but you look a little strained this evening, madame. You are not worried about driving to Bangkok? Mr Casement will take you, I think.' He had a very French formality about titles. I had tried many times to coax him to call me Gilly, but without success. Yet he would not let me call him anything but Penn.

'It is nothing,' I said. 'My leg aches a little, that is all.' I looked up at the top of the table. 'I was surprised to see Mr Casement here. It was said he was in Paris with Prince Soumidath.'

'So he was, but he has come back, as you see. He has brought messages from the Prince, for the commanders. There will be some hard bargaining.'

'He is a negotiator, then? I would have thought the Prince would have come instead, or sent the Prime Minster, or one of his sons.'

'It is too dangerous for the Prince at present. He will have to risk himself in the future, but not yet. As for the others, there is bad feeling between them and the commanders. If Prince Soumidath comes to us, he will come alone, without his sycophants. I think Mr Casement understands that, though the Prince, as yet, may not.'

I looked at the three faces at the top of the table. Peter was speaking in very rapid French, and Son Sleng and Ieng Nim had bent forward to listen with enormous attention. Son Sleng was smiling slightly, and he looked, as he often did, more like one of his own young fighters than the commander-in-chief. Ieng Nim's face was intent, but gave away nothing.

'You trust Peter Casement?'

Penn laughed. 'We trust nobody. But at least he comes to us with clean hands.' I exclaimed, but shook my head when he asked what I had said.

'Nothing, Nothing.'

I saw very little of Peter the next day, for he was in the headquarters hut with the commanders. My leg was much easier, and I spent most of the day on the river bank or walking aimlessly about the camp. For the first time I felt bored and uneasy.

At night, he came to my hut after dinner. 'Come for a walk,' he said. 'It's too early to go to bed.'

I hesitated, then I got up and started, a little ahead of him, towards the great stupa. 'I have finished my business here,' he said behind me. 'We can leave for Bangkok tomorrow.'

I said nothing until we reached the base of the stupa, then I began to climb, slowly, to spare my leg. 'Did you send orders for my husband to be killed?' I said over my shoulder.

He laughed. 'I heard you had some idea like that in your head. What do you take me for, a murderer?'

I turned, but I could not see his face in the darkness. 'I am not sure.'

He spoke very carefully. 'Listen to me, for I am not going to discuss this again. You are being stupid. The message I sent was about arms shipments. What happened was nothing to do with me, and I am very sorry about it. In any case, no harm was done.'

'You think not?' I remembered David, and how he had looked, lying on the floor in his stained pyjama trousers.

We climbed in silence towards the top of the stupa. As we reached the uppermost terrace, the clouds moved gently away towards the west, and the huge moon emerged, so that we saw below us the white bones of the city. The sweet silvery light made the stupa seem to float above a dark, mysterious sea. I felt my anger recede. What had happened before now seemed as remote as the smile of the stone Buddha which looked at us calmly in the moonlight from the corner of the terrace.

'That's better,' Peter said with relief. 'Come and sit down here, and let us be friends.'

We sat in silence, and I let the moonlight soak into my bones. There was not much room on the narrow ledge, and I felt Peter's sleeve lightly brush my arm.

After a time, I turned and saw him looking at me. His glance was oblique and it slid away when our eyes met, so that he was once again looking over the antique graveyard below. But I thought I had seen some expression of dispassionate kindness, mixed with another kind of emotion I could not understand. At once, my mood turned dark. 'What is it?' I said stiffly.

He hesitated. 'Don't become fond of me, Gilly. It would be a terrible mistake.' He smiled as he said it, to take the hardness out of it, but in the moonlight his face looked as pale as stone.

'Why? Because you only like whores?'

I was appalled to hear myself saying it.

He drew in his breath. For the first time, I had made him angry. 'Who told you that? I did not think you would listen to that sort of gossip.'

'No one told me. I saw you with the Thai woman in the market in Bangkok. You were shopping with her and the child.' He said nothing, and I went on, knowing what I was doing was suicidal, but unable to stop myself. 'Is the child yours?'

He laughed and relaxed, his anger going. 'No, I've only known Rosie for a year or two. That's not her real name, in case you're wondering. No one can pronounce her original one, she says, or at least the clients can't.'

He seemed totally unselfconscious, and I watched him cautiously. 'But she is a prostitute?'

'She is.' He sighed, and lit a cigarette. 'You're an obstinate girl, Gilly, and I can see I might as well tell you what you want to know because you will just keep asking until I do. Yes, she is a prostitute. Yes, I do sleep with her, at least when I am in Bangkok. I pay the rent for the apartment where she and the child live, and I give her money from time to time. It's not so much, you know. I live pretty much close to the bone myself.'

'How *do* you live?' This was a subject I had heard discussed more than once over drinks in Bangkok bars. The speculation tended to be rather wild, with suggestions that Peter was funded anywhere from Washington to Moscow, as well as by the Prince.

'I've told you before. I had a hefty advance from my

publisher in New York, and the Prince pays my expenses when I am travelling.' He laughed at my intent look. 'There's no mystery about it.'

I let that go, and returned to the subject which obsessed me.

'Why do you live with this woman?'

My persistence made him impatient, and he turned again and looked at me consideringly. His voice hardened. 'Why do I live with a whore, when ladies like you are offering it free? Is that what you are asking?'

What he said was perfectly just, but I could not bear it, and in anger and despair, I got up and started along the terrace, stumbling on the uneven pavement. At once, he moved quickly ahead of me, barring my way. 'Sorry,' he said. 'I shouldn't have said that. But you are bloody provoking, Gilly.'

I could not force my way past him, so I stood, trembling, and he took my arm impersonally, and drew me down so that we sat side by side on the narrow ledge.

'You have called Rosie a whore, and so she is,' he said conversationally. 'Let me tell you about her, though. No' – as I tried to get up – 'you take an interest in my affairs, and it is up to you to listen.'

He looked past me, and up into the luminous sky. It was very quiet at the top of the stupa, for the camp below had settled down and only the sentries were awake. We might have been the only inhabitants of an antique world.

'Rosie is not unique, there are thousands of women like her in South-east Asia,' Peter said, speaking slowly as though he were beginning a story for children. 'She comes from a farming area near Chiang Mai, and her parents sold her to a Bangkok factory owner when she was ten.'

'Sold her?'

'Oh, they don't call it that, but money does change hands. Rosie's parents had seven other children so they were glad to get rid of one.'

'She worked in one of those factories in the back streets,' I said almost inaudibly.

'Yes, they still exist, and they are still much the same as when Rosie worked there, twenty years or so ago. You've seen them. You know what they are like.'

I had seen them, when I went to French lessons with Mme Arnot. Her room was in a house in a maze of twisting back streets, and even at night, one could see through unglazed windows into hot, squalid rooms where children and young girls bent over God knows what small and sight-destroying tasks.

'They like children because they have small fingers,' Peter said calmly. 'The kids can do a lot of jobs better than adults, assembling transistor parts, or sewing those god-awful pictures in human hair.'

'But Rosie didn't stay in the factory?'

'She stayed until she was fourteen or fifteen, but she was doing such close work in such bad light that she was afraid of going blind. Besides, they only pay starvation wages, you know, and she had nowhere to live except a cubicle in a dormitory in the backyard of the factory.'

He had been holding my arm to keep me sitting beside him but now he let it go, and looked at me wearily. 'She didn't have much choice, except to go on the streets. Apart from anything else, she was illiterate. She still is, for that matter, but she is very fierce about the boy going to school.'

'She's been a prostitute ever since?'

'More or less. She tells me she was very pretty when she was younger, and for two or three years she managed to get off the streets when one of her clients, a well-off businessman, set her up in a flat. Then she got pregnant, and he refused to believe the child was his, and turned her out.'

'Was it? His child, I mean.'

'It was. But he was tired of her, by then, and it was a good excuse. So she went to live at the mission those

Belgian lay sisters run until the child was born. She went back on the streets again, but she's always managed to keep him with her.'

There was something irrational in what he was saying. 'You support her, yet she is still soliciting. I saw her doing it quite openly in a bar in Bangkok.' I remembered that Rosie had asked me then if I was from the mission.

If I had hoped to surprise him, I was disappointed. 'Did you now?' His Irish accent broadened as it always did when he was amused. 'I could ask you what you were doing in the sort of bar that ladies like Rosie use as their place of business.'

I was angry because he was laughing at me. 'I was waiting for someone and I saw her,' I said tersely. 'Don't you mind, that she does this?'

His amusement faded. 'Yes, I mind. But she is a free agent, and I can't stop her. She does it because she knows her looks are going, and she wants to make as much money as she can while she can. She is competing with fourteen-year-olds, you know, and it is getting harder for her every year.'

I looked at him questioningly, without speaking, but he at once read what was in my mind, as he had done more than once before.

'I am not going to turn her out, if that is what you are assuming. She knows I will support her as long as possible. But she doesn't think I am a very good bet, even in the short term.'

'Why not?'

He did not speak for a while. Then he said, his voice quite unemotional: 'She assumes that I do not have a very great life expectancy.'

A long silence fell between us. It was so still, I could hear his quiet, regular breathing as he sat beside me, and the moon, riding huge in a cloudless sky above us, bleached us and the stupa into sharp black and silver outlines. We may have sat for an hour, hardly moving, or it may have been only a few minutes, I am not sure. Time seemed to have become meaningless.

I felt drugged with the moonlight and the night, and in the end, when I spoke, my voice sounded remote.

'You still haven't told me why you live with her.'

He looked at me gravely. 'Why do you think?'

I considered what he had asked, thinking of the many conversations I had heard in bars when Bill and I had to entertain visiting wiremen from Europe, or the States, or Australia. 'Some Western men find Asian women a turn-on because they are compliant or subservient,' I said cautiously. I remembered one middle-aged New Yorker who had told me nothing had excited him as much for years as shop girls bowing to him in the department stores in Tokyo.

He laughed, this time with easy amusement. 'If you think Rosie is subservient, you should hear her berating me or the boy when she is in a temper,' he said. 'She would put a Belfast fishwife to shame.' He looked at me hard. 'And for your information, I don't get my turn-ons by bullying women. Unlike, I suspect, your husband.'

It was only a guess, but he saw at once by my face that he had struck hard. 'Well, it is none of my business,' he said politely, 'just as my affairs are really none of yours. But as we are here, alone, in this place, I will tell you what you want to know. I live with Rosie because she asks nothing of me.'

'You said you gave her money.'

He gestured impatiently. 'Don't be obtuse. You know very well that is not what I am talking about. She accepts me while I'm there, but she makes no fuss when I go away. She does not expect me to say I love her, and best of all, she makes no pretence that she loves me. Sex does not mean a great deal to her, why should it? But when we go to bed together, she responds with warmth and generosity, which is all I ask. I think she is fond of me because I am, by her standards, kind and considerate, but if I disappeared from her life, she would not grieve very much, if at all.'

'Except for the money.'

'Except for the money, of course. Why not? It's important to her.'

He looked at me with such a calm, considering look that I was ashamed of what I had said. But I still did not fully understand him.

'Is that really all you want, a relationship as casual as that?'

He sighed, with a return to impatience. 'It is very hard to convince you, my dear Gilly. Do you seriously suppose, with the sort of life I live, that I would saddle myself with a wife and children?'

'No, I don't think you would.' I tried to make my tone light. 'But you're not unique, you know, especially in this part of the world, which is full of drifters. Harry Greene lives a life which is just as erratic as yours, and probably a good deal more dangerous. He has offers from ladies, too, and I don't think he turns them down.'

'Possibly not. But Harry and I are quite different. He doesn't mind temporary entanglements, I don't want any at all. I can't afford to waste my time and energies on them, I have other things to do.' He looked at me with some interest. 'Did you and Harry sleep with each other, by the way?'

I laughed. His tone was so easy, I did not take offence. 'None of your business,' I said echoing him. Then I relented. 'No, we didn't. I don't think I am Harry's type.'

'True enough,' he said seriously, 'and that's a pity. He would be a much better bet than anyone else, if you wanted to get that husband of yours out of your system.'

The mist was beginning to gather at the edge of the trees, and a bank of cluds was assembling in the western sky, ready to march against the moon.

'Let's go down,' he said with a sigh, taking my arm. 'I want to leave early in the morning, so we should get some sleep.' At the bottom of the stupa, he bent and kissed my hands briefly. 'Good night,' he said lightly. 'Don't grieve about things you can't change. It will be all the same in a thousand years.'

* * *

I needn't have worried about feeling embarrassed on the trip back to Bangkok. We had company, in the shape of one of the senior fighters, a dour, thirty-five-year-old veteran, who was already installed in the back of the Land Rover when I came out of the sleeping hut next morning.

'A chaperon?' I said ironically to Peter, who was packing in his own gear.

He laughed. 'If you think you need one.' Penn came up then and said rather apologetically that the man wanted a lift to the border, where he had some business. 'We should have asked you first,' he said. 'The vehicle is yours.'

'Not really. It is Mr Greene's.' I was rather pleased, for I had no wish at all for any more heart-to-heart talks with Peter. Nor he, I am sure, with me.

Penn kissed my hand in the old-fashioned style when we left, and said that when we next met, it would be in better circumstances. 'I promise you that when we are installed in the capital, we shall receive you there,' he said. 'You will be an honoured guest.'

When we were some way out from the camp, I twisted round awkwardly in the jolting Land Rover to look back at the Great Temple. It was still very early, and strips of mist adhered to the top level of the trees. But against the lightening sky, I could see the terraces of the great stupa with its slender point rising to the promise of Nirvana, and I felt a sensation of most intense melancholy. I did not believe I would see it again.

Peter, for once, had almost nothing to say all the way

back to the border, and the silent presence of the man in the back oppressed my spirits. We made camp at dusk, and after a scrappy meal, Peter rolled into his sleeping bag without a word, though the other man sat up all night, his rifle across his knees. When I woke, as I did often, I could see his silhouette in the moonlight, hunched and brooding.

The next day, he dropped off just short of the border, and disappeared into the trees, sketching a brief salute with his rifle.

'What is he really up to?' I asked cautiously. 'After all, you should know.'

Peter shook his head, then cursed as we lurched into a particularly deep pothole. 'Not necessarily. I am the Prince's emissary, that's all. Son Sleng is not about to take me into his confidence about his military dispositions.'

We suddenly swung on to a stretch of made road, and he sighed with relief and braked. 'How is your leg? Would you like to drive for a while? I could do with a rest.'

When we had changed over, he lit a cigarette, and eased his shoulders wearily back against the seat. 'Something is stirring, though,' he said abruptly. 'I saw Son Sleng giving that guy a long briefing last night. My guess is that there will be a big push when the wet season is over.'

We came back to Bangkok with its noise and frenzy and suicidal drivers in the late afternoon. Even after a short time away, it seemed like another planet. At the traffic lights, the child beggars darted through the cars to thrust garlands of wilted flowers at us, or tried to reach up to clean the windscreen with dirty rags. When I gave the nearest one a few coins, three others set upon him and forced open his tightly clenched hand, while he wept and the cars honked impatiently around them. Peter shook his head at me. 'You can never live here unless you learn to accept it,' he said calmly.

He brought the Land Rover to a neat halt outside my flat, and sprang down, throwing the canvas bag which was his only luggage over his shoulder. He looked at me gravely, but did not touch me.

'Goodbye, my dear Gilly,' he said. 'I won't be around for a while, but I suppose we will meet again one of these days. Tell Harry he's a bastard for abandoning you like that.' He waved briefly, and walked away without looking back.

CHAPTER NINE

Peter was right about the big push, though he was out in his timing. It was not until I was in New York, many months later, that I heard that the Liberation Front had begun their long-expected assault on the capital.

Radio and television were full of it, and as I sat drinking coffee and waiting for David at the Rockefeller Center, I read a long account of the bloody effects of the mortaring of the city in the *New York Times*. There was a picture of a woman screaming as she held up a dead child to the camera.

When I had finished, I put down the paper and looked out through the window at the skaters swooping and whirling on the rink outside. It was warm in the restaurant, but the air, as I had walked up Fifth Avenue, had been crisp and snappy with winter. The New Yorkers were complaining about the long cold spell which refused to give way to the spring, but I could not get enough of the sparkling air. After the soggy sweatiness of Asia, it was like being slightly drunk on champagne all the time, and without a hangover.

David came in then, and sat down, ordering coffee and a sandwich. I showed him the headlines in the *New York Times*. He nodded. 'Yes, it won't be long now. I had a talk today with Rick Dawson' – he had renewed acquaintance with the American adviser we had met at Vouliphong's reception – 'and he says the United States is pulling out. No use flogging a dead horse. They learned that lesson in Vietnam.' He watched the arrival of his neatly flagged sandwich with approval. David was fond of American food, describing it as hygienic.

'Does that mean Soumidath will go back to the capital?'

'It is difficult to say. According to the Americans, the Liberation Front hasn't decided yet whether he would be an asset or a liability. It isn't the usual thing to have a Prince at the head of a socialist state, but on the other hand, Soumidath has excellent public relations value.'

I looked at him in some surprise. 'Did Rick tell you that? How does the State Department know what the Liberation Front is thinking?'

'They have their sources. Very unexpected ones, sometimes.' He ate his sandwich thoughtfully, and I could see he was not going to say any more. I did not bother to pursue it, for it was probable he was only guessing. David was rather expert at appearing to know more than he really did.

Watching him across the table, I felt a sense of incredulity that we were sitting here together, drinking coffee in reasonable amity in a New York restaurant, with the skaters gliding outside in the crackling air. Our last farewell, in the sweltering heat of Bangkok, seemed in another world.

Actually, our joint presence in New York was coincidental rather than prearranged. In the most recent of the dutiful letters I had continued to write to David during our separation (though the intervals were becoming perceptibly longer) I had mentioned, more to fill up space than anything else, that I was going to New York in March to negotiate a contract.

David had cabled back, saying he would be there too, to talk to his new publishers. He asked me to let him know the name of my hotel, and I could not think of any reason not to give it.

I had been rather nervous when Bill Geraghty asked me to go to New York for him, to haggle with Big Brother. 'Look, love, I don't want to go,' he said. 'I've been away so often this last year I can't afford to make another trip. Everybody will have forgotten my face.

Anyway, you know just about as much about this business as I do.'

That was not quite true, but near enough. A couple of months after I had come back from Khamla, Bill's wife had written to him from Sydney saying she was proposing to divorce him. He wouldn't have minded that so much, because she refused to live in Asia, but he was terrified of losing his three boys, whom he now saw every school holidays. He flew down at once to dissuade her, leaving me to run the agency.

I was thrown in at the deep end, and I was surprised how well I managed. Bill came back for a month to see how things were working out, then, reassured, returned to Sydney for a long holiday, wooing his wife with promises that within a year or two he would have made enough money to go home for good.

His wife believed him, and perhaps he believed it himself. I had seen enough of people like him to know it wasn't true. Asia is full of Bill Geraghtys, can't-go-home-again permanent exiles. 'Curry eaters,' Bill himself used to call them, with the flavour of spices on their tongues.

It was logical enough, therefore, that I should go to New York, for I had already done most of the early negotiating with Big Brother by telephone and letter. We wanted improved terms from them for the second year of the contract, and Bill thought we could get them, for we had been doing rather well, and Harry Greene continued to supply us with an occasional bit of spectacular film.

But Big Brother, more properly known as World-News, was a very hard-nosed organisation, and was trying to beat us down. 'Go and talk them into it, love,' Bill said. 'They won't be able to resist a nice girl like you.'

That was rather over-stating it, but in fact the New York people were much more amenable in the flesh than they had sounded in their letters. I dealt with one of the directors, Brideson Samuels, who, not surprisingly, was known as Sam.

Because Khamla was in the news again, Sam asked me to do a voice piece on the lifestyle of the Liberation Front in the Great Temple camp, and paid me handsomely for it. I was able to buy myself a new winter coat which I urgently needed. Everything I had was out of fashion.

'If you get back there, just let us know,' Sam said, giving me lunch at Sardi's. 'We would certainly be in the market for more of the same.'

He looked at me carefully across the table. 'You haven't mentioned him to me, but you must have met Peter Casement at some time or other.'

I was wary. 'I have met him a couple of times. My husband introduced us last year, when we were in Hanoi. We ran into him at the funeral of Prince Soumidath's mother.'

Sam raised his eyebrows. This was the first time he had heard of a husband. But he was not really interested in my private affairs, he was interested in Peter. 'How well did you get to know him?'

'Not very well.' That was literally true. 'He is just someone I seem to bump into now and again. Why do you ask?'

Sam settled back against the banquette. 'I used to know Peter pretty well myself when we were in Vietnam. We teamed up in Saigon during the Tet offensive. Those were pretty hairy times.' He beckoned to the waiter. 'I've lost touch with him since. I never seem to catch up with him now when he comes to Washington.'

It was stiflingly hot in the restaurant, but my hands and feet felt cold, and I shuddered involuntarily. Sam had turned to talk to the waiter, and did not notice.

'You must be mistaken,' I said lightly. 'Why would Peter come to Washington?'

He looked at me in surprise. 'Why not? He's still an

American citizen though he hasn't lived in the States for years. He probably has lots of buddies there.'

'But he's an adviser to Prince Soumidath.' It would have been wiser to avoid the subject, but I could not stay away from it.

Sam laughed. 'Is that what he calls himself these days? Well, there's no harm in keeping your options open.'

The waiter came up with two more martinis. Sam took a connoisseur's sip, then gave a nod to the waiter as though he had been tasting a fine wine. 'Just right,' he said. 'The last one wasn't dry enough.'

He started at the menu then looked up again. 'He's a funny guy, Peter,' he said conversationally. 'He can't keep his fingers out of a good revolution. It must be his Fenian blood, I guess.'

'Fenian?' The glass was icy in my cold hand.

'Hasn't he talked to you about his family?' He watched me over his drink. 'No, probably not, if you don't know him too well. Come to think about it, he only gets on to it late at night, when he has had a lot to drink.'

'I thought he had a pretty hard head,' I said, trying to smile. 'I've been at dinner with him once or twice, and he seems able to put away a lot.'

'Sure, but once in a while he goes at it bull-headed, and gets pissed out of his mind.' He picked up the menu again. 'Maybe he doesn't do it now, but he certainly used to in 'Nam. What will you have?'

I was uninterested in food, and agreed abstractedly with his suggestions. I remembered David had told me once he had been stuck in a hotel in Vientiane with Peter, and he had talked about his family. An image of Peter, drunk, telling David what he would not tell me sober swam up before me. It did not please me.

Sam had stopped ordering, and was returning to the subject. 'His grandfather was one of the leaders of the Easter Rising,' he said, drawing patterns on the tablecloth with his fork. 'He was shot by the British in 1916. The family moved to Belfast, and Peter was born there. When he was nine or ten, his own father was killed. I'm not sure how, Peter was pretty uptight about it, even though he was drunk when he told me, but his dad was up to his neck in republican politics. Some time afterwards, his mother died too, and Peter was sent to New York to live with an uncle. It seems to have been a really shitty business.'

Nine or ten. That was the age of Rosie's child. I wondered if he had told Rosie about his parents.

'Cheer up,' Sam raised his glass to me. 'It was all a long time ago. But if you do run into Peter again in your part of the world, tell him his old buddy sends him his greetings.' The waiter brought plates of clams, and he started to talk seriously about the AsiaNews contract.

* * *

I was very reluctant to meet David again, but our encounter went off much better than I thought it would. He was in good spirits, for he had found an American publisher for his new book, and had a handsome advance. They were in a hurry for it, with South-east Asia so much in the news, and he was taking a sabbatical to finish it.

He said nothing about the incident in Khamla, but I had gathered from other sources that it had done him no harm. An expurgated version of what had happened had reached the Western media, and David, having been shot at, was regarded as more of an expert on the region than ever, and something of a hero.

If he felt uncomfortable at seeing me again, he showed no signs of it, and went out of his way to be charming, talking easily and often with sardonic wit of the university, and of our mutual acquaintances. We seemed to be back to the relationship we had briefly had before we married, when, in the months of courtship – if you could call it that – he had exerted himself to please.

He was unusually generous, treating me to rich and rather boozy dinners in the Village, and to seats at the theatre and the opera which I could not possibly afford for myself. I was suspicious, but despite myself I felt some of the old fascination coming back. It was hard for me to be sure whether I had ever been in love with David, or only thought myself in love. Whatever the emotion was, there was still a little of it left behind.

The night before I was due to leave to go back to Bangkok, we went to the Lincoln Center to see the New York City Ballet, and walked back to my hotel through the frosty night. There was still some ice on the sidewalks, and when I slipped on a patch in my inadequate shoes, David drew my arm through his and held it firmly.

'I'm not asking you to come back to me yet,' he said, his voice level. 'I don't believe you're ready for it. But there is no reason why we can't see each other from time to time.'

'No reason,' I said cautiously, 'but it's not very likely. I want to stay on in Bangkok for a while at least. I promised Bill Geraghty that I would before I came on this trip.'

He laced his fingers through mine. 'It's not another planet, you know. I expect to be there later in the year, anyway, when I've got the bulk of the book out of the way. Presumably you wouldn't cut me dead if I should turn up.'

He gave a brief laugh as he said it, but I could tell he was serious. For the first time in many months, I felt a constriction under my breast, as though something was tightening round my heart.

I made my voice as light as I could. 'If I am there, I'll be glad to see you. I'm hoping to travel more, now that Bill is back on the job.'

He did not speak, but tightened his grip on my fingers, and we walked through the icy night in a silence which might have been companionable, but was not. There was the faintest hint of a tremor in his grip.

I was staying at a small, relatively cheap, but quite cheerful hotel in the east forties, and the clerk on the desk grinned when he saw me walk in with a man. David and I had always parted at subways before, and the desk clerk, watching me come in alone, had teased me with blunt New York candour about not having a boyfriend.

'Found yourself a feller at last, ma'am,' he said pushing the key across the counter.

I felt David stiffen at what he would be sure to see as gross impertinence, then he relaxed and smiled, said, 'Good night' to the man, and ushered me ceremoniously into the lift. I was alarmed then, and tried to free my arm, but he was holding me tightly and, short of making a scene before the grinning spectator, there was nothing much I could do about it.

'Let me come up and say goodbye to you properly,' David said softly in my ear. 'Besides, I have a present for you.'

On the fourth floor, we marched down the corridor together, more like jailer and prisoner than a pair of lovers, although a middle-aged couple who, flushed and giggly, were having trouble with their door key took us for that. 'Have a good night,' the woman said, waving at us the outsize orchid she was holding.

David took the key from my hand, and opened the door quickly, while the couple watched us, laughing. He pushed me inside, and I saw his mouth was tight. In the old days, he would have burst out in an angry tirade about ill-manners, but to my surprise he said nothing, merely helping me off with my coat, and throwing it with his own on a chair.

When I looked at the beside table, I understood why the clerk had been grinning, for a small but very elegant basket of spring flowers with the label of the florist downstairs stood beside an ice bucket, from which the neck of a bottle protruded. Automatically, I pulled the bottle up and looked at it. It was a very good German wine which he had had at dinner a few nights before, and which I had praised, saying regretfully that wine of that sort was both rare and expensive in Bangkok.

David looked at me with something like shyness. 'I wanted it to be a real farewell for you, not just a hand shake on the pavement,' he said in a low voice. 'I have something else for you, too. I went to a lot of trouble to get it.'

He took a small box from his pocket and opened it. It was an antique ring, a black opal in a rather ornate silver setting. 'Your birthstone,' David said, taking it carefully from its velvet bed, and holding it out.

I was surprised that he should remember what my birthstone was, and even more surprised by the ring itself, which was beautiful but showy. David's taste in jewellery tended to the austere, and the engagement ring he had bought me, despite my protests that I did not want one, had been a model of modest good taste.

When I did not take the ring, he picked up my left hand and slid it carefully onto the third finger. He did not ask where my wedding ring and engagement ring were, which was just as well. One of the Belgian lay sisters who ran the mission for destitute girls had stood patiently outside the Erewan entrance one night, begging for contributions to the mission. To my own surprise, and hers as well, I had taken off both my rings and dropped them into her collecting box.

The opal ring looked handsome, but its tightness on my finger gave me a sudden feeling of constriction. Pulling it off, I transferred it to my right hand. 'That makes it less committed,' I said, smiling to take away the possibility of offence.

David smiled too, though rather thinly, more in his old unreformed style. But he made no further comment, and, turning, took the wine from the ice bucket and opened it. He had even thought of asking for wine glasses, and he filled one and handed it to me. 'To our next meeting,' he said, watching me carefully.

I had already had wine at dinner, and a glass of champagne in the interval of the ballet, so I was not anxious to drink more, but could hardly refuse, as David had gone to so much trouble. He himself, by nature a sipper, seemed to be drinking unusually quickly, and silently urging me to do the same.

I sat on the bed and he on the only chair, talking quietly and easily about when he might come to Bangkok, and the trips we might make while he was there, to look at antiquities. I only half-listened, leaning back against the pillows, relaxed and languid. It surprised me that, in his presence, I felt no anxiety, none of the familiar tension which made my muscles rigid. When he tried to refill my glass, I shook my head. 'You are trying to make me drunk.' I was only half-serious, but I saw by his face that it was true.

He leaned forward, watching me with an expression I could not quite identify. 'You've changed,' he said. 'You are quite different.'

I was tipsy enough to examine this proposition unselfconsciously. 'Not really. There was always another sort of person inside me, but it couldn't get out.'

Behind his glasses, his eyes began to blink rapidly. It was a nervous mannerism I had seen before, but only very rarely. 'Because of me?' His voice was so low I could hardly hear him.

'Well, there were other factors, but being married to you didn't help,' I said truthfully. 'On the other hand I may be just a late developer. If we had stayed together, I believe I would have changed but it would have been a painful and messy process. Leaving you and living alone has made it much easier for me.'

In the half-light of the beside lamp, David looked very pale. 'Do you really live alone?' he said hoarsely.

I laughed. 'Oh, yes. I've just escaped from one

impossible relationship. It will be a long time before I put my head in the noose again.'

The wine had made me both candid and cruel. David drew back as though I had struck him, and taking off his glasses, drew his hand across his eyes. It was a very uncharacteristic gesture, and it made him look utterly defeated.

During the bitter days of our marriage I had often thought of one day avenging myself on David, and now I knew that I had done so, but there was no pleasure in it. He would have got up then and gone without a word, but I said hastily, 'I'm sorry,' and leaning forward, put my arms clumsily round him.

It was intended as no more than a token of comfort, but I saw at once that it was a mistake, because he gave a groan and at once pulled me down on the bed, burying his face on my throat, and murmuring some words I could not hear.

His skin, usually cool, was dry and burning, as though he had a fever. I tried to ease him off, but he clung to me tightly, like a child, so I did not struggle against him, even when I felt his hand fumbling to undo the zip at the back of my dress.

I let him undress me, lying supine under his touch. The fact that I did not flinch from him, as I so often had done, calmed him, and the wine helped him too, so in the beginning our bodies started to find some sort of rhythm, moving together on the narrow bed.

I had hoped, for David's sake as well as my own, that our coupling would be a slow and leisurely affair, but in the end, though he was trying hard, he could not restrain the old, fumbling angry haste, nor quite hide the desire to hurt. When I felt his frantic urgency, I deliberately willed away the heavy body lying on top of mine, and conjured up Peter instead, saying his name inaudibly over and over again into David's shoulder.

A sensation of great sweetness rushed through me, and at the climax I cried out loudly. When David heard me, he wept, and I licked the salty tears off his cheeks with my tongue, so that he wept again, and we clung together in the warm dark.

I woke just after dawn, and saw that David was sitting on the edge of the bed watching me. He was fully dressed, and I automatically pulled the sheet up to my shoulders. I felt sober, slightly hungover, and not altogether pleased with myself.

David seemed to be waiting for me to say something, and the intensity of his stare made me uneasy. 'It doesn't really make any difference,' I said at last. 'I'm not coming back to you.'

When he did not answer, but still continued to watch me, I sat up in bed resentfully. 'I cannot image why you would want to live with me again. Everything I do annoys you. In fact, I had never understood why you married me. It certainly was not for love.'

He gave a long sigh, and his body seemed to relax. The he got up and went to the window, as he had done in Bangkok. It seemed easier for him to be truthful if his back was towards me.

'No, it wasn't, at first, though I was quite attracted by you. I don't like hard, pushy women, and you seemed very young and shy and full of old-fashioned virtues.'

I was puzzled. 'But why marry at all? Domesticity doesn't seem to suit you.'

He gave a hard laugh. 'It seemed a good idea at the time. Married academics are a safer bet. Also, I'd heard, over the years, quite a bit of speculation about my . . .' he paused, then said painfully, 'my masculinity, or alleged lack of it.'

I was astonished that he should make such an admission to me. His masculinity was one thing I had never doubted. Whatever his tastes, they did not run to boys.

I got up, winding the sheet round me. 'So I was the sacrificial victim.'

He turned angrily towards me. 'How did I know that

it was going to be so difficult? I sometimes think it was even harder for me than it was for you.'

He would have gone on, but I shook my head. 'Don't David,' I said wearily. 'We are just wasting our time. It's over, and that's that.'

He accepted defeat then, picking up his coat, and throwing it over his arm. Rather formally, he took my hand and bowed over it. 'Just remember this,' he said in a low voice. 'I may not have loved you at the beginning but I do now.'

CHAPTER TEN

Bill Geraghty was full of congratulations when I came back to Bangkok with the signed contract. The terms were not as good as we had asked for, but rather better than we had hoped to get. AsiaNews would stay comfortably afloat for another year at least, and Bill put up my salary and talked vaguely of a partnership if I stayed on for a while. For the first time in my life, I was able to build up a small fund of savings, and having money in the bank made me feel reassuringly independent.

David wrote regularly, too regularly for my taste, saying nothing about what had happened in New York, but talking confidently of his coming to South-east Asia, now likely to happen towards the end of the year, and what he hoped to accomplish.

A month or so after my return, an expensive basket of flowers arrived at the office for me with a card with an Interflora logo. It said nothing but 'Love from David', with the date below.

Bill saw them arrive, and raised his eyebrows. 'What's the occasion? I didn't think it was your birthday. Isn't it in October?'

'Yes, it is.' I was equally puzzled, and it was not until later in the morning that I remembered it was the date on which we had been married. David had never marked the occasion in any way before, saying the celebration of wedding anniversaries was a bourgeois practice. That he should bother to observe the date now, at this distance, seemed ominous.

I forgot all about the flowers and David, however, when the news came through that the whole of Khamla had fallen to the Liberation Front, after the final assault on the capital. The television screens flickered continually with images of the last days of the war, and I spent hours in front of them, fascinated.

Harry Greene was one of the few cameramen who had risked staying on under the round-the-clock mortaring which had reduced large parts of the capital to rubble. He shot some marvellous film of the departure of Prince Vouliphong and his entourage, fighting each other to get aboard the choppers from the lawn of the Three Tiered Palace, the American advisers having prudently pulled out with more dignity some days before.

I had little pity for Prince Vouliphong, for according to rumour he was only too happy to depart for a comfortable exile in the South of France, as a pensioner of the Americans. Bill said cynically that if he ever ran short of money, he could always pawn his wife's jewels.

Not everyone was so lucky, and I heard with an unpleasant jolt that the vice-premier who had come to the guesthouse to apologise the morning David had nearly died was one of those who had been lined up and shot out of hand in the courtyard of the palace, after the Liberation Front entered the capital.

Harry's film running on the networks the following night showed the assault on the palace itself, prefaced by the storming of the gatehouse where I had had my handbag searched the night of Prince Vouliphong's reception. It was a remarkable sequence, with the armoured column moving remorselessly up to the inner gates, Son Sleng and Ieng Nim, in uniform, riding in an armoured personnel carrier behind the tanks. There was some sporadic shelling, and the heavy main door was broken down by a tank, but most of the defenders had fled, and it was quickly over. The red and white flag of the Liberation Front with its famous twin stars flapped from the flagpole, a women fighter having triumphantly hauled it up, and a few minutes later the two commanders and their escort appeared on the balcony where, on ceremonial occasions, Soumidath had come out to greet his people.

The young fighters swarming all over the forecourt of the palace went wild at the sight of the commanders, and a great roar went up, fusillades of shots fired into the air mingling with the cheering. Some of the fighters broke into the elephant enclosure and unchained the sacred elephants, riding them bareback, three or four at a time. The great beasts trumpeted and charged into the crowd, made hysterical by the noise. I saw half a dozen men and women go down in their path before they were driven back, and I turned away, unable to watch any more.

'Tearaways!' Bill said, opening another can of beer. 'I dunno how Soumidath is going to come to terms with that lot. He'd do better to retire to his own villa in the South of France. He and Vouliphong could get up a bridge four.'

This view was shared by most of the locally-based Asia-watchers, who said that now the Liberation Front had smashed their way to a military victory, they need not bother with Soumidath any more. Harry Greene, when he came back to Bangkok with some less urgent film, did not think that at all. He predicted we would see a royal reappearance before the month was out.

'Where the hell is Soumidath anyway?' Bill said over a late supper. 'There hasn't been a peep out of him lately.'

'In North Korea, as the guest of his old chum Kim Il Sung, waiting for the call.' In the dim light of the restaurant, Harry looked thin and rather strained. Even his taste for war and death had been tested by the last days of the Vouliphong régime.

'The Prince has a good sense of timing,' he said, signalling the waiter for another drink. 'He knows the Western press are after him, so he has taken refuge in the one place they can't get at him. That way, he can skulk in the wings, ready to make a dramatic entrance centre-stage when the moment comes.'

I laughed. 'It doesn't sound like Soumidath. In the old days he would have had the press in three times a week to lecture them on what was going on. And he would send cables to papers all round the world.' Soumidath's long telegraphed messages to editors in the West, taking them to task for misreporting, were notorious.

Harry shrugged. 'You're right. I see the fine machiavellian hand of your chum Peter Casement in all this. He's holding the Prince back now to get the maximum effect later.'

I said nothing, but Bill looked curious. 'Have you seen Peter lately? Has anyone?'

Harry shook his head. 'Not a sighting. But it's a safe bet he is with the Prince.'

I wanted to change the subject away from Peter. 'You really think the Liberation Front wants Soumidath as head of state?'

Harry smiled. 'Not the Liberation Front any more, the government of Free Khamla. That's a different can of worms.' He rubbed his face, looked suddenly weary. 'Yes, I think they will bring him back. The end was so bloody the new government is afraid the world sees them as nothing more than a gang of butchers. They need the Prince to give them respectability, so they can get the aid pouring in. Soumidath won't be anything more than a figurehead, of course, and how long he will last even in that capacity is anybody's guess.'

Harry was right. Within the month, the papers were full of pictures of Soumidath arriving back in his capital, mobbed by peasants especially (so Bill cynically suggested) trucked in from the countryside for the day.

I saw some film on television of the Prince, garlanded with white flowers, embracing Son Sleng and Ieng Nim on the balcony of the Three Tiered Palace. In the background, I glimpsed a tall, fair-haired European. He was talking to someone and had his head turned away from the cameras, but there was no doubt it was Peter.

Soumidath being Soumidath, he could not resist making his return the occasion for non-stop celebrations, and he announced, after he was formally installed as head of state, a Festival of Free Khamla to which his friends from all over the world were to be invited.

'Son Sleng and Ieng Nim are letting him have his head for the moment,' said Harry, who already had his invitation to this remarkable event. 'Pity you can't go. I hear the Prince is planning something quite specacular.'

I was envious, but I need not have been, for a few days later, I had my invitation too, a handsomely engraved card from the Prince, enclosed with a short letter from Penn Thioen, who reminded me in his most felicitous and formal French of our parting at the Great Temple when he had promised that one day I would be received in the capital as an honoured guest. 'The day has come, dear madame, much sooner than we had dared to hope,' the letter said.

Bill was pleased for both my sake and the agency's, and at once arranged for me to have time off. I sent a telex to Big Brother, offering to do a couple of voice pieces, and received an enthusiastic reply from Sam, guaranteeing more than generous terms if the pieces came up well.

'Well, Madame Herbert, you are becoming something of a celebrity in your own right,' Harry said, with a touch of malice. He was, I think, a little piqued, as he considered Khamla exclusively his own patch.

I was quite pleased at the faint note of rivalry and, with the fee from Big Brother in mind, had a long silk dress made for the reception at the palace which would open the Festival. I thought I might even wear David's opal ring, it being the only piece of jewellery of any value I owned. The reception at the Palace sounded as if it might be an occasion for showing off.

Harry and I travelled together by plane, the airport having by now been restored to something like working order, although the runway was still pitted with filled-in craters, and the Antonov-24 lurched drunkenly as we taxied in.

Penn was there to meet us, looking ten years younger than when I had last seen him at the Great Temple. His grey crew cut had grown out to a respectable length, he was dressed in a well-tailored beige safari jacket and slacks, and his broken-winged spectacles had been replaced by a new gold-rimmed pair, rather like the ones David affected. He shook my hand enthusiastically, then bent and kissed it for good measure. He was smiling, all his familiar melancholy gone.

'Dear Madame Herbert, I greet you in the name of the Government of Free Khamla,' he said formally, 'and Mr Greene also, though it is not so long since we saw him. The Prince sends you his personal good wishes, and says he looks forward to seeing you at the Palace tonight.'

A girl of eight or nine in a short white dress came forward shyly with tight little bouquets of flowers, one for Harry, one for me.

'My daughter,' Penn said, putting his hand briefly on her shoulder. I looked at him in surprise, having always, I don't know why, assumed he was a bachelor. He saw my expression.

'You do not think of me as a family man, I can see,' he said laughing. 'But I have a son, as well as this child here. He is only five, and still takes an afternoon nap, so I did not bring him to meet you.'

I said nothing, but he answered the unspoken question. 'You think I am old to have such young children? It is true. My first wife died, and I married again some years ago.'

'Your wife was not with you at the camp?'

Penn shook his head. 'Oh, no, it would not be possible. She is very delicate, very nervous, not strong like you, madame. When the troubles started, I sent her with the children to France, and she has only recently come back. Now I am learning to know my family all over again.' He took the child's hand in his, and looked at her with love.

Penn led us through the airport terminal building to the waiting car. It showed signs of hasty rebuilding, but it was gay enough, with revolutionary banners and portraits of the Prince, Son Sleng and Ieng Nim, grouped like some unlikely Trinity. The Prince was smiling, as always, the other two looked appropriately grave. Revolutionary music blared from loudspeakers, and outside the terminal building, a guard of honour was rehearsing for the arrival, later in the afternoon, of more important people than Harry and me. The guard wore smart khaki uniforms with dark red shoulder-boards, and I thought one or two of the faces were familiar, though it was hard to reconcile these well-tailored soldiers with the tattered guerrillas of the bush camp.

'The Prime Minister and the Foreign Minister also send their greetings,' Penn said when we were in the car. He meant Son Sleng and Ieng Nim, and it was typical of him to use the formal titles. I remembered that, in Hanoi, Soumidath had said he would make Ieng Nim Minister of the Interior, but Ieng Nim, Harry said, had insisted on the foreign affairs portfolio, despite Soumidath's wish to double it up with his own rather ambiguous title of head of state. He rather fancied himself as an actor on the world stage, and if it came to that would certainly give a better performance than Ieng Nim.

The capital itself, as we drove through, looked very much the same. I was surprised that there seemed so little mortar or bomb damage, but Penn confessed that arriving guests were being taken on a route which avoided the worst hit areas. 'I tell you that, madame, because you are an old friend,' he said smiling. 'We do not want to deceive you though we put on a little show for some of the others.'

Harry grunted. 'Whole streets went up in flames in the southern section behind the Palace when I was last here,' he said. 'I'll take you round tomorrow and show you the people living in what's left of their houses. Not a good ad for the revolution, Penn.' Penn Thioen said nothing, but he looked down at his daughter and tightened his arm round her waist. She was a silent child, studying us all with quiet attention, but when her gaze met her father's, she smiled.

As we came closer to the centre, I saw there were many soldiers still on the streets, not in neat uniforms like the guard of honour at the airport, but in the ragged shirts and shorts or ubiquitous black pyjamas of the fighters at the Great Temple. They were identifiable by the pink checked sweat cloths round their necks, and by a new badge of office, red and white armbands with the double star of the Liberation Front. Most of them were very young, and they carried automatic rifles slung across their shoulders, or, more unusually, the stubby submachine guns formerly favoured by the Royal Khamla Army.

In spite of the revolutionary music blaring out from the loudspeakers on the electric light poles, and the brave banners, the streets had a desolate air. Many shops were boarded up, the few people we saw hurried with their heads down instead of sauntering along and stopping every few yards to chat, and all the familiar tableaux of street life in Asia – the pedlars, the sidewalk barbers, the letter writers, the lottery ticket sellers – were missing.

Harry was looking uneasily out of the car windows. 'Hell, it's like an end-of-the-world movie,' he said. 'It wasn't as bad as this even during the shelling. Where are all the people?'

Penn coughed nervously. 'They are still afraid, so they stay at home. It was not very good for a while, when our troops entered the city. They did not always behave correctly.'

'So I heard,' I said cautiously. There had been stories of atrocities, but then there always were, and many of them turned out, as in Vietnam, to be propaganda by the departing side.

'It will be better when we can send all the soldiers back to their villages.' Penn hugged his daughter again. 'Then, you will see, things will be very different. Come back in a year, the two of you, and you will see the new Khamla rising from the old.'

Harry looked at me and pulled the corner of his mouth down mockingly, but I turned away impatiently. He was a professional cynic, and I would rather believe Penn.

We passed the Temple of One Hundred Buddhas, and I was fearful that the car would turn on to the road to the guesthouse where we had stayed before. Harry saw my sudden movement. 'Don't worry,' he said. 'A shell landed smack in the middle of it. We're not going there, it's uninhabitable.' I was relieved, for I had no wish to meet any ghosts.

In fact, we had much grander accommodation this time, in one of the cluster of guest villas nearer the Three Tiered Palace. They were built in European style and surrounded by a high wall, with four smart soldiers in the same uniform as the airport guard of honour manning the gate. 'We've been promoted,' Harry said with satisfaction. 'We are in with the VIPs.' Then he looked at me and laughed. 'They wouldn't put me in here if I were by myself, I bet. It's all in your honour. You really must have won Penn's heart.'

I shook my head at him but mercifully Penn was already out of the car, fussing over the luggage, and I didn't think he heard. He was a very formal man, and it would have embarrassed him. Certainly some feeling had grown up between us, a fondness and respect on my side. I am not sure what on his, possibly something vaguely paternal, or the relationship of a master to a pupil. If he were a Western man, I would be surer of my ground, but the longer I stayed in Asia, the more I came to believe it was impossible for Europeans and Asians to meet on any real ground of understanding. There are gulfs and ravines which cannot be bridged. Bill Geraghty said it was simple enough and I ought to stop worrying about it. 'Kipling had it dead right, kid. East is east, and west is west, and never forget it.'

I had a little suite to myself in the villa, a bedroom with a balcony overgrown with vines, a sitting room furnished in the high fashion of the 1930s, and a bathroom with a stained bathtub, into which some water actually flowed. As Penn bowed me in, with great pride, I saw out of the corner of my eye a rat scampering away down the corridor, and was glad, not for the first time, that beds in guest houses are provided with mosquito nets. At least they keep the rats off.

'What style!' Harry said, when he came into my sitting room for a drink later on. 'My rooms are not nearly so grand.'

We looked at each other, sitting primly on cane chairs, while a tiny houseboy in white shirt and trousers poured us drinks, ice tinkling in the glasses, and both of us burst out laughing. Harry was almost unrecognisable in a cream lightweight suit with collar and tie, his hair cut and carefully combed. I was wearing my new long silk dress, I had had my hair set before I left Bangkok, and for once I had put on some make-up.

The trouble was that our elegance was not going to last long. It was a stifling night, and though the overhead fan created a small tepid oasis in the centre of the room, the heat was pressing in, ready to attack. One gin and tonic was already beginning to make us sweat, and I knew that as soon as we stepped outside, we would be as wet as if we had come from a Turkish bath.

Harry wiped the sweat from his own forehead with a handkerchief. 'It will be cooler at the Palace,' he said.

'My countrymen' – he meant the American advisers – 'got so pissed off with the heat when they were here that they talked Vouliphong into having the main rooms air-conditioned. Soumidath doesn't like it, he's never happy unless the temperature is thirty-five degrees or so. But there will be so many VIPs there tonight that he will have to turn it on. Or let's hope so.'

CHAPTER ELEVEN

It was certainly coolish in the Long Gallery after the brutal humidity of the night outside, though there was such a crush that the air-conditioning would be fighting a losing battle as the night went on. I was glad I had dressed up, for Soumidath had managed to stage a brilliant and theatrical occasion, with himself as the leading actor. It was his evening, and though Son Sleng and Ieng Nim, as well as the rest of the Cabinet, were all lined up at the top of the room in matching dark blue suits, they remained hardly more than a sombre backdrop for Soumidath.

He was wearing for the occasion Royal ceremonial dress, identical with that which could be seen in paintings and miniatures of his ancestors going right back to the legendary King Jawarath. It was of yellow silk, with baggy trousers and a long over-tunic, sashed in scarlet. With it, he wore a small yellow hat, rather like a forage cap. Innumerable orders blazed on his breast, his fingers were heavy with rings, and the large ruby pinned in his hat winked in the light of the chandeliers.

Not to be outdone, many of the ambassadors present – few were resident now, most had flown in from Asian capitals – either wore national dress, or were in full rig of white tie and tails, and decorations. The Africans and Muslims looked particularly fine, and with the women in their brilliant gowns, the long dusky room seemed full of butterflies. Harry and I gave each other rueful grins. We were drab by comparison.

We made a slow circuit of the room, picking out the celebrities. Soumidath had done quite well, attracting, as well as the ambassadors, a vice-premier here, a senior minister there, even one or two minor heads of state who happened to be visiting Asia. Western Europe was well represented, as well as the Soviet Union, China and, of course, the Third World, anxious to welcome a new revolutionary régime. 'Most of them have come more out of curiosity than anything else,' Harry said, nimbly lifting two glasses of champagne off a passing waiter's tray. 'How they are going to line up when the dust settles is another thing again.'

For this evening, anyway, Soumidath had put on a splendid show. The air, warmer perceptibly by the minute, was so heavy with the scent of waxy yellow flowers in vases all along the walls that even to breathe it was intoxicating enough, without the champagne. A band, hidden somewhere just off stage, was playing Viennese waltzes, though the buzz of conversation was so loud it was hard to hear it. The Persian rugs had been taken up, and I guessed there would be dancing later.

Looking up to where Soumidath was embracing visitors, I saw behind the sober phalanx of the Cabinet, a glimpse of stone. A camèra bulb flashed, and the serene smile of a Buddha came briefly into focus.

'Now which one is that!' I said to Harry. 'The real one, or the imitation?'

Someone took my arm from behind. 'The real one,' Peter's voice said. 'The fake Buddha Prince Vouliphong had made is down in the courtyard. We are going to dispose of it ceremonially later in the evening.'

He shook hands with Harry, and bent briefly and formally over my hand. Like Harry, he was elegant in a pale summer suit, and his curly hair was still clipped very short. Without the beard, his face looked younger and more vulnerable.

'So you are here,' I said involuntarily, and he looked at me with amusement.

'Where else would I be, but at the Prince's side?'

Harry was blunter. 'I didn't think Son Sleng and Ieng Nim cared for you all that much.'

Peter shrugged. 'They don't. But the Prince insisted that at least one aide come with him, and they think I'm a lesser evil than most of the other hangers-on. At least I haven't any cousins or uncles to start plotting with as soon as I arrive.'

Harry whistled. 'They made most of the Prince's retinue stay behind?'

'That was a condition. Apart from me, there is only a secretary, and Soumidath's youngest son, who isn't quite old enough to get up to any mischief.'

Harry looked at him thoughtfully over the rim of his glass. 'Doesn't that leave you rather isolated in the event there's any trouble?'

Peter shook his head. 'We shall be all right for a while. The régime needs Soumidath to give it a bit of class, and as you can see by the turn-out tonight the Prince still has great pulling power. Son Sleng and Ieng Nim know very well they couldn't have got a fraction of these people along without the Prince as front man.'

Harry still looked doubtful. 'Maybe. But I'd watch my back if I were you. I wouldn't trust these guys as far as I could throw them.'

Peter laughed, and took my arm. 'Let me worry about that, it's my back. Meantime, come and shake hands with the Prince. He particularly told me to look out for you.'

I thought that was a bit of Irish blarney, but Soumidath did indeed greet me with exuberance after Peter had reminded him who I was, kissing my hands warmly.

Harry did even better, receiving a princely embrace, for Soumidath was well aware of his reputation in Asia. After the terrible unfolding of the most recent act of the Khamla dramas, the new régime needed all the favourable publicity it could get, but I thought that if the commanders were looking to Harry to help provide it, they were over-optimistic. He took a sardonic view of the government of Free Khamla, and besides, peace bored him. I knew he was trying to get back into Burma again, where the war lords were stirring up a new round of aggravation for the Ne Win government. He would not stay to record on film Soumidath's triumphal progressions through the countryside, as I heard the Prince now inviting him to do.

Soumidath was drunk with joy that night, and took no notice of our polite demurrals when he urged us both to stay on for weeks – for months if we wished.

'You will see the rebuilding of Khamla, madame,' he said to me, patting my arm briefly. 'It is a task to which I shall give the rest of my life. I would die for my country, do you believe that?'

He looked anxiously from one of us to the other, as though our opinions were important. Harry murmured non-committally and looked uncomfortable. He preferred his heroics on film. But I felt the tears come into my eyes, and I did something which surprised me. I took Soumidath's hand and pressed it briefly to my forehead, as his own subjects did in token of homage.

He looked at me for quite a long time without speaking, then I saw he also was weeping. Harry had abruptly turned away to speak to somebody, and had missed the incident, but behind his shoulder, Peter was watching me. He gave an awkward grimace, as though he was suddenly in pain, then he smiled at me, and I felt a slow flush creep up my neck.

Soumidath laughed, breaking the mood. '*Eh bien,*' he said, apropos of nothing. 'It has been a long journey, but we are home again, both of us.' I was puzzled for a moment, then I saw he was gesturing at the stone Buddha behind him. The Prince's mouth was smoothly curved now, in the same archaic smile as that of the image. It was said that the Buddha had been carved in the likeness of King Jawarath II, and though the sculptor had been executed for sacrilege, the statue itself was thereafter considered all the more sacred.

A small queue of ambassadors was waiting to talk to the Prince, and a couple of aides waved Harry and myself away impatiently. 'Let's go and grab something to eat before the locusts descend,' Harry said, and we went into the supper room off the Long Gallery.

'My God!' said a French diplomat, coming in with us. 'Long live the Revolution!' It was certainly a stunning sight, for (as Penn had told us) Prince Soumidath had ordered the Palace chefs to recreate a banquet given by his great-grandfather to the Emperor of Siam in 1860. That had been a formal dinner and we had to manage with a buffet, but the long tables covered with white damask cloths were loaded with more food than the peasants in the poorer villages of Khamla would see in a year.

'Let's hope nobody here tonight is light-fingered,' Harry said, closely inspecting a sucking pig reposing on a platter of what appeared to be solid gold. The plates were Limoges, and at least some of the bowls used as food containers were Ming. The cutlery was heavy silver, and so were the chopsticks laid out in neat rows. The food itself was eclectic: huge rosy lobsters squatted beside what Harry told me was barbecued monkey, a local delicacy. More sucking pigs were flanked with mounds of sea slugs and abalone and plates of rare funghi. Tiny whole birds complete with heads and claws, and meant to be eaten that way, were side by side with wonderful creations of the pastry cook's art, and enormous quivering pink and green jellies with traceries of cream. A small tree, rather like a red Christmas tree, turned out to be made of whole strawberries pressed into cream cheese over a chicken-wire frame.

'Wow!' said Harry, starting to denude the little tree. 'I haven't tasted a strawberry for years. I wonder where Soumidath's great-granddad got them in 1860?'

The drink was as lavish as the food, mainly champagne in silver buckets, filed with rapidly melting ice, and opened on request by perspiring waiters in high-necked jackets already showing dark patches under the arms. I do not like warm champagne, and in any case it was much more interesting staying sober, so I refused all further offers of alcohol, somewhat to Harry's annoyance, as he was in a drinking mood. 'Go and find someone else to drink with,' I said calmly. 'I'm quite happy.'

Peter raised his eyebrows when he came into the supper room and found me sitting alone at a small table eating slices of fresh mango. 'Deserted?' he said. 'Harry isn't a very good escort.'

As always, when Peter was close to me, my pulse rate quickened, and I could feel the actual throb in my wrists and neck, but it was a phenomenon that no longer disconcerted me. It was a chemical reaction I could not help.

'He is not my escort,' I said, helping myself placidly to another slice of mango. 'You should stop trying to couple Harry and me. We work together from time to time, and that's about it.'

Peter sat down, and speared a piece of mango from my bowl, staring at me with curiosity and, I was quite glad to see, with what looked rather like irritation. 'Do you know how much you have changed?' he said. 'How different you are to the lady I met in Hanoi?'

I laughed. 'Oh, I think so. Why are you so surprised? People do change when their whole lifestyle changes, don't they?'

He looked at me again, and his mouth turned down sombrely. 'Do they? I am not sure about that. I think my own attitudes froze when – oh, when I was quite young, and they haven't altered since. It's a bad thing that, dear Gilly.'

It was the nearest he had ever come to being confidential with me, and before I could stop myself, I reached over and put my hand over his. But his face at once turned wary again, and he gave my hand a casual pat and put it aside.

'Finished?' he said, looking at my empty fruit bowl. 'Then come and I'll show you something interesting.' I rose, but I must have looked discomfited, for he took my hand again and put it lightly on his arm.

'It's a funny night, tonight.' He spoke casually, but with an undertone of anger. 'It's making me feel morbid, and that won't do at all.' He glanced at me sideways. 'At all, at all,' he said in a burlesque Irish accent, to make me laugh, and to take the edge off his own mood.

We went back together into the Long Gallery, then into a small room beyond. Peter took me to the window, and pointed down into the great courtyard below. 'Look!' he said.

The courtyard was a big, open-ended space, formed by three wings of the Palace. There had obviously once been beds of flowers and shrubs round the three sides, but what plants there were left were trampled and broken. The courtyard was empty, though the moonlight, pouring into it from the glaring moon directly overhead, made it look as though it was filled with translucent water. As my eyes grew more accustomed to the light, I saw there was something in the middle of the space after all, a stone statue with a familiar outline.

'It's the Buddha!' I craned out further to see. The twin of the image in the Long Gallery was in the centre of the courtyard. It seemed to be raised on some sort of small cart with wheels, and it was bound with garlands of flowers. Ropes, also twined with flowers, were attached to the front of the little cart.

'It's the false Buddha,' Peter said, leaning out beside me. 'As I told you, we are going to dispose of it ceremonially later tonight. It's been a terrible embarrassment for the Prince.'

'Yes, I suppose so. Two identical Buddhas, and nobody, after a while, could be sure which was the right one.' I considered the problem. 'Couldn't he have just have had it taken away and quietly broken up?'

'Not really. It is the false Buddha, but it is also a true Buddha, in the sense that Vouliphong had it properly consecrated by the local rites, and it stood in the Temple of One Hundred Buddhas for the obligatory seven days, which makes it holy. Monseigneur believes it would bring all sorts of frightful consequences down on his head if it were treated profanely.'

I laughed, and was surprised to see he looked at me coldly, his face white in the moonlight. 'Come on,' I said uneasily. 'Don't go native on me. You don't believe that, do you?'

He gave a half-laugh himself then, and turned away. 'Oh, I sacrifice to all the gods,' he said lightly. 'I'm a prudent man, and it's insurance for a rainy day.'

'But you were brought up a Roman Catholic?' The question would annoy him but I was tired of taboos.

'That's ancient history.' He took my arm, not too gently, and turned me back towards the window. 'You haven't asked me what the Prince is going to do with the Buddha.'

'Well, what?' Obviously anything connected with his past was going to remain forbidden territory, for me at least. I turned my attention back to the statue below.

'Something we hope will appease everybody. The monks from the temple are going to perform a sort of deconsecration ceremony first. The head bonze kicked up a hell of a fuss about it, but the Prince threatened to cut off funds for a year if he didn't invent something suitable, and the old boy went along with it in the end. Then the Buddha is going to be ceremonially towed away, and sunk with appropriate blessings in the little lake at the end of the Palace gardens.'

I felt doubtful. 'That still sounds rather sacrilegious to me.'

'Yes, it's a bit risky, but the best we could think of. While the false Buddha is around the Palace, the Prince feels threatened. A false Buddha, another false Prince: I think his mind is working somewhere along those lines.'

We stood together in silence looking down into the courtyard. The moonlight had a density of its own, transparent but tangible. If I put my hand out, I was sure I would feel it lying heavy on my palm. Then Peter sighed, and started to speak. I looked at him carefully, but the band started up in the Long Gallery. The evening's dancing was beginning.

'Come and dance,' Peter said. 'The Prince will be looking for you too. He insists on dancing with every one of the women.'

When we went inside, I was horrified to see that this was only too true, and everyone was standing back while Soumidath whirled a succession of embarrassed partners up and down the Long Gallery. Every woman had only a minute or two, which was just as well, for the band played a succession of vigorous waltzes, and Soumidath was in such a wildly euphoric mood it was hard to keep up with him. When my turn came, we galloped up and down the polished floor so fast I was glad I had had nothing further to drink, and was steady on my feet.

Both Peter and Harry applauded when I came back to them, flushed, panting, but rather triumphant. 'Bravo!' Peter said, and I turned to him boldly. 'It is your turn, I think.'

But whatever understanding we had come close to earlier was gone. He had his edgy, withdrawn look, and he shook his head politely. 'Please keep me a dance later,' he said formally. 'At the moment, I'm on duty. Monseigneur is calling for me.'

It was true that the Prince was signalling to him, and I saw that he wanted to hand over his last dancing partner, the wife of an important African ambassador. She was a very tall beauty with a yellowish-bronze skin and high-planed cheekbones, and Peter talked to her animatedly, trying to crack her impassivity as he steered her round the room.

'You're wasting your time, you know,' Harry's voice

said behind me. 'I don't know what's driving that guy, but whatever it is, it's all that matters to him.'

I swung round on him angrily, but he put two fingers firmly over my mouth. 'Don't start cursing me. I'm not trying to interfere in your affairs, and I know it is none of my business. But I think it's time you cut your losses, and found yourself another feller, Gilly.'

I felt my temper cool, and a sense of dreariness took its place. My pleasure in the rich sensuality of the night drained away, and I heard Harry swear under his breath. 'Sorry, love. I didn't mean to upset you. Come and dance.'

He held me very close as we danced, more, I think, to comfort me, than out of any erotic intention. 'Pity you don't fancy me,' he said, pulling his mouth down in a parody of despair.

I laughed, enjoying the feel of his thin, nervous body against mine. 'Come on, you know I'm not your type. I'm not pretty enough, and I'm not bird-brained.'

To my surprise, he considered this seriously. 'It's not a question of looks. You're a bit frightening, Gilly. Did you know that?'

'Frightening? Don't be ridiculous.'

'Frightening might be the wrong word. Intense. Too serious. I'm the here-today-and-gone-tomorrow type.' He drew back suddenly and looked at me as we danced. 'Come to think of it, you and Peter are very alike in some ways. You are both single-minded, though he's some sort of nut, and you aren't.'

I started to speak but a series of explosions outside signalled the beginning of the spectacular fireworks display Soumidath had promised us, and we all went out on the balcony to look.

* * *

It was quite late when the Prince got round to the deconsecration of the Buddha. I think it was something that disturbed him, and he was putting it off as long as he could. But shortly before midnight the music stopped and a gong sounded, and he stood alone on the dais, looking pale and anxious. Unusually for him, his skin glistened with a film of sweat.

'There is something now that must be done if our country is to go forward in harmony and prosperity,' he said in a low voice, so that we had to strain to hear. 'What is true' – he gestured to the Buddha behind him – 'has been restored to its proper place. What is false must be banished.' He looked round the gallery, and he seemed to be begging for some sort of reassurance.

'I know all of you do not share our beliefs,' he said. 'Some are Christians, some are Muslims, some are non-believers. But please, for tonight, share with us in the ceremony which I must perform, and wish that we may have good fortune.'

He nodded to the aides, and a procession began to form up, with Soumidath at the head, followed by Son Sleng and the military commanders, then the politicals and the civil service, Penn among them. The ambassadors and dignitaries looked embarrassed, but formed themselves into the body of the procession. Harry and I and a few other non-VIPs brought up the rear. I couldn't see Peter, but Harry had spotted a more important absentee.

'Now where is Ieng Nim?' he said thoughtfully. 'I wonder what that bastard is up to.'

'Gone for a leak,' one of the invited bureau chiefs from Bangkok said, walking with us. 'I saw him on his way to the john. He's missed his cue, that's all.'

The way into the courtyard was down a narrow, winding staircase, which robbed the procession of its dignity. It became a jostling free-for-all, and I was relieved when we emerged at last into the great, luminous space with the Buddha, blanched by moonlight, at its centre. Four young monks with shaven heads stood motionless beside the flower-wreathed ropes. It was they, I supposed, who would draw the Buddha to the lake for its ceremonial drowning.

Our procession came to a shuffling halt, and some of the aides motioned us to stand where we were, as audience, while Soumidath went forward alone to the foot of the statue. As he walked slowly across the courtyard, another small procession came from a dark doorway: a very old monk in a saffron robe, and behind him, half a dozen or so of the senior bonzes of the temple.

'The Grand Abbot,' Harry said beside me. 'He's the local equivalent of – oh, well, in British terms, I suppose the Archbishop of Canterbury.'

Soumidath and the Grand Abbot met at the base of the statue and touched hands briefly, church and state exchanging greetings. Both looked strained, which was hardly surprising. In any part of South-east Asia, the deposition of a Buddha is not a thing to be undertaken lightly.

At a signal from the Grand Abbot, the young bonzes took up the ropes of the cart on which the Buddha stood. The senior monks began to chant, and the ceremony of deconsecration was under way. 'They must have had to invent something for the occasion,' Harry said in my ear. 'Bet you it's not in the Buddhist prayer book.'

Soumidath was a naturally loquacious man who never did things by halves, and it looked as if we were in for a trial by endurance. Very few of us had any idea of what was happening, though the Prince and the Grand Abbot appeared to be engaged in a pious shouting match, with the harmonious drone of the monks as a background accompaniment.

It was a serene night, with the moonlight pouring down as thick as honey, and the soft air heavy with the scent of the waxy flowers wreathing the Buddha. I remembered their perfume. They were the flowers Soumidath had piled on the bier of his mother when the old Queen had lain in state in Hanoi. Funeral flowers for a Queen and a Buddha.

Drugged by the night, I was in a half-trance when Harry turned abruptly, and stood on my foot. 'Sorry!' he said under his breath. 'But look up at the window in the far wing.' I followed the line of his finger. At first I did not see anything. Then I saw the outline of a man, and when the moonlight fell across his face I saw it was Ieng Nim. He was leaning well out and he was unmistakable.

'What's he doing up there?' Harry said quietly. 'Why isn't he down here in the courtyard?'

I shrugged. 'He's probably a good Marxist, and he thinks this is all a lot of crap.'

Harry was unconvinced. 'Maybe. But Soumidath ought to make sure that bastard has an accident as soon as it can be arranged. He's big trouble.'

I looked at him curiously. My own skin crawled whenever Ieng Nim came near me, but I had thought it was perhaps some hangover from the meeting in the Temple of One Hundred Buddhas, or the odd affair of his mutilated hand. 'How do you know?' I said.

It was his turn to shrug. 'Just a feeling. He smells bad, and I don't mean only because of his goddam finger.'

The ceremony, mercifully, seemed to be coming to its end. Soumidath and the Grand Abbot shuffled round the statue with bent heads, and the monks' chanting took a dying fall. The young men who were to pull the cart broke their pose of total immobility, and moved slightly forward, testing the strain on the ropes.

'Thank Christ for that,' an American voice said behind me, and the Prince's aides came towards us, to urge us into a processional line.

At the precise moment, two things happened. A flare went up in the darkness behind the courtyard, and two shots rang out in rapid succession. The flare made the courtyard as bright as noon, and I saw the smile of the Buddha disintegrate under the bullets.

More flares went up, enough for a small fireworks display. After the sudden, shocked silence, there was a good deal of screaming and shouting, as the monks headed back for the doorway from which they had emerged, and the diplomats took what cover they could on the long verandah which ran along the central wing of the Palace. At least it had pillars and a waist-high stone balustrade.

I saw Peter come out of the darkness, and seize Soumidath's arm. The Prince was standing at the foot of the Buddha, looking up into its shattered face. Tears were running down his cheeks, and he was making a high, keening noise. There was no one else near him, for his aides had taken cover at the first shot, though they were now unhappily dodging back across the courtyard, calling to him.

Even Peter, taller, younger and more wiry, had a struggle to move him. 'Come, Monseigneur, for God's sake!' he shouted, as though to a deaf man. 'They will kill you if you stay here.' Harry, who had been silently watching from the half-shelter of a pillar, went running forward then, and between them they half-forced, half-urged Soumidath into a doorway at the far end of the verandah.

As though this was some sort of signal, a group of men, with a few girls among them, came surging into the courtyard. They all wore the old uniform of the Liberation Army, the ragged shorts and shirts, the home-made sandals, the stained bush hats, and, round their necks, the field army's pink checked scarf. All of them carried AK-47s, and as they ran across the courtyard, they fired indiscriminately into the air. The firing echoed off the stone walls of the Palace like the staccato rattle of a thunderstorm.

The noise was tremendous, and clearly intended to frighten and deter. It achieved this effect, for looking along the verandah, I saw even the most senior diplomats and their wives were now crouched down below the balustrade on the dusty floor. I ducked down myself when a bullet glanced off the pillar I had been sheltering behind, but I was in luck. There was an ornamental grating in my section of the balustrade, and I could see most of the courtyard through its open-work traceries.

The young fighters – some of them looked hardly more than teenage children – had taken up the flowered ropes and started to pull the faceless Buddha, lurching on its cart, towards the open end of the courtyard. They pulled it so carelessly that once or twice the cart almost overturned, and as it tipped, they laughed and cheered, and I saw one of the girls lift her rifle high and fire it, as though out of sheer exuberance.

Some of the smart soldiers of the Palace guard, in their ceremonial uniforms, now came out into the courtyard, moving cautiously in single file from the darkness of the far wing, their own automatic rifles held across their bodies. I knew the officer leading them, though he looked unfamiliar in his well-cut khaki and his polished Sam Browne. He was the senior fighter who had cadged a lift with Peter and me back to the border when we left the Great Temple camp.

He shouted an order and his men fanned out behind him. Then he shouted again, this time to the young fighters pulling the Buddha. The clumsy little procession came to a halt, and the two groups confronted each other, no more than a few yards dividing them. For a few moments, there was a total silence, then the officer slowly drew his pistol, and as he did two of the young fighters, a man and a girl, took, with equal slowness, a few steps forward.

The moonlight was so bright both groups seemed to be caught in a spotlight. Then the officer began to speak, and I gripped the stone balustrade in frustration, because I could not understand what was being said.

'He is asking what they are doing, interrupting a sacred ceremony, and telling them they must go back to their camp,' a voice said beside me, in rapid French.

I looked round. Penn had come up, unseen, and was crouching beside me. Even in the dim light, I could see the greyness of his skin.

'Who are they?'

'Young fighters, as you can see. They form revolutionary groups, which we have tried to disperse, but they are impatient, and will not listen.' He gave a sigh which racked his body. 'They think we older ones move too slowly.'

'And they oppose the return of Soumidath?'

'Of course. To them, he represents the old order, and everything that is rotten and corrupt. They do not see that, in the beginning, there must be compromises. What they want is a revolutionary state, with no head, with no bureaucrats, with no religion. They will not even change those rags they wore in the jungle for army uniforms.'

'Who leads them? Those two?' I looked out through the grille at the man and the girl who were still arguing with the Palace officer.

Penn's mouth twitched in a humorous smile. 'As much as any one. They say they have no leaders, that all are equal. There are others, though, who encourage them.'

I remembered the face I had seen at the window, 'Ieng Nim, perhaps.' It was a statement, not a question, and Penn looked at me anxiously.

'It is possible,' he said curtly. 'But not openly. He is too careful for that.' He touched my arm briefly with his thin, dry hand. 'You should not speak of this to anyone but me. Do not talk to Mr Greene about it. He is a friend, but not to be trusted.'

I smiled, despite my own anxiety. In the circumstances, it was a perfectly logical statement. Harry had disappeared, and if I knew him, he had gone back to get a camera.

I looked back into the courtyard. 'So the attack on the Buddha is an attack on the Prince?'

Penn hesitated. 'In part. But it is an attack on the false Buddha, not the true one. That they will not yet dare attempt. I think it is a sort of warning that Buddhism will not be tolerated as the state religion. There have already been some murders of monks in temples in the outlying provinces.'

The diplomats and their wives were growing restive. I could hear a rippling murmur of anger along the darkened verandah. Penn heard it too, and groaned. 'This night has set us back years,' he said despairingly. 'The world will say again we are savages.'

Then he swore under his breath, the first time I had ever heard him do so, and stood up. I stood with him, too surprised to worry about the danger, for a door had opened in the side of the Palace, and Soumidath came out again and walked slowly into the light. With him, half a pace behind, was Son Sleng.

All the diplomats got to their feet as well, and stood at the balustrade, like an audience watching the play from a gallery. The shouting in the courtyard died, and there was total silence. In slow motion, the two men walked across, and joined the officer and the Palace body-guard, who at once closed round them to protect them. Penn was murmuring to himself in Kham. He sounded as if he was praying. I could see Peter further along the verandah, but he made no move to go after the Prince.

The two groups were now confronting each other near the entrance to the courtyard, the young fighters clustered round the faceless Buddha, the Prince, the Prime Minister and the soldiers in a tight knot facing them. It was an astonishing scene: ragged children towing a mutilated, flower-wreathed statue, toy soldiers round a Prince in silks and jewels. If it were not for the guns, it could have been a cut-out from a child's story book.

The Prince was arguing passionately. I did not need Penn to interpret, for I knew what he was saying. He was telling them that he was their father, that they must trust him, for he loved them as though they were of his own blood, that they must give the Buddha back to the priests, or they would bring shame on him, and shame on Khamla thoughout all the world.

Soumidath was an accomplished actor, as everyone knew who had seen him perform, but he was not acting now. For one terrible moment, I thought he was going to kneel to them and beg, but then he saw the hardness on the young faces confronting him, and he fell silent.

When he did, Son Sleng stepped forward. I had often thought him too boyish to be taken seriously as commander-in-chief, but tonight he no longer looked young. He looked deadly. He began to speak in an easy, conversational manner, in sharp contrast to the Prince's rhetoric, but at what he said, the soldiers round him began to move back, and only a sharp command from the officer halted them.

'What is it?' I said to Penn. He stared at me, all the lines sharply engraved on his face, as though he had grown ten years older. 'Son Sleng has told them that if they do not give up the Buddha at once, the soldiers will open fire.'

'But they will shoot back!'

He shook his head. 'They are caught in a trap. Look up at the roof.'

I saw where he was pointing. On the far wing of the Palace, a flat roof jutted out at first storey level, covering a guardhouse. On the roof, a small party of soldiers had silently materialised, manning a machine gun. The moonlight glanced off its brutal snout, pointed downward to rake the courtyard.

The ragged children, looking upwards, saw it too, and I thought for a moment they were going to break and run. But instead, without speaking, and as though moved by a single instinct, they slung their guns over their shoulders and linked arms, making a human chain around the Buddha.

Beside me, Penn gave a harsh sound like a cough. 'Fanatics!' he said. 'They are fanatics. They will destroy us all.'

I looked along the line of diplomats. Their own lives were in some danger, but, oddly, no one was taking cover. They stood, silent and rigid as statues, looking out into the moonlit courtyard.

Out there, nothing was moving. Then Son Sleng raised his hand, and the Palace guards brought their rifles up. The chain round the Buddha remained motionless. I could see the face of one of the girls at the front. Her eyes were closed, and her mouth was slightly open, as though she was already dead.

We all watched Son Sleng's hand, waiting for it to come down, but it remained in the air for an agonisingly long time, as though he could not bring himself to give the order.

Then, quite suddenly, Soumidath moved. He pushed aside a soldier who was shielding him with his body, and walked, stumbling a little, to the group surrounding the Buddha and stood in front of them, holding his arms wide, his back to the statue. In a low voice, without any of his usual dramatics, he said something to Son Sleng.

Penn interpreted, though there was hardly any need. 'He says he cannot allow blood to be shed. If they shoot, his own blood will mingle with that of these innocents.'

* * *

'Innocents!' Harry said later, as we stood at the window, watching the end of the affair. 'Innocents! Soumidath should have let the Army shoot the whole pack of them, and saved himself a lot of trouble later on. Look at the fucking little bastards!'

The ragged children, triumphant, were still amusing themselves using the Buddha for target practice. Though it sat serenely on its base, its face was unrecognisable, and bullets had gouged out chunks of stone from its body. Someone had raided the kitchen and brought back a bucket of offal, and grisly bits of intestine were draped round what remained of the Buddha's neck.

I turned away, not wanting to watch any more but a loud explosion brought me back to the window. One of the young fighters had tired of the slow disintegration of the statue, and had hurled a grenade. A second grenade followed, and the stone blew apart in great chunks. There was nothing left standing except the base, but one of the hands remained intact, and a girl fighter picked it up and dipped it in the offal bucket. Then she held it up triumphantly, red and glistening in the moonlight.

'Christ!' said Harry, 'Let's go and get a drink. If we are going to be murdered in our beds tonight by those yobbos I would rather not feel the pain.'

Unbelievably, the scene inside the Long Gallery was almost normal. The band was playing as loudly as it could manage, in an attempt to drown out the explosions outside. Looking at my watch, I saw it was two in the morning, but no one seemed anxious to leave, presumably not wanting to take the risk of being ambushed on the way to the hotels and guesthouses.

One would have thought the night's events would have taken appetites away, but servants were bringing fresh platters of food into the supper room, and Soumidath's guests, most of them haggard with fatigue, were eating and drinking with a kind of hysterical greed, as though trying to replenish their energies for what might still lie ahead.

I could not eat but I was thirsty, and drank two glasses of white wine in quick succession. Not surprisingly, I felt instantly drunk, but I did not care about that any longer. It was hardly the night to stay sober.

In the Long Gallery, the Prince himself had reappeared, and was making a formal round of farewell, shaking hands with the men, lightly touching the women's fingers, though here and there, when he came to an old acquaintance, he could not restrain himself from a desperate hug. He looked old and unfamiliar, no longer in the least like the true Buddha, which still smiled benignly in the half-light at the end of the Long Gallery.

'Let us go,' I heard the French ambassador's wife say to her husband. 'I cannot bear that thing smiling at us. It is like some terrible joke.'

'So much for Soumidath's triumphal evening,' Harry said beside me. The Prince himself came up to us then, murmured a goodnight, and some sort of apology, but his eyes were dull, and I do not think he even registered who we were. His aides surrounded him then, and he walked out, almost like a prisoner, through the door at the end of the Long Gallery.

But though the Prince had gone, the evening had not ended. The most senior diplomats were drifting out, but food and drink seemed to have revived many of the guests, and dancing was starting again, much less decorously now.

'Nothing like a bit of shooting to make you feel randy,' Harry said cheerfully, looking at some of the body contact that was going on on the dance floor. Nobody, I was interested to see, seemed to be dancing with their wives. A young Swedish diplomat came up, and, without asking, pulled me on to the floor. His body, pressed hard against mine, was sweaty, and he was trembling very slightly, more with excitement, I suppose, than fear.

The whole evening had taken on a drunken, rakish look, for most of the remaining men had now taken off their dinner jackets, showing braces and damp shirts, and the women's dresses, including my own pale silk, were dusty and crumpled from crouching on the verandah. Elaborate hairstyles were beginning to disintegrate, and make-up was running in the heat. The women who had worn mascara looked like clowns, with dark smudges on their cheeks.

The band rested briefly, and I managed to disentangle myself from the Swedish diplomat, though he was reluctant to let me go. He wanted to dance again when the music started, but I heard Peter's voice behind me, and turned at once.

'You promised me a dance earlier,' he said loudly. 'I've come to claim it. Tell that partner of yours to piss off.'

I stared at him in surprise. He looked cleaner and fresher than the rest of us, for although he still wore his dress trousers, he had changed into an open-necked shirt and he had put his head under the tap. His hair was wet and crinkly. Physical fastidiousness must have been an automatic thing with him, however, because he was unmistakably drunk.

Harry saw it too. 'God almighty, man, how did you manage to get in this state in the time?' he said admiringly. 'You must have been drinking triples.'

Unlike the rest of us, he had certainly been drinking spirits, for I could smell raw brandy on his breath. He was as pale as a dead man, with something of the same greyish look about the cheeks, and his pupils were so enlarged I could see my own reflection in them.

He smiled in a way that made me uneasy. 'When I make my mind up to wipe myself out, I don't fuck about,' he said, and I remembered sitting opposite Sam Samuels in Sardi's when he told me how Peter sometimes used to drink in Vietnam.

'Well, if that's your bag,' Harry said politely. Peter had taken my hand to pull me onto the dance floor, and behind his back, Harry mouthed: 'Can you manage?' I nodded, though I was by no means sure. Peter in this mood was an unknown quantity.

He might have been drunk, but it did not affect his dancing. He was one of those people whose physical coordination is so good that they can even give this gift to a more awkward partner. Perhaps it was the wine, but as we moved to the music, our bodies intertwined, we seemed to become gradually weightless. I already knew that Peter was a far better dancer than I, and I had been afraid I would not be able to follow him, but he held me so tightly and he was so fluid that we became, in a literal sense, one flesh.

Someone had turned off the air conditioning, and our bodies were pasted together as much with sweat as by the close embrace, but I did not mind. It was the first time Peter had acknowledged my body without any reservation, leaving me free of the fear that in a moment he would push me aside, following the path of his own unfathomable logic. I was not sure what was going to happen, but for the moment I was satisfied with the pressure of his hard, wiry body against mine, and I moved blindly with my eyes closed, letting him guide me.

I don't know how long we danced. Peter stopped only once, when he insisted we go into the supper room and drink a bottle of wine. I drank a glass to please him, but he poured the rest into a tumbler, and gulped it as though it was water. I think he was afraid of becoming sober.

When the band stopped at last, it was nearly dawn, and only three or four other couples were left on the dance floor. Harry had been dancing with a small Lao woman earlier, and had now disappeared, though I had not seen him leave. As the music ended, Peter stumbled for the first time and let me go. His shirt was wet with sweat, and he was even paler than he had been earlier, though I would not have thought that possible.

'What we need is something more to drink,' he said, slurring his words. 'Have you anything over at the villa?' His accent, always fugitive, was straying back to Ulster again.

I looked at him consideringly. There seemed little hope of stopping him, and there was a half-bottle of gin in my suite, left from pre-reception drinks. 'Yes, I have a drinks cupboard,' I said, truthfully enough, though there was nothing in it except the half of Gordon's. 'Let's go now. They are closing up here.'

He had some idea of a last drink in the supper room, but I took his arm firmly, and pulled him with me. It seemed likely another couple of drinks would put him out, and I preferred that to happen in private rather than in the Prince's reception room. I wondered uneasily if the Prince was calling for Peter, but thought it unlikely. If Soumidath turned to anyone for consolation tonight, it would not be a foreigner.

It was rather dark outside, for the moon was setting, and a faint smell of dawn was in the air. I was glad it was not far to the villa, for Peter was now becoming unsteady on his feet, and he leaned on me so heavily that once or twice we almost fell on the uneven ground.

There was no sign of the young fighters near the Palace, but to reach the villa we had to pass the remains of the shattered Buddha. I had hoped that by now someone would have cleared the debris away. But it was just as we had last seen it from the Palace window: the base of the statue still stood on the little cart, crushed white flowers around it, some of them stained with blood from the offal bucket. The fragments of the Buddha were scattered over a wide area, where the grenades had hurled them.

I tried to pull Peter past as quickly as possible, but he pushed me aside and, kneeling, picked up something from the rough grass. It was the head of the Buddha, still recognisable, though its features had been torn away by bullets. But the tight curls clustering round the head and the ears with their extended lobes remained intact.

Peter knelt, holding it in his hands. I tried to urge him to his feet, but he ignored me. He did not say anything, but turned the head over, smoothing it with his fingers. He made a curious noise in his throat, and for a moment I was afraid he was going to weep. I did not want that to happen, for I did not think he would ever forgive me for being a witness to it.

But he did not weep. Instead, he got to his feet in an awkward lurch, and, steadying himself, hurled the head through the air as though he was aiming for a goal. It was an impressive feat, for the head was heavy. It fell with a dull thud behind a clump of grass.

'To hell with it!' he said angrily. 'What does it matter? It was only the false Buddha anyway.'

This seemed to me a piece of supreme illogic, and I would have liked to laugh, but did not dare. Instead, I took his arm and pushed him forward towards the villa, now mercifully within sight, and he did not try to resist.

We got to my rooms as quietly as I could manage. There were other people sleeping in the villa and I did not want to rouse them – particularly Harry, though it was quite likely he had found a bed elsewhere. It was a night when a lot of barriers might well go down.

Peter seemed half-asleep, supporting himself on my shoulder, but as soon as I turned the light on and pushed him into a chair, he woke and demanded a drink. I hesitated, for now that we were safely in the villa, I would have preferred to sober him up. But he got to his feet abruptly, and I saw at once it would be dangerous not to give him what he wanted. I did not think he would hit me – though he might have done – but he had suddenly turned into a stranger, an ugly and pugnacious drunk, ready to smash anything in his way. It was not a role in which I would have cast him.

I went quickly to the drinks cupboard, but even then I was too late to stop him crashing against a small inlaid table, and sending the pair of vases on it tumbling to the floor. They broke into a dozen pieces, and he looked at the fragments stupidly, as though someone else had done the damage. I could only hope they were not priceless. Soumidath was quite capable of sending some of his treasures over to the villa.

I half-filled a glass with neat gin, and handed it to Peter. He drank it down at once, without even grimacing at the taste. 'What are you trying to do?' I said incredulously. 'Kill yourself with this stuff?' He did not answer, but simply held the glass out for a refill.

I did not argue, but poured more gin, as little as I thought I could get away with. He was obviously attempting to knock himself cold, and probably the sooner he managed it, the better. It was hardly the way I had thought, while we started dancing, that the evening might end.

The second gin seemed at last to relax him. His face lost his angry flush and his hands unclenched. He put the glass down carefully on the table, smiled at me, and said in a quite normal voice: 'Perhaps I should go and lie down for a while. The walls are going round and round and making me dizzy. I'd hate to throw up on you.'

I hastily went into the bedroom and pulled the cover down on one of the two narrows beds. I thought I might have to half-carry him, but when I looked back, he had managed to take off his shoes and socks, and had padded silently into the bedroom behind me in bare feet. I put out my hand to help him, but he pushed me gently aside. 'Goodnight, Gilly,' he said formally, and, lying down on the bed, gave a deep sigh, and at once fell asleep.

I sat on the other bed, and looked at him for a long time. After the first few minutes, though, it was not a peaceful sleep. He seemed uncomfortable, and thrashed around, murmuring to himself. It was still hot, and his shirt was pasted to his body with sweat. Runnels of sweat ran down his cheeks, like tears, and even his hair was dark with it.

I went over to the bed and sat beside him, cautiously putting out my hand, and starting to unbutton his shirt. He did not wake, so I carefully peeled off his shirt and trousers, taking my time so as not to rouse him. It was a long job anyway, for he was heavy and hard to move, but when he was free of the sweaty clothes, he seemed happier, and gave a long sigh, lying back calmly against the pillows.

His skin was still hot to the touch, so I went to the bathroom and filled a bowl with water, letting the tap run until it was as cool as, in that climate, it was possible to get it. Then I sat down on the bed again, and, using a small towel, sponged him carefully with cool water, wiping the sweat from his face, and drawing the soft towel over and over his chest and arms. In between, I held the towel to my own face, pressing it against my eyes, and nose, and mouth. Even the acrid smell of his sweat was beautiful to me.

When I had finished, I stood up and looked down at his long body, open and vulnerable to me for the first time. He had an athletic man's build, with muscled shoulders and a narrow waist, and unexpectedly sturdy legs. The little triangle of hair on his chest was as fair and curly as the hair on his head, and a small line of glinting gold hairs ran down his flat belly.

The sponging had soothed him, for he was sleeping very quietly now, so quietly that his chest hardly seemed to move, and for a moment, I had a terrible fantasy that he was dead, and I was laying him out for burial. In the dim light from the ramshackle bedside lamp, he looked like the Christ of the Deposition paintings, with his head turned to one side, and his white limbs loose and relaxed.

Then he gave another long sigh, and I turned away abruptly, going to the bathroom, stripping off my own sweaty clothes as I went, and standing so long under the shower that, even in that humid air, I felt cold. When I went back to the bedroom, the dawn was nudging at the windows, but I drew the shutters to keep it out. I pushed the second bed hard alongside the one on which Peter lay, to make a passable double, and got into bed naked beside him, drawing a sheet over both of us.

He was turned on his side towards me, and I lay along the length of his body, pressing myself against him, feeling with delight his naked suppleness, kissing his eyes and and his unresponsive mouth. He did not wake – I had not expected it – but he did fling an arm carelessly round me, and in his sleep, he said my name, over and over. It was enough to make me happy.

CHAPTER TWELVE

When I woke, it was early afternoon, and Peter had gone. I had lain awake for a long time, but when I did fall asleep, I must have slept as deeply as he. There was no sign of his presence, for a servant had been in and swept up the broken pieces of vases. My dress and underwear which I had dropped on the way to the bathroom were hanging neatly over a chair in the sitting room.

The room boy had also left a bowl of fruit and a vacuum flask of hot water on the sideboard, so I breakfasted off slices of pineapple and papaya and tea made with a dusty teabag, sitting luxuriously in my kimono. I was supposed to be taking part in a day-long programme of official events, but I did not think anyone would notice my absence.

After a while, I showered and dressed, but I did not leave the villa. I was waiting for Peter, and he came, as I knew he would, though not until dusk. He found me sitting in a long chair on the verandah, too lazy to read the book in my lap, watching instead the fruit bats wheeling against the lingering sullen glare of the sunset.

He was freshly bathed and changed and looked very composed. I noticed there were still a slight greyish tinge to his skin. 'Come inside,' he said, gesturing with a woven straw carryall he had in his hand. 'I've brought some beer. Guaranteed ice cold for at least the next ten minutes.'

In the sitting room, he took charge as if he were the host, finding glasses in the sideboard, and opening the beer competently. I thought he probably hated the idea of loss of physical control. When he was sober, he was unusually deft and economical in all his movements.

The beer was, as he had promised, ice cold, and he drank his own glass almost immediately. 'Don't worry,' he said, seeing me watching him. 'I'm not going to get drunk again. It's just that I'm dehydrated. I had a hell of a thirst when I got up, and I've been standing in the sun for most of the day watching the Prince harangue assorted delegations about their role in the future of Free Khamla.'

I looked at him in amazement. 'I thought you would have been laid out for a week, after last night.'

He smiled, without much amusement. 'No chance. I can make a quick recovery when I have to. Today of all days, I had to be on my feet. The Prince needed me.' He got up, to pour another glass of beer. 'My God, I have a head, though. How much did I drink last night? I haven't done anything like that since Vietnam.'

'Why did you do it?' I watched him carefully in the dusk. He was slightly on the defensive, but the invisible barrier with which he usually surrounded himself was no longer there. There was a shift in our relationship and for once I felt I was the less vulnerable of the two.

'For the same reason I used to wipe myself out occasionally in Vietnam, I suppose. I suddenly felt that something frightful was going to happen, and that there was nothing I could do to control it. It's a feeling of – oh, I don't know, a sort of cosmic helplessness. I've had it ever since I was a child, though only once in a while, thank Christ. As if I have to stand by, and watch the world die, and it drives me mad.'

He spoke quite flatly, but I was taken aback as though he had shouted and smashed his fists against the wall. 'Just because a few kids ran wild and shot up a Buddha?' I said incredulously.

'Not just that. Because it is a sign that things are getting out of hand here. The Prince knows it too. And he knows, as I do, that there is nothing any of us can do to stop it.'

I did not like any of this, and I got up abruptly and turned on the light. 'I think you are being morbid.'

'Probably. I've been in Asia too long, I suppose I came to Vietnam almost at the start of the war, as a very young reporter, and stuck with it right to the end. Since then, I've been involved here.' He made a sweeping gesture with his hand. 'Perhaps I should go and live somewhere where people aren't killing each other all the time.'

I watched him carefully. 'Why don't you?'

'Oh, I don't know.' He leaned his head against the high cane back of his chair, and put his hands over his eyes in a gesture of fatigue. 'I don't think I'm fit for normal life anymore. You might as well ask Harry Greene why he doesn't go home to Connecticut and acquire a wife and kids and a couple of mortgages.

I hesitated, then took my chance. 'You said to me once you were interested in the exercise of power.'

He laughed. 'I remember. And you told me the rumour was that I was setting myself up as some sort of latter-day Machiavelli. Do you still believe that?'

'I don't know,' I said. 'I'm never sure what your motives are. But I don't doubt that you are fascinated by power.'

'True enough. It's the most absorbing thing in the world.' He got up and began to move restlessly around the room. 'That's really why I stay with the Prince, I suppose. In Vietnam, wherever I was, or whatever I was doing, I was always a spectator. There was nothing I could do to stop what was happening. It just kept rolling on.'

'A sort of cosmic helplessness.'

He looked at me with interest. 'Yes, something like that. That's why it's important to me to be here. It will probably be the only chance I shall have in my life to be close to the source of power, to play some sort of small role myself in what is going on. And God knows, it's bloody small!'

I chose my words carefully. He was such a touchy man, the wrong question would make him shut up like a clam. 'I've never been really sure what that role is. What you actually do for the Prince, I mean.'

'It's nothing very mysterious. Nothing cloak-and-daggerish, if that is what you are imagining.' He came over and stared at me, then laughed ruefully. 'You've been listening to the rumour-mongers in Bangkok, dear Gilly, I can see. No, it's very simple. I am exactly what I purport to be, an adviser. I've kept up some good contacts inside and outside Asia, and I advise the Prince about external policy. I tell him what is being thought and said about Khamla in Europe and America, and other parts of Asia, and what reaction he can expect if he makes this move or that move.'

'And he listens to you?'

'Sometimes he does, sometimes he doesn't. He is very shrewd, is Monseigneur, underneath all that play-acting, and there have been one or two times when his instinct has proved a better guide than all my careful sifting of the political rumour mills.'

There was still something I did not understand. 'This – this playing a part in the power game, or whatever you want to call it. Is this really all that keeps you here?'

He smiled at me with great kindness. 'Ah, Gilly, I see you are looking for some noble motive. You don't want me to be just a sort of amoral manipulator, do you?'

I said nothing, and he went over to the window and looked out into the dusk, his back to me. 'Well, I will admit I'm sorry for this poor, bloody little country. Someone has got to stop it being torn to pieces, and I think in the short term that the only person who can do it is Soumidath. He's not the long-term answer. I don't know what that is, but the Prince at least has enough pull here to bring about some sort of truce, and enough prestige abroad to get the aid flowing in.'

He turned to face me. 'You think it's bad here? You should go up country, and see some of the areas where there has been fighting. The peasants haven't been able to get the harvest in for two years in some places, and they are literally dying of starvation. Just lying down by the roadside, or outside their own huts, and dying. Old people, young people, kids, everybody.'

He looked so unhappy that I went and stood beside him, taking his hand, and leaning on his shoulder. He made no move to push me away.

'I'm sorry for this poor, bloody country,' he said, almost under his breath, 'and I'm sorry for all poor, bloody little countries that get pushed around, and squeezed, and manipulated by blind, insensitive giants who don't give a damn about killing tens of thousands of people in the process.'

'Like your own country?' I said, speaking into his shoulder.

He released my hand, and moved away at once. 'My own country? The United States? You've got to be joking. It's one of the blind giants.'

'I was talking about Ulster.' It was a mistake. His eyes were wary, and I could see all the barriers coming down.

'Oh,' he said easily. 'I'm a New Yorker, bred if not born. I haven't lived in Ulster since I was nine or ten years old. That's a long time ago, dear Gilly.'

'Have you never been back?'

'A couple of times,' he said reluctantly. 'And you're right, it is a poor, bloody, sad place. The first time, my uncle took me while I was still in high school. The second time, I went on a reporting job for the agency, and I was glad to get out of the place. I swore I would never go back again, and I haven't.'

He went over to the table and picked up the untouched cans of beer. 'What a crime. We've let them go warm.' His voice was light and mocking.

'That's more than a crime. That's a capital offence.' Harry was standing in the doorway. We had not heard him coming along the passage, and I wondered how long he had been there. He was in an ebullient mood, and I could see Peter's spirits perceptibly change. I think he was very glad of the interruption.

'Now, *mes enfants*,' Harry said, pouring himself a glass of warm beer and grimacing as he drank it. 'Bestir yourselves. I have arranged a dinner for all visiting hacks at the Roi Soleil, and promised them you will come, Peter. No, don't groan, you are the big draw card. Afterwards, I will remind you, we are due for an evening of indigenous song-and-dance at the Palace, so there is an obvious need to get our strength up first.'

It was a good dinner. The cooking was French provincial with local overtones, and the old proprietor kept coming to the table himself to check on the dishes, and to embrace Peter yet again, and remind him of heroic evenings of the past. Harry's collection of visiting hacks included some hard-bitten and distinguished journalists, and I was amused to see how Peter played up to them, pushing a point of view here, dropping a mysterious hint there, keeping them laughing with engaging stories of life *chez* Soumidath.

It was the first time I had seen him practising his art, and he was very good at it. Tomorrow they would examine what he said in the cold light of their experience, and accept or reject it as they thought fit, but for tonight, they were charmed. I noticed also that Peter was performing an elegant sleight-of-hand with his wine, pretending he was keeping pace with everybody, while in fact he was drinking very little. In the circles in which he moved, it was a useful accomplishment.

The concert took place in the Palace courtyard, with Soumidath and the Prime Minister and Cabinet in a specially built Royal box, and the rest of us on uncomfortable gilt chairs brought from the Palace salons. It was a calm, scented night, with stage lighting provided by the moon, as the dancers went through their exquisite rituals, the tiny mirrors on their headdresses and bodices catching the light, the bells on their wrists and ankles chiming delicately. Above the sinuous bodies moving in their ancient patterns, the painted faces were withdrawn and tranced, turned to a silvery-white by the moonlight.

I wondered if I were the only person there who felt cold, though the night was stifling. The dancers, their slender bare feet smeared by dust, were moving over the same ground where, last night, the Buddha had been desecrated, and the ragged children had stood defiant under the machine gun's snout. The night's proceedings seemed to me bizarre, like some sort of further desecration, but when I looked over at Soumidath, in the Royal box, I saw he was smiling with open, sensuous enjoyment.

I suppose he was, at heart, an optimist, a cheerful man with an inexhaustible capacity for bouncing back when he was knocked flat. He would have to be, to have survived as long as he had.

Peter had been sitting throughout the concert with the tall, bronzed lady he had been dancing with the night before, and when it ended she seemed to have some intention of sweeping him off with her. Her hand was on his arm, and she was speaking to him with much more animation than she had so far shown throughout the visit. But to my relief, her husband came up and took her away, staring back over his shoulder at Peter with open dislike.

'It's a funny thing. All the women go for Peter even when he doesn't want them,' Harry said rather maliciously in my ear. 'It must be that hard-to-get signal he sends out. I'll have to try it myself sometime.'

I ignored him, and caught up with Peter as he started to walk back towards the main door of the Palace. 'Come and have a drink at the villa,' I said. Then, as he hesitated, 'You owe it to me, you know.'

'Very well.' He looked at me, his face expressionless in the moonlight. 'Go by yourself, and I'll come as soon as I can. I have to make some arrangements with the Prince for tomorrow.'

I was reluctant to let him go, fearful he would not keep his promise, but half an hour later, he tapped quietly on the sitting-room door and came in.

'Well, now, Gilly,' he said, pulling up a chair and facing me. 'It's about last night, I suppose. Are you going to tell me what happened?'

I watched him warily. 'Do you really remember nothing? How very flattering for me.'

He moved uneasily in his chair. 'Does that mean what I think you intend it to mean?' When I said nothing, he made a gesture of impatience. 'All right, let's start again. I will tell you what I remember, and you can fill in the gaps. I remember dancing with you, which was very pleasant, then I have some dim memory of coming into this room with you, and after that, of the sound of something smashing. Did I break anything?'

I laughed. 'Only two of the Prince's priceless vases. It's all right,' I said hurriedly, as he put his head in his hands with a groan. 'They were probably not priceless at all, because nobody made a fuss about them. What do you remember after that?'

'Absolutely nothing. Don't look so doubtful. It's called alcoholic amnesia, and it's said to be an early warning sign that if you keep on drinking like that you are going to be in serious trouble. Fortunately I'm only an occasional drunk, but it's happened once or twice to me before. You haven't experienced it, obviously.'

He got up and stood looking down at me. 'As I woke up in bed with you this morning, I assume we made love.' His voice was flat and expressionless, and it maddened me, and broke my composure.

'My God! Would that be such a terrible thing for you to have done? To make love to me?' I stood up and faced him, trembling with anger and humiliation. 'The way you behave you would think you were some sort of monk, and I was tempting you to break your vows. Anyway, it must have been a tremendous experience for you, last night, if you can't even remember it.'

He tried to take my hands but I pushed him away. 'Get out, Peter,' I said. 'I've had enough of you. You shame me.'

He did go to the door then, but before I could stop myself, I gave a desolate cry, and said his name. At that, he came back, and held me hard, pressing himself against me as though he was trying to fuse our two bodies together.

'Gilly,' he said, in a calm, low voice. 'Gilly, don't cry. Let's go to bed. I can't have been much good to you last night, I was too drunk. Let's see if we can manage better now.'

In the bedroom, moonlight was coming through the shutters, making geometric patterns on the floor. We undressed slowly in the silvery dark. I was still not sure how Peter felt, for there seemed a quality of reserve in him, and I hoped it was not reluctance, or worse, a kind of pity.

Now that we had reached this point, I felt my own desire drain away, and be replaced by a mixture of fear and embarrassment. Peter moved towards the bedside table and I saw he was going to put on the light, so I said, 'No!' very loudly, and he laughed and turned back to me.

In the half-dark, we stood looking at each other for a long time, neither making a move. I had seen his naked body the night before, but then it had been limp and defeated, so I was unprepared for its lean, muscular strength. His skin was very white, and, unlike Harry's, unmarked by any scars. A shadow lay across the upper part of his face like a mask, so that I could not see his eyes, but his lips were smiling.

David had made me self-conscious about my body, so that as I stood before Peter, I began to shiver as though I was cold. He came closer, and reaching out very slowly, he put both his arms gently round my neck.

He was not quite as calm as he looked, for his palms

were moist, and I could feel a slight tremor in his muscles, but his voice, when he spoke, was easy and cheerful.

'You're a funny girl. I think you're shy of your own body.' He drew back a little and deliberately looked me up and down. 'Don't underrate yourself. It's a fine, healthy body and you should be proud of it.'

I turned my face away. 'I always felt so big and clumsy beside Asian women.'

It was a mistake to have said that, because an image of Peter making love to Rosie instantly came into my mind. I knew at once that Peter had thought of Rosie too, for he almost imperceptibly retreated from me, but then he laughed and said briefly that he often felt like Gulliver himself but it was no use worrying about it.

Then, as I stood without moving, he began to caress me delicately, kissing my eyes and my breasts, running his fingers up and down my spine, nibbling my neck. 'You're like a statue, Gilly,' he said in my ear. 'Relax, that's a good girl.'

I had been afraid that some malicious spirit had entered into me and that now what I had wanted since I first saw Peter was being offered to me I would not be able to take it. But then, under Peter's insistent but still delicate touch, I felt my flesh relax into softness, and taking his head into my hands, I kissed him with joy and love.

'That's better!' he said with relief, and we clung to each other, mouth against mouth, bodies fitting as exactly as though they had been designed for this specific purpose. I heard him give a small, odd grunt and I knew that somehow I had surprised and moved him, perhaps more than he wanted.

We edged towards the bed, still linked together, then he lifted me bodily and came down with me, so that we lay facing, absorbed in a mutual exploration of lips and limbs. We were both sweating but our sweat ran together and mingled so that I did not care.

I thought I was truly relaxed, but Peter must have felt some urgency in me, for he took his mouth away from mine for a moment. 'Don't be in too much of a hurry,' he said. 'We've got all the time in the world.' In the darkness, I clung tighter to him. I knew it was true, but I was unused to the luxury of such leisured love-making.

When he entered me at last, I had the curious feeling that I had left my body, and was watching from somewhere above; that though my corporal self was abandoning itself completely to Peter, I could also see both of us, silvered by the moonlight, in our rhythmic shadow play on the bed. It was a very strange feeling and it frightened me.

Then the phantom self came back into my body to experience the final convulsive release. I started to cry out, but Peter covered my mouth with his, and murmured: 'No need, no need.'

Afterwards, when we had moved apart, he kissed me gently on the forehead, as though I was a child. Then, not touching me again, he turned on his side, away from me, and I lay listening to his breathing as he made the slow descent into sleep.

I knew it was folly, but almost without my own volition, I said in a low voice: 'Peter, I love you. Do you feel anything for me at all?'

I am not sure whether he heard me. If he did, he made no reply.

* * *

It is very hard, in such a climate, to sleep beyond dawn, and I woke when the light came through the shutters to find Peter was already awake and looking at me. I smiled at him, and stretched. It was very pleasant at that time of day before the heat came snarling into the room, and the skin grew sticky with runnels of sweat, I did not say anything, for I was happy just to lie there with Peter beside me. I knew the feel of his body, though we were not touching.

He was silent for a long time, lying on his back, looking up at the ceiling where the little geckoes, with their pale, transparent bodies, moved about their mysterious business. Then he cleared his throat and spoke.

'I didn't tell you, did I, that I saw my father die? He was shot, you know. I was only nine years old at the time.'

'No, you didn't,' I said very cautiously. I was afraid he would take fright, and clam up.

He looked at me then, but oddly, as though I was a stranger. 'Why not?' he said. 'Why not? There's no better time for it.' Then he began to speak quite rapidly, but in a distant voice, as though he was recounting a story he had learned off by heart, and which had happened to someone else.

It was true, as Sam Samuels had told me, that his grandfather had been arrested and executed after the Easter Rising in Dublin in 1916. He had a leg shattered in the fighting at the Post Office, and couldn't walk, but the British strapped him to a chair, and carried him on to the execution ground, and shot him just the same.

Peter's grandmother took her three children to Belfast, where the family had come from originally. They lived in a squalid tenement on the Falls Road, and though Peter's father, Jack Casement, was an exceptional student, he had to leave school at fifteen and find a job to help keep his mother and the two younger children.

After his marriage, he worked as a lorry driver, and he was often away on trips across the border, into the Republic.

'I had the idea, even when I was very young, that he did some sort of business on those trips that had nothing to do with the firm he was working for,' Peter said. 'The night before he went south, men always came to the house, and I was sent outside to play while he and my mother talked to them. I was frightened of the dark, and I used to sit pressed up against the door, waiting for the chance to get in again. There always seemed to be a lot of shouting going on.'

'What was he doing? Running guns?'

Peter put his hand briefly across his eyes. 'I don't know. I really don't know. I never knew how much either of them was involved, or who they were involved with. I was too young, you see, and they kept me out of it.'

'We were Roman Catholics, we were republicans, and my grandfather was one of the martyrs of the '16 Rising. My grandmother hated the Brits with as deadly a hatred as I've yet encountered in any living being but the truth about what was going on in that house died with my father and my mother.'

'What were your parents like?'

'My father was like me, a tall and fair man. My mother was tall, too, but very dark, with black curly hair. She was a beautiful woman. That's not just my prejudice, she was rather famous for it, and people used to tease my father about her looks. He wasn't bad-looking himself, but he had had acne when he was a boy and his skin was rather pitted. I think he was self-conscious about it.'

Peter was the only child, something of a disgrace for a good Catholic couple, but it was probably just as well, for money was very short. Jack Casement was in regular work, but he was supporting his mother, who was ill for a long time before she died when Peter was seven, and helping his sister, whose husband had been killed in a factory accident, leaving her with two young children.

'We lived in a flat in West Belfast,' Peter said. 'There were only two rooms. My mother and father had one, and my grandmother and I, until she died, slept in the kitchen. My mother kept everything as clean as she could, but the passageways always stank of urine and blocked drains.' He gave an odd sort of snorting sound, as though he was trying to clear his head. 'I can still smell it. It was more putrid than anything I've smelled here.'

The child was rather glad when his grandmother died. She was a fierce woman, burnt out with anger, nagging her son constantly towards some vague goal of revenge. She was also a restless sleeper, moaning and muttering, and flinging her arms wide, so that almost every night the boy woke sweating and terrified by the noise she was making. He was much happier sleeping in the kitchen alone, though for a long time after her death, he continued to wake, thinking he heard the bed in the other corner creaking, and her mad moans.

With his mother no longer there, things became a little easier, financially and in other ways as well, for Jack Casement. The men still sometimes came to the flat before his father went on trips, and Peter was still sent to play outside, but it seemed to him that the visits were far less frequent, and his mother seemed happier. They were both strict with him, driving him hard over his homework, and keeping him off the streets as much as possible. The local children were organised into gangs, and he belonged to none of them, so that he often had to fight single-handed against two or three boys who set upon him on his way home.

'When I came home with a bloody face, my mother cleaned me up, but said nothing,' Peter said. 'My father gave me some rudimentary lessons in boxing. The kids who picked on me were snotty-nosed stunted little bastards – most of them are in that area – so I didn't do too badly. It toughened me up, anyway.'

He wasn't tough enough, to keep from screaming with fear when the men broke in through the kitchen door, one night not long after his ninth birthday, and he saw the guns. There were three of them, two holding long-barrelled pistols, and the other with a cosh, and behind them, in the darkness of the alley, he glimpsed someone who looked like Michael Ahern, their next-door neighbour, though he could not be sure.

'Shut your mouth, sonny, or I'll shut it for you,' the man with the cosh said, bringing it down with a swish near his head, but he took no notice and shouted a warning. They had the inner door open by then, and Peter saw, as though in a frame of light, his mother and father stumbling out of bed.

His father was bare-chested, but in a pair of old, yellowed long johns. His mother wore one of his grandmother's flannel night-gowns, faded with washing, but considered too good to throw away. They were both still half-asleep, and they looked helpless and vaguely comic, like a surprised couple in a seaside postcard.

When his mother saw the men, she stood stock still, staring at them, her face ghostly against the tangle of her black hair. His father, one hand over his genitals, reached for his shirt which was hanging on the back of a chair, and started to pull it on.

'Don't bother with that, Jack.' The stocky man at the front waved the pistol at him. 'You'll not be needing it. It's not cold where you're going.'

'I knew what was happening,' Peter said, 'even at that age. It was long before the real Troubles started, and they weren't knee-capping people with electric drills, but those kind of kangaroo courts had been going for decades, ever since Partition.'

His father knew what was happening, too, and he shrugged, and let the shirt drop. 'What am I supposed to have done?' he said, carefully moving away from his wife. Then, more sharply: 'Let the boy go back into the other room, won't you? There's no need for him to stay.'

But the man with the cosh took Peter by the shoulder, and pushed him further into the room. 'There's every need, Jack,' he said, holding the child by the arm. 'A boy like this needs to grow up knowing how we deal with informers.'

The word fell into the room with a slow finality, like a heavy stone thrown into a pool. Each of the two groups, the man and his wife, the executioners with the child in their midst, stood silently, as though waiting for ripples to form.

'It's a terrible word in Ireland, north or south. Did you know that?' Peter moved restlessly on the pillows beside me. Sweat was forming on his forehead and upper lip, and he wiped it away with the sheet. 'Nowadays, I think they call them supergrasses, to make it sound more respectable. But it's a deadly word. Informer. And it's not only the man himself. It's his wife, and his children, and his family, branded for years to come.'

Jack Casement seemed to know that there was no hope for him, as soon as he heard the word. His gaze went blank, and his lips moved as though he was praying, though he was not a praying man. And Annie Casement moved over and put her arm round him, and laughed. It was a harsh sound, more derisive than mirthful.

'You're bloody fools to even think it,' she said loudly. 'Jack an informer? After all he has done for you? Go and look somewhere else. You've come to the wrong shop here.'

A couple of the men shifted uncomfortably, but the man with the cosh came forward. 'It's you that's wrong, missis,' he said. 'We know Jack went to the polis after his work today, and two of our boys was lifted tonight. They were boys he knew about, for he brought them over hisself.'

'Jack go to the polis?' She spat at their feet. 'Jack never went to the polis in his life! Now get out of here.'

'My father never said one word in all this time,' Peter said. 'But he saw the guns coming up, and he threw my mother hard away from him, so she fell back on the bed.

They shot him then, twice through the chest, and he was knocked back against the wall, but he slid down quite silently. My mother came at them, but the man with the cosh hit her and she fell down too. I thought she was dead.'

The boy himself remained very still, for he thought if he provoked them, they would kill him and he did not want to die. Then the leader, the man who had fired the shots, went over and dipped his fingers in his father's blood. The man with the cosh held the child, and the leader made the sign of the cross on his forehead. His fingers were sticky and wet. 'That's an informer's blood. Remember that, boy,' he said. Then they were gone.

I took Peter's hand and entwined my fingers with his. I could feel the pulse in his wrist thudding.

'Was your father an informer?'

He shook his head angrily. 'How can I answer that? I could say I can never believe he was, but how would a child of that age know? It may have been a completely trumped-up charge. It may have been that without his mother nagging him, he didn't want to go on with what small jobs he was still doing, and was looking for a way of ending it.'

'What did your mother think?'

He gave a smothered laugh. 'My mother! She had concussion and was taken to hospital. I didn't see her again until after my father's funeral. Do you know, she never spoke of it, even to me. Not once.'

While the mother was in hospital, the boy was taken in for a few days by his aunt, and the squalid little house, with two crying children, was also crowded with neighbours and acquaintances, blazing with curiosity and condolences. They tried to coax Peter into telling them exactly how his father had died, and what the men had said, but he was his mother's son, and remained obdurate.

He was not sure how he learned it, perhaps in

overheard whispers, but after a while he began to understand that someone had claimed to have seen Jack Casement going into the police station, and that someone was believed to be Michael Ahern, the next-door neighbour. No one seemed ready to say it aloud, and he thought he might have imagined it, but then he remembered something he had thrust to the back of his mind: that he had seen, or thought he had seen, Mick Ahern in the alley the night his father was shot.

He did not discuss this with his mother, for she would not even mention his father's name. He hardly saw her, in any case, for she had a job cleaning offices to keep them alive, and she rarely came home until he had eaten the supper she had left for him, and gone to bed. He could not bear to be alone in the house, and he was lucky that it was summer, for he found a hiding place behind some piles of rubbish on a vacant allotment, and stayed there reading until the light went.

Occasionally, over the next few months, some extra food appeared upon the table, and his mother had a small bottle of Guinness with her supper.

When the weather grew cold, he shivered for a while in his thin sweater and his summer shorts, but one night, there was a brand new windbreaker and a pair of long trousers laid out on his bed for him to put on the next morning. He was very glad of them, for it stopped the children mocking him at school for their poverty.

It was not long before Christmas when he came home one Friday night to find Mick Ahern sitting with his mother at the table in the kitchen. His mother worked at the weekend, and Friday night was usually their only night together, so he was angry. But he saw there was a loaf of bread on the table, and a plum cake, and margarine instead of dripping.

'Sit down, boy,' Mick Ahern said, as though he owned the house. His mother nodded silently, and he slid into his chair, and stared at the slice of plum cake she cut and put before him. He did not want to eat, but he was very hungry, and after a while, he started to cram the cake into his mouth. The man talked to him awkwardly, unused to children, asking him questions about his school, and whether he was making a novena for the feast of Sacred Heart.

'Answer Mr Ahern, Peter,' his mother said angrily, when he only mumbled an indistinct reply, but Mick Ahern smiled, and patted his arm. 'Don't worry, Annie, the boy's shy.'

He was a grey-haired man, and the boy thought him very old. His teeth were bad, with a couple missing at the side of his mouth, and even across the table, his breath was foul. He was a widower, with no children, who worked as a clerk in the trucking firm which had employed Jack Casement, and by the standards of that place and time, he was not badly off.

When the mother got up and went to the stove to make the tea, he stood up too, and, on the pretext of helping her, put his hand gingerly on her waist. She said something in a low voice, but he shook his head. 'Nonsense,' he said. 'The boy might as well get used to it.'

'She turned then, and looked at me over his shoulder. He was a small man, much shorter than she, and I could see her face very clearly,' Peter said. 'She was holding her own breath, so she would not smell the stench from his mouth. But after a while, she pushed him aside, and laughed, and sat down and poured tea for both of us.

'She said very little while we ate, but Mick Ahern talked enough for the three of us. I suppose he was a lonely man, and glad of the company. He said he was moving out of the flats. He could afford something better, and had only stayed because it was where he and his wife had spent their married life together.' Peter turned on his side, with his face away from me.

'You and your ma must come and visit me when I move to the new place,' he told the boy. 'I expect to see you every Sunday dinner, after church. Your ma has promised to cook it for me. I'm not much of a hand in the kitchen.'

When he had gone, the child looked at his mother in silence, but she drew him against her, and hugged him, and told him he must think of Mick Ahern as his uncle, for he had been very kind to them, and brought them food, and paid for the new clothes he was wearing to school. The boy was innocent enough in some ways, but it was a rough area, and he was not altogether a child. He knew without asking that his mother was paying some price for this.

'She was a beautiful woman, as I have told you, and I think any of the young unmarried men would have been glad to do as much for her.' Peter was mumbling, and it was hard to hear him. But she couldn't have accepted that. It would have been betraying my father. I suppose she was glad that Mick Ahern was small and ugly and old. She could sell herself to him, for my sake, but punish herself at the same time.'

'What did you do?' I think I knew what he was going to say before he said it, and I did not particularly want to hear it.

'Oh, I told her then that Michael Ahern had betrayed my father to the executioners. I said that he was a murderer. I had no idea whether this was true, but I told her it as a fact, saying everyone knew it but her.' He turned violently over in the bed to face me. 'I wasn't even thinking of my father, you know. I was just jealous of her – her and that terrible little man.'

I put my hand on his cheek. He was weeping. 'What did she say?'

'Nothing. Nothing much. She cleared up the tea things, and made me go to bed early, saying I must go over to my aunt's the next day while she was at work. I came home early the next afternoon, though, for I knew that something was wrong. My aunt came with me, for I had refused to go alone. She grumbled, but she came.'

Peter raised himself on his elbow, and looked at me. 'My mother was lying on the bed, fully dressed. She had shot herself through the head. It wasn't so bad,' he said hastily, as though he was reassuring me. 'Her hair was so thick and curly you couldn't see much, just a trickle of blood coming out of her ear, and dried in a little stream on her neck. I didn't even know we had a gun in the house, but when my aunt saw it lying on the quilt, she screamed, and said it was my father's pistol.'

Peter got up abruptly and stood naked by the side of the bed. He was a splendid man, and, I think, rather vain of his looks, but he wasn't thinking about his body then. I wondered if he was thinking of his father, getting out of bed, half-asleep, in his shabby long johns.

'My mother had made arrangements, of sorts. She had written a letter to my uncle – her brother – in America before she died, and gone out to post it. He kept it, and showed it to me when I was older. Jim was a lot older than she was, and she hadn't seen him for years, but he used to send her a card every Christmas, and occasional presents, so I suppose she thought it was worth a try.'

'What did the letter say?'

'Oh, a sort of wild plea for help. Rather incoherent, but my aunt Vera cabled him as well, though she could hardly afford it. He came within a week, and took me back with him. He and his wife had two girls, and hadn't been able to manage any more, so they were glad enough to adopt me. Jim had done rather well for himself, and he put me through school and college. They were both very good to me, and I'm sorry I couldn't love them.'

Peter started to pull on his shirt and trousers. 'Well, that's the story. You've wanted to hear it long enough, and now you have.'

I got up too, and put on my kimono. 'Why did you tell it to me now?'

He put his arm round me and kissed me gently on the

forehead. 'You ask more questions than anybody I've ever met. Who knows? Drink sometimes sets me off, but it wasn't that this time.' He looked weary. 'I must be getting soft, I suppose, or you've broken me down at last. Let's have some tea. All that talking has given me a terrible thirst.'

CHAPTER THIRTEEN

I was glad we had managed some sleep, for Soumidath set a punishing pace that day, dragging us out into the countryside on buses on the first of his triumphal progressions. It was a sort of mini-Royal tour, with visits to rural factories and farming areas, and long, droning speeches by village headmen, while diplomats and press drank tea in stifling halls and complained about the heat and the flies.

'Thank Christ I'm flying out tomorrow,' Harry said, watching the Prince do a ceremonial laying-on of hands while children knelt before him. 'Why don't you come with me?' I shook my head. 'I'm booked the day after, and they've told us we can't change. The plane is so full we'll probably have to stand up all the way anyway.'

He looked at me curiously. 'Where's Peter today?'

I shrugged. 'How should I know? Back at the Palace, plotting something or other, I suppose. Half his luck. At least it will be cooler there.' In fact, I knew he was having meetings with some of the older ambassadors who had declined to be shuttled round the countryside in the heat, but I saw no reason to tell Harry that. The less he knew about anything to do with Peter or with me, the better I should be pleased. I had no wish to be talked about in the bars of Bangkok.

Oddly enough, I was enjoying myself in a sort of a way, mainly because Soumidath was. He was an immensely affectionate man, and today he was gathering his people to him in the fleshly contact he loved, pressing old men to his bosom, taking children in his arms and kissing them over and over when they put their tender arms round his neck. With foreigners tagging along, we were only visiting the more prosperous areas near the capital, and there were no horrors to spoil the day.

As far as I could tell, the Prince's ardour was returned. There was nothing mechanical in the way his people greeted him. They surged close, chanting his name, and the older men and women wept to see him. He talked non-stop and excitedly, telling them, the interpreter said, that the bad days were over, there would be no more killing, and this year the sowing would be done, and the harvest reaped. Once their country had been an exporter of rice; in two or three years, it would be exporting again.

'That I will believe when I see it,' Harry said morosely, wiping a river of sweat from his neck. 'They will be lucky if they can even feed themselves within five years. The fighting isn't over yet, not by a long way.'

It was a hard day, and I was glad when we got back at dusk, and I could strip off my sweaty clothes and take a shower. I was down to the basics of a dress and knickers, but in that Turkish bath atmosphere it was impossible to stay cool.

We were being given an official dinner that night by the Civic Council, hastily appointed without benefit of elections after Liberation to try to get the capital back into working order. The Council had a big job on its hands: electricity and water supplies were still intermittent, the drains overflowed every time it rained, and in the back streets, people were living in rat-infested, makeshift shelters of bamboo and corrugated iron. The capital was swollen with refugees from areas in the countryside where the armies had fought, and Penn said one of the new administration's first tasks was to persuade them to go back to their homes.

Son Sleng and Ieng Nim were at the dinner, but not Soumidath. Peter, sitting opposite me, said it was not *de rigueur* for the Prince to come to these sort of things.

He laughed when I said I thought things had changed now that there was a democratic state of Free Khamla.

The speeches and the dinner were both mercifully short, the civic leaders, some of them rather old, not having the staying power of Soumidath. As we left the Hôtel de Ville, a grand, decaying building in French colonial style, Peter took my arm. 'I've my own car outside. I'll drive you back to the villa,' he said briefly.

He came in with me to my rooms, without invitation, and, turning on the side lights in the sitting room, closed and locked the door. 'We don't want Harry or any of his boozy chums barging in,' he said when I raised my eyebrows.

He came then and took me in his arms, holding me close and tenderly. But when I turned my head to kiss him, he moved away and sat down on the settee, drawing me with him.

He looked at me very intently. 'When are you going back to Bangkok? Tomorrow, with Harry?'

I shook my head. 'No, the day after. There is a temple tour and a visit to the old capital site at Baranyang on the programme tomorrow and I didn't want to miss it.'

'Yes, you will enjoy that. The ruins are very fine, although not as good as Vangkhorn,' he said absently. 'Listen, Gilly.' He ran his fingers through his hair and cleared his throat. 'I want to sleep with you here, tonight and tomorrow night. Can I?'

I was amazed. 'Do you really think you have to ask? Did you think I would not want to?'

He flushed. It was the first time I had seen any colour in his clear, tanned skin. 'No, I didn't think that. It's just that I have to say something to you, and I'm afraid that you will take it as – well, as some sort of snub, or a put-down.'

I had seen this coming and was prepared. 'You are going to tell me once again you don't want to get involved, and that you only like sleeping with people who don't care about you,' I said wearily.

'Don't sound like that.' He took my hands and held them tight. 'I just don't want you to get hurt, that's all. It's true what I told you before. I can't afford to get involved, the way I live. I also told you that I don't think I'm fit any more for normal life, and that's even truer. I'm not a good bet, Gilly.'

I took a deep breath. 'You really are very old-fashioned, Peter.'

He looked surprised. 'Old-fashioned?'

'You've been living in abnormal circumstances for so long you've failed to catch up with the permissive society. Going to bed with someone isn't a matter of life and death.'

He stared at me, and I could still see a faint disbelief in his face, so I smiled at him, and made my voice very light.

'Do you seriously think that if we sleep together once or twice, I will try to drag you back to Bangkok to set up house? I have a husband already, you know.'

He laughed briefly. 'That shit.'

'He's not such a shit as you think. We had a reconciliation in New York a little while ago. This is the tangible sign of it.' I was wearing the opal ring David had given me, and I waved it at him mockingly.

'Did you now?' The disbelief had been replaced by something like annoyance. 'But you wouldn't go back to him?'

'I might. And again I might not.' I hesitated, for I do not like lying, but all that really mattered to me was that I should not frighten him away again. 'As a matter of fact, I have a boyfriend in Bangkok.' When I saw his face I laughed and said. 'Did you really think I was living like a nun and waiting for the great Peter Casement to soften up?'

'Of course not.' He let my hands go, and got up to pour himself a glass of mineral water. 'Who is this man? Do I know him?' he said over his shoulder.

'No, I don't think so. Not your type. He's an English

academic, on an exchange tour at the university.' I was improvising wildly. 'Rather like David, you see. I seem to attract them.'

He put down his glass and came to me, holding my shoulders hard. 'Shut up,' he said softly. 'I don't want to hear about your other boyfriends. There's just us here now.'

As we were walking into the bedroom, he hesitated again, and drew me round to face him. 'I hope I'm right in thinking you're on the pill, Gilly,' he said lightly. 'If you're not, there's no way I am going to take any risks of . . .'

I stopped his mouth with my own. 'Of course I am. Do you take me for a complete fool? I told you I had a boyfriend in Bangkok.'

I was lying, I hadn't taken the pill since the night David left me in Bangkok, to fly back to London.

Later, as we lay languidly in the moonlight striping the bed, I took his hand, and turned my face to his. 'You didn't really tell me the end of the story.'

'The story about your mother and father.' His body stiffened in protest, but I tightened my hand in his. 'There must have been something more. When you went back to Belfast the second time, when you were grown up.'

He sighed. 'I don't know how you knew that. You're intruding into my mind, Gilly. I'm not sure that I like that.'

'You've done it to me more than once. It's only fair,' I said briefly. 'Tell me, and we won't talk of it again.'

His old defensive manner came back. 'There's not likely to be much chance of that. After tomorrow, we won't be seeing each other for some time, if at all.' He raised himself on his elbow. 'There was a sort of little epilogue. I was in Ulster for Reuters, for the aftermath of Bloody Sunday, and when I had some time I went along to the flats where we used to live.

'I had some vague idea of trying to find where Mick

Ahern had gone. I thought I might kill him,' he said conversationally.

'I tapped on the door of the flat we lived in, and a little old man with a walking stick came out. He said he was the caretaker, and asked me who I wanted. He didn't know me, but I knew him.'

'It was Mick Ahern?'

'Right first time. He was old and sick and grey, crippled with arthritis, and with a face like a death's head. His head barely came up to my shoulder. There was no way I could have touched him.'

'What did you do?'

He laughed. 'Would you believe I told him my name, and he shook hands and invited me in and made me tea. I hardly said a word, but he talked on and on about my mother, and how fond of her he had been, and how he had hoped to be able to take care of the two of us. "It was a terrible thing, she did. Terrible! Terrible! And that poor little boy," he kept saying over and over. He seemed to forget I was the boy, and then he remembered, and he squeezed my hand, and the tears came into his eyes.

'I asked what he was doing in my parent's flat, and he said after my mother died, he didn't have the heart to move to the new place, for without a woman, it wouldn't have been a proper home. He stayed in his own flat for a while, but then this one was vacant because no one wanted to live there after what had happened, and he moved in.

'"I could imagine your ma here, and it comforted me," he said. "Every week I have a Mass said for the repose of her soul, do you know that? It's an expense, now that I've retired, and the money's short but I keep it going. Ah, she was a lovely woman. I'll never forget her." When I left him, he cried again, and asked me to promise to come back. I never did.'

'So you don't really know whether he was responsible for your father's death.'

He shook his head. 'Life's not as tidy as that, dear Gilly. It's full of unsolvable mysteries, and that is probably just as well. I'm not even sure that I care any more. They are all dead, old Mick as well, I suppose.' He turned towards me, and put his hand on my breast, moving it gently as though he was searching for my heart beat. 'I'm getting old, Gilly. I'll be thirty-nine next week. My father was thirty-five when he died, and my mother was thirty. It's strange to me to think I've lived longer than either of them.'

* * *

The Bangkok plane left at noon, and Peter had been caught up all morning with discussions at the Palace, but just as I had given him up, his car came racing onto the tarmac in a cloud of dust, and he got out, looking anxious.

'I thought I'd miss you. It was hard to get away.' He sounded breathless, but he held out to me a small box made of bronze brocade with gold patterning, with small ivory clasps. 'A present from the Prince.'

I opened the box with difficulty, for my fingers were trembling. Inside, resting in a bed of ruched yellow silk was a miniature: not a true portrait, but the Smiling Buddha, done in enamel, and surrounded by a circlet of small diamonds. It was mounted on a golden pin.

I looked at Peter in amazement. 'I'm not sure how you are going to wear it,' he said smiling. 'The Prince had half a dozen or so made for the senior ambassadors. It's meant to be pinned to a sash with a dress uniform, or something of the sort. But he put one aside specially, and asked me to give it to you. You've taken his fancy, for some reason.' He took the miniature from me and looked at it critically. 'You could always hock it and buy something more suitable. The diamonds are small, but they are quite good stones.'

'Of course I won't sell it. What do you take me for?'

He laughed. 'Don't look so indignant. Come on, Gilly, you'll have to go. Everybody else is on board.' He took my hand and kissed it formally, then kissed me lightly on both cheeks, the Prince's aide farewelling an honoured guest. 'Take care of yourself.'

I waved at him with equal lightness from the plane window. But later, after take-off, I went and wept in the smelly toilet.

* * *

I had been back in Bangkok for nearly two months before I realised I was pregnant. My periods had always been irregular anyway, except when I was on the pill, and being late, or even missing out altogether was nothing out of the way. For some reason, I had not even thought of the possibility, either when I slept with David in New York or with Peter. The idea of maternity never interested me very much, and I hadn't spent much time considering it. But when I found I was nauseated every morning, and that my breasts were enlarged and tender, with darkened nipples, I went to a Thai doctor in the street behind my flat. I had no wish to go to the European hospital, and run into someone I knew in the surgery.

I had to wait a long time, with rows of bulging Thai women who looked at me curiously, and the doctor at first seemed rather hesitant about examining me. I was not his patient, he said. He did not see many European ladies. But when I sat on stubbornly, he gave way, and started to ask questions. When I slid down from the examination couch, he congratulated me, and said my husband would be very pleased.

'You are rather old to have a first child, madame,' he said. 'You must have waited a long time.' I raised my eyebrows at that, and he said hastily: 'Perhaps not by your standards, of course. But our girls often marry at sixteen, you know. By your age they have five or six children.'

He was shorter than I, and he looked me up and down admiringly. 'You are a fine, strong lady, and very healthy. I think you will give your husband a son.'

I had been going to suggest delicately to him that he might tell me, instead, where I could get an abortion, but I had not the heart. I would have to enquire elsewhere.

I did nothing for a week. The morning sickness was negligible, and I felt very well, and looked it too. The legendary bloom of early pregnancy, I said mockingly to myself, looking at my face in the mirror. But what do I do now?

I went to the bureau, and got out the only letter Peter had written me since I left the capital. It was quite light-hearted, saying simply that he had been very glad to see me, and perhaps we might meet again one of these days, though he did not expect to be in Bangkok for some considerable time. He conveyed regards from the Prince and from Penn, and signed himself 'As ever, Peter.' It was a letter a stranger might have written, and it told me nothing.

But time was passing, and I had to make some sort of decision before it was too late. I had an idea in my mind, and I had to talk to someone, so I talked to Bill Geraghty.

'I'm pregnant, Bill,' I said abruptly. We were in his office, rather late, having a beer before we went home.

For a moment, he actually looked rather pleased. 'Up the duff at last!' He reached for my hand and squeezed it. 'You're one girl I thought it would never happen to. Are you glad? No, of course you're not,' he said hastily, seeing my face. 'Not a good idea, I suppose.'

'I need your advice, Bill. I'm not sure what I should do.'

He drank his beer hurriedly. 'Yes, of course. I'm not much on advice, but I'll do my best. Who is the father, by the way? Not your husband, too long away.' He looked at me hard. 'Not Harry, for Christ's sake. At one hint of something like this, that bastard would take off for the bush, and we wouldn't see him for months. Not the paternal type, old Harry.'

'Not Harry.' I hesitated, but there was really no one else I could talk to, and I thought Bill was fond enough of me to keep his mouth shut. 'Peter Casement.'

Bill screwed up his face. 'Oh, fuck it, that's worse. The enigmatic aide to Princes. He's not the paternal type either, and he isn't even here. Have you told him?'

'No, and I'm not going to. He doesn't want to get involved.'

'He wouldn't,' Bill said angrily. 'He's famous for it. Lives with Thai whores, they say, and pays for it.' He spilt his beer. 'Sorry, love, I shouldn't have said that.'

'It doesn't matter. I knew it already. It doesn't make any difference to me.'

He looked hard at me. 'You really fancy him, don't you?'

'Yes,' I said desolately. 'Yes. But he doesn't feel the same way. Or at least he could, but he won't. Bill, I want to go back to Khamla and see him.'

'I thought you said you weren't going to tell him?'

'I'm not. I just want to see him again, before I make up my mind.' I got up and started to walk restlessly about, while Bill watched me. 'I don't know why. It just seems important to me. At the moment, I can't decide anything.'

'You mean you might keep the kid?'

'I might. It would be more sensible not to, but I might. I won't know until I see Peter.'

He looked at me impatiently. 'Christ, women! How in hell can it make any difference, just seeing him, unless you tell him and see what he says?'

'I don't know. But it will.' I sat down and drank the last of the warm beer. 'I'm going to the Khamla consulate tomorrow, to ask for an immediate visa. Will you give me a week off?'

'Of course I will. More if you want it. And I'll ask Minnie for the name of a couple of useful doctors, just in case. She's been up the duff herself, more than once.' Minnie was the half-Chinese girl he lived with. Her real name was Ming-lin, and I thought I could probably trust her.

Getting a visa wasn't as easy as I thought. The consulate did not quite turn me down, but they gave me the usual line of patter about it not being a convenient time, and how conditions in the capital were such it was difficult to make foreigners comfortable. I pressed them as hard as I dared, but they remained non-commital about when I could expect a visa to come through. I even showed them the miniature of the Smiling Buddha, but the consular officer merely admired it, and pushed it back across the table as though it meant nothing.

Bill was not in the least surprised when I told him what had happened. 'I didn't want to upset you last night, but I really didn't think you had a cat's chance in hell of getting a visa,' he said.

'Why not? There's nothing happening in Khamla, is there? Nothing out of the way, I mean.'

'Dunno. And that's partly what makes me suspicious. There's really no news coming out at all, and with a new government in power, there should be a steady stream.' He put his feet up on the desk and leaned back. 'I had a drink a couple of days ago with an AFP chap who had just come back. He said everybody was polite, but obstructive, and he wasn't allowed to leave the capital. He asked to see the Prince, who he knows quite well from the old days, and got a knock-back. The word round town is that your pal Soumidath is losing ground, and those other bastards are taking over.' He shook his head at me. 'I don't think you should go, love.'

I took no notice. I didn't know exactly why I wanted to go to Khamla, for I really had no intention at all of telling Peter about the baby. But I was obsessed with the idea of seeing him, even only once more: an aberration of pregnancy, I suppose.

That night, I rang Penn in the capital. There were still not too many phones connected in Khamla, but he had one, as a senior cadre, and had given me his number on my last visit. He had wanted me to come to his house and meet his wife, but I had put him off, reluctant to lose the chance of spending the last evening with Peter.

He answered himself, and when I told him what I wanted, over the crackling line, he sounded as reluctant as the Khamla consular officer. 'What reason could you give for requesting a visa?' His voice was faint and I had to strain to hear it. 'You cannot come as a tourist or an ordinary visitor. We are not admitting people unless they come on business.'

I had already made provision for that, ringing Sam Samuels in New York that afternoon, and selling him the idea of some voice pieces on life in the new Khamla. He had promised to send me cabled authority so I could show it at the consulate.

'That may make it possible,' Penn said when I told him, but he still sounded doubtful. 'Perhaps M. Casement can also help. Does he know you wish to come?'

'No, and I beg you not to tell him. It is meant to be a surprise. Please, Penn. Don't spoil it.' I had no doubt that if Peter heard anything of this, he would do his best to block me.

Penn was instantly suspicious. 'I think it would be better if you delayed your visit for a little while. We are all very busy now, and we would not be able to entertain you as we would wish. Leave it for a month or two, dear madame, and I shall be pleased to help you.'

'No,' I said. 'I must come now.'

There was silence for a moment, and I thought he had rung off. Then I heard a child call out somewhere in the background, and Penn said hurriedly I must excuse him for a little, his wife was ill, and the boy had woken and needed attention. He would call me back later, and with that he did put the phone down.

It was nearly midnight when he rang, and I had long since given up hope. But he sounded quite different this time, more like the old Penn, his voice coming clearly over the line. He had been thinking over my request, he said, and he believed it would be possible to arrange a visa. 'We would not do it for everyone, but you are an old friend, and we will be delighted to see you,' he said. 'You must not expect too much. As I said, we are very busy here. But we will do what we can to help you. Go to the consulate after one or two days and they will have your visa for you.'

He was over-optimistic. It actually took a week, mainly, I think, because the consular officer was sullen and obstructive. Bill, rather unusually, took time off to drive me to the airport. 'Take care,' he said. 'If you're not back within a week I'll send in a search party.'

I was surprised to see that the plane was nearly empty, and what passengers there were were officials. The supply of visas must really have been cut off. When we touched down at the other end, Penn was waiting for me, and took me straight to an official car, without bothering with immigration or customs inspection. Instead of the well-cut safari suits he had worn during my last visit, he was in an old pair of khaki trousers, with a bush shirt hanging out over them.

He must have seen me look at his clothes in some astonishment. 'The proletarian look is in fashion at the moment, madame,' he said lightly. 'All of us who have foreign-made suits are keeping them in the wardrobe.'

As we drove into town, he kept up a steady flow of chatter about the weather, and how it was likely to affect next season's rice crops. It was unlike him, and I almost ceased to listen, watching instead for glimpses of familiar landmarks. These shabby streets, steaming under the sun and scarred with war, had now for me a sweet expectancy and my life seemed divided into compartments by the drive to and from the airport.

But Penn fell silent beside me, and as we came closer to the centre of the capital, my own rising spirits drained away. Whole streets of shops seemed to be shut up, with sheets of galvanised iron dragged over their glassless windows, and a cement factory which the Prince had been filmed opening was also boarded up, with soldiers standing guard at the gates.

There were very few people on the streets – or rather there were people, but they were the young fighters of the Liberation Army, many more of them than last time, still in their ragged uniforms and with Armalites and AK-47s slung over their shoulders. They were not walking on the sidewalks but in the middle of the road, and when our driver hooted to force a way through, they parted sullenly, and a couple of them banged on the roof of the car with their rifle butts as we drove slowly on. Down a side street, another group was dragging along a skeletal white cow, which was lowing in distress.

'Our peasant soldiers, who fought so well for us,' Penn said curtly beside me. 'More and more of them come in from the countryside every day. They should be in their villages, planting the rice, but they have become used to war, and think working the land is only for old people.'

I put my hand lightly on his thin arm. He was not, I noticed, wearing the digital watch he had shown us so proudly on our last visit.

'It happens everywhere. They'll get tired of life in the big city, and go home soon enough.' I was by no means certain of that, but he looked so strained, I wanted to find some way to reassure him.

I was not at the villa this time, but at a small hotel in a side street, and Penn apologised for it. 'It does not look very nice, but they are friends of mine, and they will try to make you comfortable,' he said. 'The Grand Imperial' – he was talking about the capital's only large hotel, where foreigners usually stayed – 'is not so good now. There have been some attacks on visitors there. Nothing much, but some stone throwing, and smashing of windows, you understand. It will be safe for you here.'

I was surprised at this, but said nothing. He came up with me to inspect the room, which was small and bare, but passably clean. The bathroom had a concrete floor and a permanent dripping shower.

'Don't worry, dear Penn, it's only for a few days,' I said, laughing at his anxious face. 'I'm a veteran of jungle camps, remember.'

'Of course,' He took my hand to make his formal farewell. 'But do not fear I will leave you here to dine alone. I will call for you at six and bring you to my house. My wife is still ill, but my sister-in-law will come and cook for us. You have seen my little girl, but not yet the boy.'

I looked at him uneasily. 'I can't tonight, Penn. I will another night, I promise, but tonight I want to see Peter Casement. Is he at the Palace?'

Penn shook his head, and laughed nervously, conveying embarrassment in the Asian style. 'I am very sorry. M. Casement is not in the capital. You would not let me tell him you were coming, so he has gone away.'

I sat down heavily on the bed, feeling faint and nauseated. It was stupid, but it was the one thing I had not thought of. 'It's all right, it's just the heat,' I said impatiently, as Penn watched me with alarm. 'When is he coming back?'

Penn cleared his throat. 'It is a strange thing. I asked at the Palace, and they said he was only away for a few days, so I did not worry. I thought he would be here to greet you, but he has not returned.'

'Where did he go? Somewhere abroad?' I did not much like the way Penn was fidgeting, and letting his gaze slide away from mine. 'No, no. Only to Vangkhorn. We have some of our own archaeologists there now, and he was to discuss with them when they would be ready to receive a group of foreign experts. We want to start a programme of preservation at the Great Temple, and already we have offers of help from all over the world.'

'That should not take more than a couple of days.' I was feeling genuinely nauseous now, and Penn, in his agitation, had lit a strong-smelling local cigarette, without asking my permission as he usually did.

'So I thought.' He gave me an anxious smile, showing a new gold tooth. 'But I am sure there is nothing to worry about. the Palace says he may have also gone to the north, where there has been trouble between the peasants and the soldiers. Two village headmen have been shot, so we have heard.'

'That's no business of Peter's,' I said coldly. 'He told me his role was to deal with foreigners.'

Penn looked at me warily. 'That is so, of course. But sometimes I think the Prince employs him on other affairs, to be his eyes and ears, you know. He cannot always be sure . . .'

He broke off. 'Dear Madame Herbert, you are tired from the flight and I will leave you to rest. If you are concerned about your friend, I will make further inquiries at the Palace and it is possible I may have some news for you tonight. Do not forget, I shall come at six.'

When I had washed my face and hands, I felt better, and going down to the desk I found a boy, a student, who spoke French, and bullied him into ringing up the Palace for me. He wasn't happy about it, but I gave him a pack of the American cigarettes I had brought in for Penn. I was not sure that Penn himself was telling the truth, and there was something in his manner that unnerved me.

But after a short, shouted conversation, the boy put down the phone and said he had been told that the foreigner was not there, and they did not know where he was, or when he was returning.

'They called him that? The foreigner?'

'Yes, no more than that. Not by his name. They said I should not have telephoned for you. You must not ask me again, madame.' He tried to slide the cigarettes back over the counter to me, but I shook my head. 'Keep them,' I said, and went wearily upstairs.

Penn came promptly at six, as he promised. He did not have an official car this time, but a battered and coughing old saloon, a relic, he said, of the automobile industry the Prince had tried to start in Khamla in the sixties. The headlights made very little impression on the dusk as we drove through rutted back streets. I waited for him to mention Peter, but he did not, so I was forced to ask.

'Nothing, madame Gilly, nothing at all.' He swerved violently to avoid an ox-cart coming out of a gateway. 'Again the people at the Palace say they do not know when he will return, and I cannot press them. It is not my business, you see.'

'Could you not ask the Prince? He would surely have been in touch with Peter.' It was growing difficult not to sound too anxious.

'I have not seen the Prince for some time, madame, except at official ceremonies. I cannot telephone him, for all calls now go through the Prime Minister's office. It is said that Prince Soumidath has himself requested this, as he is busy with matters of state, but I do not know if this is true.'

He brought the car to a jerky halt in the drive of a small colonial villa, rioting vines half-concealing the peeling pink stucco of its walls, and got out to open the door for me. 'It would be a mistake to make many more enquiries, madame. M. Casement will be back at any time, I am sure. I will hear of it, and let you know as soon as he arrives. Come now, you must meet my family at last.'

Penn's wife was a surprise. For some reason, I had expected a little, dumpy, clever woman but instead saw a thin, pale girl, obviously Eurasian, lying on a cane chaise longue in a sparsely furnished salon. She was young enough to be his daughter, probably no older than I, and when she slid gently to her feet to greet me, I saw she was, by local standards, quite tall, taller than Penn.

Her hair was black and long, worn in a French roll, and her skin was not gold, but a dull ivory, lacking the ripe bloom of the region. Her sick, delicate beauty was astonishing, and Penn smiled when he saw my look.

'She is very pretty, no,' he said awkwardly in English. 'I do not say it in French, for she know it already, and it make her more vain.'

Madame Penn was murmuring a welcome in unaccented Parisian French. She had a trick of speaking very softly, so one had to bend close to hear her, and this created a curious sensation of intimacy. Penn lowered her carefully to the couch, and covered her legs with a silk shawl, though the night was stifling.

He was bubbling with joy at the meeting, and told his wife the story of how Harry and I had come to the Great Temple and lived there with the fighters. She had clearly heard it all before, but she smiled up at him with love, and put her transparent hand on my arm, as I sat beside the chaise longue.

'I envy you, madame, that you are so strong,' she said in her low, murmuring voice. 'I would have been happy to be with my husband in the camp, but I could not go. The life would kill me.' In another woman, it would have sounded like an affectation, but looking at the emaciation of her arms, her delicate, unmarked feet, and at the beautiful skull beneath the skin, I did not doubt she was telling the exact truth.

The children came in then, the girl I had met before very shy, the little boy unexpectedly strong and boisterous. Both were quite dark-skinned like their father, and it was hard to see any of their mother in them. They shook hands with me politely at Penn's insistence, and the girl made a well-schooled little speech of welcome in French. But it was clear where the attraction in that room was. They circled their mother's couch like moths, though they obviously knew they must not throw themselves upon her. She gave each of them a hand, mumuring to them in that extraordinary voice, and the two dark heads bent as close as they dared. Penn stood watching them, totally absorbed. I think he had forgotten I was even in the room until his wife reminded him with a sideways look.

Children turn me rather awkward, and I was glad that I did not have to make conversation with them over dinner, for they were sent away as soon as the meal was served. Penn's sister-in-law brought in a bowl of rice and a whole fish on a platter, then went back to the kitchen to feed the children. She preferred not to stay, Penn said, for she spoke no French.

We ate on plates on our laps, for Madame Penn did not want to sit up at the dining table. I noticed she ate very little, playing with her food, though her husband tried to tempt her with the most succulent pieces of the fish. Penn seemed preoccupied, and I was nervy and anxious, so I thought we were in for a difficult dinner.

But Madame Penn, whatever other strengths she lacked, was a skilled and artful conversationalist. The low murmuring voice filled all the awkward silences, gently probing as she asked me about my life in Bangkok, and the work I did there, telling me how she had come to meet Penn, when she was a student and he was a professor. 'Very old and very severe,' she said, laughing at him. To my own surprise, I found myself telling her I had met David in the same way, and we made little jokes about the coincidence. She did not ask anything further about my marriage and I wondered what Penn had said to her about Peter.

After a while, Penn asked her to sing, saying she would surprise me. I could see she was tired and would have preferred not to perform for us, but she made no real protest as he propped her up with cushions. Her voice was small, and not as miraculous as he clearly thought it, but it was sweet and true, even when she pushed it into the wailing head sound needed for the Khamla ballads she sang interspersed with French art songs.

I lay back in my chair and closed my eyes and listened. The heavy, languid air moved sluggishly in the salon, scented faintly with the acrid sweetness of mosquito coils. Madame Penn's high, thin voice sang the drawn-out lament of a girl who had lost her lover in some forgotten war. When it trailed away at last, I opened my eyes and saw Penn watching his wife, with the mark of tears on his cheek. I felt pleasurably melancholy, but relaxed. All my tension had gone, and with it the nausea which had been hovering early in the evening.

Madame Penn smiled at us, but she looked deadly pale, and I got up and said bluntly that we were tiring her, and I thought I should go. 'No,' she said, taking my hand. 'Please do not. I will leave you, for I go early to bed, but you must stay a little. My husband wishes to talk to you.' She gave me a strange look, as though she was begging me for something.

She shook hands formally and wished me goodnight, walking slowly to the door, with her hand on Penn's arm. But the door swung open after they had gone through, and I saw her put her arms round his neck as he lifted her, and carried her into the back part of the house.

'Your wife is very ill,' I said when he came back. It did not seem a time for equivocation, for I knew that what he was going to say to me was connected with Madame Penn.

He nodded, and sat down opposite me, clasping his hands tightly. 'Her illness began after the birth of the first child, our girl. The doctors said that she should not have another, but she insisted, for she wanted a boy.' He made an apologetic grimace. 'And I, too, of course. It is wrong, of course, and we tell the peasants that, but it is hard to get out of the old way of thinking.'

He lit a cigarette, one of the Lucky Strikes I had brought him. 'She has some sort of anaemia, you know, a very rare kind. Our doctors could not tell what was wrong, but when I sent her to France it was diagnosed. My wife was much better in Paris, and the treatment seemed to be successful. I would not have let her return had I known how ill she would become.'

'But the hospital here is reopened, and medical supplies are coming in. Can the doctors here not help her?'

'No, for the drugs must come from America or from Europe, and they are very expensive. It would be uneconomic, the hospital says, to spend so much to treat just one person. But if she does not have such medicines soon, I think that my wife will die.'

I thought that this was true, remembering the touch of Madame Penn's hand on my sleeve, so light that it was like being touched by a ghost. 'What will you do? Can you not take her to Europe yourself?'

He smiled gently. 'Oh, I have not the funds for that any longer. Everything we have now belongs to the state, did you not realise it? This house, a plantation my father had, everything. But I have sold my wife's rings, and there is enough for air fares for her and for the children as far as Bangkok.' A long silence fell in the room. Somewhere in the back of the villa I could hear children's voices but there was no other sound.

'I want you to take them to Bangkok. All three,' Penn said abruptly.

I watched him carefully in the pale light of the table lamp. 'Is that why you helped me with my visa?'

He evaded my glance. 'It is only as far as Bangkok itself,' he said stiffly. 'My wife has a relative there who works for UNESCO, a French citizen who goes quite often to Paris, to the headquarters. He will meet you at the airport and arrange everything. It is not so much to ask!'

'Of course I will take her.' It would have to wait, I said to myself silently, until Peter's return. 'But why do you not go with her yourself?'

He shook his head. 'Things are rather difficult at the moment. I do not believe I can get an exit visa. Besides, you know, it is better if I stay.' He laughed suddenly, the lines of tension breaking up on his face. 'Everyone is in a fever now, but when their blood cools, they will need some older, wiser heads. The country is being run by . . .' He broke off. 'This is boring for you, madame. Let us talk instead of when my wife can leave.'

It would take some days, he said, to obtain the exit permits, and this made me feel less guilty. By then, Peter would certainly be back. I asked Penn if there would be any problem with the permits for his wife and the children.

'I think not.' He hesitated. 'My wife is of mixed blood, as you have seen. Her grandfather was French, a general who fought the rebels here, and his blood has come out in her. It is strange, for her mother, the general's daughter, was small and dark-skinned, and her sisters are the same. Only she is different.'

'And this makes things difficult for her.'

'Only for the present. They are reviving a little cult of racial purity, you know. It often happens in the early days of revolutions, then everyone forgets about it. But just in this period people of mixed race are not so popular. They are being told that if they wish to leave the country, they can do so.' He was chain-smoking, the ashtray by his side full of butts.

'It worries me a little that my children are also classed in this category, though they show no sign of foreign blood,' Penn said. 'It is for their sake, as well as my wife's, that I am sending them away. When my wife is better, and all this nonsense has blown over, they can come back.' He got up, looking apologetic. 'But it is late, and you are very tired, I can see. I will drive you back to the hotel, and we can talk again tomorrow.'

Peter did not come back the next day, or the day after. Penn did what he could for me, taking me to see the director of the museum in the capital. He spoke English of sorts, and I got him on tape talking about the conservation work at Vangkhorn. It was something I could sell to Big Brother to justify my trip.

The afternoon stretched endlessly, though, and the evening yawned before me. Penn apologised for not entertaining me. He had a cadres' meeting which he could not miss, and his wife was staying in bed to muster what strength she could for the trip. I ate some rice and bony fowl in the dingy hotel dining room, but when I had finished it was still only a little after eight, so I went restlessly out in the dark streets, stumbling on the cracked and rutted sidewalks, meeting no one except an occasional dark figure hurrying past me with averted head.

Peter had once told me that this little city was the liveliest and most charming in that part of Asia, after dark. 'It will be again one of these days, you'll see,' he had said confidently the last time I was here.

I was lost in the maze of streets, but then I saw a temple roof dark and serrated against the sky, and I knew where I was. The gate to the Temple of One Hundred Buddhas was open, and I went cautiously into the courtyard. It seemed a thousand years since I had come down the road from the guesthouse, the message from Peter in my shirt pocket; Ieng Nim waiting for me in the darkness.

There was a light inside the temple, enough to show the two long lines of Buddhas standing serenely side by side, just as they had done that night. No one had defaced them, at least.

A shout of laughter came from the temple itself. I went silently in the darkness to a window at the far end, and looked in. The ragged children were there again, the young fighters from the bush camps in their stained and sweaty uniforms, the automatic rifles which seemed to have become part of their bodies, like an extra limb, draped over their shoulders.

They had cornered two young monks this time, boys no older than themselves, with shaven heads and the darker yellow robes of novices. The young fighters had formed a semi-circle round them, and their leader appeared to be giving some sort of ferocious sermon: the evils of Buddhism as a State religion, no doubt. The two young monks were grinning nervously, and one of them, with some bravado, was smoking a cigarette.

Some of the young fighters were growing tired of this, and began to shout. A boy who looked no more than fifteen or sixteen sprang forward, and started nudging the smaller of the two novices with the barrel of his rifle, playfully at first, but with the jabs getting harder, until the other boy cried out in panic. The leader held up his hand and seemed to be proposing some sort of joke, for everybody laughed.

The two novices did not laugh, however. They tried to back away as the rifles lifted to cover them, but the one behind came up against the steps of an altar on which a reclining Buddha stretched majestically, and stumbled and fell. One of the young fighters pulled him roughly to his feet, and the leader gave an order, which half a dozen voices repeated eagerly.

I saw then what the joke was meant to be, for both the novices, fumbling with shaky fingers, drew their robes down from their shoulders, and, untying the folds from round their waists, dropped them to the floor and stood naked in the shadow of the Buddha.

Their bodies were very small and bony, and with their bald heads and faces furrowed with humiliation, they looked like sad little old men. One may have been a little older than the other, for he took the smaller one's hand and held it tightly, while the young fighters jeered.

I had seen enough then, and I ran as silently as I could through the gate and down the road. I was not quick enough, though, to outrun a thin, desolate cry which floated for a moment on the heavy night, then died away.

When I was close to the hotel, I was stopped by an Army patrol, neatly dressed and business-like, which came jogging round the corner. 'Where are your papers, Madame?' their young officer said in heavily accented French. I had my passport in my shoulder bag, and he looked at it carefully in the dim light.

'Please go to your hotel at once,' he said curtly. 'It is almost curfew time.' I began to protest, for Penn had said nothing of curfews, but he cut me off. 'From tonight.' He gave me a perfunctory salute, with no courtesy in it. 'All foreigners must observe it. There are no exceptions for them any more.'

The next morning I woke up feeling a good deal saner and cool-headed than I had for some time. It now seemed to me more important to take Madame Penn to Bangkok than to wait for Peter. The obsessional need to see him was still there, nagging at me, but expediency was taking over. I did not like the way things were going.

Neither did Penn, who came in while I was having breakfast. 'Did you hear of the curfew?' he said uneasily. 'I could not warn you of it, because I did not know until it was too late to reach you.'

He brightened then, and said his wife was a little better, and was ready to travel. 'Even a few days ago, Linh did not want to leave me,' he said. 'But now she agrees it is necessary, not for her alone, but for the sake of the children.' He was, as I have said, a formal man, and it was the first time I had ever heard his wife's name. It was the same as that of the girl whom I had watched die in the shallows of the river at the Great Temple, and it made up my mind for me.

'I can leave at any time, even today, if there is a

plane. When will the exit permits be ready?'

He put down his cup with a gesture of frustration. 'That is a difficulty. I thought I would get them easily, but there are many delays. Some of the people in the bureaucracy are from the old régime, you know, and corrupt. They are asking for money.'

'I can let you have some travellers' cheques.' I hadn't brought much with me, but in that poor country it might be enough. Foreign currency was still at a premium.

He shook his head violently. 'No, no. I have something left, a little gold. You know what it is like here, we all keep some small bit of gold under the bed.' As he smiled briefly I saw his gold tooth flash. 'It was for a rainy day,' he said in English. 'But I think the rainy day has come.'

The real day stretched before me, as empty as the previous one. I was reluctant to leave without making one more try to find out where Peter had gone, so I walked slowly up to the Palace through the steaming morning.

At the gate the guards stopped me, but they did not seem hostile. I gave the more senior a note to take in to one of the Palace officials who had been friendly and helpful on my last visit. He was an older man who had spent some time abroad as a diplomat under the Soumidath régime, and he spoke both English and French.

I waited for over an hour in the blazing sun, standing in the dusty road. One of the guards, seeing my distress, invited me by a gesture to stand under the shade of the guardhouse canopy, but an officer came out and waved me angrily away. By the time a messenger came back with my note I was sick with heat and fatigue. The note was still sealed, and the name and title I had carefully printed on the envelope had been scored out with a heavy pen.

Penn rang in the late afternoon to say the curfew had

been brought forward to seven o'clock, and I must not leave the hotel that night. There was no news of the exit permits, though he hoped they might come through the next day. He did not mention Peter, and I did not have the heart to ask him. If he did hear of his return, he might not tell me in order that I should not put off my departure, yet there was nothing I could do but trust him.

I stretched out dinner as long as I could, but had no appetite, and at last I abandoned the attempt and went up to my room to lie on the bed under the mosquito net, fully-dressed, listening to the thin sound of a radio somewhere nearby and the high singing of the mosquitoes. The light was too bad to read, and after a while it went off, as it often did, and I fell asleep in the thick darkness.

I woke some time later to the sound of pounding feet. The light was still off, and I had no idea what time it was, but I got up and went cautiously to the window. There was a half-moon, and I could see that down below in the street people were moving in a dark stream. There must have been a couple of hundred of them, but they passed the hotel quite quickly, thudding along at a fast jog. Some of them carried torches, showing they were in the ragged uniforms of the camps, and had AK-47s slung over their shoulders.

Miraculously, my bedroom light came back on, and I put on my sandals and went downstairs. I was not alarmed, but I was desperately thirsty, so I took my vacuum flask down with me to see if I could get some hot water.

It was not until I came into the lobby that I looked at my watch, and saw that it was two o'clock in the morning. There was no one about but the young student, the son of the proprietor, who must have fallen asleep at the desk over his books, for he was stretching and yawning and looking out of the window.

'Who are those men?' He took my flask from me to

fill it from a hissing kettle he had been boiling for himself over a small spirit stove, and looked at me warily.

'Fighters,' he said, shrugging. 'They go on night manoeuvres, perhaps.'

But as I stretched out my hand to take the filled flask, an enormous explosion ripped through the night. It was so loud that we were both stunned by it, for a moment, and I dropped the vacuum flask, which went off like a bomb. A rain of small objects fell from shelves, and in the silence that followed, there was the slow tinkle of glass from a shattered window.

I thought I was going to faint or be sick, and the frightened face of the boy swam before me. Then the *patron* himself came shuffling from the back premises somewhere, a piece of batik wrapped hastily round his waist, blinking in the light.

He said something to the boy, then repeated it in his careful French for my benefit. 'It is the ammunition dump near the airport, madame, it cannot be anything else. My God, they will kill us all.'

As though the blowing of the dump had been a signal, we heard shots from somewhere not very far away, and distant shouting. The *patron* signalled his son to go into the street to see what was happening, but as the boy opened the door, we heard more firing, much closer this time, and he ducked hastily inside. He said something to his father, then locked and bolted the door. I saw that he was shaking slightly.

'My son says there are soldiers at the end of the street.' The *patron* was busy putting shutters over the windows, and spoke over his shoulder. 'Go up to your room, Madame, and turn off the light. The boy will come and tell you if the danger comes nearer.'

But as I stood by my window in the darkness, the shots and the shouting receded, like a tide going out. Towards dawn when, sleepless, I looked out again, I saw that fires were burning sullenly in the north sector of the city. Towards the airport, a great blaze made the sky as bright as morning.

As soon as Penn came the next day, I knew that the news was bad. 'The airport is closed,' he said, sitting heavily down opposite me at the breakfast table. 'The ammunition dump at the south end blew up last night – you must have heard it – and exploding shells flew through the air. The control tower burned, and the planes on the runway. All the hangars, too. There is nothing left.'

I drank my tea thoughtfully. 'But planes can still come in.'

He shook his head. 'No. The airspace over the country has been closed, by government edict, until the airport is repaired. Our planes are destroyed, and no foreign ones may come.'

I looked at him in dismay. 'Who set off the ammunition dump?'

'Who can tell?' He poured himself a bowl of tea, but his hands were trembling. 'Much of the ammunition is old and degenerated. It may have set itself off spontaneously. These things happen. But someone may have thrown a cigarette, or fired a shot . . .' His voice died away.

Then he looked up at me. 'There was trouble in the city as well. The young revolutionary fighters, many of them, came to the Palace and tried to enter it. The guards turned them back, but a number were killed. Now they have set up armed posts in the streets nearby. They are demanding that the Prince be given to them.'

'To kill?'

He looked sallow this morning, and very old. 'To kill, one supposes. But the Prime Minister will not consent. He can put down the rising, but he needs time. Prince Soumidath is safe enough.'

'And Peter Casement?' I said reluctantly.

He smiled at me. 'Oh, he too is safe enough, madame, I promise you. If he is wise, he will stay where he is, somewhere in the countryside, until this is over. They do not like him, you know, the revolutionary children. They do not think the Prince should have a foreigner at his side.'

I pushed my plate away. A familiar morning nausea was beginning to rise. 'So we cannot leave. Your wife, and the children, and I?'

He became amazingly business-like. 'But you can. You must take my car, and drive. It is only a small country, you know,' he said coaxingly. 'Within two days, three at the most, you will be over the border.'

The nausea was becoming stronger. 'It is impossible. I do not know the roads. And where would we get petrol?'

'Finding the way is no problem. My wife knows the country areas well, and we have good maps. She will guide you. As for petrol, you can buy it in the villages. News travels slowly here, and it must come by word of mouth. The government radio will remain silent on the matter of the trouble in the city.'

He took my hand and urged me to my feet. 'I will drive you to the bank to cash your travellers' cheques, all of them if you are willing. The banks are open today, but they will close if the trouble continues. Please, madame!'

His sallow skin was flushed with embarrassment, and I could not make him beg any longer. Only his despair could have made him so urgent.

* * *

We left in the early afternoon. The car was heavily loaded with food and petrol, and hearing the clutch rasp and the engine cough as Penn drove us to the exit road from the city, I thought we would be lucky if we reached the border. Madame Penn was in the back seat with a pillow propping her on either side, and the children leaning against her to support her. Her skin was a greenish-white colour, and I wondered what I would do if she died on the way. Penn talked feverishly, rehearsing me over and over on the route I must take, and I stumbled through the litany of village names. I had been afraid the children would cry, but they were as silent as their mother.

On the way out of the city we passed the hospital, a long white rambling building built by the French. It was run, I had heard, by a very old doctor, French-trained, who had lived through a number of régimes and taken little notice of any of them. He was a bully and a disciplinarian, and though the hospital could not treat a rare case like Madame Penn's, its general standards were high for that part of Asia.

Something was happening in the courtyard of the hospital, and Penn slowed down to look. Young revolutionary fighters had made two ragged lines from the main door of the hospital to the courtyard gate. There were regular soldiers there too in their neat uniforms, a small squad with an officer at their head, but they stood quietly at attention just outside the gate, making no attempt to interfere with what was happening in the courtyard.

The main door of the hospital was wide open, and through it was slowly filing a line of patients, still in their short gowns, as though they had been pulled out of bed. Most of them shuffled along, even the younger ones, blinking and bewildered in the glare of the afternoon. A couple of older men could hardly walk, and were leaning on the shoulders of frightened nurses. I saw some women with naked and frog-like babies which could only have been born a few hours ago.

The sad little procession passed between the two rows of young fighters. The boys and girls in their jungle clothes did not strike at them, but they shouted impatiently, urging them to hurry, making the fitter ones almost run. An open truck was waiting outside the hospital gates, and two or three young fighters standing beside it began to load the patients on to it, lifting them roughly up and throwing them towards the front. A young woman with her arm in plaster screamed with pain as they pushed her up, and the naked babies wailed dismally.

Penn jerked the car to a halt and, running, went to speak to the officer in charge of the platoon of regular soldiers. He was watching impassively, but he recognised Penn when he came up and saluted him.

After a minute or two Penn came back. 'It is a concession the Palace has made. The young fighters insist that the hospital become an army hospital. Patients who are dying may remain for the moment, but all others must go and no more civilians will be admitted.' He turned to his wife in the back seat. 'We are lucky, my darling, that you will soon be in Bangkok.' She smiled, and murmured something to him in her low voice, and he bent and kissed her hand. The children sat silent and rigid, their eyes fixed on the hospital gate.

'But, Penn! Where will these people go?' The loading of the truck was still continuing. I saw one old man slide to the ground and refuse to get up, even when they prodded him with their rifles. Two of the young fighters picked him up bodily and threw him into the back of the truck as though they were handling a sack of rice.

Penn smiled uneasily. 'Oh, they will go back to the countryside, to the villages. There are medical centres in each district, you know. The Prince himself set them up. It will not be so bad for them.' He drew me a little way away from the car, and spoke to me quietly.

'The old doctor, Dr Nouth, is dead, but you must not tell my wife this. She has known him since her childhood, and even when he did not have the drugs to treat her, he did for her what he could.' A little girl, about the age of his own daughter, was being loaded struggling onto the truck, and Penn shuddered and turned back to me. 'Dr Nouth would not let the fighters take the patients away. He said it was his hospital, and he would keep sick people there as long as they needed care. One of these mad children' – he gestured at the revolutionary fighters – 'struck him with a rifle butt. It was not a hard blow, the officer said, but he was a very old man, nearly eighty, and it was enough.'

I looked at the impassive squad of soldiers. 'Can they not do anything to stop this?'

He shook his head. 'I told you. The Palace is allowing the take-over of the hospital to satisfy the revolutionary group, and to keep them quiet for the time.' He passed his hand wearily over his eyes. 'It is not such a big concession to make, for it is in line with the Prime Minister's own thinking. The city is swollen with refugees. He wants to send them back to the countryside where they belong so the work of national reconstruction can begin.'

I looked over at the hospital. The wretched little exodus was dragging on. 'It's a pity he doesn't start with the revolutionary fighters themselves, instead of sentencing sick people to die.'

Penn laughed thinly. 'The young fighters are armed, that is their strength. We made a big mistake at the beginning, letting them run wild.' He gestured at the smart soldiers and their officer. '*They* did not win the war for us, you know, they are from the old régime. It was the young fighters who fought and died for a Free Khamla. Son Sleng felt he should let them have their heads for a little.' He got in and started the car. 'We must not waste any more time. The sooner you leave the city, the better it will be.'

A little way past the smouldering ammunition dump and the burned-out airport buildings, he drew up. 'I can get a bus back to the city, so I will leave you.' He hesitated for a moment, then opened the squeaking glove box. 'There is something here that I think you should take with you.'

It was a bundle tied up in an old scarf, and I unwrapped it. A heavy pistol lay in my hands, brand new by the look of it, and deadly. 'No, no,' Penn said hurriedly, seeing my face. 'You should not need to use it, it is just a precaution.' He lowered his voice again, so his wife and children would not hear. 'I think perhaps you do not understand that there are other armies than ours now in the countryside.'

'Sarr Mok's men?'

'His, and others. Most of them are no more than bandits, raiding villages for food and arms, but there are larger groups. We have sent our own regular forces out against them, but it will take a long time to sweep the provinces one by one.'

I looked at the gun lying in my lap, then I wrapped it up again, and handed it to him.

'No, Penn. I am not a soldier. I do not even know how to use it.' He tried to speak but I cut across him. 'If we run into trouble, I can kill one man, perhaps two. But there will be others, and if we have a gun, they will shoot back and murder us all.'

Madame Penn leaned forward. I am not sure whether she had been able to hear, but she had seen the gun. 'Madame Gilly is right,' she said in her low murmuring voice. 'It would be foolish to go armed.' She put her hand on her husband's arm. 'Madame herself is our best hope. When they see a foreigner, I do not think they will harm us.'

Penn made no further protest and, indeed, he did not speak again. He kissed my hand briefly and embraced his wife and children, then, without looking back, began to trudge down the road towards the bus stop. His shoulders were hunched and he looked old and tired.

I started the car awkwardly, and it went forward with a lurch. My stomach lurched too, and I wondered what Penn would think if he knew I was pregnant.

CHAPTER FOURTEEN

The roads were bad, and when we made camp that night we were already falling behind Penn's carefully drawn-up schedule. But Madame Penn guided us to a camping place beside a small stream. She remembered it, she said, from her childhood when they had come there to picnic and see the temple ruins. There was not much left of the ruins now, a few stone columns scarred with bullet holes and overgrown with jungle.

It was a calm, dry night, and I spread the blankets and pillows from the car beside the stream. Madame Penn had walked steadily enough the short distance from the road, but she lay down without protest with a couple of pillows under head when I said she could do nothing to help me. I could see in the light of the camp lantern that her forehead and upperlip were pearly with sweat, and her hand, when I took her pulse, was damp and cold.

Penn had given me some pills, so I brought them to her, with boiled water. She took them obediently, then lay back and closed her eyes. The boy, who had not spoken all day, crept up beside her and held her hand.

The girl, at a word from her mother, came to help me build the fire and heat a dish of rice and vegetables that Penn had had prepared for us. She was willing and deft. I suppose that even at her age she had to take some of the burden of housekeeping. She spoke good French, and said her brother did also, though he was sometimes foolish and pretended he did not.

I realised I did not know the children's names. Penn had mentioned them, but I had been too preoccupied to take them in.

'I have two names,' the girl said when I asked. 'In

France, I am called Fleur, and here I am called Lhaung. It means the same thing.' I repeated it cautiously after her, but I could not manage the difficult *Lh* sound, so I said I thought Fleur would be better. 'And your brother?'

'Oh, he has only one name. He is called Khim.' She spelled it for me. 'That is not so hard.'

Madame Penn had fallen asleep, and I did not disturb her until the children had finished eating, and had bedded down together under a rug. Fleur said I should not worry about the boy, she was used to looking after him and would make sure, tomorrow, that he washed himself in the stream. He was too tired tonight to be bothered.

They were already asleep when Madame Penn woke. She had promised her husband she would eat, and I carried a bowl of warm rice and vegetables over and sat beside her on the hard ground, coaxing her on from one mouthful to the other as if she was a child. She was very pale, and her eyes were shadowed, but she talked to me in her low voice as easily as if we had known each other all our lives. She spoke mainly of her children, saying they would stay with one of her French uncles while she was in hospital in Paris. 'They will be happy, for he has a house in the country. He was a *colon*, a big man in Khamla before the world war,' she said. 'He is quite rich.'

She ate most of the bowl of rice, more to please me, I think, than because she was hungry. When she had finished, I heated some water, and carefully washed her hands and face, then bent to sponge her dusty feet and legs.

She made a small sound of distress. 'There is no need, I could manage myself. Why do you put yourself to this trouble?'

Sitting there in the dark beside her, I told her of the girl, Linh, and how I had watched her die, and could do nothing to help her. I was not sure, myself, how or why these two things were connected, but Madame Penn seemed to understand me. 'It is my name also, Linh. You must call me by it,' she said in her low voice. 'We are too formal about names, we Asians.' She raised her transparent hand and put it briefly to my forehead. 'Goodnight, dear Gilly,' she said, and drifted into sleep.

Later that night, I heard a faint sound of a child whimpering, and saw that Khim was squatting by the dying fire, his cheeks wet with tears. I held out my hand, and he stumbled towards me, huddling against my arm. 'I am afraid, but I must not wake mama,' he said in French as pure as his sister's. It was the first time he had spoken to me since we left the capital.

He was shivering, though the night was warm, so I drew him under the rug, close against my side, and after a while his tears dried, and he slept. I slept then myself, for I was almost as exhausted as Linh, and I did not wake until I heard the children whooping and splashing in the stream in the morning. Fleur was shy and had wrapped herself in a piece of batik cloth to bathe, but Khim ran brown and naked from the water to kiss his mother, who had woken too and was sitting up combing her long hair. She took his small firm body in her arms, careless of his wetness, and held him tight, until at last it was he who wriggled and demanded to be let go, saying he was hungry.

We set off very early, to make the most of what coolness there was, and it was not unpleasant driving in the fresh morning, though the roads were still appalling. Penn had made an elaborate route for us, avoiding the main provincial centres, and taking us through the most sparsely settled areas of the country. 'It is the long way round,' he said before we set out, 'but it will be safe for you.'

He had however underestimated the difficulties of buying petrol. There were pumps in the villages he had marked, but the peasants told Linh their own supplies were very short, and they would only let us have small quantities even when I offered them twice or three times the normal price. There was still a reserve supply in the cans in the boot of the car, but that was for emergencies and I did not want to touch it.

When we stopped in a village to ask about petrol, Linh also asked if there had been any fighting in the area, and whether there were soldiers on the road ahead. The headman who had come out to greet us said there had been fighting last year, but the soldiers had all gone away. There were still a few stragglers about, but they were harmless. They lived in the forests, on wild game and fruit from deserted plantations, and sometimes they came into the village to barter.

In the heat of the afternoon, with Linh and the children dozing on the back seat, two of the stragglers came out of the forest ahead and stood in the road, signalling me to stop. I did not think they looked at all harmless. They were boys of eighteen or nineteen, dirty and ragged, with matted hair. One of them was bare-legged and bare-footed, with a large tropical ulcer eating into his ankle. He had a sharp, foxy face, and carried an Armalite over his shoulder. The other had swollen, mongoloid features, and stood gazing vacantly as the car approached.

The boy with the rifle unslung it and bought it up, so I put my foot down hard on the accelerator, and drove straight at them. I thought they would jump aside at the last moment and so they did, but as he leaped the gunman fired, and the car swerved violently as one of the tyres blew out. I braked hard, just managing to keep us out of the old, dry irrigation ditch at the side of the road, and the rifle was thrust in the window, hard against my head.

I ignored it, and twisted round to look in the back seat. Linh was gasping for breath, and the children were supporting her, but she smiled at me and said with difficulty that she was all right, she had just been winded by the sudden stop.

The man with the rifle was shouting at me. His head was thrust into the car, and I could feel the spray of his spittle against my cheek. 'He is asking for money,' Linh said from the back seat. 'He says you are a foreigner, and must have money with you.'

The second man called out something then in a high, sing song voice. Linh leaned forward, frowning. 'It is hard to understand him but I think he is saying he had heard that foreigners are very rich, and carry jewels and gold. He is a little simple, that one.' She made the small, knocking motion on the side of the forehead which is a universal sign for lunacy.

The fox-faced boy was growing impatient. He swung the rifle round to cover us all in turn, lingering when he came to the children, who shrank back. Linh spoke to him briefly, then turned back to me. 'I will give them my earrings, they can sell them in the village.' She wore plain gold circlets in her ears, and she began to fumble with them. 'I think we must also give them some money. Not much, perhaps, they may be satisfied with a little.'

'That won't work. Penn told me to hide the money somewhere, but I forgot. Everything we have – my money, and the cash Penn gave me – is in my wallet. When they see it, they will take it all.

I shook my head at the man with the rifle, and held up my empty hands in a gesture to indicate poverty. He laughed then, and wrenching open the car door, pulled me out into the road, sending me sprawling. The other boy was dragging the children out, and they tumbled into the dust screaming, while Linh tried unsuccessfully to grab at their hands. I called them to me, and they came running, edging behind me and holding tightly to my legs.

I was preoccupied with the children, and with watching the man with the rifle, but then I heard Linh scream. She was still lying in the back of the car, and the second man was pulling the earrings from her ears, and forcing her mouth open with his dirty fingers to see if she had any gold teeth. He had torn one of her ear lobes, and the blood was running down her neck.

Then he straddled her, his weight crushing her body, and his swollen face thrust into hers. He lifted his head, and said something to the other man, and they both sniggered.

'What did he say?' I said urgently to the children. Fleur shook her head and buried her face in my dusty jeans, but Khim answered in a low voice. 'He says the foreign woman with the short hair looks like a boy, but my mama does not.' He pressed himself against me and I could feel him trembling.

The dirty hands of the man in the back seat were tearing clumsily at the fastenings of Linh's skirt, and I saw what he meant to do. I screamed loudly for him to stop, and he lifted his head for a moment and gaped at me.

I thrust Fleur roughly forward. 'Tell them I will give them all the money we have, but your mamma must not be hurt.' She hesitated. 'Hurry! Tell them!'

She found the words then, and the boy with the rifle relaxed a little and stepped back, motioning me to the car. He spoke over his shoulder to the other man who was still crouched over Linh, and when he paid no attention, struck him hard on the shoulder with the butt of the rifle. He got up reluctantly then, wiping his mouth. Linh lay still for a moment, then she raised herself slowly, calling to the children. Her pale cheeks were flushed and she looked feverish.

I gave them the wallet then. They could have taken it any time, it was simply thrust into the pocket of my denim jacket, which was lying on the front seat. The wallet was stuffed with notes, and they shouted with excitement when they saw it, for it was a small fortune for them, I suppose. The boy with the rifle leaned it against a tree, and squatted down with the other in the dust to count the money. They counted very slowly, their lips moving, totally absorbed.

I was sorry that I had not brought the pistol Penn had offered me. I don't think, even then, I would have killed them, though I might have, but at least I could have covered them long enough to allow one of the children to grab the rifle. With two guns we might have got our money back.

I said this to Linh and she shook her head. She was wiping the thin trickle of blood from her neck with her handkerchief. 'No, that would be too dangerous. Now we must hope they will not take the car.'

I had not thought of that, but mercifully neither had they. They were too pleased with the money, and when they had divided it, they ran quickly into the forest without looking back. I helped Linh out of the car and bathed her ear with boiled water. She said she had not been hurt except when the man pulled the earrings out.

'I do not think he could have done what he meant, you know.' She kept her voice low so the children would not hear. 'He was afraid, I could tell, more afraid than I. His legs were shaking as he lay on me.'

'Well, he gave a good imitation,' I said curtly, getting up. 'Now I must try to change the wheel.'

I had seen wheels changed many times, and knew in theory how it was done, but I had never done it myself. The children tried to help, but if two peasants had not come spluttering along the road in an old pick-up, I am not sure we would have got on our way before the sun went down.

We could not pay them for their help, but I gave them a couple of tins of our scarce tinned food, and a packet of cigarettes, and they seemed pleased enough with that. When Linh told them about the bandits, they nodded and said, yes, there were many such in the forests and the roads. They themselves always went armed, and they showed us an old hunting rifle on the floor of the pick-up.

When we had driven a long way in silence, Linh

asked in her low voice if we had any money left at all.

'Nothing. I was a fool, I should have split it up and hidden some of it with the food supplies. We cannot buy petrol, so I shall have to use what is in the cans.'

'If we could get to the border, I could telephone to my cousin . . .' Linh's voice trailed uncertainly away.

I shook my head. 'And I could telephone friends in Bangkok. The trouble is, I don't think we will get so far.'

I drove as carefully as I could, husbanding fuel. There was no possibility of going back, so we might as well go on. 'People are kind, in the country areas. Perhaps they will give us a little petrol,' Linh said, holding the children close to her.

'Perhaps they will.' I didn't think there was much chance of that, but I thought we might try bartering. There was still some tinned food left, and I had a small radio in my luggage that should be worth a tankful.

We had left the low valleys and were beginning to climb sharply. Khamla has only one, massive mountain range, running from north to south in a meandering line, and we had reached it. Penn had said it was better to cross in the middle of the day, for the roads were narrow and winding, and there were often pockets of mist in the morning and evening. I looked anxiously at the sun, which was low in the sky.

Linh saw my hesitation. 'I think it is better if we go and make camp in the mountains,' she said. 'There is still more than an hour before the sun goes down. Then tomorrow, we can start very early, and reach the border in the afternoon.'

If we reach it, I said under my breath, but I nodded and urged the car forward on the twisting road, as though it was a tired horse.

The sun was at the horizon and I was looking out for a camping place when the mist caught us without warning. It was thick and cold and clammy and it wiped out what remained of the light. I turned on the headlamps and slowed the car almost to walking pace.

'Should you not stop?' Linh said anxiously. 'The fog may lift.'

'I can't stop here. We've a precipice on one side, and thick forest on the other. I'll have to go on until I find somewhere we can pull off the road.' Penn had said timber trucks came down these roads, and there had been many accidents.

About a mile further on, what looked like a side road apppeared in the headlights, but it seemed rutted and unused, so I continued on the road we were on. That was, God knows, bad enough. The mist lifted a little, and I drove on as fast as I dared, until at last we found a small clearing by the side of the road where we could stop.

It was an awful night. The trees pressed close around us, releasing a small rain of moisture, and a dank ground mist came clammily to the edge of the circle of light cast by the hurricane lantern. I could not find any dry sticks to make a fire and, apart from the tins which I would not open, we had nothing but some cold rice and a few bananas. I could not even make tea to warm us, and there was only a little boiled water left in the flasks. Khim reverted to his babyhood, and cried in a thin, high wail, saying he was frightened, and he could see the eyes of animals in the forest. Even Linh could not quieten him.

There was no possiblity of sleeping on the muddy ground, so we huddled in the car, Linh and the boy in the back seat, Fleur and I in the front. None of us had any warm clothes, and the rugs we had with us were no protection against the seeping cold of the mountains. Fleur pushed me away when I tried to hold her, and lay rigid beside me until at last she fell asleep through sheer exhaustion. I dozed a little, but woke at intervals during the night to hear Linh murmuring to the boy in her soft voice.

I got out of the car as I heard the first harsh cry of a bird in the forest, and stretched my cramped legs. The others were asleep, but I woke them, and said they must walk a little, for we would leave as soon as it was light. Even Linh made the effort to encourage the children, stumbling with difficulty along the muddy road, but insisting they must walk with her, holding each by the hand.

When the sun came up the mist retreated, and though the white curtain hovered impenetrably ahead, I could at least see the surface on which I was driving. The vertiginous drop below, which I had glimpsed the afternoon before, and which had made me feel sick, was no longer there, and the forest pressed reassuringly close in. I had no idea what we would do if we met another car, though, for the road was no longer wide enough for anything to pass.

We had been driving for an hour when Linh asked me to stop so she could come into the front seat. 'The children are sleeping,' she said. 'If I sit with you they can stretch out.'

But when the change had been made, she leaned towards me and said quietly in my ear that she did not want to worry me, but she thought they were on the wrong road.

'We should be starting the descent by now,' she said, 'but instead we are still climbing. Also there should be some traffic on the road, and we have seen nothing.' She had the map out from the glove box, and she held it out and showed it to me. Penn had marked a village on the road over the mountains, and if his calculations were right, we should have come to it long ago.

'Do you think we should have taken the other road?' I looked at her in dismay. 'I can't go back now, I would have to reverse all the way. We will have to go on until we find someone to ask.'

She said nothing, but I knew she was thinking, as I was, that the chances of reaching the border were now remote. We had very little petrol left, and were unlikely to find any.

The car reeled drunkenly in and out of deep ruts. I saw Linh's mouth tighten with the effort of repressing a moan as she was thrown from side to side. There was livid bruising on her thin arms, and on the side of her face. 'It is nothing,' she said, seeing me looking at her. 'I bruise very easily since I have been ill.'

In fact I was more concerned about myself, for I had a hard slow, burning pain in my abdomen which made it very hard to concentrate on the road ahead. If this nightmare drive went on much longer, I might not have to worry too much about whether I should keep the baby or not. The decision could easily be made for me, although what we should do if I started to miscarry in this place was beyond imagining.

All decisions were taken out of my hands, then, for the mist came down even thicker than it had before, and the car gave a tortured grunt, and stopped dead. They boy woke in the back seat, and began to wail again. The thin, high sound went through my head, and I cried out myself.

'What is it?' Linh reached over to the back and tried to hush the children.

'I don't know. We still have some petrol, so it is not that.' I tried to smile. 'I think your car has died of old age.'

I opened the bonnet and got out. The burning pain in my belly made it difficult for me even to stand, but I leaned against the car, and looked into its tangled and rusty innards. Car engines were an unknown territory to me, and I had not the slightest idea what to do.

Linh got painfully out, and stood beside me. She looked surprisingly calm. 'You are right,' she said in a matter-of-fact voice. 'It has died. My husband said it needed new parts but we could not get them. He thought it would last out until we reached the border, but it seems he was wrong.' She took my arm. 'There is nothing more you can do. Let us wait until the sun is stronger, and the mists clear. Then perhaps we may see where we are.'

She took charge, and I was glad of it, making the children play games to warm themselves, opening a tin of fruit and sharing out the flesh and the juice. We were all thirsty, and I wondered uneasily what we would do for water if we did not come to a stream.

After we had eaten, we wrapped ourselves again in the rugs and squeezed into the car. Linh insisted on taking the two children in the back to allow me more room for, she said with some truth, I was the most exhausted of all of us. I fell almost once into an uneasy sleep, and did not wake until the boy shook me violently.

'Look, madame. Look!' He was shouting in my ear, and I woke with a cry, banging my head on the steering wheel. The mist was swirling and drifting round us, as though we were caught in cloud, but through it I could see solid shapes, like dark monoliths. I felt a crawling of the skin as though I were caught in a bad dream, but then my head cleared and I saw the monoliths were merely half a dozen men standing round the car, looking in at us in silence.

They were very short, even in a country of short people, and their skins were dark, almost black, darker even than those of the most weathered peasants. Their hair grew upwards and was slightly frizzy, so that though their features were Asian, they had a negroid look. One of them spoke to us then, and though I had not expected to understand him, the intonation was one I had never even heard before.

Linh put her hand on my shoulder. 'Montagnards,' she said quietly. 'Don't be afraid, I don't think they will harm us.'

Montagnards. I remembered one evening in the camp at the Great Temple when Penn had talked at length to me, making me exercise and extend my French vocabulary, on the racial strains among the Khamla people.

In the influxes and invasions of twenty centuries or

so, most of the influences could be traced, he said, but the little pockets of mountain people scattered throughout the country remained a puzzle to anthropologists. They were of an aberrant racial strain, with different physical characteristics, and they spoke not only a different dialect but a different language to the Khamla people. Like most hill tribes they were suspicious and independent, and though they came down to the plains sometimes to trade, they remained largely confined to their own incestuous communities. The peasants called them dog-eaters, for they bred a special sort of dog for the pot, claiming that dog meat heated the blood in the mountain winters.

'Don't be afraid,' Linh said again behind me. I was not, for I saw they carried no guns. It was almost the first time in our journey that we had seen a group of adult men who were completely unarmed.

An older man, who seemed to be the leader, spoke again, this time a little impatiently. His speech had an odd sound to it, somewhere between a click and a chirp, and I looked back at Linh. She shook her head. 'I cannot understand him. It is like none of the peasant dialects I have heard.'

I opened the car door and got out, and as I did, I saw another man coming out of the mist ahead. He was a tall man, a European, with fair hair and curly beard, and I started to run towards him, for I thought it was Peter. Then he came closer, and I saw it was not. It was a much older man, in his middle fifities, and his hair and beard were streaked with grey. He was thin, but strongly built and sinewy, and his old combat jacket and khaki wool trousers made him look like a veteran soldier. I drew back a little when I saw that, unlike the montagnards, he was armed with a rifle slung over his shoulder.

He saw me looking at it and said at once in French: 'You should not be alarmed. I carry it only in case we meet a wild boar on the road. They are dangerous, but they are also good eating. We need all the protein we can get.'

He stood smiling at me, and I thought it was an odd place to be discussing nutrition. His French had a slight provincial accent, and he spoke it quite slowly, as though he was out of practice in his own tongue.

I seemed to have lost my own voice, so he came forward and shook hands briskly with me and with Linh, touching the children lightly on the cheek. They seemed to lose their fright then, and tumbled out into the road, shivering and jumping up and down to warm themselves.

'I should introduce myself,' the man said politely. 'My name is Louis Fournier. These men and I come from a village a little way off.' He waved vaguely into the mist. 'One of our people came in this morning and said some travellers seemed to be in trouble, so we set out to find you.'

Linh, more collected than I, was murmuring our names, and saying we were on our way to Bangkok, but the car had broken down, as they could see. He bent close to her, looking with interest into her face. She was very pale, but she seemed calm, and in no distress. I wondered if Penn's protectiveness sapped her vitality, for she seemed stronger and more assertive when she was away from him.

The man motioned to me to raise the bonnet again, and began to check over the engine, exploring it with his large, thin hands. After a while, he raised his head and looked at me thoughtfully. 'We have no vehicles in the village now, and I am out of practice as a motor mechanic,' he said. 'But I can tell you there is no chance of driving to Bangkok in this car. The crank shaft is broken.'

'Is there no chance of replacing it?' It was the first time I had spoken, and he looked relieved.

'Ah, I thought perhaps you did not understand French. No, of course not, madame, not in these mountains. You would probably have to go back to the capital before you would find a garage that could deal with it. Even then, I am not sure. These cars are no longer made, and there may not be spare parts for them any more.'

He looked at us attentively. The children were squatting in the mud by the side of the road, and I saw with the irritation of fatigue that the boy was about to cry. The man followed my gaze. 'I think you had better come to the village,' he said. 'We can give you food, and you can rest.'

'How far is it?'

'Two kilometers, no more. You can walk there?'

'Of course,' I said. 'The children and I can walk. But I don't think Madame can manage it. She has been quite ill.'

He drummed his fingers on the car, considering. 'We could send for a stretcher from the village, but it would take time.' Stooping, he looked into the back of the car. 'I do not think there will be any problem.'

He opened the door, and taking Linh's hand, drew her out gently. Then he lifted her, hefting her experimentally. 'She weighs nothing,' he said briefly. I think her lightness had shocked him. 'I can carry her.'

We set out in single file in the mist, the man carrying Linh at the front, the montagnards with our small amount of luggage in the middle, the children and I at the rear. Fleur walked strongly and well, but Khim could not keep up, and in the end I had to carry him. One of the men tried to take him from me, but he screamed and tightened his arms round my neck, almost strangling me.

It was hard going at first, for the way led steeply uphill, and the clammy mist closed round us, so that I felt I was suffocating. But then the path – it was so narrow it could hardly be called a road – turned downwards at last, and my breathing began to slow.

The mist was clearing as we descended, and as the

sun came out strongly, I saw we were descending quickly to a small valley, with a stream running through it, and a village clustered along the stream.

The man carrying Linh called a brief halt, a breathing-space, he said, though I think it was more for my sake than his own. 'It is not far, you see,' he said, pointing to the village. 'Ten minutes, no more.'

I stood looking down at the village and frowning. 'The road seems to stop there. It does not continue on the other side?'

He shook his head. 'If you are going to the border, you are on the wrong road, madame. This is an old logging road, not used for some years. It goes nowhere but the village.'

He watched me uneasily, and I think he was afraid that I would weep, but I was growing light-headed with fatigue and hunger, and the problem of reaching the border seemed something which would wait. Smoke was coming up from fires in the village, and it was signalling food and warmth.

Some of the women came out to meet us as we drew nearer to the huts, and to my surprise, Khim let one of them take him from me. They were even shorter than the men, some of them hardly bigger than children, but very sturdy and strong-looking. Their hair was long, and plaited with pieces of red wool, and instead of the trousers of the peasant women on the plains, they wore woollen skirts, rather long, with bands of patterned material sewn round the hem, and patterned sleeveless jackets over long-sleeved blouses. I had seen very similar dresses in the hill villages in Thailand.

The women clicked and exclaimed over the children, and I heard one or two giggles behind my back. They probably thought me freakish, in my jeans and denim jacket, trailing along behind the party of little dark men. They were kind enough, though, and when Linh and the children and I were installed in a hut at the end of the village, they brought us bowls of hot, mealy porridge, and mugs of steaming tea so strong it brought tears to my eyes. We ate eagerly, even Linh, though the children complained about the taste of the porridge. It was unfamiliar, but not uneatable, and Linh said she had tasted it before in another, though less remote mountain village.

The man Fournier came in when we finished eating. 'The villagers ask if you like the hut,' he said. 'They prepared it specially when they heard you were coming.'

I had been too tired and too hungry to notice, but I looked round now with interest, while Linh murmured suitable compliments to be passed on to the village women. The hut was passably clean, and sturdily built in the local style from thick straw matting, with a thatched roof. The floor, unusually, was of wood, and raised a little off the ground, so that at least it was dry. Our luggage was piled in the middle of the floor, and there were straw sleeping mats against the walls, with rough blankets, and thick quilts with patchwork covers.

Linh exclaimed over them, saying she had never seen them in Khamla before. 'I taught the women to make them, in the way my grandmother did,' Louis Fournier said. 'It is very cold at night here, and blankets are not enough.' He smiled in his curly beard, and again for a moment I saw a fugitive resemblance to Peter, though a glimpse of his teeth, stained and uneven, immediately dispelled it.

A couple of girls came in and took the empty bowls. They stared at me, and giggled behind their hands, and the man apologised. 'They are used to me, but they see very few European women. For those girls, you may be the first one.'

He had been sitting cross-legged on the floor, and he got up easily, in a single movement. 'I think you should sleep now. Some of the men will go with me and we will bring the car to the village.' He saw my look of surprise. 'They are very strong, you know, and used to pulling heavy weights. They can manhandle it to the top of the rise, then, if the brakes hold, I can drive it down the rest of the way.' He went to the door and looked back. 'Sleep well.'

So we did, all of us, Linh as well. The floor was hard, but the rough blankets and the quilts quickly warmed us, and took the lingering chill out of our bones. When I woke at last, I looked at my watch and saw it was nearly five o'clock. Linh was sitting up drinking tea, and I could hear the children shouting somewhere outside. Linh had washed with water the women had brought, and carefully combed her hair. She looked surprisingly fresh, and I was conscious of my sweat-stained shirt, and dusty jeans.

'The children say there is a bathhouse two huts from here. They have washed themselves, or rather, Fleur has washed herself and Khim,' Linh said, knotting her hair on her neck. I took a towel and went to look. It was certainly a bathhouse, a circular hut with a slatted roof, and outside, a rainwater tank raised on a platform. A pipe leading from the tank made a crude but effective shower, and I stood under it gratefully, letting it pour down over my head. The water was cold, colder than one could get in Bangkok even in winter, deliciously fresh and, when I caught it in my open mouth, sweet-tasting. I heard squeaking noises and giggles, and thought that the village children were watching me through a crack, but I ignored them and continued splashing.

When I was dressed again in fresh trousers and shirt, I felt strong and confident. 'Let us rest here for a couple of days, if they will keep us,' I said to Linh. I did not see there was any alternative but it sounded less alarming if I put it that way. 'Tonight I will talk to M. Fournier, and see if there is any way he can repair the car, or, if not, whether they will give us a mule and a farm cart. We saw a mule grazing near the village as we came in, do you remember?'

'You would drive a cart all the way to the border?' Her hands froze in the act of arranging her hair, and I knew she was thinking of bumping over rutted roads.

'No, no, just to the foot of the mountains, or until we found a village where we could get a lift. If we go closer to the main road, there may even be a bus service.' Perhaps I could induce Fournier to buy my little radio, or even my tape recorder, though God knows what he would do with it. It did not seem to me we could reach the border if we were penniless.

Linh looked at me across the hut, her face no longer tranquil. 'My husband will be very worried. I promised to telephone him as soon as we crossed.'

I came and sat beside her, and took her hand. 'I know. But there is really very little we can do unless M. Fournier helps us. If Penn is anxious, it will only be a few days. Besides,' I said, improvising, 'Penn told me before we left that he would not be surprised if we were held up somewhere along the way. He won't be really concerned for a while yet.'

She probably knew I was lying, but she accepted the small reassurance, and said she was tired of being inside, and would like to watch the children playing. I made a seat outside the hut for her with a rug spread on an old box, and Fleur and Khim came up shouting, three or four tiny dark village children following on their heels. A couple of grandmothers came shuffling up too, and squatted in the dust at Linh's feet, chewing betel and talking animatedly to her in their hoarse, clicking voices. Linh gave them her whole attention, putting her hands out at arm's length, as though she was trying to absorb the meaning through the pores of her skin. She began murmuring back at them in her own low tones, and I saw with surprise that a conversation of sorts was going on.

'Mama talks to everyone,' Fleur said a little jealously, leaning on my knee. She jerked away to wave, and I looked up and saw Louis Fournier coming between the huts. 'Here is M. Fournier,' I said to Linh. 'I will talk to him about the car.'

Khim, who was wrestling with one of the tiny children, laughed loudly. 'He is not M. Fournier. He is called Père Louis. Everyone in the village knows that.'

I looked at Linh in surprise. 'Père Louis? He is a priest.'

'It is very likely. I thought it mght be so from the beginning. Only missionaries come to places like this, you know, for there is no profit to be made out of them. There was some logging years ago, but nothing else, no industry, no big plantations. If M. Fournier has been here for a long time, he is almost certainly a missionary.'

I watched him come slowly up, stopping to speak to a couple of men at the door of the next hut. 'He doesn't look like a missionary.'

Linh smiled. 'I think those few who stayed on after the mission headquarters closed have become a little loose in their beliefs. They were all ordered home to France, but some refused to go. I have heard one or two were excommunicated.' She looked at the approaching figure uneasily. 'The new régime does not like them at all, these priests who have gone native. Penn says they will track them down, one by one, and make them leave.'

'Let us hope Père Louis lasts long enough to get us to the border.' He came up then, fresh-faced and cheerful, saying he had been bathing under the small fall further up the stream, it was icy but refreshing and he would recommend it. After he had spoken to Linh and the children, he turned to me politely and asked if I would care to walk round the village before the sun set.

I had realised, when we came down into the valley, that there was something untypical about the settlement, and I realised as we walked side by side what it was. Most villages in this region are a haphazard huddle of huts, but we were walking down the equivalent of a wide main street, with huts lined up neatly on either side. All the familiar squalor and stench of village life was overlaid, but the arrangement was quite geometric.

'I laid it out when I came here twenty-five years ago,' he said when I asked him about it. 'I was still young enough to be dogmatic, and I made the people pull down their huts, and line them up in orderly rows, as you can see. I dug drains and sanitation pits, and built the bathhouse which is hardly used at all, for the people prefer to bathe in the stream. As indeed I do now.'

'The straight lines do not seem to have made much difference,' I said cautiously, looking at heaps of refuse outside the huts, and a man urinating in a high arc onto a patch of vegetables. Two dogs, plumper than the usual village curs, were snuffling in a rubbish pile, and I wondered if they were destined for the pot.

His smile flashed briefly in his beard. 'None at all. It took some years, but I learned at last that you cannot impose order on natural chaos. Unless you are God, and not always then.'

We came to the centre of the village, where a hut larger than the rest stood in a clearing. It was well built, with slatted wooden walls instead of the usual bamboo matting, and a rusty iron cross jutted from its thatched roof.

'The church,' Louis Fournier said, pushing open a creaking door for me to enter. It was dark inside, and for a moment I could see nothing. Was he a missionary? I asked, as we stood there in the gloom.

His voice was non-committal. 'I was a missionary for a long time. The children still call me Père Louis, for their parents think it is polite. But now I am something much more like a village headman.' An oil lamp stood on a bench at the side of the church and he struck a match and lit it. 'Missionaries who worked in the country areas were always self-appointed headmen, you know,' he said over his shoulder. 'We saw ourselves as the source of all power, spiritual and temporal. Sometimes, when there was already a strong local chieftan, there was a struggle to gain and keep control. A bloody one, more than once.'

'Why do you keep the church open?'

'Why not? It is very useful as a meeting hall. We have a sort of parliament here, with me as prime minister. I use it also for religious ceremonies from time to time, because the people want them. And as you see, we cater for all tastes.'

He swung the lantern suddenly, and an alcove at the end of the church sprang into the light. The three figures it contained emerged from the darkness with such menace that I recoiled and stumbled back.

In the centre, an almost life-sized Jesus writhed on a cross, the body carved from a black wood which gleamed in the light, the face contorted in anger, with open, staring eyes. 'Extraordinary, is it not?' Fournier's voice said in my ear. 'It was carved by an old German who lived here when I first came. He copied the face and body from German crucifixion paintings of the sixteenth century, but made the Christ black.'

I looked back at the alcove. The Christ was flanked on one side by a stone Buddha almost as tall, a standing Buddha, grave and unsmiling, and, unusually, rather forbidding. On the other side was a smaller figure, a variation on a Hindu goddess with three sets of arms, but with the bulging belly of a fertility figure. The figure was very roughly carved and had a squat, obscene quality. 'Not the German,' I said flatly.

'Not the German. It is local work, some centuries old, because you can see the Hindu influence. I think it is the goddess Kali, converted into a deity of the region.' He turned the lantern light on my face. 'You look pale, as though you had seen a spirit. They are quite harmless, my Holy Trinity, you know.'

'I am not so sure.' I pushed the door open and went out ahead of him, glad of the last of the lingering light.

We walked in silence to the end of the village, and I saw that the car had come down from the mountain, and was parked near the enclosure where the mule was grazing. Half a dozen tiny children were squatted in the dust watching it gravely, as though it were a totem. 'Don't worry,' Fournier said, 'no one will touch it. We keep quite strict discipline here.' He tapped the bonnet lightly. 'I have checked it very thoroughly, madame. You could not take it down the mountain even if I could coax it into life for you. The brakes are defective, and would not hold on the other side of the pass.'

I looked across the road to where the mule was grazing, and he at once shook his head. 'Ah, no, madame, it is our only surviving farm animal. It does a little ploughing and we use it in the mill, but it is very old. It might get down the mountain, but it would never climb up again.'

'What shall we do? We cannot stay here indefinitely.' The sun was about to disappear below the peaks, and he took my arm lightly, and urged me back towards the centre of the village. 'Be patient,' he said. 'Rest for a day or so. There is an agricultural co-operative at the foot of the mountain, and it has two trucks, perhaps three. One of the men will take a message down. We will ask them to send a truck and a driver, if they can spare one.'

I stopped and faced him, for we were almost back to our hut, and I did not want to discuss this matter in front of Linh.

'There is a difficulty. We have no money, and I could not pay them.' I told him the story of how we had been robbed on the second day, before we came to the hills.

He watched me impassively, and without, I thought, much sympathy. We were undoubtedly becoming a nuisance. 'I cannot help you,' he said politely. 'We are self-sufficient in food, but otherwise we live at subsistence level. Our income is lower than that of the poorest peasant on the plains.' Linh came out of the hut then, and he smiled at her and said he must go, there was a meeting to discuss next week's planting. 'Don't worry, we will find a way of putting you on the road to the border,' he said over his shoulder.

The women brought us bowls of greasy stewed meat, mixed with pieces of a potato-like tuber. I thought it was probably dog, for it had an unfamiliar sweetish taste, but the mountain air had made me very hungry, and I ate quickly. The children finished their bowls without complaint, but Linh could manage no more than a few mouthfuls.

Penn had told me her stomach was very delicate, and she easily became nauseated. They kept her on as bland a diet as possible, but even then she often vomited. She had seemed reasonably well on the trip so far, but we had, after all, eaten very little which would make her ill. Later that night, as I lay awake in the darkness, I heard her retching painfully, and I got up and helped her outside so she could be sick without the children hearing.

The next morning no mist lingered, for a brisk wind blew from the higher peaks, tearing it to shreds. It was a marvellous day, with a high sky and sharp, snapping air. The stream flashed in the early sun like glass, and I went up the valley to the little waterfall and bathed in the tumbling pool, gasping with shock and pleasure as the icy water assaulted me. I stood naked in the sun afterwards, rubbing myself dry with the rough towel, and I felt enormously strong and almost happy.

I longed for a moment for Linh and the children to disappear, and my problems with them, then guilt seized me, and I dressed as quickly as I could, and went back to the village. Linh looked a little better this morning, and ate a bowl of porridge without ill results. I sat outside the hut with my own breakfast, watching the men and women file by with hoes over their shoulders on the way to the fields. Further up, a boy riding bareback was urging the old mule towards the mill. Above the village, I could see small figures moving on the terraces cut into the hillside. It was a scene of immemorial simplicity, and it filled me with peace.

A little later in the morning, I walked over to the hut Fournier had pointed out as his own. It was of the same style as the others, but larger, with a small raised verandah on one side, and an annexe at the back. There was no one in the hut, so I went to the annexe and saw it served as an office and, apparently, as a rough surgery, for an old man was sitting on a wooden box and Fournier was kneeling at his feet, carefully peeling away a pus-stained bandage.

He saw me come in and, without a greeting, motioned me to bring him a bowl and disinfectant from a nearby table. 'Hold it for me, please,' he said, and began to swab a weeping ulcer, reddish-yellow against the dark flesh. The old man cried out briefly, but made no further sound. 'I could heal it if I had some penicillin.' Fournier turned his head and smiled at me over his shoulder. 'You can send us some when you reach Bangkok.'

I looked at him with sudden hope. 'You are a doctor?'

'No.' He smeared some ointment on the old man's leg, and began to bandage it again. I saw that even the new bandage was grey with use. 'I studied medicine for a year, then left medical school to go to the seminary. It is something I have always regretted. If I was going to cure souls, I should at least have learned how to cure bodies as well.'

He got neatly to his feet, and helped the old man stand. 'I have a sort of amateur practice here, but it is all very simple. I dress wounds, and set limbs, and sometimes deliver babies, though the village women are better at it themselves. When we have spare cash, I send down the mountain for drugs, but we cannot afford much. Mainly I use herbal medicines, there is a long tradition of them here. Most of them work only by faith, but there are two or three which are very effective.'

'I had hoped,' I said in a low voice, 'that you might be

able to help Madame Penn. I am very afraid she will die if I do not get her to Bangkok quickly.'

He had been rapidly clearing bottles and dressings from the workbench, working with deft, economical movements. With his back to me, he again had a look of Peter. 'Come into the main room and I will make some tea for us,' he said, closing an instrument case with a snap. 'We will be more comfortable there.'

The hut itself was clean and sparse, with a sleeping mat and quilt rolled in a corner, and cane chairs on either side of a low table. There was some rough shelving against one wall, piled with books and papers, and, I saw, a powerful shortwave radio. 'We are not entirely cut off from the world,' Fournier said. 'Or at least, I am not. The people here do not speak enough Kham to understand the government broadcasts.'

He pushed a chair forward for me, and called, and a moment later a boy of about fifteen came in with a china teapot and two glasses. 'I allow myself a servant,' he said, watching the boy pour. 'It is my only luxury.' He touched the boy lightly on the shoulder, and smiled at him. 'He is brighter than most, and in the old days I would have trained him to be a native priest.'

'Not now?'

'Not now.'

The tea was light and fragrant, unlike the witches' brew the village women served us, and I sipped it slowly, warming my hand on the glass. When I opened my mouth to speak, he cut in quickly. 'I cannot help your friend. We talked yesterday while you were sleeping, and she told me what her illness is. But there was no need. I had only to look at her to know that she is dying.'

The word fell between us with a dull resonance. I could not speak. I could only look at Fournier, shaking my head.

'Ah, well,' he said easily, filling my glass again. 'We are all dying, I suppose. I am, in any case, not a doctor, and my opinion is worth very little. But it would have been better if you had not come on this journey. Madame would have been safer as she was.'

I watched him warily, then glanced at the shortwave radio in the corner. 'You have heard some news from the capital?'

'Not from the capital, and not from the radio. Word came up the mountain early today – it passes from village to village, you know – that the road to the border is cut. Sarr Mok's army has been driven down from the north by the government forces and has seized most of the province below us.' He glanced at me doubtfully. 'Sarr Mok is . . .'

'I know very well who Sarr Mok is. I have seen his soldiers.'

'In that case, you will know what you would face if you left here with Madame Penn and the children. There are a number of small bands who have split from the main force, and who are operating up and down the road – as far as the border itself, the villagers say. They are robbing and murdering travellers, even peasants in farm carts. A foreigner would be seized and held to ransom, and Madame and the little girl would be fortunate if they were not raped before they were killed.' His voice was quite matter-of-fact.

'My God, you are a cold bastard!' I spoke in English, and I was not sure whether he understood. But he stood up and said politely that he was sorry if he had said anything to disturb me, but it was better if I fully understood the situation.

'You may as well make yourself comfortable, madame, for I think you will be here for some time. Sooner or later, the government's forces will regain the province and drive out Sarr Mok's men. But we do not know how long that will take.' He opened the door politely for me and bowed me out.

CHAPTER FIFTEEN

It was nearly two months before the fighting died down. For weeks, even though we were protected by fold on fold of mountains, we had been able to hear the distant crump of shelling as the government army moved down from the north of the province, sweeping Sarr Mok's men before it. I think Sarr Mok must have known he was making his last stand, for the rumours that filtered up to us spoke of ferocious mortar battles, and hand-to-hand fighting. The bandits, it was said, were mining road bridges as they retreated, so that not much traffic was moving even in the cleared areas.

I was concerned that the armies might come up into the mountains, but Louis said there was not much danger, the mountain people were usually left alone. 'When Prince Soumidath was deposed, and the Americans installed Prince Vouliphong, the cadres of the Liberation Army came to the villages and tried to recruit soldiers,' he said. 'But people would not listen to them, and told them to go away. They took a few of the men at gunpoint, but they deserted almost at once and came back, and after that, there was no more trouble.'

I had grown bored with sitting around the hut, so I offered to work in the fields, and though Louis seemed doubtful, he offered no objection. The villagers grew maize and sorghum, and the potato-like tubers, and the women gathered fruit and wild greens in the forest. There were fish in the stream, and they ran a small poultry enclosure with stringy hens and geese. Louis came back from hunting with duck and an occasional pig, and if rations were low, the villagers killed one of the dogs which snuffled around the rubbish heaps. I did not much like seeing them hanging upside down with their throats cut, and a tin under the gash to catch the blood, but I ate the meat just the same.

I was not unhappy, for I was feeling very well, and the slow rhythm of the work in the fields seemed to suit me. The first few days, my muscles violently protested, but then I grew nearly as strong as the peasant women who worked beside me, stopping only for an hour or two in the middle of the day, as they did, to doze under the shade of the trees.

I was concious that at the same time as my muscles were hardening, my belly was beginning to swell. Otherwise I hardly thought about my pregnancy. The child was there, and I had to accept that it was going to stay, but it remained quiet, giving no sign of its presence. I felt quite indifferent towards it and made no attempt to spare myself during the long, hot hours in the field. I thought perhaps I was not a maternal woman, for though I was fond enough of Fleur and Khim, I was glad that they had been largely taken over by the old grandmothers who cared for those children too young to work with their parents in the fields.

Louis seemed fonder of them than I, and enrolled them in a small class he ran in the afternoons, teaching them in a mixture of French and the montagnard dialect, in which they were by now reasonably fluent.

'Teacher, doctor, priest,' I said mockingly when I came to collect them one afternoon. There was always a slight edge of antagonism between us.

'Judge and jury too.' He lifted Fleur and embraced her. I shrugged, unsurprised, for I knew he resolved small disputes between the village people. 'And executioner. Does that shock you?'

I took Fleur from him, and sent her off with Khim to their mother. 'You might at least have waited until the children were gone,' I said angrily.

'They are too young to understand.' He looked at my dirty work clothes and my hair, matted with sweat. 'Sit down, and I will bring you some tea. You should not work so much in the sun, you are not used to it.'

I sat, drinking tea, reluctant to stay, but unwilling to go. 'Why executioner?'

'Someone had to do it, and it was better me than one of the villagers.' He paused. 'The man was mad,' he said slowly. 'I had thought so for some time, but it was so rare a thing in these mountains that I could not be sure, and his wife said he had had fits like this before, and they had passed. One day when I was hunting, he killed her with an axe, and three of his children also. Some of the people were waiting for me at the edge of the village when I came out of the forest. They said he had his mother and two more children in his hut, and he threatenend to kill them too if anyone came near him.'

He sipped his tea slowly. 'I called his name, and he came to the door, with the axe in his hand, dragging his youngest son with him. I shot him before he could speak. There was nothing else I could do.'

I looked at him, then put my cup down and stood up abruptly. 'I must go to Linh and the children. It is time for us all to eat.'

My feet dragged as I walked back to the hut, for I was growing increasingly reluctant to go inside and face the spectre of Linh. She was calm enough, for in the second week Louis seeing her agitation, had urged her to write a message for Penn. He would send it by one of the men down to the village on the other side of the mountain, he said, and they would give it to a truck driver or an Army lorry passing through to take to the capital. I thought that the chances of Penn receiving it were very small, and as the weeks went by without any reply, I watched to see if Linh grew agitated again, but she remained tranquil. The gesture of sending the letter seemed to have been enough for her.

It was her physical state which alarmed me. She washed herself slowly and carefully every day, combing her hair and putting it up in the familiar French roll.

But she had become so skeletal that sometimes, looking at her in the dim light of the oil lamp, her outline seemed to fade and become insubstantial, so I felt she was already dead, and I was sharing the hut with her spirit.

She no longer went outside, but lay most of the day on her straw mat, looking out through the open door. It was difficult finding something she could eat, for any kind of meat made her retch, so she lived mainly on mealy porridge and a vegetable broth the women made her. Her bones were protruding through the skin, and her thin body was covered with bruises from contact with the floor, even when I begged another quilt for her to lie on. I asked Louis desperately if he had no drug which could help her, and he shook his head.

I became conscious that the children were avoiding her, coming to the hut only to sleep. They were frightened, I think, by what they saw in her face. One night Fleur came to me and said with her eyes downcast that Nghaim, the young woman in the next hut, had offered to take her and Khim to sleep with her own children. 'It would be better,' Fleur said, 'for I think we disturb mama.' I looked over at Linh and she nodded slightly. 'They will be happier with the other children,' she murmured in her low voice, though later I heard her weeping in the dark.

Even when the children were gone, she hardly seemed to sleep at all. We kept a small light burning, for she said she did not like the darkness, and whenever I woke myself and turned over she was propped up against the cushion from the car, and wide awake. One morning I did not go to the fields, but walked over instead to Louis's hut, and said bluntly that if he could do nothing else for her, he must find some way to make her sleep.

'You told me you used herbal medicines, and some of them were effective.' I knew very well he had a pain-killer made from a forest plant, for I had seen him give it to a village woman who scalded herself with boiling water from a cooking pot.

'She is not actually in pain?'

'I think not, but she cannot rest. You must have narcotics, this region is one of the main sources.'

'You are thinking of the Golden Triangle,' he said absently. 'That is a long way from here. There are no opium poppies in the forest.'

'Some other soporific, then. People have been brewing up opiates for centuries. Even the Greeks had hemlock.'

He laughed suddenly, showing the discoloured teeth which always destroyed, for me, his faint resemblance to Peter. 'That is not quite what we need.' He went to the door and looked out for a moment, then he came back abruptly into the room. 'There *is* a herb which induces sleep. The old women told me about it, and I brewed a tisane and tried it on myself. I didn't bother much with it, though. It has no analgesic qualities and nobody here needs sleeping draughts.'

'But you will make some for Linh?' I do not like to beg, but I faced him and met his eyes. 'Please!' I said, and he nodded without speaking.

Louis came quite late that night, long after I had given him up. He had an old metal jug in his hand, with a little steam rising from it. 'Something to help you sleep, madame,' he said lightly to Lihn, who lay propped on cushions, watching him. I got up from my sleeping mat at once, and brought one of the small bowls we used for drinking.

He carefully poured some dark brown liquid into the bowl, and held it out to her. 'It is nothing,' he said soothingly, 'a herbal tisane, that is all. It will not harm you.'

She murmured something which neither of us could hear, but she would not take the bowl from his hand. He smiled, though his eyes were watchful. 'You think I am trying to poison you?' he said, making it a joke. 'Your friend and nurse will be your taster, then.' He handed the bowl to me, and I drank without hesitation. The draught had a sourish, rather musty taste, but the instant warmth it induced was rather pleasant.

Louis took the bowl from my hand. 'It is better if you lie down and make yourself comfortable under the quilt. The tisane can work very quickly. When madame sees you sleep, I think she will drink a little herself.'

He was right about the speed with which the draught worked, though I suppose I was already deeply fatigued from a day in the fields. Louis sat down beside Linh and took her hand lightly in his, and after a minute or two, I saw their figures were wavering in the dim light, and shadows on the wall behind them were advancing and retreating in a sort of dance.

I did not see Linh take the draught, but when I woke the next morning she was lying on her side soundly asleep, and the empty bowl was near her hand. My own sleep had been heavy and dreamless, but I did not much like the way the tisane left me languid for the rest of the day. Louis offered me a draught again the following night, but I would not take it, saying I had no need of anything to make me sleep.

Linh drank it, though, without further protest, and Louis came every night after that, with his steaming jug. The tisane did not leave her listless, as it had me, but instead renewed a little of her energy, so she now went outside for an hour or two in the afternoon to watch the children playing. Fleur and Khim were running wild. They were burnt nearly as black as the village children, their clothes were torn and muddy, and their hair was matted and, I thought, probably lousy. I asked Linh if she wanted me to bring them back into the hut and clean them up, but she shook her head. They were better as they were, she said. 'Children do not like sick people, you know.' She spoke quite tranquilly, as though she was discussing someone else.

Khim no longer came to his mother unless she called

him, but Fleur drifted over dutifully when she saw her outside the hut, and kissed her cheek. One day Linh pulled her close and held her for a moment, until the child broke away and ran back to the others. I saw her face as she ran, and I knew what had upset her was the same thing which was disturbing me. Linh smelt of eau de cologne – there was a little left from the bottle she had brought with her – but behind this, another smell was emerging, very faint, sweet and sickly. It mingled with the eau de cologne, and made it nauseating. I was afraid one or other of the children would mention it, but both remained silent, even Khim, who tended to shout out anything which came into his head. I knew he could smell it, though, and it was the reason he was reluctant to come to her.

One morning when I woke early, I thought for the first time that the scent had become tangible in the hut. It was a hint, no more, and I could not be sure whether I was imagining it, but I took a towel and went upstream to the pool under the little fall, stripping and giving myself gladly to the shock of the icy, foaming water.

I usually was sure of having the pool to myself in the mornings. Louis came only in the afternoons, when I used the bathhouse, and the villagers would not swim there at all, claiming some sort of female spirit lived in the fall. But when I came out of the water, my skin glowing with heat but my teeth chattering, I saw Louis standing by the rocks, looking at me. He was intending to bathe, for he wore only a strip of cloth round his waist, his hand frozen in the act of loosening it. He had a good body, with muscular legs, and narrow but strong torso. The patch of curly hair on his chest was a yellowish-grey.

We stood staring at each other for a moment, then he moved. 'I'm sorry,' he said, 'I did not know you were here. The children said you were both still asleep.' I expected him to make one of his formal little half-bows and go away, but he did not. He came forward instead, and put his arms very carefully round me, pressing my wet body lightly against his. We stood embraced for a moment, and I felt him gently trembling. Then he released me, without a word, and, dropping his longhi, dived into the pool, swimming strongly and disappearing under the fall. I pulled my shirt and trousers on without bothering to dry myself, and went back to the hut.

I hardly saw Louis for a few days, for the men were clearing a section of the forest to extend the sorghum field. With nothing but axes and handsaws, it was hard, punishing work, and they came back at night exhausted. 'I'm not fit for conversation,' Louis said, pausing briefly at our door at sunset, shaking his head when Linh asked him to come in, and gesturing at his filthy, sweat-stained clothes.

But when the work was finished, the children came at night to tell us a holiday had been declared, and we were all going to church tomorrow. 'Père Louis will say Mass, for it is a feast day, and his name-day,' Fleur said, with the aplomb of one who had spent her early life in metropolitan France.

Linh and I looked at each other in surprise. I had seen Louis act out a number of roles during the time I had been at the village, but priest had not been one of them. 'I thought he had no faith any more,' Linh murmured.

'I should be surprised if he did.' I remembered he had told me, when we first came, that he held services from time to time because the villagers liked them. It would be interesting to see his version of the Mass, performed in front of that grotesque Trinity.

I slept later than usual the next morning, for there were none of the usual dawn sounds of the stirring village to wake me. After I had helped Linh into one of the long, loose cotton gowns she sometimes wore, I put on a dress myself, in honour of the feast day. It was the first time I had worn anything but jeans or trousers for weeks, and I felt awkward in it. 'Your hair is growing long,' Linh said, watching me. 'You should keep it so, it suits you.'

Louis came to the hut after we had breakfasted, the children trooping behind him. We were not the only ones celebrating the feast, for he was dressed as I had never seen him, in a long white soutane over his shirt and trousers. It was tightly belted round the waist, and though it had been patched here and there, some effort had been made to keep it presentable. 'It is the only clerical garment I have left,' he said, smoothing down his skirts. 'The rest were cut up for bandages, or eaten by the termites.' Bending over Linh, he took her hand and drew her gently to her feet. I saw his face change slightly as he did so, and I knew he had noticed the smell. But he said cheerfully enough that he insisted that she come to church, the villagers would be desolated if she did not do so. 'And Madame Gilly, too, of course,' he grinned at me over his shoulder.

I would rather have stayed away, but when Louis lifted Linh in his arms, and went out into the daylight, the children tugged at me, and I thought there was nothing I could do but follow. The villagers were already filing into church, and a bell, which I had not heard before, was ringing from somewhere in the roof, its tone muffled by the thatch.

Louis had rigged up an altar, of sorts, covered with a piece of batik, and a large wooden bowl stood on it, with half a dozen smaller bowls ranged around. The only light came from the open doorway, and a flickering oil lamp burned on the altar. It had a passable resemblance to the sanctuary lamp kept alight in more orthodox Catholic churches.

A cane chair from Louis's hut had been brought for Linh, and a stool for me. The children sat at our feet, and the villagers themselves stood or squatted, crowding the main body of the church. It was very warm, and the air smelled richly of garlic and sweat and manure, so I was afraid Linh would be sick. But she sat smiling calmly, and when I bent over her, she murmured that she felt very well that day. 'I shall survive if the sermon is not too long,' she said, pressing my hand gratefully.

Louis had gone out again after he had settled Linh in her chair, and a silence pressed down over the church as we waited for him. The bell still rang mournfully in the thatch somewhere above our heads. In the warm, semi-darkness, I looked up reluctantly at last at the trio of figures behind the low altar. The contorted body of the crucified Christ seemed to leap as the flame of the oil lamp leaped, though the magisterial Buddha remained still and calm. I tried to avoid looking at the dark, many-armed goddess with her huge belly, squatting in the gloom. For a moment I had the idea that her thighs were opening, and that something was moving between them. I turned and saw Linh was staring at me, her face pale. 'If she gave birth, it would be a demon,' she said in a voice so low I could hardly hear her, and I felt my hands turn clammy.

There was a small stir at the door and Louis came in, unattended, in his plain soutane. He made his way between the rows of squatting people, and stood silently in front of the altar, his back to us. The bell stopped then, and as though it was a signal, he bowed deeply to each of the images: to the Christ on the cross, to the Buddha, and to the fecund goddess. Then he turned round to the silent, waiting figures, and opened his arms wide, in the attitude of the crucified Jesus.

* * *

'What did you think of all that?' I put another cushion under Linh's back and coaxed her to sip a little more tea, for she looked very pale. Louis should have had more sense than to allow the service to go on for so long.

'It was very interesting,' she said politely. 'Some of it was Buddhist, I could recognise the chants. And there were parts of the Mass as well, I think.'

'Yes, and all in Latin, in the old rite. News of Vatican II obviously hasn't reached Père Louis, or if it has, he is ignoring it. It's a pity you missed out on the Communion.'

There had been no host, but Louis had bent over the bowl on the altar table and consecrated it, lifting it then offering it in turn to each of his fearful Trinity. When it was done, he filled the smaller bowls and the people came forward to drink, passing them from hand to hand. One of the women brought a bowl to Linh, but Louis shook his head slightly – I suppose he thought it might make her ill – so she only touched it to her lips and passed it to me. I drank a little, then, when I felt the almost immediate singing in my blood, took a mouthful more.

It must have been very close to pure alcohol, for the atmosphere loosened at once, and became much more that of a revivalist meeting, with spontaneous singing and clapping, and some shuffling dancing, though there was barely room for it. As the service continued, I noticed that priest and congregation's attention swung remorselessly away from the crucified god and the grave Buddha, and fixed itself on the goddess. I suppose the heat and whatever had been in the bowl had made me drunk, for the goddess herself seemed to grow taller, and be casting a shadow before her. Louis sang to her in a high, clear tenor, and the congregation clicked and muttered responses behind him.

'What was Père Louis saying?' Khim had come in to crouch at our feet, and Linh ran her hand over his hair, washed and combed in honour of the feast day.

'Oh, he asked the goddess to join with the other two gods, and to make the crops grow, and to bless the village,' he said vaguely. 'I could not understand all of it.' He was fidgeting, impatient to get away, for a pig was being roasted in honour of Louis's name-day, and we could see the preparations beginning.

Linh sighed, and let him go. 'He is becoming a

savage, and Fleur too. Soon you will not be able to tell them from the montagnard children.' She met my eyes. 'Sometimes I think we will never leave here.'

I turned away from her impatiently. 'Of course we will. The fighting is dying down, we hardly ever here the shelling now. Louis will send down the mountain in a few days to see if it is safe to go.'

She looked at me, but said nothing. Then she held up her arms, and I lifted her and carried her outside, where she could watch the children playing in the dust. She seemed to weigh now no more than Fleur, and I carried her as easily.

The barbecued pig was tender and succulent, and I must have eaten too much, for I woke a couple of times during the night feeling ill. The next afternoon, when I was working in the potato field digging tubers, I fainted, and two of the men lifted me by my arms and legs, as though I was Gulliver, and carried me into the shade. By the time Louis came, I had vomited, and was feeling much better, though my hands and face were clammy.

He sent the men back to work, and felt my pulse, then put his ear against my breast to listen to my heart. 'Sit for a little, you are over-heated,' he said, and I propped myself against a tree, feeling the cool wind dry my sweat.

He sat beside me in silence for a while then he turned and placed his hand firmly over my belly. 'It is time to stop working in the fields. You are not used to it, and you could lose the child.' He smiled when I started to shake my head. 'It is not just guesswork, you know. I saw you at the pool. Until then, you had fooled us all.'

'Linh must not be told. It would worry her very much.' I drew a deep breath. In a way, it was a relief that he knew.

'I will not tell her, I promise you, though you will not be able to keep it a secret much longer from her, or from anyone. If she were not so ill, she would have guessed already.' He took my hand and pulled me to my feet.

'You had better come to my hut. I can take your blood pressure, and test your urine for sugar. We should find out why you had this fainting fit.'

He was quick and expert, and I made no objection when he asked me to lie down so he could palpate my abdomen. 'The village women have taught me what gynaecology I know,' he said, probing carefully with his thin hands. 'They can tell whether the baby is well placed, and if there will be trouble during the birth. With you, it is perhaps still a little early.'

He got to his feet, and watched me as I dressed. 'I can find nothing wrong. You are a strong, healthy woman. The fainting was probably no more than heat, and too much exertion, but I think you should rest for a day or two just to be sure.'

'When can we leave? It is important for me now, as well as for Linh.'

He did not speak for a moment. There was an answer, and we both knew it, but I did not want to hear it. Then he turned, and began to wash his hands in an enamel bowl on a high stand. 'The government radio says Binhhua province has been retaken, and the road to the border will be open within a few days. I think you and the children could walk down the pass, and I would send some of the men with you to carry Fleur and Khim when they were tired. It is Madame Penn who presents a problem.'

I looked up with sudden hope. 'You said there was an agricultural commune at the foot of the mountain, and that they had trucks. If I went . . .' There was still the difficulty, of course, of what we would use for money.

He shook his head. 'No, I have already tried. The trucks are gone. Sarr Mok's soldiers took them when they were retreating. They burned most of the village too, so there is no help there.' He took my hands in his own dry, hard ones, and looked at me gravely. 'I have not been quite idle. I have also sent another message the other way, to Penn Thioen in the capital. Duan' – he meant the boy who cooked his meals and looked after his hut – 'walked for four days with it until he came to a village where army trucks regularly pass through. I gave what money I could spare to bribe one of the drivers to take the letter. So perhaps this time it may reach M. Penn.'

I felt a sense of embarrassment, for I had assumed that he was doing nothing to help us. Not meeting his eyes, I said that moving Linh remained a problem, even if Penn received the message.

'I have asked him to send an army helicopter. It could land in the new field we have cleared. There is enough space.' I started to speak, but he cut across impatiently. 'Is this so impossible? The children have told me their father is a high official in the government, an adviser to the Prime Minister.'

'Yes, but his own position . . .' I stopped. None of us had any knowledge of what Penn's position was. It was always possible that things had improved though I did not think it was likely.

Louis put his hand up and touched my cheek. 'Be patient. If Madame Penn sees you are worried, it becomes worse for her. Wait for a few more days, and if there is no reply by then, we shall have to think again.

* * *

He was angry when he came into the fields two days later, and found me working again, stooping in the sun to dig up tubers. He told me to stop, and I said I would not. He could rule the village like a tyrant if he wished, I added savagely, but he could not rule me. He said nothing more then, but stood silent for a while, watching me working. That night, though, after he had brought Linh her tisane, he stayed on against his custom, talking quietly to her about the children's education until she fell asleep. Then he looked over at me.

'Do you wish to lose the child?'

'Be quiet!' Linh was lying on her side, breathing deeply, but I was angry that he had taken the risk.

'She cannot hear us, she is heavily asleep. Though if you wish, we can talk outside. Put the blanket round you, it is cold.'

Because I was usually tired, and I did not want to leave Linh alone, I rarely went outside the hut after the dark, and I was glad to go now. It was a marvellous night, moonless, with stars blazing in a high, clear sky. The air touched us like icicles, making my face and hands tingle. I breathed deeply, feeling the clean coldness in my lungs, and my anger died. When Louis repeated his question, I answered him carefully.

'I think it would be a good thing if I did not have the child, though it is too late now to do much about it.'

'You do not want the baby?' He said again.

I wrapped the blanket round my shoulders and looked up at the burning stars. 'I am not sure what I want. I don't seem to have much feeling about it one way or the other. But the father of the child certainly does not want it.'

He had been walking too quickly, and he slowed his pace to accommodate mine. 'Madame Penn told me you were married, but she thought you did not live with your husband. I suppose then, that the child is not his.' I shook my head without speaking.

We had come to the end of the village, to where Penn's car stood, slightly rusted now by the mountain dews, a small monument to our joint folly. Louis opened the door. 'Sit inside for a little, it will be warmer.' He got in after me and we huddled together under the rug in the back seat, like a courting couple. I could feel the warmth of his body against mine, though he made no other move to touch me, and I began to speak.

In all the time I had known Peter, I had never really talked of him to anyone. Harry and possibly Penn, who had seen me with him, might know something of how I felt, but they would only be guessing. I don't know why, then, I talked to Louis so long and so frankly. It may have been the darkness, or the proximity of his warm, strong body, or the ancient pull of his priestly role: the priest as magician, who can cure ills.

When I had finished, I was disappointed, for he did not speak for a long time. Then he said, his voice calm and polite, that the situation obviously presented a number of difficulties. 'I cannot advise you, you know.' It was dark, but I could see the glint of his eyes in the starlight. 'I gave up that sort of thing a long time ago. You must make up your own mind what is best for you to do.' Despite his coolness, his body was tense, and I knew he was angry and on edge. He had not, I supposed enjoyed hearing me talk of Peter, but I did not really care for his feelings, only for my own. I felt purged and relaxed, as though I had shifted at least part of a heavy burden on to someone else.

The stars chimed with coldness as we walked slowly back. 'You have heard nothing of M. Casement then? Nothing at all?' he said abruptly, putting his hand under my arm as I stumbled on the rough ground.

'Nothing. Even Penn did not know where he was, or what had happened to him. There has been no mention of him on the government radio?' It was a long shot, but it seemed worth asking.

'No, but the radio would hardly broadcast news of a foreign adviser to the Prince. Foreigners are still not popular. The capital is calm, but there are some problems in the provinces, where the peasants are refusing to accept the new régime. The radio announced last week that a number of village headmen had been shot.' He laughed curtly. *'Pour encourager les autres.'*

I pulled the blanket closer round my shoulders. The cold was biting. 'I don't understand why foreigners are unpopular. The régime needs all the foreign aid it can get. Khamba could still accept aid and foreign experts without compromising itself.'

'That will happen sooner or later, of course.' He took a deep breath, and looked up at the sky. 'But for the moment, the government is concerned with bringing the peasants into step, and clearing out the freelance armies.' He hesitated. 'It is said the troubles in the northern provinces are being fomented by foreign agents.'

I laughed. 'The CIA again, I suppose?'

He took me seriously. 'Why not? It has happened before.'

'Yes, I know.' We were passing the church then, and I did not want to go again through the old, weary arguments about who was responsible for what in South-east Asia. I had spent too many hours listening to the endless speculation in Bangkok bars.

'Your local goddess,' I said to change the subject. 'Your goddess in there. You seem to think her more important than the other two members of your Trinity.'

He seemed surprised. 'You think so? Well, perhaps I do. She is certainly more important to the people here. Christianity is quite a late importation, you know. It only reached the mountains in the last century, and as far as I can tell, most people became converted through expediency, rather than conviction. They are polytheists, so they could easily accommodate another god.'

'What about the Buddha? Buddhism is the official state religion.'

'Or was.' He had stopped, and was looking at the church in the starlight. 'There is a good deal of anti-Buddhist propaganda on the government radio now. In any case, though we used to have a small temple and some old Buddhist monks here, it is not a religion which really suits the mountain people. I like it myself, for it is very calming, but the villagers prefer the goddess. They worshipped her before either the Christ or the Buddha came.'

'She is a goddess of fertility? That's common enough, I suppose.'

'Of fertility, and of death. That is a little more uncommon,' he said matter-of-factly. 'She presides at all deathbeds here.'

We had reached our hut. I was shivering, though not altogether with cold, and I said goodnight and went in hurriedly.

* * *

I continued to work in the fields over the next few days, though I took more care and rested for longer in the heat of midday. Linh seemed cheerful, and talked confidently of leaving the village, for, she said, Penn would soon have our message and would send some transport for us. 'Not a helicopter,' she said, laughing, 'that would be too much. But a car or a Land Rover, perhaps.'

The children came in then, relating a story about hunting wild boar that Pére Louis had told them, and Linh listened patiently, then sent them out in the sun again.

'They will miss Pére Louis. It is the only thing I regret about our leaving here.' She looked at me directly. 'I sometimes think you do not like him very much, yet he has been very kind to us. What is the matter between you two?'

'Nothing.' I rolled the sleeping mats and stacked them against the wall. 'I think he is cracked, that's all.' I had unconsciously spoken in English, and I saw she did not understand me. 'Crazy. Mad. *Fou.*'

* * *

I had lost track of days, weeks, so that even long afterwards I could not tell anyone the date on which Linh died. It doesn't matter, I suppose, the children will remember her every year during the Festival of the Dead, but it worried me at the time.

I woke a little after dawn, as I always did, and got up to bathe, then I realised the hut was unusually silent. There was no sound of Linh's breathing, or of the faint murmuring noise she made when, through the heaviness of her sleep, she heard me get up.

She was lying on her sleeping mat, under the quilt, with her back to me, so I went and knelt beside her, quietly so as not to disturb her. I need not have been afraid of waking her. She was dead and quite cold, her pale skin a bluish-grey colour, the whites of her eyes showing under her lashes, her mouth a little open, with the lips drawn well back from the teeth, exposing the gums. One arm was flung out, and beside it was the empty bowl which had contained her sleeping draught. I had watched her drink it slowly the night before, and she had gone to sleep almost at once.

I knelt beside her for a long time, until I heard the children shouting outside, then I called Fleur to the door, and told her to fetch Pére Louis at once. I think she knew at once what had happened, for she said nothing, but turned and ran quickly towards Louis's hut. Khim was coming across from the next hut, but I called to him to go and get his breakfast, and he obediently turned back.

Louis was there within a few minutes. As I saw him come through the door, I started to speak but he said it was all right, he had sent Fleur to Nghaim, and told her to stay there until he called her. I was still on my knees beside Linh, and I looked up at him. 'You knew she was dead.' It was not a question.

'I guessed. You would not have sent the child so urgently otherwise.' He knelt beside me and put his hand against Linh's cheek. 'She has been dead for some hours.' Pulling back the quilt, he lifted her slightly, laying her down again on her back, and straightening her legs and arms. 'It is necessary to do this now, for there is already a little *rigor,'* he said. 'Soon it will not be so easy.' He laid his hand to her forehead for a moment, then carefully closed her eyes. 'I will send Nghaim. She will help you tidy her.'

'No, I will do it.' I stared at him like an antagonist, and he shrugged slightly and got to his feet.

'As you wish. We will have the funeral this afternoon, late, when the people get back from the fields.'

He took my hand to help me up, but I drew back. 'You are not going to conduct a service! She would not want that. I do not even know whether she was Christian or Buddhist.'

He smiled suddenly in his beard. 'She was both, she told me. Christian in France, to please her relatives, Buddhist here. I think she would want a funeral. It would also be much better for the children. They understand death much better if it is marked with some ceremony.'

He went then, and I heated some water, and carefully washed Linh's face and arms, and sponged her legs and feet, as I had done the first night in the forest. I combed her hair, not attempting to put it up, but letting it fall over her shoulders. Then I dressed her in one of her long cotton gowns, though it was hard to do, and went to the door and called Nghaim. She brought the children, and I told them their mama was dead, and let them go in to see her. Khim hung back, but Fleur took his hand, and urged him on, and together they knelt beside Linh and kissed her, first on one cheek, then the other. Nghaim was very sensible and did not let them stay, bustling them before her out of the hut. I heard Khim give a long, high wail as she took him back to her house.

I was glad when they left, for the faint, sweetish smell which I had noticed before was becoming stronger, and I knew that Fleur, at least, had been distressed by it. I opened the door as wide as I could, and began aimlessly to tidy the hut, rolling up the bedding, and collecting

Linh's few belongings to pack. The bowl which had contained the sleeping draught was still beside her, and I picked it up, thinking I would wash it. There was a little liquid in it, dark and sludgy, much thicker than usual. I had never seen so much deposit at the bottom of the bowl before, and I put my finger in it and tasted it. It seemed very strong, so strong I spat it out at once.

I would not go to Linh's funeral. I waited beside her until two men came to carry her on a rough stretcher to the church, then I climbed up the terraces and went in to the forest, walking as fast as I could along one of the overgrown logging paths. I could not walk fast enough, though to outdistance the sound of the bell tolling. After a while, I began to run, but the path disappeared in a tangle of undergrowth, and panting, I forced my way through until I came to a small clearing, and fell exhausted, lying on my face and weeping. I could hear something heavy crashing in the undergrowth nearby, a boar probably, but I did not move. There was a loud grunting and snuffling, but after a while the noise retreated, and I sat and wiped my face. Then I went back slowly to the village.

It was dark when I came out of the forest, and I was so tired I could hardly walk, for I had missed the path once or twice, and had found my way only by the sound of the bell, still tolling slowly. It stopped as I tumbled down the terraces, but I saw Louis's tall figure walking quickly towards me.

He said nothing, but taking my arm with more irritation than sympathy, marched me towards his hut. 'I shall give you a drink,' he said, looking me up and down as we came into the lamplight. 'Then I think you should go home and wash yourself, and go to bed.'

I glanced down, and saw my shirt and trousers were muddy, and there was blood on my knee when I had fallen. When he pushed forward a chair, I sat down without protest, and took the glass he offered me. It was cognac, and I looked at him in surprise. 'For medicinal purposes only,' he said with a grimace. 'It is expensive, and has to be brought a long way. I have had that bottle for a year.'

I leaned back in the chair, in the lamplit room, and felt the spirit spread its heat through me. Lifting the glass, I watched Louis over the rim, and drank the rest in a single draught, to give me courage.

'I think you killed Linh,' I said. 'Is it not so?'

He looked at me without expression. 'I did not kill her. She killed herself.'

'But you helped her. You gave her the sleeping draught. I tasted it and it was stronger than usual.' I spoke hastily, for I thought he would deny it.

He met my eyes steadily. 'Yes. Last night, it contained three times the usual dose.' Taking my glass, he poured a little more cognac into it, and smiled as I tried to push it away. 'Don't be stupid, take it. I am not poisoning you, or trying to make you drunk. It will relax you, that's all.'

I was too tired to argue. 'Why did you do it?'

'Because she begged me. She had been asking a long time, then, these last few days, she was more insistent.' He sat back and gave a long sigh. 'She was dying, you know that. She told me the helicopter would not come, for her husband was disgraced, and there was no other way she could leave here. Without her, you and the children would have a better chance of going and it was very important for you, as well as for Fleur and the boy. Because of your own child,' he said in a low voice.

I sat up at once. 'But she did not know. You promised you would not tell her.'

He shook his head. 'I did not. She learned it from the boy. He talked of what he had heard from the grandmothers in the village. It seemed they knew of it before I did. One of them went into the bathhouse one day, and saw you under the shower, I suppose.'

'You still should not have helped her,' I said drearily.

'She told me that if I did not, she would have to find

some other way. It would have been easy enough, a knife across the wrist. She was so near death already, it would hardly have mattered, but I did not want to give her even that pain.'

'No,' I said. 'No.' I got up then, and said I was tired. I would accept his advice and go early to bed.

Louis made no move to accompany me so I walked back through the village alone, limping slightly with the pain of my cut knee. As I passed the church, I thought of the squat goddess waiting there in the darkness, and I began to weep again.

I felt a dull rage towards Louis, but I knew that, far more than he, I had longed for Linh to die. The children had wanted it too, even if they did not know it. We were all guilty.

CHAPTER SIXTEEN

I was ill myself when I woke the next morning, with a sore throat and a burning skin. Nghaim went for Louis without asking me, and he came over to the hut and took my temperature.

'I think it is nothing much, a feverish cold, perhaps,' he said. 'You should rest for a day or two.' He looked at me gravely, but did not seem to be anxious to talk. I did no more than thank him perfunctorily, and he went away, saying he would send Nghaim with food.

For a couple of days I stayed in the hut, dozing, seeing no one but Nghaim, who came with bowls of stew and some fruit. I ate a few mouthfuls to please her, but had no appetite. When I slept, I had nightmares, dreaming the old Joshua dream, but somewhere in the dark passages, Linh was there too. I could not see her but I could hear her thin, high weeping.

Whatever was wrong with me, it had passed by the late afternoon of the second day. I was tired of the dark hut and my own sweatiness, so I went to the bathhouse and stood under the shower for a long time, feeling my spirits rise as the cold water poured down over my head and body. Looking down, I saw my swelling abdomen with a sense of incredulity. Apart from the fact that I was conscious of being heavier, I felt nothing at all.

When I had dressed in clean clothes, I went slowly along to Louis's hut. He was sitting on the verandah drinking tea, and he called to the boy in the other room to bring some for me.

He looked at me warily as I sat down, but I shook my head. 'I am not going to talk any more about Linh. What I want to discuss with you is how the children and

I can leave here. Obviously it is important that I go soon, before I get any bigger.' I put my hand on my thickening waist.

'Yes, of course.' He seemed abstracted and began fiddling with his tea glass. Then he cleared his throat. 'I have some news. It came only this afternoon, so I have not had time . . .'

'News from Penn? From the capital?' I began to tremble, and clenched my hands hard together to try to stop it. 'If only you – Linh had waited a few days . . .'

'No, no,' he said hastily. 'Not from Penn Thioen. I have heard nothing. It was very unlikely he would get the message, you know. A truck driver took the letter, and the money, but the chances are that he threw the letter away.'

He hesitated, and I put my glass down impatiently. 'What news, then?' I felt an unreasonable sense of relief that Penn was not coming, for I had no wish to tell him how his wife had died.

'Nghaim's husband went to a village forty kilometres to the north some days ago to buy seed we need for the new field. He told me when he came back this afternoon that he saw a foreigner there, a tall, fair man with a beard. He said he looked a little like me. Only not so old.' He grimaced painfully.

I started to get up, then sat down again, for I was seized by dizziness. 'Like you? What nationality was he?'

'They thought French, but that is only because he spoke French. He has been in the north of the country, and is working his way to the sea coast. They say he wants to reach the port.'

'If it is Peter . . .' I was surprised at how calm my voice was.

'Don't be too hopeful,' Louis said quickly. 'As we all know, one foreigner looks much like another. But there is another thing. They told him Penn Thioen's wife and children were here, with a foreign woman, and he said he knew M. Penn.'

A cold doubt crept into my mind. 'How was all this communicated? Peter wouldn't understand the montagnard dialect.'

Louis smiled. 'The headman in that village speaks a little French, not much, but enough to get a simple meaning across. He is a former pupil of mine.'

I picked up my glass and drank the rest of my tea, for my hands had stopped trembling, and I felt very well and strong. 'Can we send a message? Would Duan take it?'

'No need. As I said, the foreigner is working his way towards the port, and he is coming this way.' He looked at me calmly across the table. 'Do not be too impatient. It will take a little time.'

'Why?' I got up, and went to the edge of the verandah. 'Why didn't he come with Nghaim's husband this afternoon?'

'Vanh wouldn't wait for him, he is too slow. He is a little lame, I think.' I swung round to face him, and he shook his head. 'Don't be alarmed, they said he was well enough. He hurt his leg, I don't know how, and he limps a bit, that is all.'

It was the evening of the second day when Peter came. I had walked to the edge of the village to watch for him, as I had already done half a dozen times, and when he came through the trees, I could not be sure at first, in the dusk, that it was he.

He was moving slowly, with a pronounced limp, and supporting himself with a stick cut from a tree branch. But as he came closer, it was certainly Peter, though a rather ragged and dirty caricature of himself. His khaki shirt and trousers were soaked with sweat, his hair had grown up round his head in an afro bush, and his thick, curly beard half-hid his face.

I went to meet him and we would have embraced, but we were surrounded by a small crowd of villagers, who had suddenly materialised out of the dusk, the arrival of a European being too remarkable an event to miss.

'So it is you,' Peter said awkwardly. 'I thought it must be.' He transferred his walking stick to his left hand, and we shook hands formally, while the villagers clicked and chirruped around us. Then he laughed suddenly, and took my arm. 'I'd kiss you if we didn't have an audience,' he said, 'but you might appreciate it a bit better later, after I have had a wash.' He looked down at himself and gave a snort of distaste.

Louis arrived then, materialising as silently as the villagers, and in the flurry of introductions and explanations, there was no chance for me to say anything more.

Peter stumbled once as we walked through the village, and his weight was heavy on my arm. I would have guided him to my hut, but Louis took charge, saying in an unfamiliar, hard voice that Peter could sleep in the annexe at his own quarters, and what he needed most was a bath and a short rest.

Louis invited me formally to join him for dinner, something he had never done before, and took Peter off to the bathhouse, leaving me half-amused and half-angry.

At dinner Peter was rather silent, mainly because he was concentrating on eating, cramming food into his mouth with frank greed. 'Sorry,' he said, catching my eye, 'but I had rather a thin time of it on the road.' He looked much better now that he was clean, and he had trimmed his hair and beard with Louis's scissors.

It was not until after dinner, when we sat drinking the last dregs of Louis's cognac, that he told us what had happened. When he had left the capital he had gone, as Penn suggested, to the Great Temple at Vangkhorn to talk to the archaeologists. Then he had heard of trouble in villages to the north and decided to have a look at what was going on, so he could report back to Soumidath.

'It was a much harder trip than I had expected,' he said. 'The countryside was swarming with bandits, and my jeep was hijacked the second day, leaving me stranded. I was lucky they didn't kill me, I suppose. Anyway, I went on on foot, across country, heading for a district where I knew the village council was pro-Soumidath. I was coming down a mountain slope after dark when I fell into a goddam mantrap and broke my ankle. I had to crawl the rest of the way on my hands and knees.'

I gave an exclamation, and he took my hand and squeezed it. 'It wasn't so bad. The people in the village remembered me from the last time I visited there with the Prince, and they were very hospitable. The local equivalent of a barefoot doctor set my ankle. Père Louis says he didn't do a bad job.'

'Much better than I could,' Louis said impassively. I don't think the sight of us sitting side by side with linked hands pleased him much, but it was hard to see his face in the half-light.

'The trouble was, after that I got malaria,' Peter said. 'It kept recurring, so what with one thing and another I was stuck for a long time before I could get on the move again.'

'Couldn't you have sent a message to Soumidath? You could hardly have been as cut off as we are here.' His hand was hot and dry, and it trembled slightly in mine.

'Ah, well, that's another thing again.' He looked thoughtfully from one to the other of us. 'We weren't really cut off, for we heard the news from the government radio, and rumours came by word of mouth. The general drift was that foreigners of any sort were none too popular with the rêgime, and what the radio called "foreign advisers" were most unpopular of all.'

Louis nodded. 'Yes, I heard such broadcasts a number of times. They seemed to be veiled attacks on the Prince.'

'Not so veiled, some of them. Anyway, it was clear enough that I wouldn't be exactly welcome if I went back to the capital, and it could be quite damaging to Monseigneur as well. So I decided to stay out of sight for the time being until things cooled off.'

'So what will you do?' Louis poured the last few drops of cognac into Peter's glass. 'Drink it,' he said when Peter made a gesture of protest. 'It will help you sleep.'

'I don't really need anything to do that, I'm dead on my feet.' Peter stretched, and gave me a half-smile which could have been meant for an apology. 'As to what I'll do, I think I'll continue heading for the port, but now there is the question of Madame Gilly and the children to consider.' His voice faltered as he said it, and I realised with relief that Louis had told him that Linh was dead.

He got up, then, and I saw he had lost his earlier animation, and was grey with exhaustion. Louis saw it too.

'Let us talk about it tomorrow,' he said, rising and taking Peter's arm. 'You are good for nothing more tonight.'

I am not sure how he meant that, but it made Peter laugh. 'True enough,' he said and, leaning over, kissed my cheek. 'Sorry, my love,' he said into my ear. 'See you in the morning.'

So I slept alone, which I had not expected to do, but I was happy just to have Peter not far away and I slept well. I had not shed the problem of taking the children somewhere to safety, but at least I could now share it. With luck, the problem of telling Peter about his own child could be postponed for a little while.

It was nearly eleven the next morning when Peter appeared at my hut. 'Sorry I haven't shown up before,' he said as he sat down beside me on the doorstep. 'I slept for – oh, ten hours at least, then I had to wait until my clothes finished drying.'

'You look very well.' It was true, he was fresh and rested, and he had hardly limped at all as he approached the hut.

'So do you.' He twisted round to look at me. 'I was too tired to register last night, but you look blooming. You're quite plump, for you.'

'It's the stodgy diet. And I eat a lot more here, because it is so much cooler.' This was a subject I did not particularly want to pursue. 'Peter, you know about Linh?'

'Yes, Fournier told me.' He took my hand and held it, his own much cooler today. 'Was it rough?'

'It was a bit. For her more than for me, of course. And it was hardest of all on the children. I've scarcely seen them the last few days, they don't want to come to the hut.' He was turned slightly away, and I wondered what he was thinking about. 'Peter, what are we going to do? Can we walk down the pass and get a lift to the border?'

He had been very abstracted, but he roused himself with an obvious effort. 'Not a chance. I talked to Fournier at length this morning and he confirmed what I knew already. Sarr Mok's army has been through the region like locusts, burning villages, taking whatever cars and trucks the peasants owned – and God knows there weren't many. We would have to walk hundreds of kilometres before we found a lift.'

'Well, that's out. The children couldn't manage it.'

He grinned uncomfortably. 'I'm not sure I could either. For one thing, we would have a very steep uphill climb before we started to go down. It would take us two or three days to get over that lot.' He gestured to the range on range of mountains to the east, forbidding even in the brilliant morning light.

'What do we do, then? We can't stay here forever.' My voice was sharper with impatience than I meant it to be, and he looked at me curiously.

'We go the other way, the way you came. It is shorter, it is all down hill, and we can pick up a lift of some sort on the main road. I have some money left, and a little gold, so we can pay.'

'But I thought you said it would be dangerous to go to the capital?'

'We are not going to the capital. We are going to the port. I know someone there with a boat who will take us to Thailand.'

I felt an immense sense of relief, but still some doubt. 'Do you think the children will be able to walk so far? It will take us some days.'

He drew a little away, facing me, and released my hand. 'Listen, Gilly, the children aren't coming with us. I've talked to Fournier, and he will keep them here until Penn can come for them.'

'No!' I said violently. 'I am not leaving them. I promised Penn that I would take them to Bangkok. I won't go without them!' To my own surprise, I began to weep and tremble, and he put his arm round me, and tried to calm me.

'Come inside,' he said. 'We're attracting attention.' I looked and saw a group of women edging closer, so I went with him.

In the dimness of the hut, he knelt beside me on the floor. 'Gilly, be sensible. For one thing, I don't believe the children will stand up to the trip. The boy might have to be carried part of the way, and both of them would certainly slow us down.'

I started to speak but he shook his head impatiently. 'That's not the only reason, though. Don't you realise how dangerous this trip is going to be? The country is still in a state of civil war. As well as soldiers, there are cowboys with six shooters swarming all over the landscape as though it was the wild west. We will be lucky if we make it ourselves to the port. Do you really want to expose the children to the sort of risks we are going to have to take? For Christ's sake, Gilly!'

I knew he was right, and Louis told me so as well later that day. 'The children would present another problem you have not yet thought of,' he said camly. 'If village people see two Europeans with a boy and a girl who are clearly Khams, they will believe you are kidnapping them. Do you not know this is propaganda the government has put out against the missionaries, that they take children from their parents by stealth or deceit? If the children go with you, you are both dead.'

'Very well,' I said tiredly. 'I can't argue with both of you. But we will have to find a way of letting Penn know where the children are.'

Peter gave a long sigh of relief. 'That won't be hard to do, once we get back to civilisation. We can telephone from the port, you know. If we can't reach him for any reason, I'll send a message as soon as we reach Bangkok. There are ways of doing it.'

'What if something has happened to Penn himself?'

'In that case, the children are certainly safer here,' Louis said. 'I can keep them until things settle down, then, if I have to, I will take them as far as the border myself.' He smiled at me, and, rather unusually, took my hand. 'But I do not think it will come to that. M. Casement has told me Penn Thioen is a survivor. He will send for the children himself when he can.'

Peter slept in Louis's hut again that night, saying it was more *convenable*, and in any case we both needed all our strength for the next day's journey. I was awake very early, and I did what I had refused to do before: I went to the rear of the church and stood by Linh's grave for a few minutes. It was unmarked, and the raw earth was sodden with rain. I turned away for I could not bear the thought of the delicate body, uncoffined, crushed by the weight of the earth.

The children were not there to see us leave, and I was very glad of that. Louis said he had sent them fishing with the men, well upstream. I did not think they would mind very much when they were told I had gone. In recent weeks, Nghaim and her family had come to mean more to them than their mother or I.

I took nothing more than the clothes I stood up in, and it gave me an astonishing sense of freedom, to be so unburdened. Louis said he would keep my suitcase for me, but I thought privately I was unlikely ever to come back to reclaim it. We both carried food and water, Peter in the canvas haversack he had brought with him, I in one of the fibre shoulder bags the women used to haul back produce from the fields.

Louis walked with us to the edge of the village. In the harsh morning light, he looked older and more lined than I had yet seen him, and though I was mad with impatience to get away, I tried not to hurry through the formal farewells.

He kissed me lightly on both cheeks and shook hands with Peter. 'I hope we will meet again,' he said politely. 'Madame Gilly, it has been . . .' He stumbled and abandoned his sentence. '*Bonne chance*,' he said abruptly and turned away, though when I looked back later, he was still standing in the road, watching us.

The further the village receded, the more my spirits rose. I felt as though, these last weeks, I had been stumbling through a dark fog, and now I was emerging into a brightly lit day. I was full of energy, and walked as fast as I could, until Peter protested.

'Slow down!' he said, and I saw he was sweating and out of breath. 'Are you trying to break some sort of record? You might remember my goddam ankle.'

'Sorry.' I put my arm lightly through his. 'I'm just glad to get away, that's all. I was starting to feel I was in prison with Louis as chief jailer.'

He shook his head at me. 'You're an ungrateful girl. You and the children would probably be dead by now if it wasn't for him. Why do you feel that way about him?'

'I don't know. Just one of those things.' I could not really tell him that I had resented Louis because he was like Peter, and was not Peter, and how easily I could have turned to him for comfort.

Peter looked at me curiously, but did not press me any more. As the sun grew stronger and the steep descent started, we were both silent, concentrating on the effort of walking. The rutted surface of the sharp slope must have jarred Peter's ankle at every step, and after an hour or two, though I was not tired, I felt the muscles of my calves and thighs begin to protest.

When we stopped at noon to eat and rest, I looked anxiously at Peter. He was white with fatigue and he grimaced as he bent to massage his ankle.

'Are you sure you are going to be able to make it?'

He laughed. 'I shall have to, shan't I. There isn't any alternative, I would never make it back uphill. We shall have to go slower than I would like. Slow and steady should do it.'

We did take it more slowly in the afternoon, but by the time we made camp at dusk, he was limping so badly I had to give him my arm for the last couple of kilometres. I spread a blanket and made him lie down while I lit a fire and heated a stew of vegetables I had brought with us.

He turned over on his side with a groan and watched me. 'My God, you're really fit,' he said grudgingly. 'I never thought the day would come when I couldn't keep up with you.'

'Serves you right for being so arrogant.' I brought him a bowl of stew, and a cup of steaming tea. 'Eat that, and you will feel a lot better.' As he ate, I knelt beside him and began carefully to massage his swollen ankle. I cherished the feeling of his flesh under my hands, even under these circumstances.

He put his empty bowl down and watched me. 'You're a funny girl, Gilly. I thought I understood you well, but I'm beginning to think I don't.' When I did not answer, he fell silent for a few minutes, then drew his foot away with a jerk. 'Don't start mothering me, though. Go and get your supper, for Christ's sake.'

I was not as strong as he thought me, and when I had eaten and packed the remaining food away from the ants, I was too tired myself to do more than lie down beside him, pressing against him for warmth under our only blanket. He was already heavily asleep and did not stir all night, though I woke often, listening to the forest noises and watching the thin moon caught in the tangle of the branches. I was relaxed and unafraid, with his warm body hard against mine, and his slow, regular breathing in my ear.

Peter managed much better the next day as the descent slackened and the road surface improved. He seemed cheerful and talked easily of the good dinners we were going to have when we reached Bangkok. The children seemed to be on his mind, though, and he cautioned me so many times not to worry about them that I begged him to stop, saying I felt guilty enough as it was.

That was true enough. I knew in my heart we should have delayed until we could have found a way of taking them with us, but the urgency of my own need to escape had overriden everything else.

Soon after noon, we found a place to rest and eat, a sloping bank running down from the road, and a narrow stream at the bottom. There was a grassy clearing on the other side, and we waded across where the stream was shallow. I knelt and started to refill the water bottles, which were running low, but when I looked round, I saw with dismay that Peter was starting to strip.

'Come for a swim,' he said, pulling off his shirt. 'That pool a bit further down is quite deep."

'Oh, I don't think so,' I said as casually as I could. 'You bathe if you want to, but the water is far too cold for me.'

'What! And you're the girl who was boasting back at the village about daily swims in waterfalls?' Peter pulled off his trousers, and came over to me, taking the water bottles out of my hands, and started to unbuttom my denim jacket.

'Time you stripped off a bit anyway,' he said, holding me by the shoulder with one hand as I started to pull away. 'You'll die of heat stroke if you wear so many clothes now we are further down the mountain. Look how you're sweating already!'

He pulled my jacket off deftly, and gestured at me, half-crossly. Then he stepped back a little, and looked me up and down, seeing for the first time, as I stood in shirt and jeans, my thickened waist and curving abdomen.

'Oh, Christ!' he said, and for a moment we stood staring at each other. Then he turned away, and limping rapidly downstream, plunged clumsily into the deep pool where the water surged and eddied in a miniature fall.

I watched him for a minute as he dived again and again under the surface, then, with a sense of relief, I stripped off my own sweaty clothes and followed him into the water. The cold was intense, and at first I felt nothing but shock, but after that, despite myself, the enormous pleasure that abandoning my body to the embrace of water always brings me.

Peter pulled himself up on the bank after a while, saying in a casual voice that I might be some sort of river spirit, but it was too bloody cold for him. Then, hesitating, he came back to the edge of the pool and held his hand out to me, and I took it and clambered out.

We stood on the grassy verge together, shivering in spite of the sun, then Peter turned his head away and said in a tired voice: 'It's mine, I suppose.'

In spite of everything, I must have hoped for a different reaction, for I felt a surge of pure anger. 'Who else do you think I've been sleeping with?'

'Well, you said you had a boyfriend in Bangkok. A university lecturer if I remember rightly.' He sounded defensive.

'I was lying. The university lecturer was completely imaginary.'

'I see.' He looked at me gravely. 'I did warn you . . .'

'I know. Actually I had no intention of telling you about the child. That was why I was in such a hurry to leave the village. I was afraid Louis would tell you but obviously he didn't so I thought if we got back to Bangkok quickly, you would go off somewhere again, and there would be no need for you to know.'

For a moment I could see in his face that this was what he would have wished to happen, and I turned from him in exasperation.

'You might do me the credit of believing I am not trying to entrap you,' I said curtly. 'You made the conditions clear at the outset. I have nobody to blame but myself, and the responsibility is not yours, it is mine.'

A long silence fell between us, then, as if he were making up his mind about something, Peter put his hands on my shoulders and drew me round to face him.

'I'm afraid that's true, Gilly. I can't take you on, you and the child. I have other things to do with my life. I can't be burdened.'

It was stupid to argue, but I could not let it alone.

'You took on Rosie and her child.'

He shook his head. 'That's different. Rosie doesn't . . .' he seemed to have trouble searching for a word '. . . entangle me.'

'And I do?'

'No,' he said, 'no. You do not, because I will not let you. It's a great pity you have taken a fancy to me, Gilly, for there is no future in it.'

I began to weep then, because I could not help it, and Peter gave a long sound which might have been a groan. 'Oh, Gilly!' he said, and put his arms round me and held me tight. We stood embraced and shivering, at first more in mutual desolation than in passion, but after a while I felt him rise against me, and we both sank slowly down on the grass, on our knees.

'It's too late to worry now, I suppose,' Peter said in such a rueful voice that I stopped weeping and began to laugh. After a moment he laughed too, and, throwing all caution away, began to kiss me exuberantly.

Our bodies were still clean and cold from the water, and the feeling of chilled flesh on flesh was delicious. We were in no hurry as we lay together in the thick soft grass, and although both of us were conscious at first of the changes of my body, we soon forgot everything but our own joy.

My own physical obsession with Peter had had no real chance to fade. In these last months, it had been constantly sparked by Louis's chance but nagging resemblance. The frustration it had caused me fuelled the fire now, and as the water chill faded and my flesh grew warm and slippery with sweat, I lost patience with our leisurely play and pulled Peter to me urgently.

The sun had moved through the canopy of trees, and was beating hard down on us. 'Come on, my darling,' I said in Peter's ear. 'Come on! I want you.'

In the end, as we moved apart, a bird gave a high, raucous scream in the forest, and Peter laughed. 'The fauna are providing the sound effects,' he said and, rolling over, lay on his back looking up at the sky.

I closed my eyes, and I must have fallen briefly asleep, for when I opened them again he was half-sitting, propped on his elbow, watching me.

'We look like some rural idyll,' he said, smiling. 'A study for water nymph and satyr, perhaps.'

I sat up and reached for my shirt.

'Pregnant water nymph, lame satyr.'

Peter got up slowly, wincing as he put his weight on his lame leg. 'Well, yes, that too, but we can worry about all that later. Our more immediate problems are waiting for us at the foot of the mountain.'

He threw me over my trousers and jacket, and began to dress with some haste. 'Time we were on the road,' he said in a businesslike-voice. I could not see his face, for it was hidden as he pulled his shirt over his head.

* * *

We reached the main road quite early in the morning of the third day. It was just as well, for we had no food left, and only a few mouthfuls of water. Peter was calm, and before we left the shelter of the trees he opened his haversack and took a wrapped bundle out. I saw with dismay that he was buckling on a pistol in a holster. Armed, he looked like a dangerous stranger.

'For God's sake,' I said angrily. 'what are you playing at? That will only get us into real trouble.'

He shook his head. 'It's very necessary. Any driver we flag down is just as likely to be armed himself. If he sees that I have money, he will take it at gunpoint, and leave us both on the road.'

'You've got a lot of trust in your fellow men.'

'These are hard times,' he said absently. 'Let's go.'

It took us over an hour to get a lift, most drivers accelerating past in a cloud when they saw two foreigners, one obviously armed. But in the end an old truck loaded with bags of rice stopped, and a couple of cautious peasant faces looked out at us, taking in Peter's gun but also the wad of money he was holding up to them.

We had no common language, as their dialect was too heavy for Peter to understand, but we managed to convey where we wanted to go, and they agreed we could ride on the back of the truck. They asked for the money then and there, but Peter gave them half and promised, in a mixture of sign language and a few words of basic French, that the rest would be handed over at the port.

It was a bumpy ride on a bad road, wedged in among dusty sacks which made me sneeze, but anything was luxury after the long walk down the mountain. Peter asked if the jolting would make me sick, but I said I didn't think so, I seemed to be impervious to all mortal ills. I could see by the way the lines of strain and anxiety faded from his own face how pleased he was to be riding rather than walking.

We stopped at the local equivalent of a transport café at noon, and Peter treated ourselves and the co-drivers to curry and rice and beer. 'That only leaves us with enough for a night's lodgings,' he said, carefully folding away his few remaining notes. 'We may not need it though, if we are in luck, and Hap Lee has a boat going out tonight.'

'Who is Hap Lee?' I ate my rice with appetite, avoiding the curry as much as possible. I had not enquired about what arrangements Peter intended to make at the port, being too preoccupied with my own problems.

'He is, we hope, the guy who is going to get us out of Khamla. He has three or four boats which go from here up the Gulf of Thailand. Any of the Thai ports will do us.'

This was news to me. 'I didn't know there was a regular boat service up the Gulf.'

'There isn't.' He drank the remains of his beer with a sigh of pleasure. 'Oh it's regular enough, I suppose, but it's not legal. Hap Lee is a smuggler. I thought you might have heard of him. He is quite well known in these parts.'

'Sounds great,' I said without enthusiasm. 'If he is so well known, why don't the authorities do something about it?'

'Why should they? He's been performing a useful service for years. The provincial authorities leave him alone, because he bribes them handsomely, and whatever régime is in power in the capital patronises him enthusiastically. He brings in shipments of arms for anyone who will pay, very high-quality stuff which the opposing sides can't always get from their patrons.'

I looked at him in dismay. 'I don't really fancy signing on with a gun-runner. It sounds a bit risky.'

He laughed. 'Don't worry. I heard that lately Hap is concentrating more on luxury goods – record players, colour TVs, western drugs, things like that. The current régime, in its present puritanical mood, can't import them openly, but there is a black market in them just the same.'

'Well, I suppose it's better than sub-machine guns.' I felt cold, thinking of the armed children roaming the countryside, and Penn and his plans for a reborn Khamla. Peter saw my face, and shook his head impatiently. 'Don't fool yourself, my darling. It happens all the time, everywhere.'

'Maybe.' I stood up. 'Come on, they are waving at us from the truck.'

We came into the port far later than we had hoped, for the truck had broken down twice along the way, and even with Peter helping with the laborious exploration of its ancient innards, it had taken a long time to get it going again. We found only one café on the waterfront still open, and the people there said none of Hap Lee's boats were in the harbour, though Hap was himself expected to bring one in the next day.

I was stiff and sore, and dead tired, and I was grateful Peter was there to do the arguing with the manager of the town's only hotel, who was summoned from his bed by the porter and was, not surprisingly, reluctant to take in two dirty foreigners with no luggage.

I don't know what Peter said to him, and I was too weary to care, but in the end, he gave way sullenly and showed us to a room with two narrow beds, a handbasin with a leaking tap, and not much else. Peter threw himself down on one of the beds with a groan.

'Do you realise you and I have almost never met under any normal circumstances?' He looked at me, as I started to pull off my clothes while I waited, without much hope, for the colour of the water coming out of the tap to lighten. 'Funerals, revolutions, bush camps, squalid dosshouses . . .'

'Perhaps that's the charm of it. Abnormal circumstances are your natural habitat. I'm beginning to think they are mine as well.' I thought of the years with

David, when life moved forward with clockwork precision, and I realised I regretted nothing.

They gave us fruit and tea for breakfast in a sepulchral dining room, and as we were finishing the manager came, gave us back our papers and said firmly that he could not put us up any longer, the hotel was fully booked.

As we had seen nobody else since we arrived, this did not seem likely, but we did not argue. Peter said to me that Hap would let us sleep on the boat, even if he was not going out again that night.

'Why do you think he will take us?' I smiled vaguely at the manager, who was fidgeting from one foot to the other, and finished my tea.

'He owes me a favour,' Peter said briefly. 'I got him out of jail once. Anyway, I have some gold, as I told you, and Hap can never resist money.'

The manager cheered up when we said we would go, and let us use the telephone in his office. Peter ran Penn's number in the capital, but it did not answer, so he tried the office at the Palace.

After he had spoken briefly, he put the phone down and shook his head. 'They say he is not there, and they asked me to give my name or leave a message. I can't do that, it's too risky for Penn. We'll leave it until we get to Bangkok, then I'll just sit on the phone until I get him at home.'

Mercifully it wasn't raining, so we spent the morning walking aimlessly round the port. It was a typical harbour town, sprawling and run-down, with a largish dock area, where rusting cranes stood idle. For once there was no military activity on the streets. The Army was fully engaged with the civil war to the north. There were a couple of small freighters at the wharves and I looked at them longingly, but Peter said they would hardly be likely to take passengers, and we had better stick to Hap.

Some of the cafés and small shops had Chinese

names above the door. 'I didn't know there were Chinese here,' I said to Peter, stopping to watch a man churning out a kind of anchovy paste on a primitive machine.

He laughed. 'There are Chinese everywhere, hadn't you noticed? Hap is one himself, of course, though he has a bit of Kham blood. He was born here, and he can't stay away. He has a house in Bangkok though, and he lives there most of the time.'

We missed seeing Hap's boat come in, for we were in the market buying some fruit with the last of Peter's money. 'We're going to starve to death if he doesn't arrive soon,' I said gloomily.

'Cheer up.' Peter peeled a lychee and gave it to me. 'If Hap said he would be in port today, he'll arrive. You can set your watch by him.'

He was right, for when we came back to the waterfront, we heard a shout from the doorway of a café. A short, fat man stood there beaming at us, and Peter squeezed my arm triumphantly. 'I told you so!'

'Peter!' Hap Lee said as we came up to him. 'They told me a foreigner was looking for me, and I was sure it was you.' His English was so heavily accented it was like another language, and he had a mouthful of dazzling gold teeth, but I was so pleased to see him I kept on shaking hands even after he would have let go.

He put a hand on both our arms. 'Come and I will buy you a drink,' he said, leading the way into the café.

'I'd rather you bought us a meal.' Peter's voice was casual, but Hap looked at him sharply.

'Broke?'

'No, not broke, but we've run out of ready money.'

Hap laughed, showing his amazing teeth, and installed us at a table with some ceremony, saying he would talk to the cook and make sure there was something fit to eat. I watched him go, a short, stocky figure in dirty dungarees.

'He doesn't look like a big-time smuggler.'

Peter smiled. 'You should see him turn up at a restaurant in Bangkok in his best summer suiting, with all the waiters bowing and scraping. He lives in a mansion crammed to the ceiling with frightful Ching dynasty antiques, and he's got a ravishing new wife, young enough to be his daughter.'

A boy in a dirty white jacket came and put bowls and chopsticks on the table, along with two clouded tumblers half-full of brandy.

I took a cautious sip. It was raw, but it raised my spirits, which had fallen rather low that morning. 'If he is already rich, why does he go on with this sort of thing?'

'Hap believes it is impossible to be too rich. Anyway, the life suits him. He likes the danger. Some people do.'

I smiled at him without malice. 'You should know.'

Hap came back then, still beaming, urging us to drink, and slapping Peter's shoulder affectionately. He was a non-stop talker, pouring out stories of recent trips in his barely comprehensible English, and swapping news with Peter of mutual acquaintances, of whom they seemed to have a great many.

I smiled politely but was more interested in the food, which soon arrived: bowls of rice topped with shrimps in a sweetish sauce, hardly *haute cuisine*, but not bad. I was hungry enough to eat almost anything.

When he had finished eating, Hap took out a toothpick and began to attend to his teeth, keeping his hand politely in front of his mouth in the Chinese manner. Peter had fallen silent, and after a while Hap cleared his throat, and said cautiously: 'I think you want something from me.'

'We want you to take us to Thailand. Any port you are heading for will do.' Hap hissed through his teeth and looked doubtful. 'We can pay,' Peter said hastily. 'I have some gold.' His voice hardened. 'In any case, I believe you owe me a favour. You told me once that if I wanted any service – anything at all – I had only to ask.'

'Yes, yes, that is true.' Hap turned to me. 'I was in big trouble some years ago, and Peter helped me.' I started to speak but he stopped me. 'It is an old story, not very nice, you would not want to hear it. But if he asks me now for a favour, I must keep my word.'

Hap's gratitude did not extend, however, to giving us a free passage. When we were sitting in the cabin of his boat, he asked at once how much gold we had, and when the little bar of gold was unwrapped from a dirty handkerchief Peter fished out from his haversack, he looked at it lovingly and weighed it in his hand.

'It is not much,' he said cheerfully, 'but it will do. Make yourselves comfortable, please. We are unloading now, and we will sail tonight.'

When he left us, I raised my eyebrows at Peter. 'Do you usually carry bits of gold about?'

'I always have some, certainly. Everybody in this part of the world does, didn't you know? It's the safest and most portable form of currency. Actually I have a little more tucked away, but I'm not about to tell Hap that.'

Hap's boat looked like a large and newish fishing boat, with trawling nets on the deck, and refrigerated holds, though it was unlikely, Peter said, that they ever held fish. The cabin was surprisingly clean and comfortable, with two berths along the sides, and a dining table and chairs in the middle.

Hap had forbidden us to come up on deck, so we dozed away the rest of the afternoon. The air in the cabin was hot and stale, and my clothes grew damp with sweat as I lay on the bunk opposite Peter, but by now physical discomfort had come to be an experience I could put to one side and largely ignore. It was peaceful enough, with the only sound the soft thud of feet on the deck above, and an occasional grunt as someone bent to pick up a heavy package.

I thought Peter was asleep but after a while he stirred and said in a low voice: 'How do you feel about the baby? Do you want it?'

'I don't know.' I lay on my back and stared up at the ceiling. 'I'm not putting you off, I really don't know. By this time, I should be experiencing all the usual emotions, but actually I feel nothing. Perhaps something will happen later on.'

He propped himself on his elbow and looked at me. 'Did you not think of doing anything about it?'

'An abortion, you mean? Yes, of course I thought about it. But then I got caught up in all this' – I gestured vaguely round the cabin – 'and now it is too late.' I waited for him to ask me why I had come to Khamla in the first place, but a wary look came over his face, and he did not.

'Anyway,' I said, when we had both been silent for a few minutes, 'I'm not keen, in principle, on the idea of having children. I had a rotten childhood. Oh, not like yours, not nearly as dramatic, but rotten just the same.'

He lay back on the bunk and put one arm over his forehead. 'I really don't know much about you, do I?' I could not see his face, but his voice was very cautious. 'What does your husband think about the situation?'

I was incredulous. 'David? He doesn't even know. I haven't seen him for months, not since New York.' At this stage, David was the last person I was worrying about. But I had often wondered what Bill Geraghty had thought – and done - about my failure to return to Bangkok. For all I knew, there may have been an almighty diplomatic row going on. On the other hand, Bill may have just assumed I had gone off with Peter, and done nothing.

It would be very inconvenient, though, if David chose to make his promised trip to Thailand about this time.

Peter turned over on his side, his face to the wall. All I could see was the hard ridge of his shoulder. 'I don't think we ought to talk about it now, we're both too tired and ragged. Let's leave it until we get to Bangkok, and we're more in our right minds.'

He clearly did not want an answer, and I did not give him one. After a while, he began to breathe slowly and regularly, but I do not think he was asleep.

As darkness fell, the activity on deck increased, and there was the unmistakable sounds of departure. I sat up gladly, holding my face to the porthole to catch the faint coolness of the night breeze. Peter got up too, and we both washed and tidied ourselves as much as we could in the tiny cubby-hole at the rear of the cabin.

Hap came down, full of good humour, and said we would soon be under way, and he would land us in Thailand by the following afternoon. 'I will send food,' he said. 'If you are going to be sick, better to have something in your bellies to be sick with.' It was a possibility I hadn't thought of, and I grimaced.

We were already moving when a good-looking Chinese boy in his early twenties came into the cabin with bowls of rice, and a dish of fresh fish and fried squid. He made easy small talk in good English with a strong American accent, and I asked him where he had been to school.

'Most recently, Berkeley,' he said with a grin. 'Have a good evening!' Picking up his tray, he went quickly out.

'One of Hap's sons,' Peter said, selecting a piece of squid with his chopsticks. 'He sends all his boys to the States for their education. I think he's got two more in college at the moment.'

'And then they come back and he trains them as smugglers?'

'Why not, it's the family business.' He drank some of the cold beer the boy had brought, and gave a long sigh of relief as the sound of the engines quickened. 'Thank Christ we're under way at last! Tomorrow night we'll have dinner in Bangkok.'

I looked at him carefully across the table. 'You're glad to be leaving Khamla?'

He raised his eyebrows incredulously. 'You must be joking! Of course I'm glad. It hasn't been exactly an enjoyable few months.'

'Are you going to try to come back?'

He looked suddenly tired, lines which I had not noticed before running down from the side of his mouth. Under the strong overhead light, I could see there was a sprinkling of grey in his fair hair. 'I don't know. I've invested years of my life in this enterprise, and I'm reluctant to give it up now.' His animation returned for a moment and his smiled flashed in his curly beard. 'Oddly enough, you know, I'm also very fond of Monseigneur. I wasn't at first, the power game was the attraction, but close up, he has a very mesmeric effect. I can quite see why the peasants kneel to him.'

'How does he feel about you?' A dull, jealous ache was settling in my breast. How stupid, to be envious of the Prince.

'He values me, because I have been very useful to him, and I have done what he wanted efficiently and without making difficulties. Apart from that, I think he feels some affection for me. He is a very affectionate man. But the Prince has only one real passion, and that is for his country. Nothing else really matters to him.'

He finished his beer, and shrugged impatiently. 'We are being much too serious. I won't be haring back over the border the day after tomorrow, or next week, if that is what you are worrying about. I'll have to wait until things cool off, and the Prince sorts out those bastards who are working to bring him down.'

'Will he be able to? Sort them out, I mean.'

He pushed his bowl away. 'Oh, I think so. I'd put my money on Soumidath any day.' But I remembered the face of Ieng Nim looking out the window of the Palace the night the false Buddha had been destroyed, and I was not so sure.

After we had eaten, I began to feel a faint nausea, and

I cursed Hap for putting the idea of sea sickness into my head. It was hardly surprising though, for the boat was rolling in a heavy swell.

I had just lain down on the bunk when I heard a shout from up above, and felt the pounding of feet running on the deck. Then there was a crack, and a long whooshing sound. I sat up again quickly. 'What's that? It sounded as if . . .'

'Yes.' Peter, who had been sitting at the table, was now at the porthole. 'Someone is firing at us. Oh, hell!' His voice rose in an angry cry.

I went over to his side and looked out. A searchlight was stabbing at us from the blackness not far off, and behind it I could just see the outline of a boat. It was long and low and seemed to have some sort of turret at the bows.

The engines of our own boat grew louder as it picked up some extra speed. But there was a flash of light and another long whoosh which felt as if it was just over our heads.

'A patrol boat,' Peter said briefly. 'Hap will have to stop. He doesn't stand a chance.' Hap had obviously come to the same conclusion, for a moment later the engines cut out, and we began to wallow helplessly in a big sea.

I began to sweat, though my skin felt cold, and a disgusting tide of nausea rose in my throat. 'I thought you said the patrol boats left Hap alone.'

'They usually do. This is a one in a million chance.' He saw how pale I was and pushed me not too gently back on to my berth. 'Don't worry. If they board, Hap will bribe them to turn a blind eye. They won't come down here.'

We sat silently opposite each other, waiting, then after a few minutes felt the dull thud as the patrol boat came alongside and nudged us, and we heard the sound of heavy feet on the deck. We could also hear Hap's voice raised in protest, and a man shouting back as a violent argument went on.

The voices came nearer, Hap still protesting. I looked at Peter and saw he had his hand in his haversack. When he drew it out, he was holding his pistol.

'Don't!' I said urgently. 'It will only make it worse for us, and for Hap. If they don't see the gun, we may be able to bluff it out.'

He shook his head but said nothing, and brought the pistol up level. Then the cabin door was roughly flung open and Hap's bulk filled the space, shielding the men behind him. I could see, over his shoulder, that there were three of them, a neat naval officer with a drawn pistol and behind him two ratings with rifles.

Up until then, I had some hope that they might have been Thais, but all of them had on their cap badges and collars the double stars of the Government of Free Khamla.

Peter took a step forward, but at the same time the officer prodded Hap in the back with his pistol and urged him into the cabin. Trapped between the two guns, Hap raised his hands towards Peter as though in appeal. His skin had turned a dirty grey, and he opened his mouth two or three times before any sound would come.

'Peter!' he said at last, his voice hoarse, as though he had a cold. 'I didn't do it. I didn't tell them, I swear to you.'

Peter had been standing as rigidly as though he was frozen into position, but at that he relaxed and, turning, threw his pistol onto the bunk and smiled at Hap.

'It's all right,' he said, 'I didn't think it was you. You wouldn't risk your boat, for one thing.' He looked at the neat naval officer who now emerged cautiously from behind Hap's back. 'You are looking for me?' he asked in French.

The officer nodded, and said in a heavily accented and tentative French that we must transfer to the patrol boat. He motioned the two ratings forward and one took Peter's arm while the other picked up the pistol from the bunk and offered it to the officer.

When, at a signal, he came over to me, Peter spoke at once. 'I will come with you, and I will make no trouble,' he said. 'But you should let the lady go on to Thailand with Hap Lee. There is no reason for her to be involved.'

I am not sure how much the officer understood, for he looked puzzled, but after a moment he shook his head, and motioned. The second rating took my arm, and we all went up on deck.

They kept us waiting while they searched the boat, though without much result for the cargo had been unloaded. The wind had dropped and the air was thick and heavy and smelt of diesel fumes. As the deck rolled under my feet, nausea drove out all other feelings, and, pushing aside the young rating who tried to stop me, I stumbled to the rail and vomited violently, the retching convulsing my whole body.

I could hear Peter's voice arguing, but they would not let him come to me. They allowed me to sit down on the hatch cover for a minute or two, though, when I had stopped vomiting, and Hap's son had brought me a wet towel to wipe my face. 'Don't blame my father,' he said in a low voice. 'I heard them talking on deck. It was the hotel manager who reported you after he saw your papers. Mr Casement's name was on some kind of list.'

I felt so sick I no longer really cared who had betrayed us. Both boats were rolling so much that both Peter and I had difficulty getting across the gap. He almost fell when his ankle gave on him and I couldn't jump because I was shaking and retching. In the end two of the ratings took my arms and swung me over bodily, and I landed sprawling on the other deck.

The patrol boat had a tiny forward cabin with a single berth and the young officer, strained and nervous, but polite, took me there and let me lie down. They kept Peter up on deck and I did not see him again during the run back to the port, mercifully not much more than an hour. Just before we docked, though, I heard some sort of commotion on the deck, followed by a thud and a cry.

When I came onto the deck, feeling better now that the pitching had stopped, I saw that the side of Peter's face was bruised, and there was a trickle of blood on his cheek.

'What happened?' I saw from the way he was standing that his leg was hurting, so I went and took his arm. No one stopped me, though the ratings on guard moved a little closer.

'I tried to go over the side a bit further out, but I wasn't quick enough. I thought I could swim to the shore and lie low for a bit until I could try for another boat.'

'What about me?'

He grimaced and leaned heavily on me, easing his leg. 'Oh, they aren't interested in you. With me out of the way, they would just put you on the first plane to Bangkok. They may do that anyway.'

We didn't waste much time at the port. When we landed, a police wagon was drawn up at the dockside, and we were hustled into the back and locked in. There were no seats so we sat down on the floor, bracing ourselves against the bumping. The only ventilation was a small grating in the door, and when we left the lighted dock area, thick, sweaty darkness enclosed us.

I felt a moment of terror, as though I was stifling to death, and I could still taste and smell vomit on my own breath. If we were going to the capital, as I supposed we were, it would take most of the night to get there, so I turned hopelessly to Peter, and lay against his shoulder for a while. But the contact made sweat spring up between us, and our skins burned with heat.

Moving away and sitting up, I asked wearily why he had really tried to jump over the side of the patrol boat. 'Surely you don't think they will do anything drastic? You're an American citizen, you should be safe enough.'

He shrugged. 'Maybe, though I'm not so sure. But anyway, I would have liked to make my exit my own way rather than theirs.'

'You think they will deport you?'

'Sure to. I don't mind that so much, but I think they'll keep me hanging round a while just to show who is boss. Then Soumidath will probably feel he has to intervene, and it's all going to get rather shitty. I don't want it to happen that way.'

'I've never been sure what Son Sleng and Ieng Nim have against you,' I said cautiously.

He sighed. 'It's not Son Sleng. He's a good guy in my book, and he and the Prince could work together well enough if they were left alone to get on with it. It's the other bastard who worries me.'

'Ieng Nim?'

Peter moved impatiently. 'He's had it in for me from the beginning, and I must say the feeling is mutual. He's got some paranoid idea of shutting Khamla off from the rest of the world and practising self-sufficiency. It won't work, of course. Soumidath will have to get rid of him or he'll wreck everything. Trouble is, he's got quite a following among the young kids.'

The paddy wagon lurched over a particularly rutted stretch of road, and I had to fight to stop myself from retching. I tried once again to lie against Peter's shoulder, but he drew away, saying in an abstracted voice that it was too hot.

Then, after a while, as though I had asked him a question, he said: 'Yes. Well, for God's sake don't tell them about the baby, or even give them any hint that there is anything between us.'

I laughed. It was all I could do, and it was better than weeping. 'I'll be telling the truth. There isn't anything. You've made it very plain.'

He hesitated, then he put his hand firmly on my arm. 'Gilly, don't get involved in my affairs. I'm saying that largely for selfish reasons. I've got enough problems of my own without having to worry about your physical safety.'

I started to protest at that, but he shook his head angrily. 'Listen to me. I hope and I believe that when we get to the capital they will simply take you to the airport and fly you out to Bangkok. At worst, they'll keep you for a day or two and ask you some questions.'

I felt chilly despite the heat. 'What sort of questions?'

'What you know about me, what I've been doing in the countryside, that sort of thing. They'll ask you about Penn, and Madame Penn too, of course.'

'What am I supposed to say?'

'Just do the ignorant, well-meaning foreigner bit. Tell them you don't understand local politics, and that you were simply trying to get out of the country the best way you could.'

'They'll believe that?'

He sighed. 'Probably not. But I'm betting that they will think you are more trouble than you are worth, and that it will save face all around just to let you go.'

There was something so strained and defeated in his voice that, laying my pride aside, I put my arms around his neck and pulled him to me. 'I have a feeling I may never see you again,' I said in a loud voice. It was a conviction which had just come into my head.

He gave me a brief hug, then pushed me carefully away. 'For your sake, I hope that's true. It would be the best thing that could happen to you.' The strain had gone out of his voice and he sounded unexpectedly cheerful. Easing himself down, he turned on his side, and put his head on his arm.

'Try to get some sleep,' he said gently. 'It will be a long day tomorrow.'

* * *

I did not think I could sleep in the jolting, stifling darkness, but I must have done, for when I woke, the wagon was pulling up and a grey daylight was filtering in through the grating. Peter was fast asleep, looking quite young as he lay on his back, his mouth slightly parted, his teeth white in his curly beard. He was very pale, and the bruises on his cheek had turned the blackish-blue of plum skins.

I shook him awake and he sat up at once as the lock grated, and the doors at the back swung open. Two soldiers with rifles motioned us down, but in the end they had to help us both, for I was so stiff I could hardly move, and Peter was limping heavily.

It was just after dawn, and a faint trace of night coolness remained in the heavy air. We seemed to be on the outskirts of the capital, and the wagon had drawn up outside a large building behind a high wall, with guards at the gate, and a watchtower just beyond. I did not need to be told what it was, it was unmistakably a jail.

Peter stared at me for a moment, then began to laugh. He looked genuinely amused, but then he abruptly stopped laughing. 'My God!' he said. 'Wait until the Prince hears about this, he will have a fit. His favourite lady thrown in the hoosegow!'

But they had no intention of taking me into the jail. A limousine was drawn up beside the wagon, and before I realised what was happening, two of the soldiers took my arms and pushed me into the back. I called out to Peter, but they were already hustling him through the gateway to the jail. He tried to turn and wave but they shoved him roughly forward and sent him sprawling. Then the limousine accelerated and we shot off in a cloud of dust as the jail gates shut.

We drove through the capital as fast as the rough road surface would allow. An Army officer sat in the front with the driver, and there was a guard beside me, a rifle self-consciously across his knees.

After a little while, we joined the road in from the airport, so I knew where we were. It was too early for many people to be about, but desolation hung in the air like a miasma. Large-eyed cows with bony hips wandered aimlessly along the streets past shuttered shops. The terrace of an open air café which had retained a few pretensions to smartness was littered with broken furniture, as though a tornado had selectively passed through. In the open doorway of what looked like an abandoned house, a naked child with a swollen belly sat wailing hopelessly.

I tried to speak to the officer in French, asking where we were going, but he did not answer. His head and shoulders remained rigid, and he did not even turn. In any case, I found out soon enough. The car turned up a familiar street and drew up before the villa where I had stayed with Harry when we had come to Khamla to celebrate the Prince's return. It was familiar and reassuring, a little like a homecoming.

I was exhausted and still very nauseated, so I made no further protest when they took me inside, pushed me into a room and locked the door. It was quite dark, for the shutters were closed, and I stumbled across and opened them. The window had been jammed shut and would not move when I tried to push it up, and in any case, there was an armed guard in the garden, just outside. He shook his head and motioned me back with his rifle when he saw me at the window.

CHAPTER SEVENTEEN

I was not uncomfortable in the days I spent at the villa. The bedroom they had put me in was not nearly so large or well-furnished as the one I had had before, but it had a bed with clean sheets below a ceiling fan which worked when the power was on, and there was a shower with occasional hot water.

Having nothing better to do, I took showers three or four times a day, and washed out all my clothes. In that humidity, they took a long time to dry, so I made my self a sari out of one of the sheets. This obviously shocked the guard who came in with food and tea, but I did not care.

The worst thing was the boredom and the inactivity. I was not hungry, but at least the arrival of the food tray three times a day broke the monotony. Though I felt very tired, I seemed to have lost the capacity to sleep, and there was nothing to do but lie on the bed staring at the ceiling, or walk relentlessly up and down the small room, waiting for the grate of the key in the lock which meant another meal time had arrived.

I tried to talk to the young soldiers who brought the food, but none of them spoke French. In any case, I suppose, they were under orders not to speak to me. If this was what solitary confinement was like, I thought, I cannot imagine how people bear it for years on end. I should go mad very quickly.

I suppose I had never realised before what it was like to be completely deprived of anything to read. Even in the mountains, Louis had had a small stock of carefully preserved books to which he rather reluctantly gave me access. Translating some of the more obscure philosophical and theological works had done wonders for my French.

By the afternoon of the second day, all my clothes were more or less dry, even my denim jacket, though they had the clamminess that nothing but a drying cupboard can deal with in that region. I dressed slowly and combed my hair. It was quite long now, and badly needed trimming. When I looked at myself in the dim, speckled mirror in the bedroom, my clothes were crumpled, but I was at least clean and relatively tidy. I was like Peter, I did not care to appear in public in a disorderly state.

It was just as well I was fully dressed, for at dusk the door opened abruptly, and the officer who had been in the front seat of the car came in. He looked me up and down and nodded approvingly, then said in French I must come at once, we were going to the Palace.

It was eerie, driving through the silent streets, under the huge moon which turned the Palace, when we came to it, into a spectral outline in black and white. With the officer beside me, I walked slowly across the moonlit, empty courtyard where the ragged children had amused themselves destroying the false Buddha. It seemed a long time ago as though in another life.

We went across the verandah, and up the side staircase to the Long Gallery. I hesitated in the doorway, feeling an extraordinary reluctance to go in, but the officer took my arm and urged me forward.

I had never seen the Long Gallery before except *en fête,* full of people and conversation and music. Empty and dimly lit as it was now, it looked sombre and surprisingly shabby. The rugs were ragged around the edges, the silk of the curtains frayed, and cracks ran across the stucco on the walls. It had the look of a room deserted many years before, and as we walked slowly the full length of the gallery, I looked with anxiety at the Buddha standing in the shadows at the end. I had a fantasy that it would be defaced and mutilated, or its features eaten away by time like the Buddhas at the Great Temple, but as we came closer I saw that it was intact, the stone unmarked, the smile as benignly archaic as ever.

We skirted the Buddha, and behind it the officer opened an unobtrusive door in the panelling. It led to a small ante-room where a couple of Palace guards in their under-shirts, their jackets hung on chairs, were smoking and drinking tea out of tin mugs. They got up quickly when they saw the officer, but he motioned them to sit again, and led me across the room to another door on which he rapped loudly. A voice from the other side called something, and my escort opened the door and motioned me through, remaining outside himself.

I was surprised, after the semi-darkness of the Long Gallery, to find myself in a business-like room lit with fluorescent tubes. It was obviously one of the Palace's smaller reception rooms now converted to an office or meeting room; there was a desk piled high with documents and a set of filing cabinets at one end, and a long table with chairs set round it at the other.

Prince Soumidath was sitting at one end of the table, with Son Sleng and Ieng Nim on either side of him. The Prince appeared to be signing a pile of documents, and empty tea glasses and overflowing ashtrays showed that the session had been in progress for some time.

When I came in, the Prince half-rose as though to greet me, then changed his mind and sat down heavily again. He looked sallow and tired and pudgily overweight, as though he had not been out of doors for a long time. He wore one of his old embroidered shirts, but untypically, it was crumpled and none too clean, and I could see a thin film of sweat on his neck.

By contrast, both Son Sleng and Ieng Nim looked healthy and alert in high-buttoned cotton bush jackets and slacks. Neither moved as Soumidath gestured me to a chair against the wall near the door. Son Sleng did not look up, fiddling instead with some papers in front of him, but Ieng Nim watched me carefully, his chin supported on his hand. I saw that the stump of his mutilated finger was now pink and clean. After I sat down, he turned back to the Prince, and began to talk to him in a low voice.

No one seemed to be going to take any further notice of me, and I was not sure why I was there. Then I looked towards the other end of the room and saw that a man half-turned from me and taking something from a filing cabinet was Penn Thioen. He was wearing what looked like a discarded fighter's uniform, and his hair was cut to short grey bristles, so that he looked disturbingly like a convict.

When he saw me he hesitated, then with an obvious effort came to me and touched my hand briefly in the most formal of handshakes. When I started to speak to him, he shook his head and at once moved away, taking some papers to the Prince, then standing well back behind his chair. I had the feeling he was distancing himself from me as much as possible, and this frightened me.

For a few minutes, there was no sound but the rustle of paper as the Prince turned over the sheets Penn had brought him. We seemed to be waiting for something, and I knew what it was when the door opened without any ceremony and Peter came in. He was unescorted, but before he turned and closed the door, I saw a soldier in the other room.

He did not see me at first, for I was sitting to the side of the door, and all his attention was concentrated on the Prince. '*Bonsoir,* Monseigneur,' he said cheerfully, and gave a little, almost satiric bow. 'I hope you are well.'

'*Bonsoir,* Peter,' Soumidath said uneasily. 'We have not seen you for some time.'

Peter shifted his intense gaze for a moment from Soumidath's face, and stared first at Son Sleng, then,

en more deliberately, at Ieng Nim. 'No,' he said, with hort laugh. 'Well, I have been in the countryside, but ore recently in Khanchan prison.'
A dull red rose in Soumidath's cheeks. He motioned Peter to sit down at a chair at the table. I could see he s very angry. 'I did not know you were back in the pital,' he said in a low voice, his head bent over his pers. 'I was not told until this evening.'
Peter shrugged and sat down. He looked dirty and hevelled and I knew he would hate that, but herwise he seemed much as I had last seen him. The uises stood out on his cheek, but they were no worse an they were before, and his face was otherwise marked. I could tell, though, by the way the lines ran wn from the corner of his mouth, and by the careful y he had moved across the room, that his leg was rting him.
He took his time settling into the chair, then looked a leisurely way round the room, greeting Penn with a ile that was not returned. Then he saw me and his dy tensed, but after a moment he relaxed, and dded to me as though to a stranger.
'Madame Herbert,' he said formally. 'I thought you ould be back in Bangkok by now.'
I shook my head, but said nothing, as there seemed thing to say. Like Penn, Peter was obviously distanc-g himself from me, for my own protection or for his, I as not sure which.
Son Sleng moved impatiently and said something to e Prince, and Peter at once turned his gaze back to the p of the table.
'Is this yet another interrogation session. Mon-igneur? I've had enough of that in the last few days. r am I on trial?'
'Do not be ridiculous, Peter,' Soumidath said irrita-y. 'No one is on trial. But I have agreed that certain atters must be cleared up before you leave.'
Peter raised his eyebrows. 'Leave? Does that mean

you no longer want me as an adviser?' His voice wa sharp with irony, and I shut my eyes in exasperation Don't, Peter, I said silently. Don't antagonise th Prince. Don't push the others too far. Just let then throw you out and be done with it. I hoped tha somehow I might get this thought across to him, bu when I opened my eyes again, I saw the look c obstinacy and anger on his face.

Peter started to speak again, but Son Sleng inter vened. 'We are all agreed that some questions abou your activities need to be asked,' he said coldly. 'We ar not satisfied that you have always acted in the bes interests of the country.' I noticed that he did not say c the Prince.

Peter looked again at Soumidath. 'Is that what yo think, Monseigneur? Do you believe I have worke against you?'

The Prince had the look of a man who was bein forced into a corner, and I was afraid his anger woul turn against Peter. 'These matters have been investiga ted by the Foreign Ministry,' he said in an almos inaudible voice, his head bent, fumbling with hi papers. 'Ieng Nim has raised some queries . . . ' H tailed off, and fell silent.

Peter stiffened again, and pushed his chair back wit a rasping sound that made us all jump. Then he gave brief, hard laugh. 'Let's hear from Ieng Nim, then,' h said loudly.

Ieng Nim took his time, while all of us waited. H carefully polished a pair of glasses and put them or then opened a file in front of him and began to tick of points on the first page. I think he would have liked t draw the agony out even further had not the Princ snapped something at him.

He cleared his throat then and looked at Pete 'During the time you were working for the Prince, yo visited the United States on several occasions?'

'Certainly,' Peter said readily. 'Why not? I hav

elatives and friends in New York, and the Prince knew was going to see my family. There was no secret about .'

'But you also visited Washington, is it not so?' Ieng Jim turned over another page of his file, and leaned ver to show it to Soumidath. 'Here are the dates, Monseigneur.'

Peter had turned very pale, and the plum-coloured ruises stood out lividly on his cheek. 'I have friends in Vashington,' he said with a defensive note in his voice did not like. 'People in the press corps I have known or years.'

'And you also have friends in the State Department.' : was a statement of fact, not a question. 'You talked to eople in the State Department, and that was some-ning Monseigneur certainly did not authorise.'

Peter hesitated. 'It is true I went to State once or wice and talked to people there.' he said slowly. 'It is lso true the Prince did not know I had done so.'

Looking at Soumidath, I knew Peter had lost the ame. The Prince's embarrassment and unease had een replaced by a burning anger.

'You knew I wanted no contact with the United tates.' He stared at Peter as though he had never seen im before. 'Why did you go against my wishes?'

Peter stared back at him anxiously. 'Oh, Mon-eigneur, it was nothing very serious,' he said, trying to eep his voice light, but not really succeeding. 'I was ıst trying to keep the channels of communication pen, in case you wanted to use them at some time in ıe future.'

'You think I would talk to Washington again?' Hard ed spots of colour burned in Soumidath's cheeks, and I ıought of the many times I had heard his diatribes gainst the United States for its betrayal of his country, nd I despaired.

Peter seemed to think he had gone too far to retreat. 'ou feel this way now,' he said doggedly, 'but you

cannot cut yourself off from the West forever. The bes
hope for Khamla is to remain unaligned, but tha
doesn't mean you can't . . . '

'Can't what?' Ieng Nim said quickly, before th
Prince could reply. 'Accept aid?'

Peter took a deep breath. 'Accept aid, as long as it i
without conditions. Monseigneur knows how to pla
one side against the other. He has done it before.'

Ieng Nim smiled, with delighted malice. 'Those day
are gone, when we prostituted ourselves. Now w
accept aid from nobody. Is that not so, Monseigneur?

We all looked at Soumidath, but he said nothing. Hi
face was still darkly flushed, but I saw a faint doub
move in his eyes. I was not sure what it meant, it coul
have meant anything.

Ieng Nim appeared to think he had proved his case
'Very well,' he said in a satisfied voice, and turne
another page of his file. 'Let us now look at what yo
have been doing for the last few months.'

'That's easy,' Peter said ironically. 'Very little excep
being holed up in a village with malaria and a broke
ankle. Certainly nothing that should worry you.'

Ieng Nim went on as if he had not spoken. 'You wen
from here to the Great Temple at Vangkhorn?'

A little colour had come back into Peter's face
'Certainly. I went, as Monseigneur asked me to do, t
make arrangements for the visit of foreign experts.'

'But after that you went to the north of the country
That was something you were not authorised to dc
Prince Soumidath had no idea of it. Since then we hav
not seen you.'

Peter looked at him warily. 'I only intended to b
away a few days. There were rumours of trouble i
Akhchang province, and I went to see what wa
happening.'

Son Sleng leaned forward and spoke for the first time
'For what reason?'

Peter hesitated. He was being lured on to dangerou

ground and he knew it. 'I thought Monseigneur might like a first-hand account of conditions in the north,' he said cautiously.

Son Sleng looked angry, though I had the feeling it was with the whole situation rather than with Peter. 'It was not your business. Monseigneur employed you to advise him on foreign affairs, not to meddle in internal politics.'

Peter gestured impatiently. His face was drawn, and he eased his leg cautiously in front of him. 'Do you have to go on with this charade?' he said, looking directly at the Prince. 'If you wish me to leave Khamla, Monseigneur, it would be simpler just to tell me so.'

But it was Ieng Nim, not Soumidath, who replied. He settled his glasses half way down his nose and gazed over them primly. 'We have not finished yet. There is the question of your activities in Akhchang province.'

'Jesus Christ!' Peter said wearily. 'How many times have I got to tell you I was laid out for weeks . . . ' A note of hoarseness and strain was coming into his voice. Ieng Nim heard it, and looked up triumphantly from his notes.

'So you say. We think you were actually trying to organise a counter-revolutionary force in the area.' He smiled with what looked like genuine amusement. 'We have already had the so-called Third Force during the civil war. This would, one supposes, have been a Fourth Force.'

Peter shook his head violently from side to side. 'You are out of your mind. Why would I want to organise yet another bloody army? Hasn't there been enough fighting already?'

'Your American bosses don't appear to think so,' Ieng Nim watched him across the table quite benignly. 'They were offering arms and equipment for this Fourth Force.'

'Ah,' said Peter with a short laugh. 'The US bogey man reappears. Why was Washington interested in setting up this counter-revolutionary army?'

'To overthrow the Government of Free Khamla, and install a puppet régime. You can hardly deny it has happened before.'

Peter flushed. 'What has happened in the past is irrelevant.' He shifted restlessly in his chair and looked directly at Soumidath. 'Do you believe this nonsense, Monseigneur?'

The Prince did not reply for a moment, then he shuffled the papers in front of him and brought one to the top. It was obvious that he had already read it.

'I must believe some of it,' he said unhappily. 'There is a statement from the headman of the village where you stayed.'

'A statement?' Peter stared at him unbelievingly.

Ieng Nim intervened. 'A confession, if you like. The headman was brought to Khanchan prison some weeks ago.'

Peter got to his feet, too quickly, for his leg gave way under him, and he had to hold on to the edge of the table for support. He spoke again directly to Soumidath, ignoring Ieng Nim.

'Monseigneur, you must not accept this. You know as well as I do that a man can be forced to say anything under interrogation. You also know what methods Ieng Nim would use.' He looked then across the table with a slow, murderous rage in his eyes.

I could see Soumidath was growing very tired of a game which was being enjoyed by no one in the room except Ieng Nim. All he wanted was to finish it, and by the looks the two men exchanged, so did Son Sleng.

'The statement was clear enough,' the Prince said tersely. 'I am assured it was made without coercion.'

'Send for the headman. Speak to him yourself.' Peter leaned forward urgently. 'Let me speak to him.'

'That is impossible.' Ieng Nim's face was deliberately blank. 'He had a heart attack and died in the prison hospital. He was an old man, you know, too old for this sort of business.'

Peter sat down slowly. His eyes clouded over, and he did not speak for a minute. Then he turned again to the Prince, his look now an appeal.

'Monseigneur!' he said. 'Until recently, I have been with you all the time, working in your office in the Palace. How could I have been in touch with my "bosses" as this fool' – he nodded with loathing at Ieng Nim – 'calls them?'

Soumidath was again forestalled. 'Greene, the American photographer, and Mme Herbert have been in and out of the country,' Ieng Nim said smoothly. 'Greene certainly brought messages, and Madame also, though she may not always have known she was being used as an intermediary.' This last was obviously a sop to Soumidath who at once looked relieved and smiled vaguely in my direction. He leaned over then and asked a question I could not hear.

'Oh, Penn Thioen told us,' Ieng Nim said, nodding at Penn who drew back a little from his post behind Soumidath's chair. 'Mme. Herbert persuaded him to help her with a visa, on the excuse she was reporting for an American newsagency. But when she arrived, he says, she was interested in nothing but seeing M. Casement.' His mouth turned down briefly. 'He is her lover,' he added in a conversational voice.

The word fell into the room with an ugly shock. It stopped me when I tried to speak, and it defeated Peter, who leaned forward and put his face in his hands. Penn himself gave a short, angry cry then turned away, averting his face to avoid my eyes.

Soumidath glanced briefly at me, then away again with something like pain. 'Let us end this,' he said with distaste. 'We have heard enough.'

Ieng Nim shrugged. 'As you wish, Monseigneur, though there is more I could say.' He flipped rapidly through the pages of his file as though reluctant to waste valuable evidence, then closed the cover with a resigned air.

Peter sat back, blinking as though he had been asleep, then got up slowly, grimacing as the weight came on his foot. Ieng Nim rose too, and stared deliberately at Peter with a half-smile, before turning to the Prince.

'M. Casement must leave the country at once and not return,' he said. 'You trusted him, Monseigneur, but you should not have done. There is no doubt he betrayed you to the Americans.'

The two men stared at each other, and Ieng Nim's smile grew wider. He had seen something in Peter's face that he wanted to see.

'He betrayed you,' he said again, in a very loud voice. 'He is a traitor.'

* * *

It is very rare to enter fully into someone else's consciousness, but that is what happened to me then. I could see into Peter's mind just as if our two personalities were fused, and though I suppose I must have got up and moved towards him, I completely lost any experience of being in my own body.

I said I could see into his mind, and I mean that literally, for Peter's head was filled not with a normal thought process, but with the projection of a vivid visual image like something flashed on a cinema screen.

He was seeing a dingy room in Belfast, and his own father standing beside the bed in his old long johns while he tried to protect his genitals with his hands while a nine-year-old boy who could do nothing to stop what was about to occur, heard voices accusing o treachery and betrayal.

What happened after that remains confused in m mind. They said later that Peter tried to kill Ieng Nim and there is no doubt that it was his intention, for h was no longer a nine-year-old boy but a tall, powerfu man, who wanted, in some confused way, to wipe out y another death, what had happened all those years go.

Certainly there was murder in his face as he moved ound the table towards Ieng Nim, quite slowly, but vith deliberation. They told me afterwards that he had icked up a sharp paper knife that was on the table. I lon't think he did, but I can't be sure, and anyway it lidn't matter. He could, quite easily, have killed Ieng Nim with his hands.

Soumidath did nothing, standing as though en-ranced. Penn and Son Sleng moved to stop Peter, but oth were small men, half his size, and he flung them ff when they clung to his arms.

Ieng Nim, trapped between the table and the wall, aw his death coming to him and, moving backwards to ain time, he gave a great shout, which rang out all over he room.

It must have reached the guardroom beyond, for the loor crashed open, followed almost at once by the ound of a shot. I did not see who fired, for it came from ehind me, almost deafening me, so that I put my ands over my ears and screamed.

It must have been a risky, glancing shot that the uard fired, for Peter was almost on top of Ieng Nim. The bullet took him full in the chest, and the force of it arried him backwards, as though he had been blown by strong gust of wind.

He did not fall at once, but drew himself up with a ook of immense surprise. Then, linking his hands, he ressed them hard against his chest, as though he was rying to staunch the flow of blood.

I tried to get to him, but the room now seemed full of eople, with more shouting guards running in from the nteroom, and the table was in the way.

Then, as though at a signal, the shouting stopped and he room fell silent. We could hear Peter's bubbling reathing, as he took a couple of steps backwards in low motion. I was close now, just across the table, but

he did not look at me at all. All his attention wa
concentrated on the Prince.

'Monseigneur!' he said in a bewildered voice, holdin
out one reddened hand. 'Monseigneur?'

Soumidath stood immobile behind the table. His lip
parted and he seemed about to speak, but nothing cam
out but a low groan. His hands tightly gripped the tabl
edge as though he was willing himself to remain still.

Peter continued to stare for a moment, then his knee
folded under him and he slid quite slowly to the floor
When I managed to push past Soumidath, and to shak
off Penn who tried to stop me, I knelt beside him an
took his hand, but he was already dead. I did not nee
Penn murmuring in my ear to tell me so, for Peter'
eyes, though they were open and staring straight int
mine, were blank and lightless, like those of a blin
man.

I have some fragmentary memories after that o
hands dragging me bodily away from Peter, though
tried to cling to him; of Ieng Nim huddled in a chai
looking grey and sick; of Penn and one of the guard
pulling me by force through the anteroom into the Lon
Gallery and then down to the car. There is only on
thing I remember clearly of the end of that night: as w
moved down the Long Gallery, the two men urging m
on, I managed to twist round for a moment, and lool
back. In the shadows at the end of the gallery, th
Buddha smiled serenely, its lips in the familiar archai
curve. But above the smile, its eyes were sightles
sockets, as blank as Peter's had been in death.

* * *

Some time after dawn, the young officer who ha
escorted me to the Palace the night before came to th
villa, and, averting his eyes from my face, said ther
was a plane leaving for Bangkok at eight, and he woul
take me to the airport.

He called to someone through the open door, and a waiter in a white coat came in with a tray of fruit and eggs and tea. I could not eat anything, though he urged me to, but I was very thirsty, and drank several glasses of tea.

The officer coaxed me to go to the bathroom and wash my face and comb my hair, talking to me as if I were a child. Looking at myself in the speckled mirror, I was surprised to see how normal my face appeared. I was pale and my eyes were a little swollen, but otherwise it was an everyday self which stared back at me. I turned away in disbelief. It seemed inconceivable that the night should have left so slight a record on my face.

Departure was not a complicated business. I had nothing with me except a small handbag. But before I got into the car which was drawn up outside the villa, I asked the officer to wait a minute, and stood looking round the tangled garden.

There was a white, waxy flower growing almost wild in the garden beds, and its strong smell hung obtrusively on the wet, hot morning air. I recognised the scent. White flowers like these had been piled on the bier of the old Queen, the Prince's mother, on the day when I met Peter for the first time. I turned away angrily and got into the car.

The young officer tried to make polite conversation on the way to the airport, but I did not answer him. I was looking out at the streets, familiar to me now, and full of landmarks. Something very strange had happened. Only a few days before they had been deserted and desolate, now they were full of people.

There were a few soldiers with rifles walking slowly along the side of the road, but they were relaxed, their rifles slung carelessly over their shoulders, and I saw a group of them jostling each other to buy hot boiled dumplings at a food stall.

Mainly, though, the crowds were the ordinary early

morning ones, people on their way to work, peasants setting up market stalls, peddlers bent under shoulder poles, an open air barber cutting hair.

I looked out at them in terror, then shrank back inside the car, closing my eyes. It was as though time had been frozen here, and at Peter's death, some sort of magical signal had been given which had set the world turning again.

They had managed my arrival at the airport very well, for the plane was already on the tarmac warming up when the officer escorted me through the terminal without any formalities.

Penn Thioen was waiting at the exit door. He held out his hand to me, but I would not take it, and after a moment he let it fall.

'It was never meant, you know,' he said without preamble. 'The Prince would never have permitted it. Never! You must believe that, madame.'

'What *was* intended?' I was almost too tired to care, but it seemed important to him.

'Only that Peter would admit something – anything! Even what he said about talking to people in the State Department should have satisfied them. The Prime Minister and the Foreign Minister were both anxious that he should be discredited with the Prince.' He shook his head. 'They thought Monseigneur listened to him too much.'

I looked at him dully. 'The Prince would have listened to you, too. Why did you not tell him none of what Ieng Nim said was true? You know Peter, you have been very close to him.'

He turned his face away, and did not meet my eyes. 'I was not sure myself, what was true and what was not true.'

For a moment, I was jolted into anger. 'You cannot seriously believe that Peter was working against the Prince!'

He looked at me then, and I saw there were tears in

is eyes. 'I don't know. There was some evidence, more han you saw.'

'Faked evidence.'

'Perhaps.' He gave a gesture of frustration. 'I don't now, the Prince doesn't know. No one knows, now.' He took my hand this time, and held it. 'I did not speak gainst Peter,' he said in a low voice. 'They asked me to, out I refused. I told them nothing, except that you had eemed anxious to see him when you came the last ime. That was true, was it not?'

'Oh, yes, it was true.' His frail, dry hand still lay in nine, and I pressed it slightly.

'Can you make sure Peter is properly buried?' During he night, I had fallen briefly asleep, and I had dreamed hat the ragged children were mutilating his body, as hey had mutilated the Buddha.

'It is already done.' I could not see his face, for he owered his head, but there was something in his voice which made me sick.

Penn started to speak again, and I had to concentrate o hear what he was saying. 'There was another reason why I could not speak too much for Peter,' he said, numbling so that it was hard to hear him. 'I have not seen my wife and children yet, you understand. Son Sleng told me he had had inquiries made, and the police have located them in a village about 100 kilometers east of here. But he said I would not be able to go to them until this business with Peter was over, so I could not take any risks . . . ' His voice tailed away.

The plane was ready to leave now, and the young officer came forward and urged me towards the steps, holding my arm firmly. 'Don't mistake me,' Penn said, half-running to keep up with us. 'I am not blaming you. I know if you became separated from them on the road, and you had to go on alone, there must have been a good reason.'

I turned then, and stared at him stupidly. 'It's all right, you mustn't worry,' Penn said hurriedly. 'They tell me Linh and the children are quite well.'

I tried to stop but we were at the foot of the steps, and a steward had come down, and, taking my other arm, urged me towards the doorway. 'Hurry, hurry, madame,' he said impatiently. 'The whole plane is waiting for you.'

At the top of the steps, the officer let me go, and ran quickly down the stairs. The steward had a tight hold of my arm, but I pulled myself free and turned round.

'Penn!' I called, standing in the doorway. 'Penn Thioen! Your wife is dead.'

But he was turned away, walking back to the airport terminal, and though he jerked round at the sound of my voice, I am not sure he really heard me over the noise of the jets.

* * *

When I came into the terminal at Bangkok, Bill Geraghty was waiting for me. He was red-faced, sweaty and untidy, and looked as if he had just got out of bed.

He stared at me incredulously, as though I was a ghost. 'Thank Christ I got here in time,' he said nervously. 'I had a call only about an hour ago to say you were coming. Dunno who it was, some guy who wouldn't give his name.'

I did not speak, and he continued to stare at me, dropping his eyes compulsively to my waist. Then he reached into the pocket of his safari jacket, pulling out a folded piece of paper.

'This came for you last week,' he said awkwardly. 'I didn't know what to do with it, so I opened it. It's from your husband. He's arriving tomorrow.'

THE END

FOLLETT

THE MAN FROM ST PETERSBURG

It is 1914. Germany has armed for war. England, unprepared, faces certain defeat unless a secret alliance can be made with Russia. The Czar's envoy has just arrived in London. But so has Feliks who has come to leave his mark on history – with a single bullet! As Feliks closes in on his unsuspecting victim, he meets the woman he had loved – and lost – years ago in St. Petersburg . . .

'AN EXPERT IN THE ART OF RANSACKING HISTORY FOR THRILLS' *Time*

'Thoroughly well-researched and exciting . . . a strong plot with some surprising twists and four well-portrayed main characters' *Punch*

'RIVALS FREDERICK FORSYTH AND JEFFREY ARCHER' *The Standard*

0 552 12180 0

£2.50

CORGI BOOKS

FREDERICK FORSYTH

THE MASTER STORYTELLER

The Day of the Jackal

One of the most celebrated thrillers ever written, THE DAY OF THE JACKAL is the electrifying story of an anonymous Englishman who, in the spring of 1963, was hired by Colonel Marc Rodin, Operations Chief of the O.A.S., to assassinate General de Gaulle.

'Mr. Forsyth is clever, very clever and immensely entertaining' *Daily Telegraph*

'In a class by itself. Unputdownable' *Sunday Times*

More than 7,500,000 copies of Frederick Forsyth's novels sold in Corgi.

0 552 09121 9

£2.50

CORGI BOOKS

THE KEY TO REBECCA
by Ken Follett

'Our spy in Cairo is the greatest hero of them all' Field Marshal Erwin Rommel, September 1900.

He is known to the Germans as 'Sphinx', to others as Alex Wolff, a European businessman. He arrives suddenly in Cairo from out of the desert, armed with a radio set, a lethal blade and a copy of Daphne du Maurier's REBECCA – a ruthless man with a burning, relentless conviction that he will win at all costs.

The stakes are high, for the survival of the British campaign in North Africa is in the balance. Only Major William Vandam, an intelligence officer, and the beautiful courtesan, Elene, can put an end to Wolff's brilliant clandestine reports of British troop movements and strategic plans . . .

In this desperate race against time, as Tobruk falls to the Panzer divisions and the sky of Cairo is blackened with fragments of hastily burned security documents, Vandam and Wolff become locked in a deathly struggle which will determine who wins – and who loses – the greatest war the world has ever known . . .

0 552 11810 9 £1.95

THE FOURTH PROTOCOL
by Frederick Forsyth

'A triumph of plot, construction and research. As good as any Forsyth since the Jackal'
The Times

THE FOURTH PROTOCOL is the story of a plan, dangerous beyond belief, to change the face of British society for ever.

Plan Aurora, hatched in a remote dacha in the forest outside Moscow, and initiated with relentless brilliance and skill, is a plan that in its madness – and spine-chilling ingenuity – breaches the ultra-secret Fourth Protocol and turns the fears that shaped it into a living nightmare.

A crack soviet agent, placed under cover in a quiet English country town, begins to assemble a jigsaw of devastation. Working blind against the most urgent of deadlines, and against treachery and lethal power games in his own organisation, MI5 investigator John Preston leads an operation to prevent the act of murderous devastation aimed at tumbling Britain into revolution.

THE FOURTH PROTOCOL is outstanding – for sheer excitement, for marvellous storytelling – a mighty entertainment and a superlative adventure.

'Forsyth's best book so far'
Washington Post

0 552 12569 5 £2.95

NO COMEBACKS
by Frederick Forsyth

A rich philanderer plans to kill the husband of the woman he loves in NO COMEBACKS, a skilfully contrived piece with a savage twist in the tale. It is the title story in a marvellously exciting and varied collection by a master story-teller.

To this, his first book of short stories, Forsyth brings the narrative power and the wealth of meticulous detail that have made his novels bestsellers around the world.

"The ten stories vibrate with drama and the shock of the unexpected . . . chillingly effective" *Publishers Weekly*

"A diverting collection of short suspense fiction that should both surprise and delight Forsyth fans" *New York Times Book Review*

0 552 12140 1 £2.50

THE DOGS OF WAR
by Frederick Forsyth

The discovery of the existence of a ten-billion-dollar mountain of platinum in the remote African republic of Zangaro, causes Sir James Manson – a smooth, ruthless City tycoon – to hire an army of trained mercenaries whose task it is to topple the government of Zangaro and replace its dictator with a puppet president.

But news of the discovery has leaked to Russia – and suddenly Manson finds he no longer makes the rules in a power game where the stakes have become terrifyingly high . . .

0 552 10050 1 £2.50

:HE DEVIL'S ALTERNATIVE
y Frederick Forsyth

'Whichever option I choose, men are going to die.'' This is he Devil's Alternative, and appalling choice facing the 'resident of the USA and other statesmen throughout the vorld.

ıs the gripping story gathers momentum, the reader is ransported from Moscow to London, from Rotterdam to Vashington, from a country house in Ireland to the world's iggest oil tanker which threatens to pollute the whole of the Jorth Sea. The climax is the most exciting that even this ıaster story-teller has contrived, and the last-minute urprises in the concluding chapters take the breath away.

552 11500 2 £2.95

'HE ODESSA FILE
y Frederick Forsyth

'he life and death hunt for a notorious Nazi criminal nfolds against a background of international espionage nd clandestine arms deals, involving rockets designed in iermany, built in Egypt, and equipped with warheads of uclear waste and bubonic plague. Who is behind it all? 'dessa. Who or what is Odessa? You'll find out in THE 'DESSA FILE . . .

In the hands of Frederick Forsyth the documentary thriller chieves its most sophisticated form – Mr Forsyth has roduced both a brilliant entertainment and a disquieting ook'' *The Guardian*

552 09436 6 £2.50

A SELECTED LIST OF FINE NOVELS AVAILABLE FROM CORGI

THE PRICES SHOWN BELOW WERE CORRECT AT THE TIME OF GOING TO PRES HOWEVER TRANSWORLD PUBLISHERS RESERVE THE RIGHT TO SHOW NE RETAIL PRICES ON COVERS WHICH MAY DIFFER FROM THOSE PREVIOUSI ADVERTISED IN THE TEXT OR ELSEWHERE.

	No.	Title	Author	Price
☐	11353 0	**THE WHISPERING DEATH**	*Daniel Carney*	£1.
☐	11592 4	**UNDER A RAGING SKY**	*Daniel Carney*	£2.
☐	10808 1	**THE WILD GEESE**	*Daniel Carney*	£1.
☐	11831 1	**WILD GEESE II**	*Daniel Carney*	£1.
☐	12610 1	**ON WINGS OF EAGLES**	*Ken Follett*	£2.
☐	12180 0	**THE MAN FROM ST. PETERSBURG**	*Ken Follett*	£2.
☐	11810 9	**THE KEY TO REBECCA**	*Ken Follett*	£1.
☐	12569 5	**THE FOURTH PROTOCOL**	*Frederick Forsyth*	£2.
☐	12140 1	**NO COMEBACKS**	*Frederick Forsyth*	£2.
☐	11500 2	**THE DEVIL'S ALTERNATIVE**	*Frederick Forsyth*	£2.
☐	10244 X	**THE SHEPHERD**	*Frederick Forsyth*	£1.
☐	10050 1	**THE DOGS OF WAR**	*Frederick Forsyth*	£2.
☐	09436 6	**THE ODESSA FILE**	*Frederick Forsyth*	£2.
☐	09121 9	**THE DAY OF THE JACKAL**	*Frederick Forsyth*	£2.
☐	12380 3	**OTHER WORLD**	*W. A. Harbinson*	£2.
☐	11533 9	**GENESIS**	*W. A. Harbinson*	£2.
☐	11901 6	**REVELATION**	*W. A. Harbinson*	£2.
☐	12160 6	**RED DRAGON**	*Thomas Harris*	£1.
☐	10595 3	**DUBAI**	*Robin Moore*	£2.
☐	12417 6	**THE SALAMANDRA-GLASS**	*A. W. Mykel*	£2.
☐	11850 8	**THE WINDCHIME LEGACY**	*A. W. Mykel*	£1.
☐	12584 9	**DEADLY GAMES**	*Fridrikh Neznansky & Edward Topol*	£1.
☐	12307 2	**RED SQUARE**	*Fridrikh Neznansky & Edward Topol*	£2.
☐	12583 0	**SUBMARINE U-137**	*Edward Topol*	£2.
☐	12541 5	**DAI-SHO**	*Marc Olden*	£2.
☐	12357 9	**GIRI**	*Marc Olden*	£2.

All these books are available at your bookshop or newsagent, or can be ordered direct from th publisher. Just tick the titles you want and fill in the form below.

Transworld Publishers, Cash Sales Department, 61–63 Uxbridge Road, Ealing, Londor W5 5SA

Please send a cheque or postal order, not cash. All cheques and postal orders must be in sterling and made payable to Transworld Publishers Ltd.
Please allow cost of book(s) plus the following for postage and packing:

U.K./Republic of Ireland Customers:
Orders in excess of £5; no charge
Orders under £5; add 50p

Overseas Customers:
All orders; add £1.50

NAME (Block Letters) ....

ADDRESS ....

....